Cover design by Benedict Wordsworth

Copyright © 2013 Tom Brown
tombrownbooks.wordpress.com

ISBN-13: 978-1490441085
ISBN-10: 1490441085

First published 2013

STRANGE AIR

Tom Brown lives in Crystal Palace, and likes to write novels. He doesn't have a grand plan, preferring to ward off success by writing about whatever interests him at the time. His first book, the genre-busting *So Long, Shakespeare*, threw together two of his keenest passions – Shakespeare and *Star Wars* – in a 'deliciously playful science-fiction satire' (*Around the Globe* magazine). His second novel, the macabre historical thriller *Strange Air*, was written after he heard about the Victorian skeletons that lurk in a railway carriage beneath Crystal Palace Park.

ACKNOWLEDGEMENTS

Strange Air is inspired by two true stories: the little-known tale of a Victorian engineer whose pioneering air-powered railway came within days of changing the history of London's public transport, and the chilling experiences of a young woman who, in 1978, fell down a hole in Crystal Palace Park and vindicated a notorious local myth.

The novel would not have been possible without the help of numerous people, many of whom may not be aware of their contributions. In particular, I'd like to thank the staff of the British Library, London Metropolitan and Parliamentary Archives for assisting with my research, and the good folk of the Virtual Norwood and Sydenham Town online forums, whose enthusiasm for the Crystal Palace and its environs helped clarify many points of detail. I should also like to acknowledge the work of London blogger Ian Mansfield, whose own research into the Waterloo and Whitehall Railway unearthed one or two valuable points which I had missed. Anyone wishing to learn more about the air-powered railways should read his eBook *London's Lost Pneumatic Railways*, as well as hunting down Charles Hadfield's *Atmospheric Railways*, which was my bible during the early days of this project. Finally, I'd like to thank my editor Lucy Ridout for her invaluable suggestions, and above all Helen Fuller for first telling me about the myth of the Crystal Palace Park skeletons, and then providing unstinting support as I spent five years piecing together their back story. This book is for her.

Strange Air

'Impossible: a word formerly much in use, even among persons of intelligence, but which is now considered to indicate paucity of information, limitation of intellect, and the absence of all grandeur of conception.'

John Vallance, early champion of air-powered railways, 1824

Chapter 1

Wednesday 13th November, 2013

The Fresh Air Suburb.

Every morning those were the first words I read, as I crawled out of bed and stared, bleary-eyed, at the poster opposite. The phrase was arranged round some pseudo-mythological illustration, elongated in an alien font which I'd decided was *fin de siècle*, if only because the date given at the bottom was 1900.

> The Fresh Air Suburb: Exceptionally healthy
> because of prevailing wind from the coast. 380 feet
> above Thames therefore out of the valley fogs.

Big claims. On the few good days they gave reassurance; on the bad, of which there were many more, they rubbed salt into my wound. The poster had been a last-day 'Keep Calm and Carry On' gift from my old work friends. Though I didn't much love the design, I'd hung it up to remind me of them, as well as the supposed merits of my unfamiliar new home.

Now, of course, the poster resonates for all sorts of wonderful reasons. But even as this day began – the day my life changed forever – the words bristled with double meaning because it was so bloody cold in my flat.

'Fresh air suburb, my foot,' I moaned, harnessing my

dressing gown across my stomach – not exactly washboard, but no worse a beer belly than most thirty-four-year-old men – before creaking to the lounge and cranking up the central heating. Like the rest of the flat, the room had gone to seed, smothered with stuff I'd extracted from removal boxes: back issues of *Fortean Times* and *SFX*, a couple of fantasy novels I had on the go, paper maps of the strategy game I'd been playing on my PC . . . Whatever I'd needed for company, left wherever I'd needed it.

Not that it mattered. Today was the day. Or rather, tonight the night – the designated end of my lethargic honeymoon, after which I'd knuckle down: unpack the rest of my stuff, find myself a thrilling new line of work, and bravely face the light after so long in the subterranean shadows. Or something like that.

The flat was a top-floor conversion in a grand, neo-gothic house from the late 19th century. It wasn't exactly pristine, but then I wasn't really the house-proud type. Besides, it had been a bargain at the price, and had a satisfying air of history about it.

Opening the lounge curtains, I said a weary hello to the suburban slopes of Sydenham, then headed into the kitchen. Last night's dirty plates sat by the sink, but for me to roll up my sleeves I required the promise of food. I'd bought a week's supplies when I moved in, and thanks to some ingenious juggling of leftovers I'd made them last a whole fortnight. Now, though, I was facing genuine famine, and really *did* need to visit the supermarket.

Or did I? Even as I dithered between walking and catching the bus, I remembered the chicken noodles I'd found the previous night, lurking in a box of saucepans: more than enough, I decided, to see me into tomorrow.

Feeling the first hint of a wheeze – inevitable, given the temperature – I returned to my bedroom to grab my inhaler. I took a couple of deep drags, and let my eyes fall on the trees in the park that backed on to the house's shared garden.

The branches were all deathly still, despite the raw early-winter wind wreaking havoc with the leaves on the lawn below. Without thinking, I sank onto my bed and watched, enchanted, while my medication took effect.

It wasn't the first time the trees had seduced me. Although I'd hardly been busy over the preceding fortnight – gaming, reading, eating ready meals, gaming some more – my hobbies could easily swallow up hours, even days at a time. But for some reason, those trees had the power to distract me from anything. I must have squandered an hour or two each day just staring at them, beguiled by their lifelessness, and wondering what lay in the park beyond.

This occasion was no different. Captive to the trees' uneasy magnetism – wanting to indulge their promise of sanctuary, but deterred by their unwavering blankness – I lost all track of time. When I was finally roused by a summons from my phone, my teeth were chattering and the gaunt, stubbly face that stared back from my bedroom mirror had turned so purple that I had to blink to check I hadn't frozen over.

I answered my ancient brick of a mobile. It was Dave, my oldest friend from work. At my leaving drinks, he'd promised to visit this evening to help me explore some local pubs. This was the thing on which I'd become fixated: a night of real ale and gossip to lift me from my slump. Yet now, from Dave's first, faltering greeting, I knew he was ringing to cancel. His apology was garbled, but the gist was that he'd been offered overtime and couldn't turn it down – a bit tactless, since his depot was only undermanned because I'd been shown the door.

Whatever. The real cause of his no-show was that he was a tube man, born and bred, and couldn't bear coming so far south. This I knew, because I was once the same. Before the move, I'd never been further south than Brixton – that being as far as the underground took me – and in a sense I still hadn't. Hence why today would have been special. My first night out, with my old companion in tow, to see what my new, healthier neighbourhood had to offer.

But what of it? He couldn't be bothered. Despite being the very one who'd proposed the 'fresh air suburb' for my convalescence, the sod couldn't actually face visiting.

'So anyway, mate,' he said with unconvincing camaraderie. 'How's it going up there?'

'Good thanks,' I replied. 'Keeping busy.'

'What's the area like?'

'Not bad. Nice pubs, decent shops. Good sort of people, too.' This was all speculation; the only time I'd actually left the flat was to buy milk from the nearby newsagent. 'I really think it's going to work out.'

'Did you apply for that job at Southern?'

I hesitated.

'You know the deadline was last Friday.'

'Was it?'

'Oh, for Christ's sake, Eric. I thought you were going to do that?'

'So did I.'

'It's the perfect solution!'

'I thought so too. When I left. But now . . .'

I looked again at the trees. Out of nowhere, they were stirring, their branches disturbed by the whistling wind, as if they were gesturing to me. For a moment the wind relented, and the branches returned to rest, but then the gale redoubled and they motioned again. I felt a flurry of excitement.

'Now what?' asked Dave.

'Now, I'm not so sure. I worry it wouldn't be the same.'

'How do you figure that? Same job, isn't it? Just above ground.'

'Maybe.'

'Seriously, mate. You can't dick around. Not after what's happened. It's not like other times when you leave a job . . .'

I tuned out. All I could think was that the trees were moving; at last, the park was showing signs of life. I needed to react.

'Sorry Dave,' I said. 'Someone at the door.'

I ended the call and threw on the first clothes I found. Before I knew it, I was downstairs, out the door and in the garden. The trees felt suddenly, enticingly alive; it was like I was being invited into the park. Without hesitation, I walked across the grass, and opened the back gate.

I can't say what I was expecting. Solitude? Company? Oblivion? It could have been all those things; it could have been none.

What it absolutely *wasn't*, however, was what I was about to get.

Chapter 2

Monday 3rd May, 1847

Thomas's epiphany came swiftly and without warning, on board the 3.56pm from London Bridge to Croydon.

Standing on the edge of a sweaty crush, third carriage from the front, he began the journey in a mood as foul as the air that rushed upon him. His woes had come as a pair: first, having his belongings snatched on the crowded bridge; then, persuading the station staff to exhibit some kindness and let him board without a ticket – a predictably demoralising exchange which eventually procured a grudging third-class return.

The late spring sun was beating down incessantly, its sweltering power magnified by the stale city air. Thomas's movements were not his own amid the scrum, and for want of easy access to his handkerchief he used his palm to mop the perspiration from his bearded face, trying and failing to reset his footing in the process. Suited and shiny-booted, with his top hat clamped under his arm, he cut an incongruous figure in the open-air coach, which creaked under the weight of bedraggled workers travelling home after a hard day's labour.

He returned his hat to his head and took a restorative breath, only to splutter on a lungful of oily smoke. His hat, duly dislodged, flew away in the engine's streaky trail, triggering a commotion in the coach behind as the workers dived to catch it. He laughed gamely as it was passed circuitously back, each link in the chain offering a witticism on how such wagons were no place for the neatly dressed.

Below, the edge of the city was sliding by. The tangled streets and ramshackle Bermondsey houses gradually thinned into patches of faded green, until finally a windmill signified that the countryside proper was beginning. The factory roar subsided, and Thomas picked out the passengers' voices against the clatter of the train.

'The man's a monster!' exclaimed one, with a hoarse cockney growl. 'We might as well be digging our own graves.'

'That's exactly what we're doing,' agreed another. 'No way is that tunnel safe. We're working too fast to secure it, and Freddy's not standing up for us. Way it's going, we'll be buried alive before the week's out.'

The comradely conversation cut cleanly through the noxious black smoke from the loco as they crossed the junction at Corbett's Lane, and powered into Kent over the Grand Surrey Canal. On either side, farms, cottages and copses arranged themselves in sun-drenched harmony, but the airy beauty was throttled by the squalor of the uncovered carriage. Hanging his head over the side, Thomas lamented that such decent, hardworking men still had to endure the misery of shuttling to work in these murderous wagons. More than ever, he felt impatient to move to London and start improving the life of the common man – if not by fixing this particular injustice, then at least by addressing comparable social scandals.

'You wanna watch that, sir,' said a voice. 'Another train comes past and never mind your hat – it'll be yer head comes flying off, and this time it won't matter if someone catches it!'

Thomas looked towards the source of this advice: a fresh-faced lad, with cropped, sharply parted hair and a generous expression. His unusual youth was emphasised by a pressed white shirt whose brightness contrasted with the sooty overalls of his fellow passengers.

'Of course,' said Thomas. Smiling, he stood upright and

tilted his head from side to side, acknowledging it was still intact. 'Thank you.'

The boy grinned but, being so short, was soon sucked out of view by the churning crush. Resuming his surveillance of the passing countryside, Thomas's thoughts drifted to what he needed to examine on arrival in Croydon, and how best to note down salient details.

A short while later, the driver applied his brakes and they rolled up alongside a platform. New Cross looked a sweet enough village from down on the tracks, but couldn't possibly account for the numbers alighting from the smarter carriages further back. They, presumably, were heading to the market haven of Peckham, whose stationless sanctuary was only a short distance away.

The open-air wagons shed a mere handful of passengers and Thomas lapsed back into thought, only belatedly noticing that they hadn't continued on their way. Peering down the side of the train, he spotted some people attending a complication with the locomotive.

'Oh for heaven's sake,' he murmured, spirits darkening once more. 'What in the name of Robert Stephenson . . . ?'

'Here we go again, lads,' said one of those on board.

There was a disgruntled groan; the hitch clearly came as no surprise.

'Fear not, pal,' said a more sprightly voice. 'It's the last day of this nonsense. Decision came last night: now the line to Epsom's ready, it's full steam ahead.'

The wagon rocked as its occupants stamped their approval. Cutting through the jubilation, however, was the young man from earlier, his snow-white shirt highlighting his sorrowful face. Whatever strange problem had plagued this service for so long, its remedy wasn't good news to everyone.

At the front of the train, the uncoupled loco was chugging away, seemingly relieved of its duties. Intrigued, Thomas unbuckled the gate and jumped onto the platform. Breathing in some welcome lungfuls of fresh air – confirming that, at least in today's stillness, the notorious city stink hadn't yet drifted this far south – he joined the guard and stationmaster as they saw the locomotive on its way.

A handsome red 2-2-2, the *Sydenham* looked a picture of health: recently polished on the outside and, to his not uneducated ears, operating faultlessly on the inside. After 20 yards, it veered down a short siding towards a turntable, and so revealed – a little further down the mainline – a solitary passenger carriage, which two horses were hauling *back up* the tracks. A uniformed driver was stationed on an open platform at the front, and it was he who wound down the brakes to stop the empty carriage directly in front of Thomas's train.

The guard leapt onto the tracks and coupled the two, while the driver collected his bag and dismounted. The insignia on the latter's hat, belonging to the London, Brighton and South Coast Railway, was shining proudly, and his buttoned black tailcoat and white trousers were quite spotless – at odds with the grubbiness that unavoidably went with the job.

'Last trip for me,' he said, patting the stationmaster on the back. 'Thanks for your patience this past year.'

'Likewise, son,' said the stationmaster, rounding up the horses. 'You find yourself a good spot back on the locos.'

'Oh, that I will!'

The driver set off towards the other end of the passenger coach, which now became the front. Following him, Thomas found that the vehicle was indistinguishable from any other second class carriage, but for the platform at its rear – an oddity which, he now discovered, was mirrored by a matching stage at the *front*.

It was onto this that the driver climbed, dumping his belongings in a small covered compartment. Everything here was identical to the opposite end: bare but for an iron safety bar at the front, a protruding brake handle, and some kind of barometer on the back wall, protected by an overhanging roof. Like the driver's uniform, all the apparatus was incongruously clean.

'Forgive my ignorance,' said Thomas, 'but what exactly is happening?'

'Can't you see?' replied the driver. 'We're swapping that majestic locomotive over there for this insufferable piece of rubbish.'

Thomas looked again at the driver's carriage. 'But what use is this, next to the locomotive?'

'You might well ask.'

'But how does it . . .' Thomas hesitated, not wanting to sound ignorant. 'How does it *go*?'

The driver pulled out his watch and checked the time.

'I'm sorry,' said Thomas. 'I'm not local.'

'So? I thought this was notorious throughout the land.'

'This?'

'The atmospheric.'

The words resonated in Thomas's head. *The atmospheric.* He'd read about it – a new mode of railway propulsion involving depressurised air – but had been too immersed in other matters to pay attention.

'We're changing from steam power to air power?' he asked, incredulous. 'Halfway through the journey?'

'Madness, isn't it?' said the driver. 'But yes, from here to Croydon – the full 7-and-a-half miles – it's atmospheric all the way.'

Thomas squinted through the simmering haze. Two men were busy either side of the tracks, arranging a pair of ropes around a succession of small capstans. But it wasn't this archaic ritual that struck him. Rather, it was the belated recognition of an extra line, emerging from a set points and stretching into the distance beside the two mainlines.

At first glance, it was like any other railroad, albeit unusual in being separated from the main up and down tracks – running to and from London respectively – by a wooden fence. On closer inspection, however, this 'atmospheric' line was quite exceptional. Two standard rails ran on either side, but in the middle was a tube: gun-barrel-straight, a foot in diameter, and continuing, uniform with the rails, as far as the eye could see.

'We tried to be patient,' said the driver, 'but the novelty soon wore off. That's why it's back to the locos. That's why, this time tomorrow, you'd be halfway to Croydon by now.'

'You don't seem sad to see it end,' said Thomas.

The driver leant on the safety bar and spat onto the tracks. 'Well, you know. The idea's elegant enough. Occasionally it even works quite nicely. But by God, these hold-ups!'

'Why not have this leading carriage already attached? That way you could just detach the loco and be off.'

'See the vacuum tube up ahead?'

Thomas nodded: even from a good 20 yards away, the sizeable pipe was unforgettably visible.

'Powers-that-be only went and laid it too low.'

'Too low for what?'

The driver stamped, and Thomas knelt to discover an astonishing assembly suspended from the base of the carriage. It was around 15 feet long, running centrally under the floor. At its front, protruding beneath the head of the coach, was a bell-shaped, leather-coated piston. Further back, attached to a central iron rod, variously sized wheels were positioned at different heights.

He gazed again at the atmospheric track and deduced the driver's meaning. Clearly, the vacuum tube had been laid so deeply in the ballast that the under-carriage piston – needing to slide through it – had had to be hung absurdly low, meaning the carriage couldn't cross points without crashing into the intersecting rails.

'They fixed it up ahead,' explained the driver. 'Installed special points that move the rails out of the way. But they could never afford that up at London Bridge, so we have to come this far by steam, then swap the loco for this piston carriage. And with only the one line, we're having to wait for the up service, even though we're ready to go.'

'It's a nonsense,' agreed Thomas.

'Just goes to show,' said the driver, 'even the best make a pig's ear of it sometimes.' He sat down on his perch, legs dangling over the edge. 'Old William Cubitt's your man for this mess, but Samuda, Brunel – they've all had a hand in it.' He unwrapped a boiled sweet and popped it into his mouth. 'Me, I reckon the success gets to them. Start inventing for the hell of it. I mean, the loco's not perfect. Stinky filthy, and it's murder when they break down. But they're beautiful things, and they bring a lot of good. So why change? Especially when there's so much else wanting an engineer's attention.'

These last words chimed with Thomas. As the two trackside workers reached them, attaching their ropes to the piston carriage, he felt his progressive instincts challenged by this decidedly backward invention. But since it was his life's calling to be curious, he thought he might as well capitalise on the continuing delay.

'Would you mind if I took a closer look?' he asked.

The driver shrugged. 'Do as you please, mister. Just don't be delaying us any further – if you get my meaning.'

Thomas went across to the atmospheric track, and crouched to examine the central vacuum tube. On a pillar by its side was a barometer, like the one on the driver's platform. The tube itself was of cast iron, reinforced by fins which snuggled inside the sleepers. Running lengthways along the top was a leather strip, covering the all-important slot. It was about 7 inches wide, hinged on one side and reinforced by thin iron plates on the other, obviously intended to stop the leather being sucked into the tube when the air inside was depressurised.

Thomas knelt down, wincing as his legs brushed the hot iron rails, and inspected the circular flap of leather at the mouth of the tube, clearly designed to shield the vacuum within from the air pressure outside.

'Quite extraordinary,' he muttered, so engrossed that he didn't notice the faint buzzing that had begun to fill the air – nor indeed the silent shape of the rapidly approaching train.

Chapter 3

I stepped into the park and looked around. Still, I had no idea where I was going, let alone why, but in my loneliness I didn't care. Over the preceding fortnight, the inertia of the park had made it a kind of soul-mate. Now it had reached out with those quivering branches, I was happy for it to lead me on.

Immediately ahead was a raised patch of land, dimly resembling a burial mound in its incongruity and sparser spread of trees. I turned right, heading round the base of this rise, until I joined a path that descended gently from right to left. Through the bare trees I saw sloping lawns and a lake, but the dense woodland, enveloping me on all sides, made it tough to gauge the park's size.

Entranced by the rustle of wind in the trees, I turned left and headed downhill. The leaves were thick and crisp underfoot, infinite shades of brown speckled by frost. While a few still clung to the scraggy branches, I remember thinking that even the stubbornest stragglers would surely be blown down before the day was out.

The burial mound reappeared, this time on my left, after which the woodland soon gave way to a lush lawn, overlooked on the left by more grand, late-Victorian houses. Relishing the expansive silence, I followed this boundary to the exit at the bottom of the hill, where I turned to mosey up a striking tree-lined avenue. Ahead of me were two enormous structures: on the left a stadium; on the right, a squat sixties structure, much like an aircraft hangar. Behind it loomed an ugly brown tower block, while beyond that was the district's iconic transmitter, towering over the scene like an emaciated Eiffel Tower.

It was hard to believe that these motley landmarks shared the park with the countrified charms of the wood. More than any other London park I'd visited, the place lacked any single identity. From one deserted section to the next, it seemed random, confused, collectively lost – and I felt right at home.

I veered to the left of the sports stadium, and meandered dreamily through an intricate landscape of paths and bridges, criss-crossing murky ponds inhabited by sinister, sculpted monsters. Shortly after that, I reached the railway station – tracks dug deep into a hillside cutting – whereupon the higher levels of the park unfolded on my right.

The transmitter stood in the far corner, guarding its domain with an industrial glower. Below it, the slopes had been flattened into two imposing terraces that reached for hundreds of yards across the park. The front of each was secured by mighty stone walls, arcades and balustrades, with the higher level adorned by two life-size classical statues – one both armless *and* headless – and the lower broken up by a symmetrical arrangement of empty plinths. Both terraces were accessible at their central point by grand old staircases, though no such steps connected the upper terrace to the dense woodland that blanketed the highest ridge of all. Once again, the whole scene was magnificently deserted.

I skirted the edge of the terraces, and chanced upon a lonely brick building whose black-on-white sign identified it as the local museum. A smaller, more begrudging notice said admission was free, so I scaled the stone steps and entered.

Inside was a high-ceilinged, intensely silent hall which compensated for the absence of visitors or staff with abundant old photos, paintings and newspaper cuttings. Stupidly, it was only now, gazing at the scale model that dominated the room, that I twigged how my new suburb gained its name. Until then, the only connection I'd made had been with the football team, and 'Crystal Palace FC' was just a given. Now, however,

I realised that the name referred to an *actual* palace, which hadn't just dominated but defined the grounds through which I'd been wandering.

The model purported to show the Crystal Palace in its prime, stretching north-to-south along the highest level of the park like the most immense greenhouse imaginable – a virtuoso study in iron and glass.

The main body of the structure was long and relatively thin. It looked as though rectangular glass containers had been stacked in a series of orderly piles, diminishing in number as they rose. On top of this resolutely perpendicular base, an arched roof, labelled 'The Nave', ran lengthways down the building, intersected by three arched 'Transepts' – two at either end, and one, twice as big as the others, in the centre. Here, at the Palace's imposing peak, the building was at least six or seven storeys high, but taller still were the Pisa-like water towers at either end. The whole thing had a mesmerising symmetry – from the individual panes of glass to the wings that reached into the gardens from the north and south extremities of the main building.

Beneath the Palace, the rest of the grounds swept downhill in a harmonious array of paths, statues and fountains. The whole place looked positively Utopian, a world removed from what it had become. Of the hotchpotch features I'd just seen at first hand, only the model monsters – misshapen dinosaurs, apparently – remained intact from the vision laid out in the model.

I stepped away, and wandered round the edge of the room, where the walls were covered in a dazzling collage of disparate imagery. Pictures of the Palace interior showed everything from a mighty concert stage to replicas of ancient Egyptian sculptures, tropical foliage and hot air balloon demonstrations, while photos from the grounds illustrated a range of sports – archery, cricket, rifle shooting – alongside a crazy-looking flying machine, a water park, and even some kind of underground railway.

There were plenty of cards explaining the place of each image in the Palace's history, but I found it hard to take everything in. Partly this was just the effect of so much new information, but it was also an inability to see past my sadness at what the Palace and its grounds had become. Each time my eyes landed on some new forgotten treasure, I felt that little bit angrier that these riches weren't actually there for me to explore.

Just as I moved to the last of the wall displays – 'The fatal fire, 1936' – the silence was broken by the creak of floorboards. I looked round but, as far as I could see, the room remained empty. Telling myself it was just the wood resetting itself – something to do with the freezing temperatures – I noticed one of the glass cabinets in the centre of the room, and went to take a closer look. Inside was a range of quaint ceramic souvenirs depicting the Crystal Palace and its gardens: jugs, mugs and plates which had been salvaged, it said, from the 'infernal conflagration' of 1936.

This returned my mind to the final wall display, so I turned back to where I'd been seconds before.

'You here for the tour?'

'Jesus Christ!' I exclaimed.

I was staring at a man, well into his seventies; possibly even older. His withered face was dominated by a deep-set frown, and a neglected beard had grown to various lengths amid the wrinkles. He looked painfully skinny. In fact, I was sure I could see the outline of his bony body beneath his fluffy, full-length black coat. Clutching a concertina, attached to a strap he'd slung over his shoulder, he was standing right in front of the panel about the Palace's fiery destruction.

'Well?' The man's voice was loud and bassy, despite his scrawny frame. 'Are you here for the tour?'

'I'm not here for the tour.' My heart was still pounding from the shock.

'You're *not* here for the tour?' he said, seemingly incredulous.

'I'm not.'

'But you're here now.'

'I am.'

'It's two-thirty.'

I glanced at my watch. 'It is.'

'Two-thirty is when the tour starts.'

He grabbed my arm and dragged me out the door, pointing to a sandwich board at the bottom of the steps. It said 'Next Tour, 2.30pm'. I was sure it hadn't been there when I arrived.

'Daily tours,' he said, 'two-thirty prompt.'

'Yes,' I replied, as reasonably as possible. 'I'm here at two-thirty. But that's just coincidence.'

He glared at me with piercing brown eyes, his chiselled cheeks glowing white beneath scraps of beard. Shaking and wheezing, he looked all set to explode when, quite unaccountably, calmness fell upon him and, trotting down the steps, he went on his merry way.

'The Crystal Palace,' he began, talking to nobody but the park itself, 'was first constructed in 1851 in Hyde Park. Its purpose was to house Prince Albert's Great Exhibition: a uniquely ambitious celebration of international art, history and industry. After the exhibition, the Palace was painstakingly dismantled before being re-built, in a vastly enlarged form, here at Penge Place . . .'

His voice faded away as he walked further into the park. For a moment, I wondered if I shouldn't catch him up and become his audience after all. But I'd been enjoying my solitary introduction to the Palace's history, and instead found myself heading back into the museum.

Except that the door to the museum was now shut. Some-how, the old man had locked the place up when he dragged me out. Astonished at his dexterity, I turned back to shout after him, but he was now out of sight as well as earshot.

Sighing to myself, I strolled back down the steps. If nothing else, the eccentric old man was certainly at one with his surroundings: a relic who had seen better days, displaying only a surreal flicker of former sense.

Following his route along the higher of the two terraces, I gazed over the suburban flatlands of Beckenham and Bromley, their drabness blending seamlessly with the melancholy of the foreground. Memory of the model loomed large, and I felt a strange surge of pity for a pair of sphinxes, poised on rectangular plinths either side of a stone staircase. Like the park's surviving statues, they'd obviously been there since the Palace's glory days. But whereas the fellow atop the nearby terrace wall had been relieved of his head, the poor sphinxes had been doomed to retain theirs, watching unblinkingly as decades of deterioration took their toll.

'Well, your neck bone's connected to your shoulder bone . . .'

Fading up from nothing, a deep, gravelly voice drifted through the freezing air.

'And your shoulder bone's connected to your arm bone.
Your arm bone's connected to your wrist bone,
And your wrist bone's connected to your hand bone . . .'

At first, the song seemed to come from all around me. But as I wandered here and there, the voice became louder and its origin clear: a fenced-off depression, beside the busy road and just next to the woodland that occupied most of the Palace's former site.

'Now hear . . .'

The singer took a breath. I was pretty sure it was the man from the museum.

'. . . the word . . .'

Another deep breath.

'. . . of the Lord.'

He obviously wanted me to find him, so I looked for a route down. Unable to find a way through the fence on this side of the road, I spied an interruption in the wall opposite, and crossed to discover a flight of stone steps descending to an isolated concourse that appeared to lead nowhere. As I headed down, however, I found four arches feeding back *underneath* the road. Here was a passageway that had once connected the Crystal Palace to – well, to what exactly?

The arches were blocked by iron gates, and led not into four separate tunnels but one larger passageway of startling beauty. The ceiling was patterned with red and cream tiles that curved upwards from octagonal pillars, each merging with the next like some lost Mediterranean cathedral.

The song returned, reverberating through the spacious subway as I squeezed through a gate that was hanging off its hinges. The echo from the vaulted ceiling amplified my footsteps, and I instinctively imagined myself as part of a huge crowd, surging towards the Crystal Palace, impatient to explore its innumerable wonders.

I emerged into a roofless square. A half-collapsed wall rose in front, framing a pair of arches that led up to ground level. On either side were recesses, all bricked up or empty, except the one closest on my right, where a shadowy figure was slouched against the wall.

'Well, your neck bone's connected to your shoulder bone . . .'

I stepped closer. Sure enough, there he was: the old man from the museum, having reached the first stop on his lonely tour of the park.

'And your shoulder bone's connected to your arm bone.'

His eyes were closed as he sang, and he was accompanying

himself on a concertina. Oblivious to my presence, he botched part of the tune on the latter, then repeated the notes over and over, making the same mistake every time.

After several unsuccessful attempts, I decided it was time to say something.

'I'm sorry about—'

'You shouldn't be down here,' he growled, eyes snapping open as he suspended his latest effort.

I raised my hands in peace. 'I assumed you wanted me to find you. You know, to take the tour.'

'This isn't part of the tour.'

'It should be.'

'It's off-limits. It's just where I come to think.'

'And sing,' I said. 'It sounded good.'

His face flickered with a smile. 'I sing alright,' he conceded, 'but . . .' He stroked his concertina. 'Well, she's the problem. Different note on the push and the pull.' He illustrated, holding the same button as he squeezed in, then out. 'Strange air,' he sighed. 'Strange, strange air.'

'What's your name?'

Ignoring my question, he turned the concertina over, as if searching for a solution to his problems.

'I'm Eric,' I said. 'I'm new to the area.'

'You are?'

'Pretty much. Moved in a couple of weeks back.'

'Then why on earth not take a tour?'

I held out my arms. 'I'm here now, aren't I?'

He commenced a pianissimo instrumental of 'Dem Bones', full of fluffs and smudges.

'Why did you move up here?' he asked. 'Work?'

'In a way.'

'What is it you do?'

'I'm a tube driver.'

He stopped playing. 'How so? No depots nearby.'

I gave a rueful smile. 'Well, that's just it. *Ex*-tube driver.'

He fixed me with his eyes. 'You sound sad.'

'Sad doesn't cover it. Dream job, it was. I'd been obsessed with the underground since I was a kid. The maps, the tunnels, the ghost stations, the hidden bits of track – knew it all by the age of twelve. I had the models, of course, but I always wanted to play with the real toys. I went to university to please the parents, then got the job aged twenty-two. Not a dissatisfied day since.'

'The darkness didn't trouble you?'

'It was all I ever wanted.'

'And the loneliness?'

'I occasionally got frustrated. Wished it was cleaner, safer, more efficient. But as I've discovered since leaving, loneliness comes with boredom, and I was never bored on the tube. Always in motion, oblivious to surface events, people whizzing by in a blur. The novelty never faded.'

'If you loved it so much, why did you leave?'

I tapped my chest. 'Awful asthma attack. Four months ago. Almost killed me.'

'Ah.' He grinned. 'So you moved up here for the air?'

I laughed. 'How did you guess?'

'Not much else to recommend it.'

'Really?' His frankness surprised me, given his ties with the museum. 'I thought the park was rather captivating. A bit sad, certainly, but—'

'Sad? It's downright diseased. Can't you tell, wandering around? Can't you sense the loss?'

My mind filled with the image of the two grand staircases, sweeping up to nothing but empty space.

'I'm not just talking about the Crystal Palace either,' he went on. 'I'm talking about all that's come since. Truth is, from that first fire in 1866 the place was doomed. Blaze after blaze there was. 1866, 1923, 1936, 1950. All eating away at that great old greenhouse, till not an iron column or pane of glass remained.'

I began to shiver. As tour guides went, the old man was clearly more realist than salesman, but I liked him for his honesty.

'Of course,' he continued, 'once the Palace was gone, they tried making something of the park it left behind. But everything here rots in the end.'

'What did they try?'

'You name it: motor racing, a dry ski slope, concerts down at the bowl. But it was no use. Just as the Palace itself wasn't allowed to survive, so nothing survives in the Palace's place.'

As he spoke, I gazed up, out of the subway. The giant transmitter was just visible over the walls, its white tip disappearing amid a descending mist.

'How about you?' I asked, turning back. 'How long have you been in the—'

I stopped. The old man was nowhere to be seen. He'd vanished with the same improbable ghostliness with which he'd first appeared in the museum.

Unnerved and yet also oddly charmed by his antics, I headed back through the subway. I knew what he meant about the eerie atmosphere – I'd felt that oppressive absence – but his insinuation of a curse, plaguing the Palace and all that followed, was obviously just the result of too many years spent pondering the park's unhappy history. Besides which, it was obvious that he revelled in the creepiness: dashing around in the Palace's absent shadow, dumbfounding its visitors, practising his song but never noticeably improving.

I started back up the steps, smiling at the old man's mischief-making. A moment later, however, my amusement ceased as I reached the roadside, and the song came again.

'Your arm bone's connected to your wrist bone,
And your wrist bone's connected to your hand bone . . .'

Of course, I told myself, he was just playing games: hiding somewhere, doubtless delighting in my confusion. And yet there was something not right about the sound. It was one voice, but it arrived on the icy air as if emanating directly from the landscape. There was no immediacy to it; just faintness and echo, as if expressing a dying memory that belonged to the whole of the park.

I set off across the road, and the music started to fade. In its place, memory of the old man's words reverberated in my mind.

'A different note on the push and the pull,' he'd said. 'Strange air. Strange, strange air.'

Chapter 4

'Mister!'

Thomas glanced up. A sun-silhouetted figure dived towards him, clattering him off the railway track and into a heap on the siding. Looking up, he saw what he'd somehow missed: a five-coach atmospheric train, complete with its own piston carriage where the loco should have been, speeding silently over the spot where he'd been crouching mere moments before.

'So quiet,' he whispered, climbing to his feet as the up train arrived in the station. 'How can it possibly be so quiet?'

'It's alright, mister,' came a half-broken voice. 'You're not the first, although I s'pose you may be the last. The silence startles everyone first time they hear it.'

It was the young lad from the carriage; the one who'd looked so sorrowful at talk of the atmospheric's demise. His white shirt had been scarred by the tumble, but his pale cheeks were aglow with excitement.

'I saw you walk down here, sir. I could tell you weren't savvy with the ways of the atmos. And heck, I could already see the up train coming down the slope, so I thought someone had better get you out the way.'

'First my head, now my life itself.' Thomas helped the young man up, grateful for his concern, without which he'd have been better acquainted with the underside of an atmospheric piston carriage than even he should have desired. 'Please believe me, had I any money on me, it would be yours. Alas, I was unlucky enough to—'

'Mister, it's fine. You weren't to know the stealth of the atmos.'

'It really is the most extraordinary thing I've ever – or rather *never* – heard.'

'Bit different to the locos, eh?'

'There's something quite ghostly—'

He was struck by a shrill, other-worldly whistling.

'That's the vacuum tube, sir,' explained the boy. 'They send the telegraph signal the moment the up train passes through, so now the engine at Forest Hill is sucking air out the tube. The hissing's because the valve's still not up to snuff.'

'You mean as the vacuum increases? Air is getting past the leather, into the tube?'

'Right, sir. It's been a big problem, especially on this stretch, where you need a high vacuum to haul her uphill.'

They set off back to the station.

'Do you work on the line yourself?' asked Thomas.

'Not *on* it, sir; *by* it. My dad owns The Greyhound at Sydenham Station, so I've got to know its workings quite well. The steamies still go past, but there's magic in the atmos. Sometimes my dad wants errands run into town, and I take every chance I get!'

They reached the front of their train, where the driver was examining his barometer.

'Pressure's ready,' he called. 'All aboard!'

Back in the carriage, Thomas watched as the trackside capstans, attached by rope to the piston carriage, began to turn. With a silent smoothness that belied its weight, the train resumed its motion.

'So what about you?' asked the boy. 'Why are you riding the atmos today?'

'I'm on my way to the Old Town.'

'Are you?'

'Indeed I am.'

The young man studied the engineer's handsome attire.

'I'm guessing that's a professional curiosity, sir. What is it you do?'

'I'm a civil engineer. Presently I'm working on the canal down in Canterbury, but my real passion is sanitation: improving water supplies and drainage. Hence why I'm off to Croydon. The Old Town is reputed to be the best place to observe the most challenging squalor—' He checked himself, remembering the likely provenance of his fellow passengers. 'And I am passionate about correcting that.'

By now, the train had reached the points. The trackside workers unhooked the ropes from the piston carriage as it passed.

'Yes, we have our railways, our bridges, our canals,' continued Thomas, 'but now we must attend to the *ramifications* of those improvements: unimagined overcrowding in towns ill-equipped for the load.'

The front of the train was now on the atmospheric line, heading by its own momentum towards the vacuum tube.

'Word is that the government's preparing to act at last. I want to be primed for when they seek inspectors to evaluate—'

His ears were assaulted by a short, sharp bang – and a smooth surge forward.

'No cause for alarm, sir,' said the young lad. 'Do continue.'

But Thomas couldn't speak; already, he was too enraptured by the ethereal acceleration.

He listened and looked ahead, to the piston carriage and beyond. Instinctively, he sought signs of visible or audible strain, whether from a taut cable being laboriously wound round a drum, or a locomotive wheezing with effort. But there was nothing; not one hint of motive force. It felt like the carriages were moving of their own free will, propelled by an energy within the iron and wood that had no extraneous impact but to move them forward, ever faster, until it felt like they were floating, or rather flying – coaxed inexorably forward by some sublime magnetic magus.

He shut his eyes and recalled how the leading coach had

veered onto the atmospheric track. He imagined its under-carriage piston entering the vacuum tube via the circular shield – an event which must have created the bang just before. Then he pictured what lay behind the piston head, and how the wheels on the rod had obviously lifted the leather valve from the tube and allowed air to rush into the vacuum – an atmospheric commotion that pushed the piston and its carriage forward, bringing with them all seven passenger carriages of the 3.56pm from London Bridge to Croydon.

He reopened his eyes, expecting the visceral thrill to diminish now he had thought through the mechanics. But if anything, the sense of ecstatic unreality only intensified. Here was an immaculate union of design and execution, the ingenuity of the theory made manifest in the poetry of the experience.

'You like it, sir?' asked the boy.

'It is quite marvellous.'

'Just you wait,' said a red-faced worker, looming over the boy's head. 'Any second now . . .'

The train began to slow; they were onto the incline.

'Please don't judge it on this,' begged the boy. 'It's not perfect, but it could be improved.'

'How so?' snorted the red-faced man. 'Doing away with the hill?'

'What hill?' chimed one of his mates. 'It's only 1 in 100. The locos have it in no time. And to think they said *this* would be its greatest strength. *So much lighter, without a loco: perfect for slopes!*'

The workers collapsed into derisive laughter, but the lad stayed fixed on Thomas.

'If things were different, sir,' he said, 'the atmos would be more efficient than a loco. If there was a second line to double the service and lighten the loads. If we had bigger tubes, better engines, less vacuum leakage. The system wasn't designed to meet this kind of demand.'

'Listen, mister,' said the red-faced cynic. 'The whole line

was suspended for six weeks when they changed the valve, and I've lost count of how often the pumping stations have failed, meaning they have to rescue us with locos. There've even been times when we've had to get out and push the bloody thing!'

'It's madness,' agreed his pal. 'All you want from a train is to go from here to there. You don't care how, just as long as it happens as quickly as bloody possible!'

This last comment silenced the zealous young lad, and no more was said until they reached Forest Hill.

As the driver brought them to a standstill, Thomas's eyes fell upon one of the network's several pumping stations. An elaborate gothic structure, with a chimney disguised as a spire, its actual earthbound purpose – using the power from a steam engine to exhaust air from the atmospheric tube – was known only by a deep droning and the odd sooty worker, flitting in and out. The incongruous architecture betrayed the engineers' high opinion of their whimsical system, and doubtless only accentuated the banality of its operational failures.

The driver released his brakes and the train slipped forwards. Moments later, another succinct explosion announced that the piston had entered the next stretch of tube.

As before, they gained speed quickly, and this time, unencumbered by any slope, the acceleration continued until they reached 40-odd miles an hour – highly impressive, given the weight of eight carriages. The velocity whipped up a wind of such vigour that conversation was prohibited, and Thomas was free to revel in the dual rushes of air: that blowing over him in one direction, and that flooding into the tube in the other, pushing them on. It was so invigorating that he found himself not only forgetting the flaws and excusing the hubris, but wondering if the obvious comparisons with cable-operated railways, and other outmoded systems, weren't entirely misplaced. If anything, this felt not like the past but the future – steam's natural successor.

'This is me, sir,' said the boy as they pulled into Sydenham. 'I know there are problems, but there's a magic in it, don't you think?'

'Most certainly.'

'You agree it's an improvement on the loco?'

'Potentially.'

'But just think if this line had been allowed to grow: all the way down to Epsom and up to London Bridge.' He jumped onto the platform. 'Just think if all them other schemes had worked: atmos up and down the country, even through the heart of London.' The train slid forwards, towards the next section of tube. 'Just think, sir.' The boy raised his voice. 'Just imagine how great it would have been!'

The piston banged, the train accelerated, and the young man passed out of sight, his passionate pleading lost on the air.

Bewitched by the serenity that sucked them on, Thomas gazed up at the lush green grounds of Penge Place, sweeping down to the railroad and sporadically covered by patches of the Great North Wood.

It was true, quite evidently, that the workers weren't going to miss the atmospheric, and there had clearly been a surfeit of hopeless operational failures to justify their disdain. But for Thomas, the reality of the thing mattered less than the principle. And it seemed absurd that such a clean and peaceful experience should default to one in which passengers were openly assaulted by the bestial fury of a steam locomotive. Yes, steam was cheaper and faster, but the working man deserved better even if he didn't realise it. It was simply wrong to rely on his being accustomed to filth, and so happy to suffer for a faster journey, when an alternative had been devised. Never mind that this was as yet slow and unreliable. If any part of people's lives could be improved – if the means were there – then the opportunity had to be made to work.

He ran his hands over his face, conscious that it didn't become him to oppose the majesty of the locomotive. And indeed, maybe his argument wasn't so much with steam as with the open-air wagons? After all, if only all passengers could be carried in covered coaches, then surely the mode of traction became irrelevant?

But this surge of feeling wasn't just about the workers. It was about the perversity of steam locomotives bringing the foulness of the metropolis to the fields, farmlands and suburbs that provided sanctuary from city squalor – and the converse potential of air power to bring freshness *in* to the city centre. This was about the whole essence of what civic transport should be.

The train swept silently through fields of golden spring, and Thomas realised he was falling in love; besotted by the beauty of the atmospheric's spirit and the elegance of its engineering. Though their acquaintance had been brief, its purity attracted him as urgently as any invention he had known. It was impossible to say how, but even at this depressing juncture, riding a line which had failed abjectly, and without any atmospheric expertise to his credit, he knew that one day he would find a way of using air to improve the lives of his fellow citizens.

For the moment, however, his priority was sanitation. This was a sphere whose time had come, and a committed study of water supplies was key to getting on. As the train slowed ahead of Norwood Station, his thoughts were again of Croydon, of his trial inspection, and the manoeuvrings required to be appointed to the rumoured Board of Health.

And yet, even as his mind filled with water, his heart lingered on air, and on the discovery of that which was all around him but whose potential, until today, he had never contemplated: the fathomless power of the atmosphere.

Chapter 5

'Strange, strange air.'

The old man's song had faded, but the words he'd spoken continued to echo round my head as I stood on the edge of the park – its atmosphere strange indeed – wondering where to go next.

On my right was a busy bus station, with a few pubs, shops and cafés just beyond. I started towards these, figuring some normal human company would do me good, but halted after a few paces. For all the old man's oddness, wandering in the shadow of the Crystal Palace had begun to ease the loneliness that had been pulling me under. The park breathed with a sadness that spoke of better days, and the affinity I felt was hard to resist.

I decided to head back to the museum and – fully expecting its resident eccentric to re-appear – insist on taking up his offer of a full tour. But before I'd got halfway, the temperature dropped still further, bringing a moisture into the air that immediately started troubling my lungs. Having idiotically left my inhaler at home, I had no choice but to cut short my wanderings and get back to the flat.

I turned onto the main road and tracked the park's perimeter from the outside. Beside me, the wood gave way to a grassy enclosure containing the four divergent legs of the giant transmitter. My eyes followed the steel curves up through several hundred feet until they were cut off by the mist, which was thickening as fast as it was descending. Over half the structure was already missing, and it wouldn't be long before the clouds devoured the peak of the hill itself.

With my breathing getting shallower by the second, I took the first downhill turning I could, intersecting a caravan park on the left and the transmitter complex on the right – singularly failing to register the lane's narrowness until some old brick ruins appeared beside me, identified by a disappearing sign as 'The World's Oldest Aquarium'. Heart sinking, I realised that the curving lane was returning me to the park.

I turned to retrace my steps, only to find the mist rolling over the trees and tumbling down the lane. Predatory and insistent, it filled me with an intense yet irrational fear. Hearing again the old man's song on the air – *'Now your wrist bone's connected to your hand bone . . .'* – I let the mist push me back onto the Palace terraces, where the hazy suburban sea of south-east London once again arranged itself before me.

Guessing my direction as best I could, I bore left into unchartered territory, glancing back briefly to see the transmitter – along with the whole upper stretch of the park – now entirely cloaked in white. As I did so, the old man's song faded away as imperceptibly as it had returned.

Of all the areas in the park, this new section was the most carefully landscaped. Bordered by woods and etched with paths, the lawns swept down to a leaf-covered pond. On the far side of the water stood a concert bowl, its rusty roof agape over the stage like a half-opened laptop, flanked by two decrepit speaker towers. Involuntarily, I found myself imagining the far-off echo of a rock concert, and as a wider tarmac road joined my path, this mingled with the pulsing drone of motor racing, reverberating round the rolling grass banks. In my head, at least, the grounds resonated with ghosts of the past, as invoked by the old man in the subway. The effect was so vivid that I momentarily forgot the advancing mist, and the icy clouds that soon billowed around me, whiting out the concert bowl and ensuring that only the next few metres were visible.

Ignoring a sign pointing to the 'Maze', I continued down the main path. The silence was punctuated only by the gentle lapping of a lake on my left, which was itself soon deadened as the mist reached saturation point. Now, there was no longer even any ground beneath me. Instead, the moist air swirled like plumes of steam, and it was as if my torso, arms and thighs were gliding effortlessly through the clouds. Either that, or my body was being swallowed by some cold, silent, smoky inferno.

Then I slipped. Unable to see the path curving away, I slid on some mud, and skidded down a slope. I came to rest horribly light-headed, wheezing through the otherwise immaculate silence as I got sheepishly to my feet. Staying on a level, I kept walking until the ground rose and my feet hit a solid path. I sent a relieved sigh billowing through the mist, only to realise that the path was covered with ice.

Cursing, I jumped into the adjacent mud and clambered up an incline. By now I was perilously close to an all-out asthma attack. The dizziness was terrible – I could feel the park spinning, even though I couldn't see it – and I'd completely lost my bearings. Walking in a circle, desperate for my inhaler, I prodded the mud with my foot. I'd ended up on the peak of some kind of mound, and was dithering over which direction to take when the sound of a bus, pressurising its air brakes, pierced the misty silence. It was only brief, but loud enough to pinpoint a road, not far off.

This was all the encouragement I needed. Within moments, my wheezing subsided, and I wondered how I'd let the conditions conspire to leave me feeling so vulnerable. Facing the road, sensing the warmth of home, I put my left foot forward and brought the right one through.

Except that I couldn't: my foot wouldn't budge. Somehow, it had become stuck so stubbornly that, as I lurched forward and back, the danger wasn't toppling over so much as snapping in two. I tightened my thigh and jerked up from the knee, but no sooner had I freed my foot than my whole leg was pulled back down.

I stumbled backwards. My ankle slid into the mud, and my jeans tightened and tore round my buttocks. Crying out, I yanked my leg upwards, but this time it was even more of a struggle and took several attempts to pull my foot free. Finally liberated, I hopped to the left, only to be tugged violently back as my unseen foe – a squirrel? a dog? some kind of fox? – grabbed my right shin. With a vice-like grip, it pulled me down with gigantic force.

I toppled to the right, slapping shoulder-first into the mud. My foot gave its assailant the slip and I flipped onto my bum, scrambling away as a flash of brilliant white shot up, a foot above the ground.

I heaved in a gasp of horror and astonishment. For what I was looking at was no animal; it was no living thing at all. The whiteness was the white of bone, and the bone belonged to a human hand: a skeleton's hand, glowing in the mist above a slender wrist, all of a piece, functioning together, yet with nothing between each bone. No ligaments, no tendons, no muscle: just air.

It paused, upright and motionless. Then the fingers began flexing, as if sniffing for a scent. It turned its palm slowly towards me, periscope-like, before emerging further to reveal the elbow joint. A second later, with impossible speed, it lunged and grabbed my ankle.

Off I slid again, skidding helplessly as the arm withdrew. Writhing and screaming, I plunged my hands into the ground and locked my arms to provide resistance. For a few inches this achieved nothing, but soon the accumulation of mud around my wrists stopped my downwards slide. I transferred my energies into my lower body, drilling my other leg into the earth to provide a pivot, while heaving up the captive limb as powerfully as possible. At last, the icy grip of the skeleton's hand failed, and the lower half of my leg reappeared.

Crawling away, I watched the arm thrust up again and

reach towards me, fingers pinching the air in the wake of my retreating foot. Finally, once I was a good few yards away, the arm flipped back to the vertical. After another moment's periscoping, the open palm looking this way and that, it shot back down into the ground.

I froze, not daring to move in case I triggered another assault. Staring at the spot from which the arm had emerged, I listened to the gurgle of mud and water as the ground reset itself. The seconds became minutes, and a silence fell over the scene. It seemed that the hand had relented. Nervously, I exhaled, sending spectral wisps through the air as I checked for signs of disturbance elsewhere in the earth.

All seemed calm, so I stood up. My breathing was still impaired, and I realised how lucky I'd been to have avoided a full-blown seizure. I turned to walk away, but couldn't resist glancing back at the hole through which the hand had appeared. To my amazement, not only was there no trace of the arm, but the hole itself had vanished. The mud was level and entirely still, indistinguishable from the surrounding earth, but for one of several footprints I'd left behind.

Certain of nothing but my shock, the sound of traffic seeped back into my mind. I tip-toed towards it, steadiness restored with each unimpeded step, until my way was blocked by a wooden fence. The mist was lifting around me, and I didn't have to follow the boundary more than a few metres to the right before reaching the gate that led into my garden.

A minute later, I was back in my flat: home, at last, from my stroll round the park.

Chapter 6

Ten years after his revelatory trip on the atmospheric, Thomas decided that it was time to begin.

The men of the papers were chatting jovially in a pen at the foot of the stage, while a modest crowd had built up behind them. Most importantly, the time was approaching 7.30am, and the passing traffic was nearing its peak.

Waiting beside the wooden platform he had assembled, furnished with two little tables that laboured under piles of pamphlets, Thomas prepared for his entrance. The stage faced the north-eastern corner of the square, where the first hints of summer's warmth had provoked an unwelcome display of colour from the blossoming trees and flowers. He hadn't exactly wished for wind and rain, of course, but the notion that being on the city streets at this hour was in any way tolerable, let alone moderately pleasant, was hardly conducive to his arguments.

Pleasant, however, it undeniably was, with the sunlit view dominated by the district's two magnificent landmarks. On the right stood the white Portland stone of the opulent new church of St. Pancras, while off on the left was the more earthbound Euston Arch – 200 yards away but strikingly severe, its stone pillars and Doric façade looming over the intervening houses with all the pride of the age.

Brushing a butterfly off his hat, Thomas adjusted his necktie, ensuring it was just so, then straightened his waistcoat and hat. A few years ago, working as a superintending inspector for the General Board of Health, he'd faced far more hostile crowds without the faintest anxiety. Now, however, he could no longer hide behind his institution. This was nobody's scheme but his own.

He climbed onto the stage and introduced himself. The pressure pulsed through him as he described his four successful years at the GBH, visiting towns and reporting on their despicable hygiene, then recommending solutions for improving drainage and water supplies. It was hard not to sound immodest as the rumble and clatter of the streets forced him to raise his voice, but no matter. He was enormously proud of his achievements and, besides, only the boldest attitude would suffice if his ideas were to be heard above the figurative din of rival schemes.

Certainly, his resonant voice was proving an effective magnet to those thronging along the Euston Road on his left, and Upper Woburn Place on his right. Before long his corner of the square was full, and people outside were having to peer through the trees to watch. Clearly his talent for public speaking, so powerful in herding the poor for the GBH, remained potent.

'But why am I here,' he asked, 'distracting you at such an awkward time?' He held out his arms. 'Look around, and there is my answer. A sea of people, possessed by the need to get to work fast, but prevented by the stasis on the streets: a paralysis so insufferable that you happily seek this moment's sanctuary to escape the clutches of over-priced omnibuses and sluggish stagecoaches.

'And who can blame you? Bring me the sound-minded man who thinks it acceptable that your progress to honest days' labours, in factories, workshops and offices, is hindered by the miserly crawl of advertising vans, wagons on their way to market, or private carriages occupied by one or two gentlemen at most. Truly, I would love to meet such a man, for no such man exists.'

The crowd was at least a hundred strong: an ocean of rapt white eyeballs.

'But of course I do you a disservice to think you'd ever dream of using so-called *public* transport. Sensible souls as you are, you've long since realised that the only practical option is to put one foot before the other; to become one of two hundred thousand travellers trudging across town, in at morning then out at night, leaping over horses' mess, dodging waterfalls from overhead windows, paying to cross bridges, weaving between the stalls, and trying above all to *avoid each other*. For ultimately nothing delays us more than the sheer number of people making the same daily pilgrimage – a swarm swelled immeasurably by that otherwise most wonderful invention: the railway.'

The crowd in the square was still growing, and the lines outside were several bodies deep.

'Now please don't mistake me. It thrills me that, just over there, one can board a train and be in our great Midland cities within hours. And doubtless it excites those of you who travelled in by train this morning, that the railways afford you the luxury of working in London while living elsewhere.'

He gestured towards Euston. 'But look again at that mighty arch. Conceived as a gateway to our capital, has it not instead become a barrier? A symbol of how our great termini – Paddington, Euston, King's Cross, Fenchurch Street, London Bridge – represent the end of the line in the profoundest sense? That fateful decree a decade ago, insisting the railways stop short of the city centre, has created a ludicrous problem: stalemate on our roads, and pavements congested not just with those walking in from the outskirts, but those brought part way into London by the railways, only to be deposited short of their destination. For them, the situation is doubly absurd.'

'Hear, hear!' cried a man at the front of the crowd, just behind the press enclosure. 'I come up from Brighton for meetings in Paddington twice a week. Takes as long from London Bridge to Paddington as from Brighton to London Bridge!'

Thomas smiled as a dozen others bellowed out variations on the same theme. Realising that the crowd was fully encircling him – a good two or three hundred bodies – he raised his hands to quieten the cacophony. There was real momentum to his speech, and he had to make it count.

'Now since the railways are culpable for this mess,' he resumed, 'ought we not demand of them a solution?'

'Yes we bloody well ought!' shouted a woman. 'Get them all to extend their lines into town, build a central station, have done with it!'

'Ah yes,' said Thomas, 'that would indeed be the most obvious remedy. Alas, not only is it now impossible, given the density of stubborn landowners blocking the way, but it is also rather inflexible, in such a rapidly expanding city. Far better, surely, to have an entire railway network *within* the central area. One which offers *numerous* station stops, while minimising the destruction of property. A railway, in other words, which must be built either above our heads or below our feet.'

The faces in the crowd were uniformly expectant: listening attentively, hoping he might be their saviour.

'Above or below,' he said again. 'That is the question. And it's one to which Charles Pearson *thought* he had the answer. Now Mr. Pearson is a lawyer, so his selfless intent was never in doubt, but I think we all struggled to comprehend the benefits of a scheme that would have brought *extra* chaos to our streets by digging them up, laying tracks and tunnels, then re-covering them and demanding we descend like moles into the darkest depths of the earth.'

'Intolerable!' came a cry from outside the square.

'Unthinkable!' yelled someone else.

'And there you have it.' Thomas smiled. 'I clearly needn't repeat the protests of medics and priests, horrified at what pestilence and demonic peril awaited us underground, not to mention my fellow engineers, unanimous that laying such apparatus was impossible, given the sewers and pipes clogging up the London clay. Indeed, there were so many objections, it's hard to believe it has taken so long for this embryonic "Metropolitan Railway" to reach the brink of collapse. But even if we do not mourn its passing, Mr. Pearson's preposterous proposals have at least shown that there is only one answer to the critical question – above or below?'

He reached for a pamphlet. Hitherto he'd attacked popular targets. Now, he had to convert the crowd's easily excited ire into enthusiasm for something new.

'For all our benefits, I have formulated *A New Plan for Street Railways*.' He showed off the pamphlet. 'A simple system – affordable, clean, safe and reliable – which will get our city moving in the most unobtrusive way.'

'Enough of the grand claims, Mr. Rammell!' bellowed a man in the press enclosure. 'Give us the details, and let us form our own opinions.'

Thomas looked down to discover that the heckler was none other than John Herapath of the *Railway Journal*: arguably the most influential railway journalist in the land. Smiling politely, he opened the pamphlet and did as Herapath asked.

'It all begins with the trackwork,' he explained, 'to be built 14 feet above the pavements. With no outer work or parapets, it will consist solely of the rails: narrower gauge than normal, fixed on one side to the buildings themselves, and supported on the other by thin, cast-iron columns rising from the kerbstones below.'

He glanced round; the crowd seemed genuinely intrigued.

'The railway may be built – and extended – with a fraction of the fuss proposed by Mr. Pearson's moles, and will pose no obstacle to movement or light. Since access will be from stations on the higher floors of new or existing buildings, none protruding beyond the frontage plane of their native street, the railway will only ever be noticed when a train glides by, casting its fleeting shadow across the scene below.'

'How very appealing,' said Herapath. 'One just worries how such rudimentary trackwork is to support the weight of the locomotive-driven trains to which we are accustomed.'

Thomas tensed up; the journalist was playing a mischievous game.

'Mr. Herapath makes an astute observation,' he said, raising his voice to guard against what was to come: the trickiest part, no doubt, but also the most precious to him. 'Indeed my trains will be lighter than the norm. How so? Well, firstly, since they will only ever be used to transport passengers, they can be built to a far less heavyweight specification. Secondly, the carriages will be exceptionally plain, eliminating all unnecessary luxury. And thirdly, the mode of power will be atmospheric.'

He tried not to falter, but couldn't help it – taken aback by the number of people who tutted, groaned or rolled their eyes. Within moments, an exodus began.

'Dear oh dear, Mr. Rammell.' Herapath smirked as he looked around. 'Was it something you said?'

As so often with men of the press, John Herapath's power was proportionate to his size. Being very portly indeed, many believed that his opposition to atmospheric power had been instrumental in scuppering the original 1840s lines. That was a precedent which Thomas could ill-afford to repeat – hence his determination to involve Herapath from the start, persuading the journalist of the progress he'd made.

'It won't be like the atmospheric railways of the past,' he said.

'Shame!' returned Herapath. 'I had such fun mocking them!'

'In the countryside, don't forget, its noiselessness and cleanliness were squandered in the largely deserted surroundings – whereas here, in the deafening, toxic metropolis, such qualities will be cherished. Practically, too, shorter, more regular stops will mean the atmospheric tube can be laid in more manageable sections.'

'I can vouch for the atmospheric's silence,' said Herapath, raising his hand. 'Exactly as peaceful as you'd expect from a train incapable of forward motion!'

There was now a queue of people waiting to leave the square, while those that remained looked increasingly restless. Thomas felt his panic rising.

'I don't deny the old atmospheric had its failings,' he continued. 'But my new system remedies every single one. So the closing valve, which seals the vacuumed tube, has been significantly improved, while I will also install a vacuum reservoir between the air pumps and the tube. The engines will therefore be more reliable, since they will operate continuously, not in fits and starts, to exhaust this reservoir. What's more, the trains won't be delayed waiting for air to be sucked out of the tube, since there will be a vacuum on tap.'

The crowd was half what it had been five minutes before.

'How will the railways actually operate?' asked a man.

'Poorly!' cried Herapath, much to the amusement of his acolytes in the press.

'They will not be like traditional routes,' replied Thomas, 'running from a to b, with an up line and a down line. Rather, each will constitute an endless course, much like a racetrack. In some cases, the circuit will be contained within a single street, with trains passing up one side and down the other. But when the streets themselves constitute a natural circuit, the routes will pass along successive roads, turning with the natural flow, then returning down different streets to reach the original starting point. In these cases, an outer ring will carry trains one way while an inner ring, on the opposite side of the street, will take services in the other direction.'

He was feeling nauseous now, doubting every word that left his lips. Nobody was watching from outside the square; those within numbered less than a hundred. Following Herapath's example, the journalists had begun packing away their notepads, sniggering among themselves – doubtless at

Thomas's expense.

'Stations will be half a mile apart, enabling trains to move simultaneously from stop to stop at 20 miles per hour: not just more convenient, but one hundred per cent safe. After all, with every train moving in the same direction, propelled by atmospheric power, collisions are literally impossible.'

'Give up, Mr. Rammell!' shouted Herapath, as he led the other journalists away. 'The old atmospheric railway embarrassed far more accomplished engineers than you. If you have any sense, you'll steer well away from it in future.'

Thomas took a deep breath. It felt futile to conclude, but he was determined to finish what he'd started.

'My intention,' he went on, voice cracking, 'is to begin with this very thoroughfare, connecting the termini of the Great Western, London and North Western, and Great Northern Railways, with a view to extending to the City and south of the river.' He took one final breath, the humiliation almost over. 'A prospectus to that effect will shortly be issued, and in the meantime you may collect copies of my pamphlet.'

There was no applause; no murmur of enthusiasm or even derision. Instead, he just stepped back and watched the few remaining spectators walk away, happier to re-join the chaos on the streets than dwell another second in the company of him and his *New Plan*.

Chapter 7

After returning from the park, my top priority was to see off my asthma. I took a couple of drags on my trusty blue reliever inhaler, and chased them with two more on the preventative brown one. The big attack four months before had left me unusually susceptible to more like it. Though I'd had no trouble since moving house, the suddenness of the day's exertions, after so long cooped up inside, made me extra cautious.

I took off my mud-encrusted clothes – the jeans, ripped in several places, were a lost cause – and after a long, soothing shower, went to my bedroom to watch darkness creep over the park.

The mist had lifted completely, leaving the twilight clear and, I guessed, bitterly cold. As the minutes passed, my sphere of recollection expanded. I pulled back from the skeleton hand, pinching wildly yet connected by nothing but air, and brought into view the falls and slips, the imagined sounds, the museum man with his crazy talk of curses and unceasing rendition of 'Dem Bones', sounding like it came from the whole of the park. My asthma had left me distinctly light-headed, and I wondered if my imagination hadn't gone into overdrive. Though I'd clearly struggled with *something* – my ruined jeans confirmed that – it was surely nothing more than tangled twigs and roots, scrambled into skeletal form by memory of the old man's song.

I turned away from the window. Confident that the hand

had only ever existed in my head, a wave of relief washed through me, and I became aware of a crushing hunger. I knew I had the noodles I'd uncovered earlier, but the more I thought about it, the keener I was to set my idiot mind straight. After the weeks of solitude, I didn't want my torpor compounded by some silly waking nightmare. For my own good, I had to get out. I pulled on my winter coat and set off for the supermarket.

Outside, the star-sprinkled sky was brilliantly clear, dominated by a full moon which softened the streetlamps' orange glare. The chill pierced my bones, and I strode briskly up the road, ignoring the gloom of the park on my left.

Reaching the top of the hill, I walked through the moonlit shadows of the great transmitter, its vertiginous steel gleaming cleanly above, until the pubs and cafés of Upper Norwood came into view ahead. The road was busier now – rush hour was upon us – and the cacophony only intensified as a set of wailing sirens split the roar of traffic: three fire engines, followed by a pair of ambulances and a vanload of police, whizzing past and disappearing down the far side of the park.

I arrived at the fence enclosing the ruined subway, and looked into the park. A distinct amber glow hovered in the night air, off to the right, and I felt suddenly ill-at-ease – seized once again by the notion that the park was playing tricks on me.

I walked on a short way, then stopped again. Determined to forget the earlier nonsense in the wood, it seemed wrong to let my fear get in the way of curiosity.

Taking a deep breath, I turned into the park and began walking towards the light. I skirted the subway – the ground frozen to a crisp – then descended a level until an avenue of trees came into view on my right, framing the museum. A violent inferno was engulfing the little building.

'Get back!'

A throng of firemen spilled out of the surrounding woods, waving me away. I did as I was told, stepping back through the monstrous, flickering shapes that the fire projected onto the grass.

Once I was a safe distance away, I turned to watch, and the fire-fighters did the same: powerless to save the lonely brick building, and all the history contained within. Given the time of day, it seemed safe to assume no one was trapped inside – the fleet-footed old man, I figured, would have escaped in good time – but I felt saddened nonetheless.

'Told you.'

I jumped.

'Place is cursed.'

The museum man stepped up beside me, concertina held close to his chest.

'Last remaining building of the Crystal Palace,' he said. 'Now it's gone the same way as the rest.'

'I'm sorry,' I said.

'Sorry?' He turned to face me, eyebrows rising. 'Why should *you* be sorry?'

'It's where you work, isn't it?'

'Oh.' He looked back at the burning building. 'Well, I wouldn't say *work* as such. It's where I spend a lot of my time.'

'That and the subway?'

He nodded. 'Pretty much.'

'Well, either way. You have my condolences.'

He shrugged. 'Just one more conflagration to add to the list.'

'Do you know how it started?'

'Do I know?' He laughed and unlocked his concertina. 'Of course I don't. Nobody does. Nobody ever *will*.' There was a great whoosh as he drew air into the instrument. 'That's the pattern, son. No Palace fire has ever been satisfactorily explained.'

'Really?'

'Not a single one. Theories aplenty, but that's all they are: speculation. Nobody's ever produced any hard evidence. Not a shred. That's why I say: place is cursed. Has to be.'

He wandered off, leaving me to eavesdrop on the firemen's chatter. For all the old man's supernatural innuendo, there seemed little doubt among the professionals that the blaze had been sparked by local kids, misbehaving with leftover fireworks from Bonfire Night. But just as I was about to make my own way out of the park, I heard the old man's song, receding into the distance:

> 'Well, your neck bone's connected to your shoulder bone,
> And your shoulder bone's connected to your arm bone.
> Your arm bone's connected to your wrist bone,
> And your wrist bone's connected to your hand . . .'

There was an explosion at the heart of the fire, and my mind filled with the vision from earlier: the skeleton's hand, reaching and clasping. Instinctively, I ran after the old man, who was limping uphill, towards the subway.

'Good grief!' He squeaked the concertina shut. 'What the devil?'

'Your song,' I panted. 'Something that happened . . .'

'Happened?'

I hesitated. 'In my imagination.'

I knew I shouldn't tell him, but I needed to tell *someone*. I hoped it might banish the vision from my mind.

'It was after I met you earlier. The mist brought on my asthma, and I ended up back in the park, dazed, on this tiny little mound . . .'

He stared back, unblinking. 'And?'

'And this thing . . .' I raised my wrist and waved it around, tethered at the elbow. 'This human hand, white and bony like a skeleton . . . It burst through the mud and tried to pull me in.'

The old man grinned, his eyes glistening in marvel. 'Where did this happen?'

'It didn't happen.'

'But where did you *imagine* it happening?'

I waved vaguely in the right direction. 'Somewhere over there.'

'Over towards the Sydenham gate?'

I shrugged. 'Could be.'

He shoved me aside, limping down the terrace steps and setting off towards the landscaped part of the park.

'You're not actually going looking for it?' I shouted.

'Why on earth not?' he called back. 'Just your imagination, remember?'

'But it's dark. It'll be dangerous in the woods!'

'The moon'll guide us well enough.'

'What if it's icy?'

'Come on!' He quickened into a fitful run. 'I need you to show me where it didn't happen!'

I had no choice. Not to follow would mean admitting that maybe I hadn't imagined the attack after all. I had to trust my conviction: return to the wood before the horrors took deeper root in my mind.

I set off in reluctant pursuit, re-joining the old man by the rusty concert bowl, its leafy pond absorbing all light and giving nothing back. The flames from the museum had become obscured by intervening trees, but the moonlight readily penetrated the barren branches overhead.

'One thing I don't understand,' he said, as I drew level.

'What's that?'

'About your job.'

'Go on.'

'If you loved it so much – why not take your chances and continue?'

'I would if I could. But truth be told, it wasn't my choice to leave.'

'You got sacked?'

I nodded. 'It was my own stupid fault. I'd struggled with asthma ever since I was a kid, but I was damned if it was going to ruin my dream. So when I did the medical form for

London Underground – well, let's just say I might have forgotten to mention the state of my lungs.

'For twelve years, I kept it in check. I'd dose up on my brown inhaler religiously; use the reliever occasionally in the cab. But back in July, this desperately hot day did for me. Worst attack I've ever known. I passed out, the train was stuck in a tunnel for over an hour.' I hesitated, thinking back to what little I remembered of that fateful day. 'Course, it all came out after that, and I had no comeback. I'd not been honest; I'd put others' lives at risk. I had to go.' I let out a long, lingering sigh. 'Who knows? Perhaps if I'd been honest initially . . .'

We were behind the lake that backed on to the music stage. On our right was a depression which I recognised as the slope I'd fallen down, shortly before my imagined entanglement with the undead.

'I miss it,' I said simply, conscious of getting carried away in the old man's attentive, amiable company.

'What are you going to do now?' he asked.

'My friends keep saying I should get a job driving overground trains. That was my plan, moving up here. But I've come to realise: it wasn't the driving trains that I loved; it was being underground.'

I looked to my right, and spotted the point where I'd re-joined the frozen path. From here, it was easy to determine the slope I'd staggered up – the same little peak which had caught my eye when I first entered the park: oddly bald, like some kind of burial mound.

'This is it, right?' asked the museum man. He was already heading towards the top.

'Must've been.' I stayed glued to the path.

'And tell me: what did you do to provoke the – ahem – hand?'

'I did nothing to *provoke the hand*. I was just standing there, about to walk off, when my foot got tangled up.'

'In your imagination,' he said.

'Yes,' I replied sharply. 'In my imagination.'

'Hmm . . .' He stroked his beard. 'How to stir *le main* from *le mud*? A little Morris dancing perhaps? A stern military march? A hop, a skip, a jump?'

He tried each in turn, unlocking his concertina and squeezing out a histrionic instrumental of 'Dem Bones' while howling with laughter. His entire motivation in dragging me to the wood appeared to be to mock me, and I didn't mind one bit. The frivolity helped restore my composure, and it wasn't long before I too was striding up the bank. The mud had frozen to a crust, and the absence of the earlier moistness – the sense that the ground was sucking you in, which had surely shaped my hallucinations – only strengthened my resurgent confidence.

'Come out, come out wherever you are!' I bellowed, leaping around on the peak as my companion sang along to his tune:

> 'Now your shoulder bone's connected to your arm bone,
> And your arm bone's connected to your wrist bone.
> Your wrist bone's connected to your hand bone . . .'

'Wait!' I shouted.

The old man stopped. A powerful silence descended, broken only by the distant cooing of owls.

'With the ground so hard, I should be able to see my footsteps from earlier. If we test each in turn—'

'Great idea!'

Together we kneeled and prowled: scouring the area, finding plenty of footprints, but provoking nothing untoward.

The old man sighed. 'What a shame.'

'I'm sorry,' I said, as I spotted one final footprint that had eluded us both. 'In all seriousness, though, I'm glad you led me up here.' I peered closely at the mark. 'The memory would've haunted me forever if I'd not had the guts to—'

I couldn't finish. Just as I prodded the final footprint, there was a grisly gurgle, and a hole slurped open. Before I could react, two bony hands shot up and grabbed my skull, jerking me into the ground.

Within seconds my entire head was submerged, the downwards movement halted only by my shoulders refusing to fit inside the hole. My eyes were clamped shut against the mud, and the moist earth seeped into my nostrils and mouth as the bony fingers dug into my scalp. The rest of my body was splayed out on the cold earth, neck and spine screaming in agony. Just as it felt like my head was about to be ripped clean off, my shoulders squeezed themselves into the hole and the rest of me flipped to the vertical.

Instinctively I wanted to fight back – to squirm and kick – but I knew this would only hasten my descent. Instead I stayed static, sinking a further few inches, ever more desperate for air, until the pressure around my head suddenly eased, and I was able to breathe again.

The thin atmosphere smelt almost unbearably putrid. As the hard fingers shook my skull, urging my podgy belly through, my shallow, wheezy breaths echoed back at me. Astonished and terrified, I realised that I was entering an underground chamber – and it was bigger, *much* bigger, than any kind of coffin.

My torso squeezed into the space, leaving only my feet above ground. Both my arms flopped past me and swayed in the cold air, while the space vacated by my belly allowed a little moonlight to sneak through: not much, but enough to bounce off the angular outline of my attacker and confirm that the phantom arms belonged to an entire skeleton. It was kneeling on the floor with the skull staring up at me, expressionless but for its default, demented grin, and the glare of its empty eye sockets.

For several seconds I gazed back, unable to look anywhere but into the hollow depths of the skull. It was only when *it* looked away from *me*, gathering strength for a redoubled assault, that I realised I couldn't actually see the rest of its bones because they were covered by clothes – baggy men's clothes, through which its spiky skeletal framework was unmistakeable.

It was this that set me off. A bone-chilling shiver shot through me, and I screamed like never before. Surely this had to be a nightmare; and surely, in realising it, I'd wake up.

It wasn't to be. Instead, as the moonlight spread, dusting the chamber with faint silver rays, I discerned the shocking outline of yet more skulls, belonging to skeletons sitting upright on either side, held together by the same impossible force that was sustaining my attacker. Unlike him, these others were motionless, but they too were fully clothed: bony bodies draped in knee-length coats and full-length dresses, complete with neckties, waistcoats and shawls.

Unable to take any more madness, I seized my assailant's forearms, visible because his oversized sleeves had bunched up at the elbows, and was about to push him away when something grabbed my ankles, hauling me up so powerfully that the skeleton lost his grip and collapsed to the floor.

For a moment I was ascending, but then the skeleton scuffled to his feet and grasped my head again. Before I knew it, I was going back down.

'Eric!' The museum man's voice was faint. 'Can you hear me?'

'For Christ's sake!' I cried. 'Pull harder!'

He took me at my word. Up I went, more quickly than before, and soon the nape of my neck was touching the soft mud of the hole. But then the skeleton counterattacked, yanking me back down. I tried to prise the bony fingers off the side of my skull, but the ongoing tug of war made it difficult to get the right purchase. Finally, I summoned enough strength to peel off the palms from below, handing the old man the initiative. Shutting my eyes as the mud closed in, I slid upwards, awash with relief as my torso, head, then lastly my flailing arms squelched out of the hole, and my rescuer dragged me to safety.

'Good Lord above!' he exclaimed. 'What the devil is it?'

I sat up and saw the skeleton's hands snapping at the winter air: bones bright and unmuddied, fingertips tapping. The arms emerged as far as the elbows, swinging round in a frantic, last-ditch attempt to retrieve their prey.

'Don't worry,' I panted, digging my inhaler out of my pocket and taking a deep drag. 'We're out of reach.'

'But what if the whole thing comes up?'

'It won't. Will it?'

A moment later, the arms grew dispirited and the motion died. This time, however, as they sank back into the earth, something checked my relief: a faint, hoarse human whisper.

'Eeeh, reek,' came the voice, as the hands disappeared. '*Eeeh, reek.*'

'Did you hear that?' I asked.

The old man didn't answer.

'What was that?' I persisted. 'What did it say?'

The gurgling hole disappeared, re-sealing itself with frost.

'Eric,' said my sidekick.

'Yes?'

'That's what it was saying.'

I shuddered. '*Eeeh, reek,*' it had croaked. I fell back against a tree.

'Well, come on,' he said, eyes aglow. 'Tell me what you saw.'

'Some kind of room.'

'A room?'

'A tomb, I guess.'

'Intact?'

'Seemed to be.'

The old man gasped.

'The skeletons were sitting upright on either side.'

'More than one?'

I nodded. 'But that's not even the weirdest thing.'

'No?'

'Their clothes; each them was dressed in old, shabby clothes – like from some costume drama.'

'And they're alive?'

'Only one was moving. But they all seemed to be *together*. Like some force is preventing them from falling apart.'

My bearded friend was totally spellbound. 'Incredible.'

'Which part?'

'All of it. But especially the suddenness: like some reflex action, the moment you touched that spot – bang!' He thumped his fist into his palm. 'Immediate punishment.'

The words had hardly left his lips when – bang! – an explosion echoed across the park.

'The museum,' he said instinctively – but already his face was lighting up with the flicker of flames.

'The museum's on the opposite side of the park,' I replied. 'Whereas this . . .'

We jogged down to the path and gazed through the trees at the lake, alive with colour as it reflected the blaze which was engulfing the disused concert platform on the opposite bank.

I turned to the old man in astonishment. How could such a fire have started, let alone taken hold, so quickly? Arson seemed the only explanation, but why bother to destroy something so useless? Was someone on a mission to rid the park of its relics? Had somebody been inspired by the museum incident – or were the same people responsible for both? None of it made sense, least of all the question of how the culprit had got the bowl burning with such ferocity.

It was then that the coincidence hit me – and, going by the dawning horror on his face, my companion too. Not the coincidence of the two fires themselves so much as the coincidence of each of the two fires happening immediately after my two struggles with the skeleton.

Without a word, we parted: the museum man limping round the back of the lake; me, sprinting downhill, giving the skeletons' peak a wide berth, and taking the first exit I found.

Back in my flat, I looked out of my bedroom window. The flames from the park flickered through the trees, and the smoky glow obscured the starry sky. Feeling unfeasibly like a criminal – like the arsonist who had remotely triggered both infernos – I stood, dumbfounded, and stared. Could it really be that, in disturbing the skeletons' rest, I had provoked them so much that they were taking out their anger on the park?

The thought was ludicrous, but each time I dismissed it, the idea returned with greater insistence. Two encounters; two fires. The symmetry was unignorable.

I watched the fires burn. As I watched, I trembled. And as I trembled, I made a vow.

Never again, for as long as I lived, would I set foot back inside that park.

Chapter 8

Ten hours after descending from his self-made stage, Thomas sat dejectedly in his study on Trafalgar Square. He stared past the uncollected pamphlets and out of the window, dimly discerning Nelson in the twilight.

The greatest frustration wasn't in failing but in not understanding why. He knew well enough when the tide had turned, but whether the cause was mere mention of the atmospheric, Herapath's malicious interjections, or a failure of his once-dependable skills of persuasion, he couldn't tell. And if he couldn't diagnose the problem this time, how could he prevent similar catastrophes in future?

Perhaps the answer was simply that there should be no future. Who was he to be bothering busy minds with visionary schemes? There was no escaping the fact that this wasn't his specialism, and in the crowded field of railway schemes the very least one needed was a reputation. Yes, he was a civil engineer. And yes, he felt the urgency of his calling most rarely. But for all that he perceived continuity between his work for the General Board of Health and his *New Plan for Street Railways*, the world was too swamped with the schemes of better-known engineers to heed such affinities for itself. If the ebbing away of his audience had demonstrated anything, it was that the quality of his proposed railway mattered nothing next to the fact that he had no claim on people's imaginations.

There was a knock at the door. He hadn't been expecting

anyone and didn't especially want visitors. But as the knocking came again, curiosity compelled him to squeeze past the pamphlets and answer.

'Hello there,' said the gentleman at the door.

Thomas could scarcely believe it.

'I see you recognise me, so I shan't indulge in the tiresome modesties of introduction. You needn't worry either. I was at Euston Square earlier. I heard all about your *New Plan*.'

Thomas shut his gaping mouth and blushed, shocked that this man, of all men, had witnessed his ruinous presentation.

'Do you have a moment to discuss it?'

There was no doubt what was coming, but Thomas consented anyway.

'Do forgive the mess,' he said. 'I haven't had a chance—'

'Never mind that,' said the man, silhouetted against the sun as it set over Pall Mall. Though his features were in shadow, Thomas readily imagined the flowing grey locks and regal forehead, together with those inquisitive eyes and tufty sideburns. It was easily overlaid since any right-minded British citizen knew of Sir Joseph Paxton and his mighty Crystal Palace, built in Hyde Park for the Great Exhibition six years previously, but latterly relocated to the slopes above Penge and Sydenham.

'I know why you're here,' began Thomas, bothered not by thoughts of Paxton's *magnum opus*, but another of his glass-and-iron schemes: an enclosed, circular, ten-mile arcade which he once proposed to carve through central London. Along with shops and a road carrying dedicated traffic, the arcade was to have contained an overhead, eight-track atmospheric railway, running in opposite directions on either side.

'You must believe me,' continued Thomas. 'Any similarity between my *New Plan* and your Great Victorian Way is purely coincidental. Though I took heart from your plans, my ideas were formulated *before* I heard of your own designs.'

'Oh, please.' Paxton stepped forward and threw his features

into relief. 'These resemblances do nothing but flatter me. As for whether they occur by accident or design, surely such questions make a mockery of our craft? Great public works are not accomplished from bursts of inspiration. They are part of a natural continuity, a collective progress spanning generations. If I am to accuse you of stealing my ideas, then you must accuse *me* of stealing from Mr. Moseley, whose not dissimilar scheme went before Parliament at the same time as my own – and both he *and* I must be grievously indebted to Mr. Clephan, Mr. Pearson, or any of the many who, at the height of the railway mania, thought to use air to suck trains around our metropolis. We are all part of the same continuum, and I defy you to show me an intelligent engineer who would wish it different.'

Thomas smiled. Paxton was every bit as kind as his reputation suggested.

'Goodness,' he went on, 'if anything, I admire your proposal because it reacts so strongly *against* the Great Victorian Way. Whereas I was too proud to make the concessions to practicality required by Parliament, you addressed its failings: forsaking grandeur for simplicity.'

Thomas's grin broadened further. This was too good to be true.

'You really think my *New Plan* might work?'

Paxton folded his arms. 'Let me put it this way. In an ideal world, an overhead atmospheric railway, in the rudimentary form you imagine, is the only civilised solution. Alas, our world is *not* ideal, and I am here to tell you that it is never going to happen.'

Thomas's heart sank. 'But why?'

'Because it has been decreed. Parliament's approval of the Metropolitan in 1853 signified its commitment to a subterranean future, and it will countenance no more overground schemes as a result – even if the Metropolitan itself fails.'

'But that's absurd,' replied Thomas. 'Nobody – not one single citizen – wants to travel underground.'

'Yes, but does anyone *want* to travel above ground? You saw the reaction earlier. Ultimately, people just want these decisions made for them. That's why Parliament exists: to make a choice and stand by it.'

Thomas stared out at the square. 'So what is there to do?'

'Lift up your head and work on. Hence my coming to visit you: to ensure your humiliation this morning doesn't put you off.'

Thomas faced his guest. 'Go on.'

'You are clearly a man of standards, Mr. Rammell. You possess that rare quality of caring more about people than profit. And given that you are ploughing a furrow I too once explored, I felt moved to offer you some advice: honest words about where you stand, and where you should go next.'

'And where might that be?'

'I have already told you: underground.'

Thomas laughed.

'I mean it. A good engineer works not with the world as he would like it to be, but the world as it *is*. Your task is to embrace the subterranean reality and express yourself within it; to take your *New Plan* and think what qualities might usefully be adapted. For although Parliament has decided the railways shall go underground, there is yet one crucial decision to be made.'

Thomas felt his heart quicken. 'The mode of power.'

'Precisely!' Paxton began pacing, his enthusiasm infectious. 'I've been around long enough to know what happens. Even if the Metropolitan weathers its present financial crisis – even if it doesn't, indeed; even if another company assumes its mantle – the pattern will be the same. Such will be the pressure to achieve the extraordinary feat of building railways beneath our feet, the means of actually powering them will only be addressed as an afterthought. Once they come to it, they'll either lack the money to explore different methods, or the investors will be too eager to open.' He placed his hands on Thomas's shoulders. 'Truly, I would stake my life – I'd stake the Crystal Palace itself – on the fact that when our first underground railway opens, it will be powered in the most readily available way: the only way we really know how.'

Thomas stared back. 'They wouldn't dare.'

'They'd have no choice.'

'But these will be short journeys, with no need for such brute force. As for the practicalities – the emissions alone would prove fatal!'

'It sounds ghastly,' agreed Paxton, 'but that is the inevitable compromise. And since it is unsustainable, it is likewise certain that, in time, a different mode of propulsion will be required.'

'So I continue refining the atmospheric,' said Thomas. 'The vacuum chambers, the improved valves, the lighter carriages – and then I step up . . .'

Paxton was shaking his head. 'The atmospheric is over. You saw the damage it did this morning. Its stigma will never be overcome – and to some extent, deservedly so. Even with improvement, the apparatus remains fundamentally inelegant.'

'But air is clearly the solution – *especially* underground. It's the only option in such a repugnant environment.'

'Then your challenge is to devise something new. A means of harnessing air sufficiently superior to the old design that people forget their bad memories.'

Thomas felt his imagination spark back into life. After all, it wasn't the atmospheric system so much as air itself that inspired him – so why accept that the 1840s model was the only way of doing things? Why not go back to first principles, come up with something truly different, in the quest to sweeten the otherwise unpalatable prospect of subterranean transport?

'It's a challenge I accept,' he said. 'And I am indebted to you for showing me the way. How can I ever thank you?'

'By succeeding,' said Paxton. 'I share your absolute faith in the power of air, Mr. Rammell. It is nothing short of a necessity, if we truly want to civilise our thriving capital.' He set off across the room. 'In which spirit, I've a small donation to set you going.'

He opened the door to reveal a young man: mid-twenties, smartly dressed, with greased-down hair and a pale face. Thomas knew instantly that they had met before.

'You looked terribly lonely up there today,' explained Paxton. 'This young gentleman is the perfect remedy. His name is Billy Gray, and he has as sharp a mind as you will find in an assistant. I met him a few years ago at his father's public house in Sydenham, and he's worked for me at the Palace ever since.'

Mention of Sydenham completed the memory. 'How wonderful to see you again,' said Thomas.

'You've met before?' asked Paxton.

'On the old Croydon atmospheric. Billy saved my life. I was charmed by his enthusiasm for the railway.'

'Me too.' Paxton grinned. 'Why else do you think I fell in love with air power?'

Billy bowed towards Thomas. 'It'd be a pleasure to work for you, Mr. Rammell.'

Thomas smiled. 'I'd be delighted to have you by my side.'

'Then you have your challenge and you have your man,' declared Paxton, turning as he left the room. 'Now all that remains is for you to rescue us from the horror of underground steam.' He paused in the doorway. 'Good day to you, Mr. Rammell – and good luck.'

Chapter 9

I can't say if the radio was real. I thought I'd switched it off, but maybe not. Certainly, it was possible they were discussing it; I was tuned to a London station.

There hadn't been any more fires in the forty-eight hours since the concert bowl went up, which came as a relief to everyone except me. Not that I wanted to see the park burn; but with every fireless minute my own guilt grew, and I became ever more convinced that the arsonist was no one else but me – incredibly, impossibly, unavoidably me.

Presumably this was why, if the radio wasn't real, it filled my head as if it was. Either way, when someone piped up that they hoped the 'Palace pyromaniac' would suffer for his crimes, I awoke with a start – and heard only silence. Perhaps my radio had timed out; perhaps I'd dreamt it. All that mattered was that I was wide awake, in the middle of the night, with a thumping heart and an uncanny sense that something had disturbed me.

I looked around. I'd left the window ajar and the curtains had been sucked outwards, but everything else was unchanged from when I went to bed. Concluding that I'd let my dreams get the better of me, I rose and parted the curtains, reaching to shut the window.

'Eeeh, reek.'

I dived back into bed and threw the covers over me. Shivering and sweating, I waited, holding my breath, then lowered the sheets. There was silence. I breathed out.

'Eeeh, reek.'

This time I leapt up, flung open the curtains, and slammed the window shut. The voice had sounded distinct and immediate: there was no way it had come from within the park. Either the skeleton had risen from his tomb or someone was outside, playing a trick on me.

It was then I twigged. Clearly, the old museum man had somehow found out where I lived, and was now in my garden, regaling me with his warped idea of a joke. Sighing with relief, I pressed my face against the glass and sought him out in the moonlight. Seeing nothing, I eased the window open and looked down. Still, nobody was there.

'Eeeh, reek!'

More distant this time, the withered croak now seemed to be emanating from behind the garden wall – quite possibly from the skeletons' mound, which was only a few metres inside the park. Confused, I shut the window. Was my theory just wishful thinking? The voice was identical to the one two days before, but I hadn't been out of my flat since, let alone into the park.

Perhaps someone else had got entangled with the skeleton? But if that was the case, why was it saying my name? And how was the sound carrying so far?

It could only be the man from the museum. Freak that he was, he'd clearly overcome his fright, and was yet again exercising his morbid humour at my expense.

I sat on my bed and bit my nails. I didn't appreciate the prank, but I'd been sending myself mad, stuck in the flat alone, going over what had happened. I needed someone to talk to, and since my nameless, concertina-wielding companion was the only option, I pulled on some clothes and went into the garden.

'Hello!' I called. 'I know it's you. You can come—'

'Eeeh, reek.'

I had to hand it to the old fellow: the impression was accurate enough – gravelly, properly pleading.

'Give it a rest,' I said, opening the back gate. 'I can tell it's you.'

'*Help us.*'

I chuckled – a nice little embellishment, that – and walked round the base of the skeletons' mound to the path on the opposite side. The frosty mud twinkled in the moonlight.

'Eeeh, reek. Help us.'

The voice definitely originated at the top of the slope, where the attacks had taken place, but the area seemed to be deserted. The old loon was obviously hiding behind one of the trees.

'Where on earth are you?' I asked.

The answer, when it came, was soft, sorrowful, and so feebly distended that it lasted for several seconds.

'Traaaaaaapped.'

'Please,' I whispered, falteringly. 'You're scaring me now. Where are you?'

Nothing but silence.

'I said: *where are you*?'

'Right here, old boy.'

I spun round to see a shadow walking up the path behind the lake: an unmistakeable silhouette, with his concertina slung over his shoulder. Open-mouthed in terror, I turned back to the slope.

'What's up?' asked the old man. 'I was walking through the park when I heard you—'

I edged away from the mound, fearing the skeletons were about to spring up and throw themselves upon me.

'*Don't leave us!*'

The words filled the darkness, wrapping themselves around me as unforgivingly as the bony hand two nights before.

'Don't leave us?' repeated the museum man, as I reached him. 'But surely they *want* to be left? Left in peace.'

Together, we backed away.

'*Don't go.*' The voice was ever more menacing. '*DON'T GO!*'

We turned and ran as fast as the old man's legs would carry

him, not daring to look back as we steered ourselves round the back of the lake, the path speckled with the moonlit shadows of overhead branches. Finally, the remains of the concert bowl appeared on our right.

'Open ground!' cried the old man.

We headed onto the lawn that sloped down to the bowl, its frosted iron ruins twinkling like a lunar iceberg, adrift in a jet black lake. We stopped and looked back. I don't know what we were expecting. The sight of several skeletons, all marching to capture us? Or just one maniacal hand, sliding through the ground, snapping for its prey? Either way, nothing appeared, and we slumped onto the frozen grass, back-to-back in exhaustion and bewilderment.

The peace didn't last long. Out of the stillness came the sound of a great gust of wind, like the park was heaving an enormous sigh, although neither the air nor the silhouetted trees were moving. My insides tensed up. I somehow knew what was about to happen.

A second later, the tip of the giant transmitter ignited, bursting vividly and audibly into flames which multiplied instantly. Five or six gigantic fireballs rolled down the sloping sides and into its body. Within moments the whole structure was engulfed like a monstrous industrial Wicker Man.

'Don't leave us,' whispered the old man. 'Don't leave us – *or else this*!'

I stood up and said nothing. For all I wanted to protest – I hadn't disturbed them this time; I had done all I could to leave them in peace! – the pattern was unignorable. There *was* a connection, yet it wasn't the one I feared.

'It's not the disturbance that upsets the skeletons,' I said, feeling the fire's heat in the air. 'It's the walking away: the ignoring them. The hands reaching up aren't some freak reflex. It's because they actually want me down there.'

'To die?'

'To *help*.'

'To *help*?'

'That's what they said. *Help us.*'

'But help them with what?'

My eyes were watering as the heat thawed my freezing face. 'It's personal. That's all I know. Somehow they've locked onto me. It's *me* they want down there with them.' I gazed at the blaze and my body tightened as if the skeleton's hand was inside me, squeezing its knuckles around my heart. 'They're not going to stop until they have me.'

'How can you be certain?'

'Because of this. They summoned me, I ran away, and now this: punishment for not doing their bidding; a deterrent against ignoring them; *proof* that it's never going to stop!' I looked in panic at the old man. 'They say they're trapped: well now they've trapped me too!'

'What do you mean, *it's never going to stop*? Surely you can just move? Go where they can't get you?'

'This started, here tonight, with them calling out to me while I was asleep. Their words penetrated my dreams, woke me up! Yes, I played along and entered the park, but even if I'd stayed in bed, even if I hadn't woken up, they'd still have done this. Ignoring them is what provokes them, and I don't have to hear or be near them for that. Christ knows what leaving Crystal Palace altogether would make them do!'

High above us, the steel latticework of the giant transmitter began to groan from the heat.

'Then there's only one thing for it,' said the museum man. 'Embrace your responsibilities. Go back down the hole and—'

'Get buried alive?' I burst out in exasperated laughter, angered by his unruffled logic. 'You know who should really go down there?'

'Who?'

'You!'

'Me?'

'Yes!'

'That's quite impossible.'

'Why? You're the one who persuaded me to go back. I was

perfectly happy to let them be, but you made me look interested. You even told them my bloody name! Which, now I come to think of it, is doubly rich, since you've never deigned to tell me yours!'

'I would very gladly go down there,' he replied calmly, 'if only they'd invite me. As it is, they want you – and as you rightly say, there's no getting away from it.'

He walked away as the creaking above intensified. The top of the blazing transmitter had now shrunk, shrivelled and lost its balance, and was leaning dangerously towards the wood that covered the former Palace site. Frozen in shock, I watched as the uppermost quarter wilted and gave way, crashing to the ground and igniting the trees – just yards from the main road.

It was an unignorable statement, and left me in no doubt: like it or not, there could be no more hiding.

'I have to do this,' I said. 'I've no choice. I have to do what they ask.'

The old man stopped and turned. 'Really?'

'Really.'

'You mean it?'

Quite in spite of myself, I nodded. 'I mean it.'

'Then I'll help you.' He stood up straight and raised his head, braced for the challenge ahead. 'Like you say, we're in this together.'

I smiled, grateful for his solidarity. 'But where to start? *Help us*, they said – but what do they actually want me to do?'

The old man wandered back towards me, puffing out his pockmarked cheeks. 'Well, surely there's only one thing you *can* do for a bunch of stranded skeletons.'

'Which is?'

He put his hand on my shoulder and grinned. 'Help them out of their hole.'

Chapter 10

Thursday 24th March, 1859

It was two years since Paxton had inspired Thomas to take his *New Plan* underground, and he was finally ready to make his next move. Standing outside St. Margaret's Church, his heart was full of hope as he gazed at the latest wonder to join the myriad spires, domes and towers of London's skyline.

For many months the structure had been steadily rising at the northern end of the building to which it was wed. Until recently the clock faces had been masked while the finishing touches were put to their Roman numerals. Now, however, it was finally on display: the largest four-faced clock ever constructed, surrounded by stone, brick and iron work of consummate elegance. Its proportions and decorative balance – intricate ornamentation, but not overblown – provided the ideal finish to the neo-Gothic magnificence of the Palace of Westminster itself, while delivering an indulgent riposte to the starker beauty of the Abbey opposite. Though the mighty bell wasn't yet ready to signal time to its citizens, the clock tower itself was already greatly loved.

'The best view is coming down Whitehall,' said a voice. 'Exquisite, how the clock converses with Nelson.'

Thomas looked down to discover that this fulsome praise emanated from the very man whose exit from the Palace he had been awaiting: one whose immense black beard, billowing beneath narrow eyes and slick, wiry hair, failed to conceal a bemused grin.

'The guard said you'd been asking for me.'

Thomas offered his hand. 'My name is Thomas Webster Rammell, civil engineer.'

'An awfully impromptu introduction,' said Josiah Latimer Clark.

'I tried to make it otherwise. I wrote letters, called at your workshop – but you are a busy man. When I read you were sitting on the committee, I resolved to find you in person.'

'You have a suggestion? Something regarding sub-aqueous telegraph cables? Because it would be better to appear before the committee than accost me in the street.'

'It's not that,' said Thomas. 'Rather, it's something you worked on a few years ago. I believe an exchange of ideas could prove mutually beneficial.'

Latimer Clark looked doubtful. 'I'm off to my workshop in Waterloo. You may trot along if you wish to bother me further.'

Before Thomas could respond, Latimer Clark was on the move, dodging the carts and horses as he crossed the road.

'Rammell, Rammell, Rammell,' he murmured, once Thomas was back in earshot. '*A New Plan for Street Railways*.'

They turned the corner towards Westminster Bridge, Thomas skipping to keep pace. The new tower rose serenely on the right, its black and white clock faces gazing to all four points of the compass, far above the bustle.

'I remember the précis in *Herapath's Railway Journal*. An abject failure, as I recall.'

'It was worth the cost of pamphleteering,' said Thomas, touched that someone at least remembered the *New Plan*. 'But I didn't push it hard. I quickly realised my error.'

'Which was?'

'Thinking overground. Back then, the Metropolitan was floundering, and I thought that subterranean railways wouldn't happen. The engineering challenges seemed as insurmountable as public opposition, and I personally couldn't abide the thought. A dark, dirty, airless railway, deep below the streets, with the rats and the sewage? It ran against everything I championed at the Board of Health.'

'So now the Metropolitan has overcome its difficulties, you are reconciled to its charms?'

'I'm reconciled to *some kind* of subterranean railway. But not how they're planning it.'

Latimer Clark raised his bushy eyebrows as the river fanned out around them.

'It's a question of power,' explained Thomas. 'My *New Plan* proposed an atmospheric mode of working—'

'Then no wonder you failed!' Latimer Clark's beard blew into Thomas's face as the river winds launched their assault. 'How could you ever have hoped otherwise?'

'Because I wasn't thinking about expediency; I was thinking about what was right. In principle, atmospheric power was clean, safe, silent: considerations that were of paramount importance then, and even more so now.'

'Atmospheric power may be *clean*, but its reputation could scarcely be dirtier.'

'Dirtier than that of an underground railway powered by steam?'

They were halfway across the bridge. The billowing chimneys loomed large on the south bank, tarnishing the clear blue sky with their plumes.

'Your aims are commendable,' conceded Latimer Clark. 'But I fail to see their relevance to me.'

'It's to do with the pneumatic tubes you designed for the Telegraph Company – sucking felt bags and messages through tiny tubes, using the object itself as a piston, pushed into a vacuum by inrushing air behind.'

Somewhere beneath his beard, Latimer Clark frowned. 'Those tubes were merely to facilitate the smooth running of the company. I have no interest in air power beyond that convenience, and I fail to see what my tiny tubes have to do with subterranean passenger—'

He halted, lurching forward on the spot.

'That's right,' said Thomas with a smile. 'My suggestion is to scale up your designs, so the tiny tube becomes a railway tunnel, and the objects inside become trains, doubling as pistons, with air working across the whole transverse surface of the vehicle.'

Latimer Clark studied the pavement. 'Preposterous!' he proclaimed, darting off before stopping again. 'Is it?' He looked at Thomas. 'Yes it is!' And off he went, double-quick across the remainder of the bridge.

'It's no more preposterous than what you've already built,' argued Thomas, keeping pace. 'Since it relies on indisputable facts of the atmosphere, and is entirely contained within a tunnel, scaling-up simply *must* work.'

'The laws of physics are slippery beasts, Mr. Rammell.'

'But don't you see the magnificence? If people are to be whisked around in these claustrophobic tunnels, let's turn them to our advantage. Let's use them to create railways where air is constantly fresh and collisions impossible. Railways which function with a civilised, silent, regular reliability unimagined by those who made us go underground.'

They were off the bridge now, enveloped by factories and workshops.

'You make a persuasive argument,' said Latimer Clark.

'I do. And as it resonates with you, it will resonate with passengers, allaying their fears of travelling underground.'

A train wheezed over the viaduct ahead. Latimer Clark studied it as they turned into York Road, heading towards the terminus of the London and South Western.

'Do you intend to offer pneumatic power to the Metropolitan as an alternative?'

Thomas shook his head. 'The exactitude with which trains must fit within tunnels will make it hard to adapt existing lines. Far better to challenge the Metropolitan outright.'

Latimer Clark tamed his beard, the furrows on his brow

marking a steady accumulation of doubts. 'How do you solve the other problems: overcoming people's prejudice towards atmospheric power; raising the necessary funds?'

'It's all covered in my plan.'

'Your plan? Your new *New Plan*?' Latimer Clark's upturned cheeks suggested a smile.

'I propose to scale up pneumatic tubes by degrees,' explained Thomas. 'Since we already know they work, there's no reason why, in enlarging them, we should not alight upon an intermediate solution: a small, goods-only railway which we can develop free of popular prejudice. Such a network would readily turn sufficient profit to fund our passenger railway, while its very success would belie the atmospheric doubters.'

'Whose goods would it carry?'

'Her Majesty's.'

Latimer Clark laughed. 'Ah, yes. I should have guessed.'

'I'm serious,' insisted Thomas. 'I've read how much the Post Office liked your early designs; how they investigated whether pneumatic tubes could be enlarged to propel mailbags beneath the capital's streets, between their depots.'

'I can't deny it's an elegant idea,' said Latimer Clark, 'but that investigation was conclusive. Yes, it showed such a system would be welcome and, with 15-inch tubes, just about viable. Alas, it also revealed the cost to be prohibitive.'

They stopped outside Latimer Clark's workshop.

'That was a mere four years ago,' he went on, 'and they were desperate to make it work, saving themselves from the congestion above ground. Why should this be different?'

'Because we'll remove the element of risk. Four years ago, they were exploring it independently; the costs of construction and operation would have been theirs. My proposal is to develop a goods railway ourselves, then hire it out to them and anyone else wishing to use it.'

Latimer Clark leant against some railings.

'But then the question of cost returns,' he said. 'And if it was deemed too great by the Post Office—'

'We'll find ways to lower it,' said Thomas. 'For a start, I'm working on a cheaper means of exhausting air from larger tubes: a giant fan which brings in air from the tube and, by centrifugal force, casts it out at the periphery. The genius being, it doubles as a flywheel, meaning the engine power is employed more efficiently than anything hitherto used in atmospheric propulsion.'

'Which is all very well,' said Latimer Clark. 'But I still don't see how you can fund development without guaranteed custom.'

'The idea is to request a series of pledges. First, a written word of good faith that the Post Office will inspect a demonstration line. Then, an advance agreement that we'll have the pleasure of their custom once the full-scale network is working.'

'Oh, Mr. Rammell. Your naivety is exquisite to behold. *Pledges,* you say?'

'I concede it's a risk. But a bigger risk is not acting.'

'My friend . . .' Latimer Clark chuckled condescendingly. 'You will never find backers willing to take these risks. No one has forgotten the mania; how the bubble burst. Speculative railway ventures no longer attract men of sound mind.'

'Then perhaps mine is unsound,' said Thomas. 'But I still believe there exist men of principle, who understand that occasionally the first consideration must be people, not profit. Clearly, it is not desirable to stake private money on such ventures. Ideally, Parliament would act in the public interest. But since our lawmakers long ago condemned us to the Metropolitan – and the steam that will inevitably power it – the challenge falls to men of private means and public spirit. I am one such man, and I *will* find others like me. I cannot guarantee profit or success. But I can promise the satisfaction that we will at least have tried.'

Latimer Clark trotted up the steps. 'I wish you well, Mr. Rammell. Alas, I am just too busy with other things.'

'But I can't do it without you.'

Latimer Clark pulled open his door. 'Then you shan't do it. That is settled.'

'Wrong!' Thomas was shouting now, his courtesy spent. 'What's settled is that you *are* part of this. Like it or not, you have invented the solution. I have been working on this for over two years, and I know: there is no better alternative to underground steam than the power of air, and there is no better application of air than the model you developed.'

Latimer Clark dropped down a step. 'So you only want my support because I own the patent on what you require?'

'I want you to realise that, together, we hold the key to civilising this city. This is about more than merely proving a point. This is about fixing London: relieving our streets of overcrowding and creating a subterranean network through which our fellow citizens can travel with certain safety. The men who achieve this will be renowned throughout the world. In a hundred years' time, people will thank them as they now thank Stephenson.'

Latimer Clark stared at the steam billowing from beneath the roof of Waterloo Bridge Station. 'You have my permission to develop the tubes however you wish.'

'You'll work with me?'

'I shall be there for support, and to refine those details most allied to my expertise. But given all my other commitments, you should take the lead.' He offered Thomas his hand. 'Does that sound tolerable?'

Thomas accepted without pause. Latimer Clark's indifference wasn't what he'd been expecting, but no matter: he had what he needed, and he'd given nothing away. It was the ideal outcome.

Agreeing to meet the following week to discuss their respective designs, the two men parted and Thomas walked away, spirits soaring. As he strode back onto Westminster Bridge, returning the mighty clock tower to his view, he felt a tightening of the bond between him and the sprawling metropolis. London's streets were all in chaos, and those permitted by Parliament to deliver the cure were nothing more than quacks, their charlatanism soon to be exposed for all to see.

The city needed a saviour like never before.

The city needed him.

Chapter II

'Eeeh, reek.'

The summons came as soon as I got out of the van, and for the first time in a while I felt genuinely anxious. In the hours before, I'd come to hope that I might never hear from the skeletons again, since even planning to obey their orders felt so ridiculously obliging that they'd surely spare me the rest. But when I heard that whisper, the second I set foot outside the park's Sydenham gate, I knew that the gesture alone wouldn't suffice. The skeletons were serious about the assistance I had come to provide.

Our plan to 'help' hinged on what little we knew. Somehow, the skeletons had ended up buried under Crystal Palace Park. This being less than ideal, they considered themselves to be not entirely at rest. So our job was to afford them the dignity they had been denied. We were going to exhume them, cushion them in coffins, and bury them properly.

None of which would have been even remotely possible without Bill.

Bill was someone the old man knew through the museum, and was lucky enough to own a grand old Victorian house that backed onto West Norwood cemetery. He was younger and fresher-faced than his aged friend – who I'd at last discovered was called Tom – though I never found out what he did for a living. The two men apparently shared a fondness for absurd, impulsive adventures. While I'd been leaning towards calling in the police, or even archaeologists, Tom insisted that seeking such help would be to disobey the skeletons, who had asked for me personally and whose tempers weren't to be tested. His mate Bill, he said, was a much better bet: discreet, dedicated, and able to supply all we needed at a moment's notice. We only had to ask.

So ask we did, and Bill concocted a plan. Just round the corner from his house, he revealed, was a large timber yard. He could easily buy the wood and knock up, say, nine makeshift coffins within forty-eight hours. His large garden, meanwhile, would provide the ideal resting place for the skeletons, backing on to the cemetery and sharing its peacefulness. All that remained was to fill the coffins and transport them the 2 miles from Crystal Palace to West Norwood, for which Bill had his van. In a flash, the near-impossible became so readily achievable it was as if my two cohorts had been waiting for it their whole lives.

Checking no one else was around, we unloaded the essential tools – spades, forks, a great heap of rope – and dumped them in a wheelbarrow. The moon was shining brightly, but we still made full use of our torches. Tom and I led the way while Bill pushed the wheelbarrow behind.

'Eeeh, reek,' trembled the voice, as we walked into the wood and the frosty mound rose up on our right. 'Come. *Help us.*'

Feeling the familiar chill return, I glanced back at Bill. Despite this being his first encounter with the chuntering undead, he looked supremely unbothered, and the three of us headed uphill in silence.

We stopped just shy of the peak. I took a moment to imagine the tomb within the raised earth. My idea was to fix the sight in my mind so that, once inside, I could better remind myself where I really was: an otherwise peaceful park, a mere stone's throw from home, close to a busy road.

'Eeeh, reek. *Enter.*'

The voice sounded more threatening than ever – disturbed, perhaps, by the others' presence, or anxious that I might yet run away.

'Come on,' I said, heading to the summit. 'Let's get this over with!'

'*Eeeh, reek,*' repeated the voice, helping me find the spot immediately. '*EEEH, REEK*!'

'Alright!' I exclaimed. 'Blimey. I'm coming as fast as I can.'

I took off my coat to reveal my old tube overalls. Along with the sturdy walking boots I'd bought earlier that day, I figured these were ideal – built for heavy use, and less likely to tear in the event of any tussles that might ensue. The idea was that Tom and I would evacuate the skeletons while Bill shuttled coffins to and from the van.

'Prepare the apparatus,' I commanded, guarding the skeletons' spot while the others fetched a rope ladder from the wheelbarrow. Tom laid the lower rungs on the ground directly in front of me while Bill took the other end – a single line of industrial-strength rope – and coiled it round a nearby tree. With this in place, I pulled on the goggles we'd purchased from the timber yard, and double-checked my inhaler was in my pocket.

'All set?' asked Tom, spade in hand.

'Just about,' I answered, fighting hard to suppress the memory of my previous struggles; insisting to myself that this time would be different. This time I wasn't going to resist but co-operate. I'd do whatever the skeletons wanted. And that meant there was nothing to fear. With a bit of hard grind, we'd be done in the park within the hour, and have the skeletons buried, and the nightmare over, before dawn.

'Tie me up.'

By this stage, Bill was already off, walking back to the van to collect the first couple of coffins, apparently not caring to see me enter the tomb. It was left to Tom to lift up the ladder and – roughly at its central point – hook it over my head and round my waist.

'Ready?' he asked.

Gripping the rope firmly, I nodded. Beneath me, Tom's

torch shone on the critical point – a puddle of ice, in which I saw my goggled eyes reflected above an anxious frown. The moment had come. It was time to lean forward, step onto the ice and—

Immediately it was there, exploding through the earth: a snow-white wrist, unsullied by soil, fingers snapping at the air.

'Eeeh, reek! Eeeh, reek! Eeeh, reek!'

Such was its unfettered energy – wild, excited, triumphant – it took the fingers a while to get their bearings. Every inch of me wanted to seize the opportunity and withdraw my leg. But somehow I not only left it there but brought the other one through.

The hand took hold and pulled my ankle down. I shut my eyes, breathed in, and adopted the stance I had rehearsed: head and shoulders raised, arms fully extended by my sides, hands desperately clasping the rope ladder.

My entry was relatively smooth. Within a second the mud was squelching around my waist, and within two my head passed below ground, the earth belching as I displaced trapped air from pockets of soil. The cold, wet mud pressed into my face, squeezing into my ears, mouth, nostrils – even past the seal of my goggles – but it wasn't long before I slipped through, hitting the floor of the tomb feet-first and crumpling into a heap.

I lifted my goggles, spitting, snorting and shaking my head to clear my orifices, then took a precautionary drag on my inhaler, worried that the thinness of the air might aggravate my asthma.

With both the moon and Tom's torchlight subdued by the hole, it was hard to make out the rest of the tomb. All I could see was a retreating skull, hovering above dark clothing as it settled a few feet away – with several other skulls glimmering faintly all around.

'Are you OK?' cried Tom, his voice distant and muffled.

I felt a tugging on the ladder: confirmation that my lifeline was intact, and that the old man was ready to rescue me at any moment. Looking up, the top of the hole was a dim speck of yellow, 15 feet above.

'What's happening?' he shouted.

'Not a sound, now I'm in.' I rose to my knees, struggling not to retch as I tasted the foulness in the air. 'They're all just staring at me. How about you? Any sign of fires?'

'Bill's back with a coffin,' replied Tom. 'Otherwise, not a peep.'

This cemented our suspicions. The skeletons didn't mind being disturbed; it was being ignored that enraged them. Now they had me where they wanted me, they were happy to sit back and watch me toil on their behalf.

First, I needed to see what I was doing. I called up for one of the torches, but without the skeleton's assistance Tom could only push it so far before his reach failed him and the torch got stuck sideways in the mud. Needing to climb up and dislodge it, I untangled myself and let the ladder hang straight. I put my foot on the second rung and pushed myself up – at which point a cold, bony hand clasped my thigh. Looking down, I saw a skull staring up at me, the muted light glinting off its long, lopsided teeth. It said nothing, but I got its meaning well enough.

'I just need the torch.'

I stepped down a rung in reassurance. The skull tilted doubtingly.

'I'm not going anywhere, I promise.'

Little by little the skeleton let go, lurking nearby as I reached up, into the hole. The opening was so narrow it was a miracle I'd squeezed through, and though the sides were squidgy, the torch was firmly jammed. To break it free I had to tug so strongly that, once it gave, I lost my grip on the ladder and fell backwards towards the floor.

I braced myself for impact, but no impact came. Instead, I landed softly, two hard yet cushioning palms bringing me gently to rest. Snapping my eyes open, I saw the skull right above me, its eye sockets gazing down as it slipped its knuckles from under my body and padded into the darkness.

I'd been saved the concussion, but my mind was nonetheless boggling. Two days before, I'd been convinced that the skeletons were trying to ingest me into the earth so I might rot like them. But now, having taken them at their word, they were coveting me as their saviour. And as I realised this, I thought how sad those gaping sockets seemed – full of longing for their former powers of sight – and felt the first hint of a new kind of obligation: not just one of expediency, but pity.

'Need the spade?' shouted Tom.

I shone the torch on the nearest body, which was sitting beside another, shorter skeleton. Their knuckles were interlocked, and the smaller skeleton's head was on the other's shoulder: a loving pose finished off by a tattered old umbrella with a woodworm-ridden handle propped between them. The sight was strangely moving, like their love had lasted a thousand years.

I looked more closely at their ashen clothes. The garments were variously torn, worn and threadbare, but the total decay of the bodies meant that both skeletons still appeared to be comprehensively dressed. The gentleman had a woollen coat, shirt and necktie hanging limply over his clothes-hanger shoulders, while his trousers had become so oversized that, below the knobbliest of knees, his footwear was completely smothered. As for the lady, the shawl around her shoulders was of a piece with the cobwebs that connected her to the wall, while her clumped-up blouse gave no clue of the ribcage beneath. Her skirt sank between two fully extended, cucumber-thin legs, at the end of which her dull white toes poked through the wasted leather of her boots.

I shone the torch further afield and counted the silver skulls. Just beyond the nearest pair was a trio of older skeletons – two women and one man – while opposite them sat a lone gentleman, who I recognised as the taller skeleton who had pulled me in and broken my fall moments before. He was sitting slightly apart from another trio, consisting of a man, a woman and, squeezed between them, a much smaller male skeleton.

A chill shot through me on seeing the latter, and then again, as I realised there were nine skeletons in total – exactly the number Bill had anticipated. They were lined along two benches, running down either side. Each was sitting upright, with the women all in dresses, and the men and boy in something like formal wear. There was headgear too, but none was being worn. Instead, the bonnets and top hats sat loosely in the skeletons' laps, as redundant in this oddly civilised underground tomb as the walking sticks and brollies they all possessed.

I couldn't guess the date exactly, but I'd seen enough Dickens on TV to know immediately that these were Victorian costumes. But it was only a moment later that I realised this wasn't fancy dress. These were actual Victorian men and woman; this, a Victorian tomb, from back when the Crystal Palace was brand new. They and it had been lying here, dead and alive, for – what? – one hundred and fifty years.

'Why are you here?' I asked softly, figuring the direct approach was at least worth a shot. As my question went unanswered, however, it became apparent that, like their movement, the skeletons' husky chatter was reserved only for summons and not explanation.

I noticed some torchlight bouncing back through the cobwebs above their heads, and realised that the sides of the tomb consisted of several dusty, fractured panes of glass, separated by wood panelling. Mounted upon these divisions were old-fashioned gas lamps, their glass blackened but each still intact and roughly upright upon bronze perches.

Coupled with the seating arrangement, these trappings pointed to only one possible conclusion about the nature of the tomb, but the thought was so ludicrous that I couldn't process it without checking the rest. Flicking the torch down, I saw that the floor was covered by a thick layer of soil which occasionally rose into bigger mounds, speckled with chunks of wood and brick: remnants of the curved wooden roof, parts of which had buckled or given way completely – as in the case of the hole through which I'd entered – and of brickwork that apparently separated it from the soil above.

Sensing that this held the key to confirming my suspicions, I walked to either end and found two sets of sliding glass doors, cracked in places but still perfectly sealed. Each led onto an open ledge, but the accumulation of debris prevented me from seeing anything more. Instead, I kneeled through the net of cobwebs on one of the brown leather benches and wiped the dust from the window.

Sure enough, there was the outline, so familiar to me, of a tunnel: one whose bricks had been pushed right up against the windows, providing a layer of armour which had somehow saved the railway carriage – for there was no denying that's what it was – from the landslip outside.

Here, then, was part of a Victorian train. Ornate, weirdly modern in its seating design, and with unusual front-and-back appendages, the carriage was home to nine well-to-do, dead-but-undead Victorian passengers, stranded in an imploded tunnel which had miraculously spared them from a soily burial.

It was all making sense. Except, of course, it made no sense at all. For even if you overlooked the upright, animated skeletons, what had a train been doing in a tunnel in the grounds of the Crystal Palace to begin with – and why just one carriage? Above all, why had the passengers been left to rot after disaster struck?

'Well?'

Tom's voice gave me a shock.

'Do you need the spade or not?' he shouted.

Breathing deeply, I declined the old man's offer. There were no significant build-ups of earth to dislodge, and I was hoping I'd be able to lift each skeleton out wholesale, since that's how they were operating, rather than having to scoop up sets of individual bones.

'Oh, and by the way, there are nine of them,' I added, 'so we've just the right number of coffins.'

'What luck,' said Tom. 'I guess we'd better make a start before our fortune changes.'

I nodded. Extraordinary as my discoveries were, knowing for certain that the skeletons hadn't been left there deliberately, but were the victims of some bizarre railway accident, only confirmed what needed to be done.

I turned to the nearest skeleton: the gentleman half of the loving couple. Propping my torch on a pile of earth, I slid my hands under his legs and back. My skin tingled as I felt the hard outline of his exposed bones, and I murmured a few words of reassurance – for me as much as for him. Then, finding my balance and exerting a little pressure, I started to lift him up.

One hundred and fifty years late, the rescue operation had begun.

Chapter 12

'Please relax, sir,' said Billy Gray. 'Your incessant twitching is making me nervous. Stay calm.'

'I am calm!' barked Thomas. Things had moved on apace since he first met Latimer Clark two years before, but none of it would matter if today's events did not go as planned.

He checked his watch again. The train should have arrived five minutes ago, but the line threading up from south London remained tantalisingly clear, and the only sound in the air was that of a *down* train, chuffing mockingly over the Victoria Railway Bridge as it approached the opposite platform.

Unable to wait any longer, Thomas paced past the station house and stood at the top of the staircase. At the bottom was a path leading back under the arches towards Battersea Park, but Thomas's eyes were fixed on this side of the bridge: the portion of Battersea Fields that had remained untouched by Sir James Pennethorne's designs for the gardens across the way, having instead been appropriated by the Southwark and Vauxhall Waterworks Company. Just in front of their reservoirs – currently producing an unwholesome stink – were a couple of acres of disused land, right on the riverside and free from development. It was in this weedy wilderness, offered cheaply by the London, Brighton and South Coast Railway, that he had erected the apparatus of his vital experiment.

'Really, sir, I can escort him down,' said Billy. 'Surely you should be relieving everyone of your partner's civilities?'

Below them, Latimer Clark was weaving among the guests, introducing them to the company's directors. Even from a distance, his professorial fastidiousness was clearly no substitute for Thomas's natural charm. Though of course no amount of *bonhomie* could match a successful demonstration, it was important to create a good impression so that the project would be talked up as more than just a whimsical curiosity.

'Very well,' sighed Thomas, and he was about to set off when the up train finally appeared, doubling the racket brought by the departing down.

Given its leisurely purpose, Battersea Park and Steamboat Pier Station wasn't especially busy on weekdays, and only a few people alighted before the train continued on towards Victoria. But among those few was the unmistakeable silhouette of Sir Joseph Paxton, completing his half-hour journey from the Crystal Palace.

'Oh really!' The great man laughed, ebullient as ever. 'You needn't have waited.'

'I'd not have it any other way,' said Thomas.

'And how splendid to see you again, young man,' said Paxton, turning to Billy as they set off down the stairs. 'Can it really be four years since I bestowed you upon Mr. Rammell? I take it he's looking after you—' He stopped, distracted by what lay beneath them. 'Oh, my. How utterly magnificent. A larger worm was never seen by man!'

Thomas winked at Billy, 'worm' being the metaphor that everyone invoked on seeing the cast-iron tube for the first time. Beginning inside a large wooden shack, adjacent to the stairs, the pipe trailed for a quarter of a mile around the open ground.

'I take it the key men are here?' asked Paxton, as they reached the cracked soil. 'Sir Rowland Hill, Secretary to the Post Office, present and correct?'

Thomas shook his head. 'Alas, no.'

'Oh really? But I thought—'

'He and the Postmaster General cancelled yesterday evening. Truly, sir, I cannot fathom their apathy.'

'Too much pressure?'

'Possibly. But really, we've done all we can to *avoid* pressurising them. We even changed our name, fearing the "Pneumatic Parcel Post Company" might imply a formal connection!'

'Ah, Thomas,' said Paxton, with fatherly warmth. 'If there's one thing I've learnt, it's that the greater one's vision, the harder it is to communicate to others until it's ready for everyone to see. You are quite right to be seizing the initiative. Do not be swayed by their disregard.'

Ignoring the tube's circuitous route around the grounds, the three men headed directly to its end: a brick-bordered shallow by the river, where Latimer Clark was busily exercising his awkwardness.

'Apologies for the delay,' said Thomas. 'But I wanted to greet Sir Joseph in person.'

Seeing who was suddenly in their midst, the guests queued up to ingratiate themselves with Paxton: first the journalists, then half a dozen influential engineers, and finally the eight directors of the Pneumatic Dispatch Company – those high-minded men, led by the Duke of Buckingham as chairman, who had vindicated Thomas's conviction that a plenitude of such beneficent individuals still existed.

'To explain our aims today,' began Thomas, once the pleasantries had ended, 'the first objective is plain enough: namely, to astound and excite our directors, and thus encourage them to dig ever deeper into their venerable pockets to fund a line that the Post Office would pay to use. But there is also a second reason why Josiah and I have summoned you here—'

'Where, pray tell, *are* the Post Office?'

The question came from John Herapath – the journalist who had so ruthlessly torn apart Thomas's *New Plan*, both in person and in print.

'The Post Office are very busy, Mr. Herapath,' replied Thomas. 'They're relying on wise men like you to pass judgement on their behalf. Then, if the boot fits, I dare say they'll grace us with their presence at the appropriate stage.'

Herapath stared unflinchingly back, but said no more for the moment.

'As I was saying,' resumed Thomas, 'this experiment isn't just part of a private goods-carrying venture. This is the first step to overcoming entrenched public scepticism about the magnificent power of air. What you are about to witness is a wholly new application of such energy; one which will ultimately carry not just goods but people themselves.'

'Oh joy!' scoffed Herapath.

'That is why we have invited so many of you today, and that is also why we intend to open the line for public demonstrations throughout the summer.'

'Show us what you've got, Mr. Rammell,' said Herapath. 'And then we shall be *delighted* to advise the public whether to pay you a visit.'

Thomas glanced at Paxton, who offered a reassuring nod.

'The cast-iron tube is laid in 9-foot sections socket-jointed together,' he explained, standing beside the open end of the course. 'Hence the ribs you see punctuating its exterior. Overall the length is 452 yards, the height 3 feet, and the width 2 and a half. The tracks are fully integrated: little 2-inch ledges, jutting out where the arch meets the base to give a gauge of 2 feet.'

His guests took turns to peer in and check this for themselves.

'What exactly is the benefit?' asked the Duke of Buckingham – a thickly-bearded fellow, short and stout, with impeccable business acumen.

'Put simply,' replied Thomas, 'it removes the need for separate tracks, to be laid separately within the tube, and to go wrong, separately, within the tube.' He smiled at Buckingham and the other directors. 'Money, time, inconvenience: all are saved as a result.'

Billy signalled to the shed, from which several assistants emerged wheeling three wooden platforms over the hard ground, each bearing a long, narrow shrouded object. Behind them followed three more helpers dragging smaller carts, piled high with cloth bags, and behind *them* trotted a sprightly brown terrier.

'This is all decidedly funereal,' sneered Herapath. 'Are those coffins atop those wheels, Mr. Rammell? You'd do well not to invoke such morbid *tableaux* when all similar schemes have long since been consigned to the ashes of time.'

Thomas smiled back. 'Like Lazarus . . .' He strode to the first of the arriving platforms and whipped off the cover. 'The atmospheric rises!'

There was a fascinated murmur as the first of the unveiled trucks was lifted onto the tracks and pushed to the mouth of the tube, whose transverse shape it matched. The bowed sides of the open-topped vehicle were of sheet iron, and its four wheels were each of 20 inches diameter.

'Is that indiarubber surrounding the back end?' asked John Fowler – a brilliant civil engineer, roughly Thomas's age, who happened to be chief engineer on the Metropolitan Railway, construction of which had begun the previous year. As well as overseeing their underground tunnels, Fowler was rumoured to be frantically investigating possible alternatives to traditional steam power.

'It is indeed,' replied Thomas. 'The rubber provides the seal that enables the wagon to move through the tube, ensuring that the air pressure in front remains different from that behind. In so doing, it also protects the cargo from air disturbance.'

'We have left a slight gap between the rubber and the tube,' said Latimer Clark. 'Three-eighths of an inch – just to minimise friction.'

'The singularity is inspired,' remarked Paxton. 'So much

more efficient than the under-carriage pistons that powered the old atmospheric.'

'That isn't saying a great deal, Sir Joseph,' returned Herapath.

'But it is indisputable,' said Thomas. 'What's more, our indiarubber is many times more durable than the leather used in those old tube-top valves.'

Herapath grunted doubtfully, but the general mood seemed positive as Thomas's men loaded the cloth bags into the open carriage.

'Sacks of cement,' he explained. 'Enough to bring the total weight to one ton. A challenging load to begin – wouldn't you agree John?'

'Absolutely,' replied Fowler.

Thomas whistled for his dog. 'Albert!'

The faithful Scottish terrier came and sat, tail wagging, in front of his master, who took a cut of meat from Billy and placed it on top of the bags. Eyes aflame, Albert licked his lips.

'Wait there like a good fellow,' said Thomas to his dog, before turning to his guests. 'Gentlemen, please follow me to the engine house.'

They set off across the sun-baked earth, and Thomas explained the design of the course.

'It replicates the challenges of tunnelling under London's streets, dodging imaginary sewers and pipes with a series of curves, the most daunting of which has a 100-yard radius. That's over there, where the tube sinks into the ground, becoming invisible for a short way before rising up, as you can see, on a gradient of 1 in 22 – matching that of Holborn Hill, which we hope soon to negotiate for real.'

They arrived outside the shed, into which the tube disappeared. Billy grasped the rope handles and swung open the large wooden doors.

'Behold the beating heart of Mr. Rammell's pneumatic dispatch!' he declared.

'Oh my,' said Fowler. 'What an extraordinary-looking

arrangement.'

Thomas stepped inside and took his guests through the layout. 'So here we have the continuation of the tube, which ends after 2 yards, giving way to a run-off track 15 feet long—'

'With a much-needed pair of buffers at the end,' observed Herapath.

'Now, now, John,' urged Paxton. 'Wait till you see it in action.'

'The fan looks mightily impressive,' said Buckingham.

'Why thank you,' said Thomas, crossing the narrow walkway that led over the tracks, onto a wooden stage. 'I can't deny I'm proud of it. One of the largest ever constructed.'

'Size isn't everything, Mr. Rammell,' said Herapath.

Thomas grinned back at the rotund journalist. 'It is on this occasion.' He looked up at his handiwork. 'The fan consists of two convex discs, both made of sheet iron, each a full 21 feet in diameter. Note this big fat duct that rises from beneath the stage, and feeds into the centre of the fan, along with this axle, which is turned by the apparatus here.' He stepped up to a wooden platform in front of the fan. 'The axle is attached, via a crank, to this long, sloping cylinder, which is powered at the base by a steam engine.'

Billy joined Thomas on the stage, firing the engine into life and filling the shack with a steadily intensifying drone as the cylinder worked the crank, and the axle turned the discs. Within moments, the fan was revolving so fast that it looked to be spinning backwards, producing a gale of wind which forced the engrossed onlookers to reset their footing.

'Gracious!' exclaimed Buckingham, as the rotative fury grew. 'You really can feel the power in the air.'

Thomas climbed down from the stage and stood beside his guests as Billy went about his work, examining one of two barometers mounted on the wall above the engine, alternately increasing and decreasing the latter's power, and with it the speed of the fan. Finally, he crossed to the opposite wall, where he pulled a lever beside the tube.

'What's happening?' asked Fowler.

Thomas raised a hand. 'Wait and see. All will become clear presently.'

A hissing joined the din of the fan, and Billy returned to the engine, this time examining both barometers. Thirty seconds later, he made one final adjustment and gave his master the nod.

'All set, sir,' he shouted.

'Follow me, gentlemen!' Thomas grabbed a green flag and returned into the sun.

50 yards away, Albert was still sitting by the carriage, transfixed by the cut of meat. Thomas waved his flag, whereupon his assistants pushed the truck into the tube, letting a slight downwards incline take over. The terrier became more frantic as he kept pace, yelping and jumping as his longed-for meal disappeared into the darkness.

'Any second now.' Thomas produced a watch from his pocket. 'Wait for their green flag.'

His brow moistened. Of course this had worked in private trials, but until very recently failures had outnumbered successes. Though the power source itself was reliable, the same was not true of the tiresome peripherals: the valves, engine and barometers. The danger was that the press, and Herapath in particular, wouldn't distinguish between incidental mechanical mishaps and the system of which they were a part.

The green flag was raised.

'Here we go,' said Thomas, starting his stopwatch as Albert set off, trotting beside the tube and following its course as it sloped upwards before curving gently towards the river. Initially, he was still barking and wagging his tail, but as the tube levelled out parallel to the Thames, he accelerated into a silent sprint.

Thomas smiled as his plan took flight, greeted by a mix of 'Oohs', 'Ahhs' and 'Splendids'. Paxton especially seemed entranced by the hard-running hound. 'Unspeakably ingenious,' he enthused, once Albert reached the end of the straight and began curving back round.

'Heaven knows what he hears,' said Thomas. 'The travelling truck makes no outward sound.'

As Albert sped up and slowed in tandem with his concealed quarry, it was supremely easy to imagine the little wagon rising and falling, turning a little way left, then a little way right, as it sailed through the tube.

'Down the back straight, Albert was approaching 40 miles per hour,' said Thomas. 'Impressive for both dog and truck!'

Soon, Albert was once again heading away, approaching the severest curve of all.

'Down she goes,' said Thomas, as the tube sank into the soil and Albert ran directly above, growling at the ground itself. 'The downward slope gives a burst of acceleration before we enter the sharpest curve – testing the carriage against severe centrifugal force. And yet the dog keeps going, because the truck is so perfectly integrated with the tube.'

Albert was now sideways on, at the farthest point of the bend.

'A short level stretch to dissipate momentum from the descent, then into the 1 in 22 gradient. And though the dog does slow, he does not slow much. The power of the vacuum, effectively sucking the truck into it, is easily sufficient.'

Still running at a commendable pace, Albert veered round to head directly towards them, darting to one side to allow the tube to emerge from the ground, then accelerating again as the tube levelled out.

'Good boy!' yelled Thomas. He turned to his guests. 'Quick!'

They all darted back inside, followed swiftly by Albert, who careered round the corner and crashed into his master's legs. The iron shutter covering the end of the tube opened, and a moment later the truck burst through, whizzing across the run-off track and slamming into the buffers. Leaping straight onto the bags, the heroic hound triumphantly gobbled up his meaty treat.

The Duke of Buckingham initiated an enthusiastic round of applause, and Thomas grinned at Billy: they had judged the pressure, and thus the speed of the run, to perfection. He glanced at his watch.

'452 yards in fifty seconds!' he announced. 'An average speed of just under 20 miles per hour.'

He couldn't tell if his words had been heard, such was the ovation. Even Herapath was clapping, albeit with raised eyebrows.

Thomas beckoned to a nearby assistant. 'Have the next truck filled with *two* tons of cement. Tell them to raise their flag when it is ready.'

The assistant ran off, taking Albert back to the start, while others began unpacking cement from the first truck, which they then lifted off the rails.

'So come on, Thomas,' said Fowler. 'Tell us exactly how it works.'

Unable to contain his childlike excitement, Thomas leapt up to the stage and turned off the noisy engine.

'So obviously we have the engine and fan,' he said, 'but also, out of sight beneath us, we have the vacuum chamber, feeding into the centre of the fan via this iron air duct – and a similar one on the other side. At the moment, with the fan off, the pressure in both tube, chamber and fan, is as per the outside world. But the moment I do this . . .' He turned on the engine. 'The fan – or rather the *Pneumatic Ejector* – revolves. And as it revolves, it works a wonderful magic.'

He looked up at his invention. 'Note the convex shape of both iron discs, closing in on each other like a sea shell. They are held together by four ribs, which are driven round by our 30-horsepower engine. As the discs spin faster, the laws of centrifugal action force air outwards from the centre: a process aided by the ribs, which funnel air out of the fan, thus creating the breeze you can feel. As the air flows out, it is naturally replaced, through the ducts, by inflowing air from the chamber below.'

'I see,' said Fowler. 'So by altering the engine power, you alter the fan's speed – and thus the amount of air being extracted?'

'Precisely,' said Thomas. 'For this run, we want the same pressure as last time to show how different weights respond under identical circumstances.'

He adjusted the engine and studied the nearest of the two water barometers.

'And there it is.' He glanced at the gauge on the engine. 'At 169 revolutions per minute, the fan sustains our desired pressure in the chamber.' He looked out of the doors. 'Meanwhile, the red flag at the start confirms the carriage is loaded – all set to enter the tube, once the tube is ready.'

Billy pulled the lever on the other side of the stage.

'So opens the valve between the tube and the chamber,' said Thomas. 'The everyday air from the tube flows into the depressurised chamber and joins the exhausting process caused by the still-turning fan.' He examined both water barometers. 'Then we simply compare the pressure inside the tube with that inside the chamber, and soon enough, with minor adjustment . . .' He turned the engine up a notch. 'Equalisation occurs, and the tube is sufficiently depressurised to begin.'

'Why not have the fan communicating directly with the tube?' asked Buckingham.

'The vacuum chamber allows us to exhaust the tube far more quickly,' replied Thomas, 'while also serving as a buffer, placing less strain on the engine and fan, as they can be kept in constant use over several runs.'

He climbed down and grabbed his flag.

'The old atmospheric suffered because the pumping engines exhausted the tube directly, meaning they were always starting and stopping. Our method is much kinder to the mechanics.

'And less expensive,' added Latimer Clark. 'After all, sustaining a nominal vacuum requires less energy than repeatedly draining air from scratch.'

Thomas waved his flag. 'My signal – a flag for now, but an electric telegraph in time – confirms the tube is sufficiently depressurised. The truck is now pushed forwards, as you can see, with the natural slope taking it into the tube.' He waited for the truck to disappear. 'The green flag signifies that it has passed the entry valve, which henceforth stays open, providing the differential needed for the wagon to move forward, into the vacuum.'

He started his stopwatch, Albert set off in pursuit of a fresh chop of meat, and those at the shed watched the obedient terrier take another turn around the course.

'It's slower, of course,' said Thomas, as Albert reached the home straight and they headed back inside. 'But how long would it take to transport 2 tons of mail 452 yards through crowded London streets?' He stopped his watch as the truck reappeared. 'Probably not as little as eighty seconds. That's for *two* tons, remember, versus fifty seconds for one: twice the weight, but far from twice as slow.'

'It's undeniably efficient,' said Fowler. 'But weight isn't everything. Not all Her Majesty's mails are as homogenous as bags of cement. Much is fragile, and one recalls with alarm your first run, in which the bags scarcely survived the impact with the buffers. How effectively can you temper your system?'

It was a good question. So good, indeed, that Thomas had his answer fully prepared.

'The pressure is minutely adjustable,' he replied, 'and it's just that flexibility which I shall demonstrate in the final run.' With great care, he produced a clinking wooden crate from beneath the stairs. 'My most precious family china,' he explained, pulling out some cups and saucers. 'What I propose is to couch these amid a ton of cement bags – giving a comparable weight to the first run – but this time decreasing the pressure to allow a safe, yet successful, progress through the tube. Billy, if you'd like to turn down the—'

'Wait one moment,' interjected Herapath. 'I think I may have a better idea.' He turned to address the crowd. 'Mr. Rammell proposes to illustrate the flexibility of his system, but with a challenge he himself has issued. To what extent can that be a true test of flexibility? As with the others, this third run will have been so meticulously rehearsed, we may as well salute its success here and now.'

Thomas met Herapath's mischief with a smile.

'While of course I oughtn't interfere, still less *demand* anything, I wonder if a more meaningful test wouldn't be for *me* to specify what cargo is carried on this final run.'

Thomas nodded, unperturbed. As long as they gauged the weight correctly, there was no cause for concern. But as the journalist's eye peered down towards Albert, hungrily finishing off his latest meal, Thomas's pulse suddenly quickened.

'Oh, how terribly sweet,' said Herapath. 'Mr. Rammell hesitates to trust his cherished hound to the vagaries of his pneumatic tube. Clearly, it is neither as flexible *nor* as safe as he'd have us believe. No matter, Mr. Rammell: stick to what you have practised. I apologise for over-estimating the capability of your railway.'

Thomas stared at Albert. The smog of panic was clogging up his brain.

'I'll do it,' he said, provoking a gasp from Latimer Clark, and open-mouthed surprise from Herapath. 'There's no reason why we can't. Albert, boy – back to the start!'

The trusty dog tore back into the sunlight, little knowing the groundbreaking challenge that lay ahead.

'He'll be the first living creature we've had inside the tube,' said Thomas. 'But I'm sure he'll be equal to the task.'

'Very good,' said Herapath, grinning.

'*Thomas.*'

Latimer Clark spoke through gritted teeth, but Thomas paid no attention. Instead, he issued instructions to his men. First, he dispatched someone to the start to explain that

Albert was to be lifted into the third truck and padded with cement bags. Then he ordered the second wagon to be removed from the run-off track. Finally, he instructed Billy to re-pressurise the chamber by as much as necessary to safely yet swiftly carry Albert through the tube.

'Are we not going to weigh him?' asked Billy.

'Trust your instincts,' replied Thomas. If they were going to respond to Herapath's challenge, they had to do so with gusto. 'Use our prior tests as a gauge, and where they don't suffice, just do what feels right. Oh, and Billy: look like you know what you're doing.'

With sweat dripping from his brow, Billy began turning down the fan.

'Thomas,' said Latimer Clark. 'I simply *must* speak with you.'

Thomas held back a scowl. What was the point of playing brave if his partner kept undermining him?

'If you'll just excuse us for a moment,' he said, smiling towards his guests.

'The man is a notorious bully,' hissed Latimer Clark, once they were out of earshot. 'He's a steam-man, naturally antagonistic towards atmospheric power.'

'So?'

'So, for want of any real criticism, he's provoking you into making a mistake. Don't fall for it. Just see the china safely through, and he'll have to write favourably for fear of seeming out of step. Let's not overreach ourselves. It's been a good day.'

'But how much *better* would it be if we met this challenge? I know he's a bully, but the Post Office *are* unusually stubborn. This is just the kind of confident gesture we need to get them – and others, new supporters, new sponsors – to take us seriously.'

'It's a goods-carrying system, Thomas. A nascent one at that. Neither of us knows how a living, breathing creature will cope with the pressure differential. Yes, it is sufficiently small that one wouldn't *expect* problems, but can we be sure?'

Thomas looked his partner in the eye. 'Albert will be fine.'

'But if he's not—'

'He *will* be.'

'But if he's not – you'll lose more than your dog. The whole scheme will be obliterated in an instant.'

'Then so be it! At some point, Josiah, we will have to expose ourselves to a degree of risk, especially if we are to one day carry people in these tubes.'

'For heaven's sake, Thomas, just for one second can we *please* think about the present? Focus on the Pneumatic Dispatch at its most basic before worrying about changing the world?'

Thomas glowered at his partner. 'The present *is* all I'm thinking about, and it is my considered decision – as *lead engineer* – that this demonstration is necessary to startle the Post Office into co-operating.'

Having pulled rank, Thomas met Billy at the entrance of the engine house. The estimates had been made and the air pressure in the tube adjusted. Back at the start, Albert – tail hanging limp between quivering legs – was being lifted into the final truck.

'I hope you've judged this correctly,' murmured Thomas, as the cushioning was loaded on.

Billy wiped his brow. 'Me too, sir.'

The truck was pushed forward until Albert's whimpering, audible from 50 yards away, grew muffled as he passed out of sight. A raised green flag signified that the truck had entered the vacuum and begun winding through the tube. Suppressing his guilt – all that running around, and *this* was how Albert was rewarded! – Thomas checked his watch and tried to be excited on the dog's behalf.

'The world's first pneumatic traveller,' he proclaimed. 'Not to mention the world's first subterranean rail passenger! A pioneer who'll be remembered for centuries to come.'

Herapath roared with appreciative laughter.

'How long should I be expecting this to take?' Thomas whispered to Billy.

'Assuming the carriage is as you instructed, sir, about seventy seconds.'

He turned towards the tube, unsure where to land his eyes. For all his outward bravado, he couldn't stop the horrifying visions entering his mind. Looming over everything was the fear that Albert had already been asphyxiated by the disparity in pressure. It seemed unlikely, the vacuum being far from absolute, but it wasn't impossible. And even if he *was* still alive, that didn't make him safe. Billy had been understandably cautious. What if he had re-pressurised the tube too much? The truck would fail to make it up the steepest gradients, and Albert would bake before they could locate the truck and crack the tube open. Conversely, if Billy's panic had caused him to re-pressurise too little – what then? What if Albert crashed into the buffers with comparable speed to the first truck? The impact would kill him immediately – assuming of course, he hadn't already been suffocated.

Thomas glanced at Latimer Clark, whose anxious face was a timely reminder of the importance of looking confident. It would be no good Herapath *et al* talking up Albert's trip if they also mentioned that both inventors looked utterly petrified while it unfolded. But as Thomas gave the spectators a smile of serene assurance, it was clear that no such posing was necessary. Every last one was staring at a slightly different point of the course, visibly enthralled by the silent magic of the system. Could it be that each was imagining himself in Albert's place, being sucked towards his destination by an invisible power source many yards away? Were they too feeling the wonder that had begun to shape Thomas's life, and that he so desperately wanted to inspire in others?

The howl of a nearby steam train returned Thomas's attention to his watch. A minute had passed since Albert had entered the tube. He led everyone back into the shed and stood by the empty tracks, straining to hear the hissing that would herald Albert's approach.

'Any moment now,' said Billy.

The seventy second mark ticked by, and still there was no sign. The fear returned that, dead or alive, Albert was trapped in the tube, and as eighty seconds elapsed, Thomas began trembling. What had possessed him to commit Albert to the tube so senselessly? Latimer Clark had been right, and now he was facing the consequences of his cruelty: excruciating humiliation, followed by the lifelong bitterness of avoidable failure.

He turned to his guests, about to concede defeat, when a rumbling shook the room – followed swiftly by a hissing. Holding his tongue, he looked back to see the hatch swing open and Albert roll merrily through, tail flapping as he lay proudly amid the bags of cement.

'Magnificent!' exclaimed Paxton. 'Quite simply magnificent!'

Overjoyed, Thomas checked his watch. 'Eighty-eight seconds, and not a hair out of place!'

Kissing the buffers – pressure judged to perfection – the truck stopped and Albert leapt out.

'You little genius!' cried Thomas, patting the intrepid dog. 'What do you say to that?' He looked around. Everyone – *including* Herapath – was elated. 'Precious cargo, perfectly dispatched!'

'How is his breathing?' asked Fowler.

Thomas listened. Albert's panting was no more frantic than would be expected, given the excitement.

'If anything, he's cooled down a bit,' said Thomas, as Albert made a beeline to get back into the truck.

'Well, well,' said Herapath, his cynicism clearly cracked by Albert's enthusiasm. 'If it has the hound's blessing, then it has mine too.' He offered his hand to Thomas. 'You have swayed me, Mr. Rammell. The pneumatic is quite enchanting.'

Thomas grinned – first at Paxton, then at his company's directors – and accepted Herapath's hand with gratitude for the challenge which the journalist had issued. Around them, the shed filled with excited chatter. Thomas turned to a bewildered Latimer Clark.

'Courage, Josiah,' he said, patting his partner on the back. 'That's all it takes. A little bit of courage – and behold what progress follows.'

Chapter 13

Even now, reason demanded that the bones would simply fall apart. But as I began to lift, the magical bonds held firm. One bone came with the next, and the gentleman skeleton's posture remained perfectly rigid. As I raised him up, his partner's skull, resting on his shoulder, was pushed out of the way and she sat upright of her own accord, slipping her knuckles out of his and laying them in her lap.

With the taller body balanced in my arms, I prepared to move him into the middle of the carriage – the intention being to wrap him in the rope ladder and have Tom pull him up. But before I'd brought him more than a few inches, the female skeleton shot out her stick-thin arm and clunked it against her partner's ribcage, pushing him back onto the bench. With my arms stuck beneath him, I tried dragging him away laterally, but again the lady skeleton lunged and pulled him back.

Undeterred by her possessiveness – they'd held their loving pose for well over a century, so the pain of separation was understandably acute – I tried gathering the woman herself, only for her man to dive in and ensure that she too stayed put.

'Oh, for Christ's sake!'

'What's up?' asked Tom.

'This couple down here. Clingy.'

'Are they heavy?'

'Not especially.'

'Then bring them up together!'

I reached around their backsides, hoping to haul them into a fireman's lift, one over each shoulder. But as I started to pull, both skeletons slammed their shoulders into my back, trapping my head in the space between them. Taking the hint, I slid my hands out and they allowed me to escape.

The pain in my spine brought the beginnings of panic. Leaving the original two behind – if they wanted to stay, so be it – I tried one of the adjoining trio, but they too were unwilling to leave.

Confusion mounting, I looked to the opposite bench and spotted the solitary gentleman who had first pulled me in, set apart from the family of three. Could it be that, without a partner, he might be permitted to leave? And if so, might that reassure the others that there was nothing to fear?

I gave it a go. Sure enough, none of those nearby moved as I picked up the lonely bones. Holding up his trousers, I hauled the poor fellow over my shoulder and felt a surge of relief: at last, the beginning of the end!

I started towards the ladder but immediately checked myself as every other skeleton slowly rose up and encircled me: staring, saying nothing. I continued forward, hoping to be allowed through, but the cordon of bobbing skulls stepped up in defiance. Infuriated, I set the skeleton back on the bench – at which all the others retreated.

'They don't want to leave!' I cried. 'Every time I pick one up, the others stop me.'

'But that's absurd! Why wouldn't they want rescuing?'

'*Too late for rescue.*'

I froze: this last voice wasn't Tom's. I flashed the torch from skull to skull.

'Shall I come down?'

Too late for rescue. The bitter, venomous wheeze ricocheted round my mind.

'That's it! I'm coming down.'

'No!' I shouted. 'Together, they're far stronger than us.

Besides, I want you up there to pull me up if something happens.'

'What do you mean, *something happens*?'

I hesitated, not knowing the answer. 'I just think it's safest.'

'But if we're not lifting them out, what *are* we doing?'

I lit up the nearest skull. 'I don't know who you are,' I said, as firmly as I could. 'But you *do* know who I am. Even though I only stumbled on you by accident, I've given in to your threats and come down to help. Surely I'm owed an explanation?'

The skeleton stared lifelessly ahead, immaculately uninterested.

'Look, you've obviously been stranded here, and that needs fixing. Right? We're all set to make it happen. We've got coffins, a van, a perfect patch of land . . .'

Still nothing. Just the blank voids of its eyes and a full set of orangey-brown teeth, clamped unevenly together.

'Then what?' I sank despairingly onto the floor, staring at the hole above. 'Please, just tell me what to do, and I'll . . .'

I trailed off, noticing that the hole – narrow when I entered; narrower still once the mud had reset itself – seemed smaller than ever. Shining the torch up, my flesh crept as I saw the dim outline of overhanging trees being slowly eclipsed by glistening mud.

'Tom?' I yelled, longing to see his weathered face. '*Tom*! Can you hear me?'

It was no use. I could tell from the changing acoustic that my words were no longer reaching the surface. I was going to have to fight my own way out.

Grabbing the rope ladder, I hugged the torch close. The light fell on the solitary gentleman skeleton, whose skull twisted sharply towards me.

'Too late,' he growled, teeth chattering up and down, impossibly eloquent in the absence of lips or a tongue. '*Too late*!'

I climbed the ladder, wishing I had Tom's spade to wedge the hole open. The gap was down to a few inches, and I knew I'd be risking my life to continue. But given that the alternative was rotting to death with a small army of ungrateful skeletons, I reached into the hole, praying that no sniping hands grabbed me from below, and that the moist earth above would expand to ease me through.

I squeezed almost my entire arm in, gripping the rope, but the sides continued to contract, crushing my arm with unnatural force. Yelling in agony, I wriggled my tingling, bloodless arm back out, so avoiding the even worse fate of rotting to death with a small army of ungrateful skeletons while dangling broken-armed from the roof.

The hole squelched shut. Swaying limply on the ladder, I heaved in a series of shallow, wheezy breaths.

The skeletons had eliminated my only escape route. Though the holes in the damaged roof and tunnel remained, the mud was solidly separating the carriage from the surface. That much was bad news.

The good news, I realised, was that Tom and Bill were still above me, equipped with an arsenal of spades and forks. Although the skeletons seemed to be controlling the soil, there was no reason why – with the spadework of two sizeable men – their resistance might not yet be overcome. If I just waited, my accomplices would surely dig through. And if they proved unequal to the task, then they'd summon reinforcements – extra people or even machinery. Peering down at the skeletons, all staring back up at me, I felt certain that, unlike them, I wouldn't be forgotten.

Before this knowledge had time to crystallise into consolation, however, the rope snapped in two and I thudded to the floor, the lower part of the ladder following in my wake to entangle me like a straitjacket. Looking up, I saw uninterrupted black where the gap had been. Not even the shortest little length of rope remained to help me communicate with the outside world.

I shone the torch around. Desperate tears worked themselves into my eyes as the still-staring skulls tilted to one side, as if sympathising with my predicament. At first I had a good mind to scream back at them, outraged by their sarcastic pity, but then a thought occurred. What if their show of empathy was actually a clue as to why they had postponed their rescue by trapping me in their tomb?

'I understand,' I whispered. 'I understand your suffering.'

I spoke with mounting confidence. Clearly, they had laid me low so I'd empathise with what they'd endured. I simply had to acknowledge this, from the bottom of my heart, and then we could all move on.

'I admit, when I came down, I didn't really care. I was only worried about myself, and getting you off my back. But now I truly appreciate the horror of your entrapment. And I promise: when it comes to burying you, I'll do it with genuine, heartfelt compassion.'

The skulls held their reflective poses.

'So if we could maybe just, you know, crack on? If you could reopen the hole and—'

Their mouths dropped open and the air filled with the husky cackle of laughter. Mute with terror, I tried standing up, but the tangled ropes pulled me back down. The skulls roared even louder, their jaws rattling open and shut, punctuating the mirth with the tapping of teeth.

I buried my face in my trembling knees until the laughter stopped, whereupon I sensed the nine bodies gathered close around me. Fearing that they were about to strip me of my flesh, I braced myself for an unhappy end. But instead of raining down blows, they shot out their hands and pressed nine cold, bony fingers against my quivering head.

'Eeeh, reek,' they chorused. 'Help us.'

With the drilled uniformity of a military unit, they marched back to their benches. Rather than resume their slouches, however, all nine sat down independently and upright – no rested heads, interlocking arms or hand-holding, but stiff, straight backs and skulls held high. Their legs, too, were no longer tucked up or splayed out immodestly, but set firmly at right angles with a hand on each knee or, in the case of the ladies, demurely folded one over the other, hands in laps.

I pulled myself out of the ladder and stood up. The mud above was still sealed, the roof and windows remained cracked, but *something* was changing. It wasn't material, but rather a silent energy, working against me. It was so gentle, arising so imperceptibly, that at first I thought it might just be dizziness. But as the energy increased, ever more serenely, it became tangibly, inescapably real, pulling me in *one particular direction*. I ran round the carriage, balancing here and there in spasms of disbelief, then checked through the glass to see the bricks and dirt as static as ever, pressed hard against the sides.

The mysterious momentum tightened its grip. I steadied myself against the sliding glass doors and shut my eyes, desperate to trust my senses, but disoriented by their mixed messages. There was no doubt that the carriage was still stuck in the earth. But there was also no denying it was moving – accelerating like a train, albeit one blessed by a smoothness that made it quite different from any railway I'd ever ridden.

I blinked my eyes open and saw the two ranks of skeletons leaning to one side in response to the carriage's motion. It was time to accept the impossible. The carriage, after all these years, was moving: going somewhere despite going nowhere. And though the how, why and where of our journey left me more confused than ever, there was one detail of which I was instinctively certain.

They, the skeletons, were the passengers; and I, being alive, was their driver.

Chapter 14

They were only an hour into the day's exhibition, with another four still remaining, but Thomas didn't mind. It was well over a month since Albert's heroics had inspired the engineer himself to take a ride in the tube – whereupon he immediately began inviting others to do the same – but there remained profound satisfaction in standing outside the engine house and watching people spill over from Battersea Park. Having heard of the therapeutic thrill to be experienced on the other side of the railway tracks, they came by the dozen to savour the pneumatic curiosity for themselves, forming a patient queue in the mid-August sun that wound round beside the tube itself.

The familiar hissing summoned Thomas back inside, whereupon the shutter flipped open and the tube ejected one of the three iron trucks. He peered over the rim of the carriage and helped out a tall young man, squeezed in among blankets and cushions.

'Sir, allow me to introduce Thomas Webster Rammell,' announced Billy from the wooden stage, where he was operating the Pneumatic Ejector. 'The inventor of the Pneumatic Dispatch!'

The man stepped out of the wagon and shook Thomas's hand. 'Many congratulations, sir. Such an invigorating contraption! The effect on the lungs is most restorative, and I am pleasantly cooler too.' He reached into his wallet and produced a threepence piece.

'You're sure the trip was satisfactory?' asked Thomas.

'Most certainly. In fact . . .' The man returned to his wallet. 'Take double, for ridding me of my headache!'

Thomas bowed as he added the money to the day's already considerable takings. It had proved a masterstroke, inviting people to take the trip for free and then offer a voluntary fee of threepence. Naturally, the odd scoundrel refused, but many more paid extra as thanks for the pick-me-up.

'How was it, darling?'

Thomas looked round. The man's wife – slender, fair-skinned and dark-haired – was standing just inside the shed.

'Quite enchanting, dear,' replied the man. 'You really must try it.'

'Oh, no,' said the woman. 'I get so anxious in enclosed spaces.'

'But that's the joy of it! One doesn't feel enclosed; one feels liberated. Yes, my ears popped at the start, but after that, there was just this remarkable floating sensation, as though the carriage were somehow rising up.'

'That's because it was,' said Thomas. 'As the air works across the whole back end, it counters gravity and lifts the wagon off the rails – so reducing friction, and increasing the speed.'

'But I'm pregnant,' said the woman. 'Isn't it a little danger-ous?'

'On the contrary,' said Thomas. 'Nothing could be safer.'

'Even in this weather? It must be so hot.'

'Not at all,' said the man. 'There's even a soothing breeze that squeezes its way in.' He took his wife's hand. 'Honestly, dear, you must try it. It's like the old Croydon atmospheric, but better because you're actually inside the tube. Imagine! No jolting, no jerking. Just that wonderful smoothness, luring you round the course.'

The woman looked at Thomas. 'Is it really that good?'

Thomas laughed. 'Oh, I couldn't possibly say.'

'Come on, dear.' The man dragged his wife back into the summer sun. 'I'm going round again, and this time you're taking a ride too!'

A pair of helpers began returning the empty truck to the start, where the next traveller was already in his wagon, awaiting confirmation that the tube had been sufficiently de-pressurised. Resuming his silent lookout, Thomas felt greatly saddened that their lease was expiring, making this the last day of demonstrations. Yes, it was important to move on, sticking to the plan – goods carriage first, passenger carriage second – but the past weeks had given him a tantalising taste of the future.

'So frustrating,' he sighed, as Billy raised the flag that sent the next passenger on his way. 'Yes, the Metropolitan might have started construction, but I genuinely think we could yet overtake them – if only we could make it all happen sooner. We've not done a thing to formally advertise these trips, yet look at the enthusiasm!'

'Patience, sir,' said Billy. 'Everything is progressing as planned. The Postmaster General has at last expressed his interest, and we've drawn up a proposal which he's bound to accept since we'll be shouldering all the risk. In the meantime, John Fowler's had no luck finding a viable alternative to steam, meaning that the Pneumatic Dispatch Company will be thriving, all set to scale up, just as the Metropolitan opens and suffocates every last one of its passengers.'

Thomas nodded. Billy was right. The plan was perfect as it stood, and all that mattered was that the Battersea demonstration had achieved its primary purpose of attracting the Post Office's interest.

The hissing came again. Thomas returned inside to greet an old man whose tearful gratitude for the 'revivifying trip' was underlined by the generosity of his voluntary fare.

'Afternoon, all.'

Thomas turned to see the Duke of Buckingham, the PDC's

chairman, standing in the entrance, flanked by Latimer Clark. He hadn't been expecting either, and bid a hasty farewell to his latest satisfied customer.

'Quite a little industry you have going on here,' said Buckingham with a smile. 'Your enterprise is most commendable, Thomas. No one could ever fault your commitment to the cause.'

Thomas was immediately fearful. Buckingham's bearing was almost valedictory, and it only got worse as the chairman led his engineers behind the shed, away from the din of the Pneumatic Ejector, and the prying eyes of the queue.

'I would tell you not to look so worried,' said Buckingham. 'Alas, your dread is well-founded.'

'What's happened?' asked Thomas. The thick air closed in quickly now they were away from the breeze of the fan.

'I've just come from seeing the Postmaster General,' explained Buckingham. 'He says the Post Office refuses to enter into any binding agreement – let alone one lasting twenty-one years.'

Thomas felt suddenly weak. '*What*?'

'I know,' said Buckingham. 'It defies belief.'

'But we made it so easy for them. We removed every ounce of risk. All we asked for was their agreement to use the network to transmit mails along the given routes.'

'He insists that we should construct the network first,' revealed Buckingham, 'free of any pledge and not building on GPO property. They will then *consider* using it once it is ready, basing their judgement on an initial trial period.'

Exasperated, Thomas leant against the engine house wall and roared with frustration.

'Naturally I challenged him,' continued Buckingham. 'Surely he understood that we couldn't possibly expand our authorised capital to £150,000 – let alone attract new funders – without a binding pledge? And surely there was no risk in offering that pledge, since they'd only have to use the system if it worked?'

'And what did he say?'

'That they don't want to close themselves off to other solutions.'

'But there is no better solution than what we've devised!' exclaimed Thomas.

'Indeed,' said Buckingham, 'but there was no arguing with him. I just needed to get something; at least a sliver of a pledge. So I offered an all-round compromise. I suggested we construct the branch line between Euston Station and Eversholt Street, and that they agree – for just a year – to use it to transmit mails between the two points. Then, if the savings prove satisfactory, they guarantee their custom for the larger network – from Euston to St.-Martin's-le-Grand via Holborn, including the other branch line at Holborn, and the sub-network at St.-Martin's-le-Grand – at which point, we publish our prospectus and expand our capital as planned.'

'And his response?'

'A series of caveats. First, that the Post Office be allowed to cancel the arrangement at a day's notice. Second, that they be charged only a nominal usage fee. Third, that we don't build on any Post Office property. And fourth, that the whole thing is subject to an inspection which the Postmaster General himself will conduct.'

Thomas laughed in bewilderment, but also some relief. 'Well it's far from ideal, but it's hardly terminal. From what you said originally, I feared—'

Buckingham was frowning.

'Alas,' he went on, 'our real difficulty is funding even the modest line between Euston and Eversholt Street. As things stand, we've nothing left to pay for what is, effectively, a second trial.'

'A second trial,' repeated Thomas. 'But isn't that the solution? Simply to transplant the machinery from here to there? Yes, we'd need another 100, 150 yards of tube – but other than that, the transfer will be straightforward.'

Still, Buckingham was frowning.

'What?' asked Thomas. 'Am I forgetting something?'

Latimer Clark stepped forward. 'Our current apparatus is enough to propel carriages in one direction, Thomas; but how on earth are we to bring them back again?'

Thomas felt the blood rush to his cheeks. Of course: the second engine house, required at the other end of the tube to suck trucks the opposite way to the first – as opposed to manually hauling them, as at Battersea.

'Aside from the machinery itself,' continued Latimer Clark, 'there's the expense of finding and leasing properties big enough to contain the fans. With the Post Office decreeing that we can't use their premises, those are our costs to absorb. One engine house we can just about cope with. But two?'

Thomas lifted his hands to his head. He was dying inside.

'None of us foresaw the extent of the Post Office's resistance,' said Buckingham. 'But unless we can drastically reduce the costs – remove the need for that second engine house – then I fear the end is upon us.'

Thomas said nothing. In the brilliant late summer sunlight, the darkness of panic was enveloping him.

'Excuse me, sir.'

Billy was poking his head round the corner.

'Our next passenger is about to arrive.'

For want of anything better to do, Thomas went back inside. The fierce breeze blowing off the Pneumatic Ejector came as a welcome relief, and as the latest traveller rolled into the shed, he found himself gazing at the outer rim of the Ejector, whence the wind came.

'Allow me to introduce Thomas Webster Rammell,' proclaimed Billy. 'Inventor of the Pneumatic Dispatch.'

Without diverting his eyes from the fan – there being something in the air that told him to keep looking, keep thinking – Thomas shook the passenger's hand.

'Thomas?' asked Buckingham, who had followed him into the shed, along with Latimer Clark. 'Are you quite sure you're alright?'

'One will suffice,' he said, slowly and softly.

'One what?'

Seized by inspiration, Thomas pointed to the outer edge of the fan. 'All we need do is build an outer casing to capture the air being blown out and channel it away. Then we feed that air into the pipe – but *behind* the truck, so blowing it back down the tube.' He clapped his hands, astounded by the brilliance of the idea. 'We suck it one way, then blow it back the other – all courtesy of the same Pneumatic Ejector!'

'So we only need one engine house for the branch line?' asked Buckingham.

'Precisely. It will require some modification – new pipes, valves, plus a supply of outside air when blowing – but the costliest things are all in place. Best of all, it will save us money when we build the full network, as we'll need only half the fans we originally planned – no longer one at every station, but one at every *other* station.'

'That's all very well, Thomas,' said Latimer Clark, 'but in terms of the immediate future: what would we need at Eversholt Street?'

'Just a small room. Somewhere to load and unload the trucks, with a nominal amount of telegraph equipment to communicate with the main engine house at Euston.' Thomas looked to his chairman. 'What do you think, sir? Is that achievable?'

Buckingham stared up at the magnificent machine, its true potential only now starting to reveal itself.

'Eminently so,' he said, grinning. '*Eminently* so.'

Chapter 15

It was about thirty seconds into the journey – if I can call it that – when the acceleration ended and we glided on at a constant speed. It was also around this point that the carriage showed the first physical sign of motion.

Of course, I say both these things, but neither was quite so straightforward. For a start, I only *inferred* our continued movement because deceleration hadn't followed acceleration; the silence and serenity meant that there was nothing to show we were actually in motion. As for the physical change, it was nothing so simple as the debris ahead making way for what felt so vividly like our advancing train. This alteration was subtler: seemingly prompted by the motion, yet independent of it, energised by a force all of its own.

It was hard to spot amid the dusty haze, but once I saw one I saw hundreds: little particles of soil drifting upwards, rising to the roof of the carriage like backwards snow. I tried collecting one, a centimetre in diameter, but as soon as I opened my palm it continued magnetically on its way, nestling in a patch of earth above where the roof had cracked open. It was as if the carriage had conjured a weird kind of weightlessness – one so negligible that only the soil broke free of gravity's clutches. I illuminated the floor and watched the particles rise from diminishing mounds, further exposing the chunks of brick and wood whose collapse had admitted the soil.

The force of motion returned, and once again it felt like we were floating through some intergalactic vacuum, free of earthbound ties like friction, air and noise. The effect was so beguiling that it took me several seconds to notice that the force, which had earlier pulled me backwards, away from the direction of movement, was now pushing me forwards.

I shone the torch around. The soily procession had ceased, and on either side the skeletons were resuming their customary poses – skulls on shoulders, hands interlocking. I instinctively guessed what this meant and, sure enough, was soon able to stand up straight, swaying neither forwards nor back.

Without any bump or braking, the journey was over.

Bar the soil that had drifted up to the roof, the carriage was exactly as I'd originally found it. Not only that, but a familiar squelching was coming from the mud overhead. Heart quickening, I looked up and saw a beam of light shining through the reappearing hole, making a perfect circle on the floor. At first I assumed it came from Tom's torch, but then I registered its unusual whiteness. Stepping into the light, I saw a glorious full moon directly above: a bony bauble, hanging on the branches of the trees.

After the horror of being cut off, and the craziness of our impossible journey, I could hardly believe my sudden, straightforward good luck. For all that I'd feared the skeletons wanted to make me suffer, they were apparently content just giving me a flavour of the misery that they'd experienced. Now, rather than make me a permanent victim, they were going to put me to far more sensible use and let me do what I'd originally intended.

'Tom!' I yelled, standing in the lunar spotlight. 'Everything's fine! I'm ready to come up!'

I checked round. My one obstacle was the ladder having been cut in two, but Tom could feed down the rope to which it had been attached. Between him and Bill they could easily pull me and the skeletons up.

'*Tom*!'

Still nothing. I wondered if my mysterious journey hadn't lasted longer than I realised; whether I'd actually been gone several hours, and if Tom hadn't grown tired of waiting. Alternatively, perhaps he'd failed to dig down manually, and had gone to seek assistance, not expecting the hole to reappear in the meantime.

An owl cooed cleanly through the night as the outside air seeped in, chilling the musty interior. Keen as I was to get moving, there was nonetheless a strange, solemn tranquillity as I waited. For the first time I felt no threat from the skeletons, and I was about to take my patient place on the cobwebbed benches when something sharp prodded my spine.

I turned to see a skull right behind me, then spun back to see the other skeletons all up on their feet, approaching. There was a breathless pause as they encircled me. Then, on some unspoken command, they lifted their arms and pointed at the hole.

'Oh, I see,' I said, with an uneasy chuckle. 'Well, yes – *quite*. We all want to get out as soon as possible, but I've no way of getting us up—'

In a flash, all nine crouched and grabbed my legs: eighteen bony hands, pressing in from my ankles up to my groin. I cried out as their collective grip squeezed the blood from my limbs, but the pain was only temporary. Once they'd all latched on, they propelled me upwards at such speed that my entire body slid through the hole with perfect ease, and I was sent several feet into the air before gravity pulled me back to the muddy earth. I landed upright, feet either side of the hole, and breathed in some delicious lungfuls of fresh air. Dropping to my knees, I peered into the carriage, moved by the skeletons' solidarity.

'Good job, everyone!' I cried, as the bones shimmered below. 'You wait there while I get the rope!'

I was about to turn away when one of the skeletons pushed its skull into the hole, filling the space with its stare.

'Fetch her!' it growled, teeth clunking, before retreating into the darkness.

Fetch her? The instruction made no sense. Other than me, there was only Tom and Bill, and they weren't anywhere to be seen – neither them, indeed, nor the tools we'd brought along. In seeking help, they'd obviously taken everything with them, not wanting to arouse suspicion.

I turned through a circle and called their names, noticing how different everything looked. It wasn't just the sudden thawing of the ice and frost. It was the trees – the branches lower, the leaves denser – and the nearby path, more muted in the moonlight than I recalled, as if composed of darker gravel.

'Fetch her!'

The words came again, with added urgency. Could it be that someone else had recently disturbed the carriage? Was her presence also required for the exhumation to proceed?

'Fetch who?' I asked.

The familiar hand shot through the hole, jabbing its finger in all directions – 'Fetch *her*!' – before disappearing back into the earth.

I listened for signs of life. The park was as quiet as it had been before I'd entered the carriage, but for the distant crackle of fireworks. This was a bit unusual, given the hour, but I thought little of it and moved away, going slowly to reassure the skeletons that I wasn't fleeing.

I scanned the distance and checked behind nearby trees, becoming increasingly distracted by how different everything seemed. Even the ground no longer felt like bare mud, but overgrown grass, brushing against my legs – a hunch confirmed as I was suddenly shoved face-first into it.

'Alright!' I cried, pinned to the ground. 'I'll fetch her. Just tell me where to look!'

'Who are you?'

I froze. These were living words: sharp and prim but brightly, wholeheartedly alive. What was more, they were spoken by a woman.

'What do you hope to achieve, giving people such a frightful shock?'

She turned me over. I saw only her silhouette against the moonlight.

'And what in heaven's name are you wearing?'

I shielded the moon with my free hand and discovered that I could have asked the same of her. The dress she wore beneath her big black coat was dark, full-length and plain, with a white lace collar peeking out: not unusual in itself, but weirdly unsettling when combined with her startling blond hair, permed and rolled to toupee-like perfection.

'*Well*?'

'These are my old work overalls,' I said. 'I wore them to dig.'

She glanced at the hole. There was a good chance she was pretty. Certainly, she was youthful, with a smooth complexion and big eyes. But her expression was fearful, and her body was trembling.

'You're obviously angry,' I said, 'but as far as I'm concerned *you* assaulted *me*. Whatever freaked you out, *I* had nothing to do with it.'

'You expect me to believe that?' She tightened her grip on my shoulders. 'You just said you dug down there. Why not admit the rest?'

'I have no idea what you're talking about.'

'You know exactly!'

'Know what?'

'The hand!'

My eyes widened. 'The *hand*?'

'That skeleton arm: grabbing me just now, tugging me into the earth.'

I stared back, mute with astonishment. Of course it wasn't me, I wanted to say, but *neither* was it the skeletons; I'd been with them until moments before.

I was about to shake my head when she shook it for me,

slapping me crisply across the cheek.

'That's for preying on vulnerable young girls as they walk through the park at ten o'clock at night!'

'*Ten o'clock*?' I repeated. 'But it was midnight when I arrived! That's some walk round the park. Two hours and counting. And by yourself, too! Asking for trouble.'

'What rubbish,' she said, checking her watch. 'It's eight minutes past ten precisely. As for being by myself, what of it? I'm simply going from here to there, and the park is the quickest way. It's perfectly safe, so why oughtn't I?'

I opened my mouth, but wasn't sure which question to ask first.

'And yes,' she continued, 'I *know* it's out of bounds and I shouldn't have been here but then neither should *you*. Even if your peculiar uniform means you're some kind of guard, that's no excuse to punish trespassers by giving them such a fright.'

'The park is *out of bounds*?'

'For heaven's sake.'

'Why is the park out of bounds?'

Slowly, she lifted her hands from my shoulders and rolled off, kneeling by my side.

'Why are you pretending?' she asked. 'Everyone knows the park is closed. It's been closed for a very long time.'

'Closed for the night?'

'Closed *permanently*.'

'But why?'

'*Why*?'

'Fetch her! Fetch her! Fetch her!'

The disembodied wheeze splintered the silence.

'You've got people with you!' exclaimed the girl, clambering to her feet and backing down the hill. '*Fetch her*? What are you trying to do? What have you got down there?'

Her terror was understandable. After all, my lunatic subterranean cohorts and I were indeed to be feared, assuming I followed their obscene instructions.

'Eeeh, reek! Fetch her!'

The interventions were fast becoming counter-productive, causing the girl to turn and sprint off uphill.

What was I to do? I had to obey the skeletons, but I couldn't possibly chase the poor thing, still less assault her and drag her back to suffer whatever morbid fate lay in store. I desperately wanted to bellow defiance down the hole, refusing to become the skeletons' man for hire on the surface. But before I could mount any show of resistance, the familiar white hand shot up and aimed itself at the retreating girl.

'Fetch her!'

'Why?'

'Fetch her!'

'Or else?'

'*Fetch her*!'

The skeletons chorused this last command together, cramming nine white arms through the hole at once. I stumbled back, dazed, through the tangled grass, and headed onto the heavy gravel.

For better or worse, I was in thrall to those below ground – a mobile extension of their bony arms, enslaved to do their bidding.

I had to do as they commanded.

Chapter 16

'How was your journey?' asked Latimer Clark.

It was eighteen months after the last day at Battersea, and Thomas was standing proudly at the Euston end of his first working line. The weather outside was gloomy, with just a hint of snow. Inside, gas lamps bolstered what little light came through the windows. The wintry cosiness was aided by the animated chatter of the crowd on the other side of the tracks: assorted luminaries and curious members of the public, invited to add atmosphere to the occasion.

The room was slightly bigger than the Battersea engine house, and just about accommodated the enlarged Pneumatic Ejector, which now had a flat, circular iron casing that concealed the iron discs. This captured the gale blown off by the fan, funnelling it into iron air ducts beneath the platform. It also provided convenient placement for the dials and barometers that controlled and monitored the air pressure in the vacuum chamber and tube. The external engine was now hidden behind the fan.

Elsewhere, the scene similar to Battersea. The tube entered and ended in identical fashion, its ingenious shutter designed to swing open as incoming trucks approached, prompted by the change in air pressure. The only visible addition to the trackwork was a pressurised air chamber, accessible through a flap on the wall opposite the tube's entry point, that provided a buffer for over-shooting trucks. As for other apparatus, the flags had been superseded by Wheatstone's electric telegraph, mounted on the wall above a thicket of levers whose number had multiplied in proportion to the increasing intricacy of the pipes and valves that organised the flow of air.

'I said, how was your journey?'

Thomas sensed provocation. 'Straightforward,' he replied. 'I walked.'

'Did you indeed?' said Latimer Clark. 'I took the Metropolitan from Farringdon – and most civilised it was too. Well lit, thanks to that ingenious gas supply. Not as noisy or as smelly as feared. Busy, yes, but commodious. And with such regular services that the crowds never became unbearable. Above all, it's fast.'

'I'm glad,' said Thomas. 'And yes, I too have tried it – several times – and I can't deny that, bar the breakdown on day one, it is thus far without major fault.'

'Without major fault? People are positively besotted by it!'

'It's only three weeks old. The novelty is all. Besides, Londoners have become so desperate for quicker journeys, they're predisposed in its favour.'

'But what of the apprehension? Even the most impatient passengers feared subterranean travel.'

'Well, in those cases I should imagine expectations were *so* low that they were pleasantly surprised – if only that they came out alive; that the Devil didn't get them.'

Latimer Clark shuffled fastidiously. 'Your ambition remains undented, then.'

'*Our* ambition,' corrected Thomas. 'And no. If anything, I am *thankful* to the Metropolitan for reconciling people to underground travel – and convinced they'll soon start asking why they shouldn't enjoy such convenience without all the unpleasantness.'

'But there is no unpleasantness.'

'Trust me, Josiah. When curiosity fades and complacency

sets in – among drivers, signalmen, passengers too – there will be delays, accidents, deaths, with ever greater frequency.'

'Thomas, *please*.' Latimer Clark lowered his voice to a fervent whisper. 'As a civil engineer, your eagerness for the Metropolitan to fail is unbecoming.'

'You think I should concede defeat?'

'I think you've a stubbornness which impairs sensible judgement. Ours is just one vision among many. It would be foolish to jeopardise our reputations by staking everything on it as the odds lengthen against us.'

Struggling to suppress his annoyance, Thomas dragged Latimer Clark behind the Pneumatic Ejector.

'Now listen to me, Josiah,' he said. 'I do not *want* the Metropolitan to fail; still less do I want anyone to suffer in its doing so. Should the day come when it reigns unequivocally triumphant, I will happily salute Charles Pearson and all who have followed him. My point, however, is that such a day can never come. At some point, the use of steam will cause numerous catastrophes which render its future use impossible. The only question is, when? My own view is sooner, rather than later – and that is a belief which happens to be—'

Thomas hesitated. He had planned to have this discussion later, but his partner's negativity was drawing him into the matter prematurely.

'Happens to be what?' prompted Latimer Clark.

'My belief,' repeated Thomas, 'happens to be shared by our directors.'

Somewhere beneath his beard, Latimer Clark frowned. 'Say that again.'

'It wouldn't need repeating, if only you'd attended the meeting last week. Now the Metropolitan is here, there is no more time for caution. We must seize the initiative with the Pneumatic Dispatch – both for its own good, and to graduate to passenger carriage as soon as possible.' He peered round the side of the Ejector. There was still no sign of the VIPs. 'We just need today to go as planned.'

'Today,' asserted Latimer Clark, 'and the coming weeks. It could even be months before the Post Office gives us the commitment we need.'

Thomas shook his head. 'This is what the directors agreed. As long as the Post Office agree to use this trial line, we will publish the prospectus and start building our longer line with or without a formal pledge of custom.'

Latimer Clark's eyes narrowed with disapproval.

'You think it's reckless,' observed Thomas. 'But at some point, we must stop waiting for others to commit and simply commit ourselves: say that the time for the Pneumatic Dispatch is now, or never at all. There are other clients besides the Post Office. The railway companies, Pickfords, Chaplin and Horne . . .'

The beard was trembling. 'I can't believe you did this without me.'

'You had more pressing business.'

'I thought the directors shared my caution.'

'They did. I won them round. They are now fully prepared to invest additional funds. What's more, they firmly believe that, with this trial in progress, other shareholders—'

'But we've worked so hard!' exclaimed Latimer Clark. 'We've come so far, and yet there you go, jeopardising everything because you cannot bear to see the Metropolitan getting ahead.' He drew his hands over his face. 'The success of the Pneumatic Dispatch is guaranteed – as long as we avoid impatience. Exercise the proper prudence, and it will itself be revolutionary.'

'I see no merit in prudence.'

'But things must be done in their proper order. That is just the way of business. Act rashly, and the Post Office will deem us amateurs. Wait for their formal blessing, and—'

'From the off, Josiah, they've been constitutionally averse to formal ties.'

'But now they will *see* how beneficial the system is!'

'And that's not something they could have imagined after

Battersea? These are intelligent people. Their reluctance to commit in advance is clearly endemic.'

'What harm in waiting to see?'

'The harm is that we miss our chance to give people the trains they deserve!'

Latimer Clark looked to the heavens in frustration.

'This is the real problem, Josiah,' said Thomas. 'You've never really cared for my bigger plans. All you've ever wanted is a tidy, profitable goods-carriage service.'

'Incorrect. When we began, I absolutely shared your grand ambitions. But now the Metropolitan is here, working well, we must protect what is most attainable.'

'And I am not threatening that. Why would I? I need the Pneumatic Dispatch as much as you. The difference is, you want it for itself; I want it as a stepping stone.'

Latimer Clark turned away, letting his head fall against the shield of the fan.

'Look, I know you would have counselled differently,' said Thomas. 'And if my actions irk you to desertion, I can only apologise. But if you can overcome your frustration, you have my pledge it will be the last disagreement we have, at least regarding the Pneumatic Dispatch. Henceforth, every detail will be yours alone to decide.'

Latimer Clark turned back. 'It will?'

'Indeed so,' said Thomas. 'Assuming the Post Office give us their blessing today, the directors have given me permission to channel all my energies into working up plans for the first passenger lines, leaving you to oversee the expansion of the Pneumatic Dispatch.' Smiling, he put his hand on his partner's shoulder. 'I was going to tell you, Josiah, but I wanted to wait until after the demonstration. I thought it would make the surprise all the sweeter.'

Latimer Clark took a deep breath, as if thinking things through, but Thomas knew it was just for show. The arrangement suited them both.

Moments later, Latimer Clark held out his hand and the

two men were reconciled.

Returning to public view, Thomas found Sir Charles Rich – among the PDC's most esteemed directors – escorting the Post Office delegation into the station. The visiting party was only two strong, consisting of Sir Rowland Hill, the Post Office Secretary, and Lord Stanley of Alderley, Postmaster General. Neither looked especially pleased to be there. Both, indeed, were scowling as they reset their modest deployments of hair, dishevelled by the breeze outside.

'I should explain,' said Rich, accompanying them over the tracks. 'Our guests have just suffered the terrible indignity of having their hats stolen outside the Eversholt Street station.'

'Dear oh dear,' said Thomas, shaking their hands in turn. 'You have my sympathies. Alas, such are the streets of London: safe for nothing – neither a gentleman's hat nor, indeed, Her Majesty's mails!'

He smiled at his guests, who singularly failed to see the humour in his clever, calculated remark. No matter, he told himself. They would get the joke presently.

'Good afternoon, everyone,' he began, 'and an especially warm welcome to our guests from the Post Office, here to satisfy themselves that this little line is worthy of use. Limited space prevents me from escorting everyone to the subterranean station at the other end, but Lord Stanley and Sir Rowland have just come from their own private inspection. Perhaps they might confirm that the tiny room consists of a bare minimum of machinery?'

'It is so,' said Sir Rowland: a stout fellow with wide, roaming eyes, forever seeking out signs of fault, whose achievements in education and postal reform had made him a hero to many.

'Lord Stanley?' Thomas turned to the politician. 'There is merely the telegraph, the run-off track and the buffer chamber. Correct? No power source, anywhere in evidence?'

'Indeed so.' Lord Stanley bowed, looking altogether less impressive than his colleague. Similar in height, though less portly, he made a more obvious effort to please, but felt less convincing. Thomas attributed this practised sheen to his politician's instincts, and felt certain that Sir Rowland presented the greater challenge. If only his approval could be won, the Postmaster General would surely follow.

'It is confirmed then,' he resumed. 'The only power source for what you are about to witness is here, in the iron casing behind me.'

Thomas nodded towards Billy, who disappeared behind the Pneumatic Ejector and eased the machine into life, its noise stifled into a dull rumbling. Four assistants filled the two open trucks with cement bags and wooden planks, while Thomas went to the far wall and operated the telegraph.

'Contacting Eversholt Street,' he explained, 'saying they should expect the consignment in just over a minute.'

He had scarcely finished sending the message when Billy's voice cut through the hum.

'Pressure ready, sir.'

'Move the carriages forward!' ordered Thomas, checking the telegraph to add: 'Message from Eversholt Street: "Track clear. Standing by to receive."'

Less than a minute had elapsed since the Ejector had begun turning. The hushed concentration of the crowd was unwavering as Billy opened the shutter, and the assistants pushed the trucks into the tube.

'Time: twelve thirty-eight and twenty seconds,' announced Billy, going to stand guard at the telegraph.

There was a burst of hissing as the wagons passed the entry valve and the air being funnelled out by the Pneumatic Ejector rushed into the tube, blowing the trucks towards their destination.

'Imagine the traditional scene at this point,' said Thomas. 'The mail carts have been loaded and the horses have taken their first tentative steps along the road. So far, so satisfactory. But soon they are halted by the junction with Seymour Street, where the traffic streams to and from

Camden. The driver twiddles his thumbs, while those guarding the mail fend off loiterers wanting to make away with precious Post Office cargo. On a good day, the wait will be ten seconds; on a bad, up to ten minutes. Let's be generous and call today a good day: the horses are off again, steady in their progress up Seymour Street.

'But no sooner are they on the main road than some tiresome obstruction intervenes: a spillage from another horse-drawn cart, or a thoughtless altercation between pedestrians. Our mail men are consigned to sit in traffic – tempers flaring all around – until the obstruction is cleared and the jam of vehicles is allowed to progress, inch by uneven inch, down the malodorous road, still only 50 yards from the point of departure.'

'Arrived, sir!' declared Billy, checking the telegraph. 'Time: twelve thirty-nine and thirty seconds. Journey accomplished in exactly seventy seconds.'

There was a burst of applause from the crowd.

'Reverse the Ejector!' commanded Thomas.

This prompted a scuffle of feet behind the iron casing, together with the clunk and clatter of several levers being pulled.

'So let us say the cart is now 70 yards from the start,' continued Thomas. 'Let's imagine it has had the good fortune to see several competing vehicles spill off into a side road. It has the chance—'

'Pressure ready!' came a cry.

'Eversholt Street ready!' announced Billy. 'Trucks loaded and ready to enter.'

'Stand back from the tracks!' ordered an assistant.

'Sending message!' shouted Billy. '"Euston prepped and standing by."'

'So sorry for the interruptions,' said Thomas, smiling. 'As I was saying—'

'Trucks in!' declared Billy. 'Exactly one minute after the trucks arrived at Eversholt Street, they are on their way back.'

'So our horse-drawn cart is now 150 yards from Euston, a quarter of the way to Eversholt Street, enjoying a stretch of open road, and getting a good pace up. But what now? One of the horses has a problem? Or is it the cart – one of the wheels, come loose on the cracked ground? Either way, the consignment has stuttered to a halt and several mailbags have been jolted overboard. The problem is easily remedied, but there is still a delay as the bags are loaded back on. Finally, the cart resumes motion and is within sight of the halfway point when—'

The hatch flew open. The two trucks were travelling so fast that they whizzed straight across the room and through the hatch, where they were finally halted by the buffer of compressed air, which cushioned the shock and pushed them a short way back into the engine room. There was a brief silence as the trucks came to rest, followed by an audible gasp as two top hats appeared from within, held aloft by human hands.

'Lord Stanley and Sir Rowland,' said Thomas. 'Your hats, safely returned by two gentlemen pioneers.'

Stanley and Sir Rowland watched with delight as Thomas helped up the two travellers: in the leading carriage, the Duke of Buckingham, perfectly composed, and then Sir Joseph Paxton, his aged face aglow with exhilaration.

'Wonderfully comfortable,' he declared, stepping out of the carriage to more applause, 'and utterly invigorating.'

'Apologies for the theft,' said Thomas, as he passed the hats back to Sir Rowland and Lord Stanley. 'But I wanted to show that the Dispatch is fit to carry even the most precious cargo.'

Stanley was bursting with excitement, and Sir Rowland, too, seemed genuinely stirred, satisfying himself as to the spotlessness of his hat before popping it back on his head.

'Where is the horse-drawn cart now?' he asked.

'Just arriving at Eversholt Street.' Thomas grinned. 'If we're being optimistic.'

Sir Rowland looked approvingly at the trucks, while Thomas acknowledged the ongoing cheers, explaining how the system worked and proudly proclaiming the ingenuity of the Pneumatic Ejector: its unique ability both to blow the cars away from Euston and then, at the pull of a lever, suck them back.

'Well, Mr. Rammell,' said Sir Rowland. 'Though you have rather over-estimated what we needed today, it has certainly been entertaining. Assuming Lord Stanley has no objection' – the politician shook his head – 'we shall use your line as agreed. However, if your elaborate display was intended to get us to agree to something more, I fear I must disappoint you.'

Thomas bowed. 'We have learnt not to expect any promises.'

'Of course I am not ruling it out. As the weeks go by, we may well be so impressed that we will happily supply the assurances you need to press ahead with your bigger plans.'

'Very kind of you, Sir Rowland, and of course we will always welcome such a pledge. You should, however, know that we are now sufficiently confident to proceed with a longer line, from here to the City, immediately, even without the guarantee of your custom.'

'Really?' Sir Rowland glanced at Latimer Clark in surprise. 'Well, well. What commendable assuredness. I look forward to seeing what comes of it.'

Keen to maintain the show of *brio*, Thomas gestured for Sir Charles Rich to escort their guests out to discuss financial arrangements without further ado. He then turned to the crowds and declared the demonstration over, resisting the demands of several enthusiasts to climb into the trucks and take a ride for themselves.

'There'll be time enough to travel through these tubes in the future,' he said. 'And on a far more impressive scale, I assure you.' He smiled at Paxton. 'Shan't be long now, I promise: shan't be long now.'

Chapter 17

I could do this, I told myself, as long as I remembered it wasn't actually *me* doing it. The skeletons had ordered it; the skeletons were responsible.

The girl's head-start meant she was already out of sight by the time I began my pursuit. I scoured the trees for movement as I ran, stepping off the gravel and onto the grass to accelerate.

After a short while I caught sight of a small pedestrian gate on my right, resolutely locked with clusters of industrial padlocks, and reinforced with extra iron and barbed wire. I recalled what the girl had said – 'Closed for a very long time' – as some twigs splintered behind me. Turning, I saw her in the woods, running back downhill. She'd obviously been spying on me through the trees.

'Wait!' I yelled, following her down to the path behind the lake. 'What happened to you happened to me too, except *I* ended up inside. That's why I'm here.'

The girl slowed and turned – still backing away, but looking me in the eye.

'I don't know what they want,' I said. 'Well, I do – they want *you* – but I don't know why.'

She let out a sarcastic laugh.

'Whatever it is, I'm not so sure they're necessarily evil.'

She laughed again. I wasn't doing brilliantly with the reassurances.

'Put it this way,' I continued. 'If they'd wanted to attack me, they'd have done so by now. As it is, they're up to something bigger. God knows what, but they clearly need *you* just as much as they need me.'

It was no use. The girl raced away, disappearing into darkness as the trees overhead blocked out the moonlight.

Reluctantly, I gave chase, the burden of my mission weighing heavier than ever. There was no way I could persuade her into co-operating when I myself hardly believed the facts. To succeed, my only option was to somehow strong-arm her back to the scene of her terror.

Passing the maze, the trees thinned to readmit the moonlight. Ahead of me, I'd fully expected to see the girl sprinting up the slope, where the open lawns rose to the transmitter. But not only was she out of sight, the entire park was transformed. The concert bowl and transmitter had disappeared completely, while the lawns had gone to seed, thick with weeds and nettles. Litter and lumps of metal were strewn everywhere, making a wasteland of what had been the most elegantly landscaped part of the park.

With no sign of the girl ahead of me, I headed into the centre of the park on the level below the two walled terraces. Here, as elsewhere, my surroundings were maddeningly changed. More battlefield than park, the paths and lawns were covered with shards of scrap metal, glinting like broken glass in the moonlight. Spotting the girl in the distance, running along the front of the lower terrace, I broke into a cautious run, slaloming around the obstacles that blocked my way, then taking some stairs up to the same level as my prey.

I headed towards the central path, counting six dried-up fountains arranged across the full length of the terrace, three on either side of the path. Each was surrounded by a cordon of ghostly statues, who appeared to be guarding a decrepit array of urns.

Feeling distinctly disoriented, I raised my eyes to the upper terrace, where the two classical statues I'd spotted on my one previous expedition had been joined by a host of others, posing atop the balustrades. The spectacle was eerie yet utterly captivating, not least because the upper statues were silhouetted against a starry sky – the dense wood that had previously covered the highest level of the park, where the Crystal Palace once stood, having now disappeared.

Astonished at how it all felt more dead *and* more alive, both older *and* younger, I turned to look downhill. Below me, the sports complexes had vanished, and the central path – formerly a dull concrete walkway, feeding a dreary sixties car park – was now a weedy avenue, sweeping up through a derelict circular fountain basin, and bridging a wide pathway below. Faded advertising hoardings suggested that, in less overgrown times, the latter had once been part of a motor-racing circuit – the same one, I figured, that Tom had mentioned as belonging to the dim and distant past.

Ever more certain of my predicament, I reached the central avenue, and turned to face directly uphill. Ahead of me, just below the upper terrace, an old-fashioned bandstand looked for all the world like it was materialising from thin air – and so, in a way, it was, for the white of the moon had now begun to mingle with the flicker of orange, emanating from off on the left. The light made flames of the weeds and left no room for doubt: despite all that had changed, the skeletons were up to their old tricks.

I turned slowly to my left. There, about 150 metres away, was a fragment of the Crystal Palace: flat-roofed, a mere three-storeys high, and extending no further than the width of the lower terrace itself, but unmistakeably part of Paxton's masterpiece – glass stacked upon glass, held firmly in place by iron. As was apparently customary with the Palace, it was currently being annihilated by rapidly advancing flames.

The whole thing seemed impossible, but also strangely inevitable. Here I was, watching the destruction of a part of the Crystal Palace which hadn't existed the previous day and which, to the best of my knowledge, hadn't stood at all for many decades.

My stomach tightened with guilt, but it made no sense to blame myself. According to logic, the skeletons' vengeful deeds were reactions to being ignored or disobeyed. But this time I had left the carriage under orders, so why the punishment?

As if in answer, the girl walked into view. She was silhouetted no more than 100 yards from the burning building, standing stunned as if linking the fiery catastrophe to her strange adventure in the wood. Though she couldn't be sure of the truth, I knew it for a fact: this fire wasn't my fault but hers; punishment for fleeing the skeletons.

'It's the southern wing,' came an excited voice. 'The last part still standing, and now it's done for too!'

I turned and saw swathes of people streaming onto the terrace, seeking the source of the smoke that sent clouds into the clear night sky. The women were in full-length coats and flat shoes; the men in well-fitting suits and caps. As they approached, I met their questions about the start of the fire with one of my own.

'Just tell me,' I said. 'What's today's date?'

They all stared back in bewilderment, but for one capless young man whose jet-black hair, slickly side-parted, twinkled in the light. His eyes weren't focused on me but on the fire, and he gave the answer with an air of distraction.

'24th October.'

'What year?' I asked.

'What year?' he repeated, glancing at me briefly before looking away again. 'It's 1950. Obviously.'

The shock came in waves: first, confirmation that the skeletons had whisked me back in time; then, the year itself. 1950 was one of the years Tom had mentioned when describing the unexplained fires that had sequentially consumed the Palace. This blaze, I realised, was a piece of history. And so, presumably, was its cause: the girl disturbing, then deserting, the skeletons. Most extraordinarily of all, her actions had created some kind of portal – a hole in time through which I had passed.

'Oh, dear God!' The young man started forwards. 'It's Emily!'

This triggered a stampede towards the fire, which I grudgingly joined. Walking slightly behind the masses, not daring to think how much harder my mission had just become, I found myself in the company of a dishevelled old man in tattered cloth trousers and a moth-eaten tweed jacket. His face was scarred, and a few shapeless orange teeth angled through his flaky, desiccated lips. Beneath his jacket he wore a greying white shirt, unbuttoned by virtue of there being no buttons attached, but he showed no signs of feeling the cold. Instead, he just stared dead ahead, consumed by sight of the fire.

'I don't believe it,' he whispered, tears rolling down his cheeks. 'It's happening again. Again, after all these years.'

'There! That's the man!'

The shrill cry came from within the crowd, prompting the onlookers to separate into two lines. At the end of these stood the young lady, with the slick-haired man by her side.

'This fellow?' he asked, eyeing me up and down.

I raised my hands in peace, but he was already on his way.

'It's not as it seems,' I pleaded. 'I can explain everything.'

The man came closer, menace writ large on his face, but stopped as he spotted something over my shoulder.

'This gentleman causing you trouble, sir?'

I turned. A police officer was coming to my aid.

'Other way round,' hissed the young man. 'This bloke's been stalking my Emily through the park. Hiding under-ground, the devious bastard. Used some sort of . . .'

'Used what, sir?'

'Some kind of mechanical skeleton arm to attack her.'

The bedraggled old man gave a gasp.

'He had others with him!' shouted the girl.

'That's right,' said her man. 'Others down the hole, wanting to entrap her and have their rotten way.' He stepped up to the officer. 'Honest, sir: you've got to arrest him, right this minute!'

The constable faced me – a moustachioed little fellow whose sweaty face twinkled in the firelight. 'Well?'

I bowed respectfully, wondering how to reply. Should I tell them about the skeletons and seek clemency on the grounds that my actions weren't my own? Or should I fabricate a cover story to keep my mission alive – and the skeletons' secret safe?

In truth, there was no choice. I was cornered, fair and square; I had failed to 'fetch' the girl. My only chance of success had been to catch her before she left the park, but now the cavalry had arrived there was no getting her back to the carriage – neither now nor in the future. However happy or otherwise I'd been to do the skeletons' bidding, my crazy voyage had come to a clunking halt and it was their fault: first, for frightening the girl from the very place we needed her, and then for igniting a fire that attracted the attention of the entire neighbourhood.

It was time to return my loyalties to the living.

Chapter 18

The train slowed to a halt, its screeching brakes resounding through the station at King's Cross. Clutching two rolls of paper to his chest, Thomas braced himself against the crush. It was a full seven months since the Post Office line from Euston to Eversholt Street had opened, and he was hoping that today's meeting would finally herald the next big breakthrough.

'Be patient!' he implored, as the man whose armpit he'd been nuzzling pushed past and tore one of the sheets. 'The train's not going anywhere till everyone's off.'

The man turned and scowled.

'I just . . .' Thomas was struggling, not for words but air. 'A little consideration?'

'Yesterday we were halfway into the tunnel before everyone was off!' the man shot back. The doors opened and he barged forward, scattering those in front onto the platform.

Thomas bit his tongue as enough people alighted to relieve the suffocation. Though there were still no vacant seats – those which had become available had been swiftly claimed, not all of them by the most in need – and though the sulphurous smoke weighed heavy on the lungs, even he had to concede that breathing a little was preferable to scarcely breathing at all.

He steadied himself and joined in the coughing as the train

continued westwards. Billy was approaching down the well-lit carriage, having become separated in the boarding scrum at Farringdon.

'How late are we?' asked Thomas, as a burst of noisy acceleration caused some passengers' belongings to tumble from their laps.

'Still just about on time,' said Billy, stepping over outstretched feet and stray luggage. 'Incidentally, sir, I haven't yet said congratulations. I didn't honestly think you'd convince him.'

'I was a little taken aback myself!' said Thomas, laughing. 'But it just goes to show: now is the time. The appetite for change exists on all sides. With him on board, the directors can't possibly—'

There was an ear-splitting bang. Instinctively assuming a collision, Thomas and Billy dived to the floor ahead of the shockwave, but the impact never came. Instead, the train slowed more gently, with the engine's roar replaced by hissing, faintly audible over the carriages' clatter.

'Engine breakdown,' said Thomas, as he stood and wiped the soot off his papers.

Consternation swept through the carriage. Those standing stamped their feet, while those sitting stood, let fly a few choice words, then sat back down when it looked like someone was making a play for their perch.

The train stopped and the minutes passed. The air grew thicker as the smoke from the loco worked its way down the tunnel and sneaked inside the carriages. Finally, a door was wrenched open and the red face of a guard glowed dimly in the dark.

'Apologies,' he muttered. A plume of smoke gathered round him, then billowed inside to exacerbate the wheezing and retching. 'Not certain when we'll be moving again – if at all.'

'Thanks, mister,' shouted a young man. 'That's a fat lot of use!'

'Well worth letting the smoke in for,' quipped another.

'I'm doing my best,' said the guard.

'You do realise we're paying for this so-called service? Way things are, we'd be better off paying to trudge through the streets like we used to!'

'Yelling at me isn't going to help,' said the guard. 'I'm as powerless as you.'

'Then why not find us someone who can actually do something?'

The altercation continued to intensify, but Thomas was becoming distracted by a distant rumble.

'Oh no,' he said. 'Come on, man!' He reached for the guard. 'Get in here now!'

'Don't you dare touch me, mister!'

'*Listen*!'

The carriage fell silent, allowing the guard to register the sound of a train approaching along the tracks on which he was standing. He climbed in and slammed the door shut, but no passing train materialised. Instead, the sound of brakes screamed down the tunnel, followed by a deafening crash. A second later, the coach was shoved violently back, and the passengers fell to the floor like dominoes.

'Curses,' muttered the guard, expertly managing to stay upright. 'Signalman must've dozed off and a train come up behind.' Wearily, he opened the door and jumped back out. 'It's only 200 yards to Gower Street. You'll have to walk. Just give us a second . . .'

He wandered off, leaving the passengers in a daze – as much from his reaction as anything else. Apparently, not even the combination of breakdown *and* collision could ruffle the Metropolitan's routinely-imperilled workers.

Confirmation came that the eastwards signal at Gower Street had been changed, and the passengers spilled onto the tracks. The smoke made it impossible to see more than a few yards ahead, and Thomas and Billy weren't alone in pressing handkerchiefs to their faces to filter out what toxicity they could.

Though the distance to the platform was short, the funereal pace left Thomas late for his appointment. Even when they finally reached the station, the ordeal wasn't over, for the eastbound locomotive had filled the platforms with smoke while it waited. It wasn't until they were halfway up the stairs to the exit that the air finally began to clear, and the passengers were able to breathe life back into their lungs.

Thomas and Billy crossed the Euston Road, then headed under the Euston Arch into the terminus itself. There, in a meeting room off the Great Hall, Latimer Clark, the Duke of Buckingham, Sir Charles Rich and the PDC's six other directors were discussing the extended line from Euston to St.-Martin's-Le-Grand in the City, construction of which was to begin within the hour.

'Apologies for my late arrival,' said Thomas, taking his place. 'Due entirely to the shortcomings of the Metropolitan, I might add.'

Buckingham smiled as he sorted through his papers. 'Your arrival is timely. We sped through discussion of the Eversholt Street branch, and as for the longer line, I am delighted to hear it could be ready within three months.'

'By Christmas, yes,' said Thomas. 'Josiah really has done a wonderful job.'

'Splendid,' said Buckingham. 'All of which good news brings us to what you've been up to these past few months.'

Thomas spread his sooty papers on the desk, tethered by paperweights which Billy supplied.

'Before I begin,' he said, 'I should like us briefly to ponder the Metropolitan.'

'What of it?' asked Buckingham.

'Well, we all know the service has declined since those first few weeks, when it was under such scrutiny. Breakdowns, delays and collisions have become ever more frequent, wearing away at the public's patience.'

He rose and set off round the table, keen to engage all the directors.

'But the problems themselves aren't as striking as the Metropolitan's reaction. Rather than remedying the faults responsibly, they've become defensive. For want of being able simply to ignore choke damp, they claim that the putrid tunnel air is actually *good* for you. They counter newspaper reports of collisions and breakdowns with figures illustrating how beloved their railway is.'

'But how does this relate to us?' asked Buckingham.

'It plays into our hands,' explained Thomas. 'It ensures that disillusionment will grow, and with it desperation for an alternative.' He raised a cautionary finger. 'But only for now. Soon, passengers and profits will diminish because of the bad service, and they'll have to smarten up their act. I believe that time is a year away at most and, once it comes, our opportunity will have passed.' He eyed each director in turn. 'But we do have a window: one where success is ours for the taking.'

There was a murmur of enthusiasm – some directors even tapping the desk – while Buckingham sat forward keenly. 'So how do we begin?'

'Two separate railways,' said Thomas. 'Sister companies to the PDC, with distinct identities but shared profits, directors and shareholders. The first is the Oxford Street and City Railway. It has the great merit of achieving something new in terms of traffic-relief while challenging the Metropolitan for many of its passengers.'

Thomas passed the top sheet of plans to Buckingham, and the other directors gathered round.

'Its primary purpose is to decongest Oxford Street and High Holborn. As you can see, it begins beneath Her Majesty's Marble Arch, at the junction of Edgware Road and Oxford Street. From there, it continues eastwards beneath Oxford Street, Regent's Circus and the junction with Tottenham Court Road, then directly below New Oxford Street and onto High Holborn. It doesn't deviate from its eastern course until Gray's Inn Lane, where it curves north-east to join Greville Street, skirting Fox Court as it continues below Charles Street, then terminating at Victoria Street, on the western side of Farringdon Street Station. Length is 2 miles, 3 furlongs, 2 chains and 30 links.'

'That's a considerable distance,' said Buckingham.

'Yes,' acknowledged Thomas, 'but it's easily constructed. By progressing under established thoroughfares for most of the way, we will have to demolish only a handful of properties.'

The directors nodded approvingly.

'The real elegance, however, is the interplay with our rivals. The Metropolitan runs north-west from Farringdon Street to King's Cross, where it turns westwards beneath the Euston Road, all the way to Paddington. Our railway, on the other hand, runs *south*-west from Farringdon Street to High Holborn, whence it progresses westwards all the way to the Marble Arch – scarcely half a mile from Paddington.'

'A perfect parallel,' observed Buckingham.

'Quite so. Besides reclaiming Oxford Street and High Holborn from traffic, and giving people to the *south* more civilised transportation, we'd be creating a battleground between the two west–east thoroughfares. This battleground is large enough to justify each railway, yet sufficiently small that many of its workers and residents will be able to make a choice. Do they proceed at the mercy of steam – or would they rather be whisked along, unfettered, by the power of air?'

The directors signalled their understanding and, apparently, contentment, but as yet asked no questions.

'My other proposal, the Victoria Station and Thames Embankment Railway, challenges steam more directly, competing for uncharted territory. This time the battleground is the Thames Embankment. Construction of this begins next spring, and will inevitably integrate a subterranean railway to speed people along the north bank of the river and leave the thoroughfare free of congestion. But what form will it take? John Fowler wishes to extend the Metropolitan south-east to Tower Hill and south-west to South Kensington, then connect these with a new subterranean railway, the Metropolitan

District, running west-east through the Embankment to complete his "inner circle".'

'A similar scheme is also proposed by the Metropolitan Grand Union,' added Latimer Clark.

'Indeed so,' said Thomas. 'Both would be powered by steam, and I am adamant that both will be rejected in favour of our alternative.'

'My goodness,' said Sir Charles Rich. 'Such confidence!'

'How can you be so certain we will prevail?' asked Buckingham.

'Because our principles echo those that have brought the Embankment to the brink of construction,' said Thomas. 'The aims of Joseph Bazalgette and, before him, Sir Joseph Paxton in reclaiming land from the river are only partly aesthetic. Just as significant are the sewers that will run below ground, improving standards of safety and cleanliness in exactly the same spirit as the pneumatic railway.'

'Will our route also connect with the Metropolitan?' asked Buckingham.

'Alas, the two are incompatible.'

'But completion of that inner circle seems so obvious.'

'That is a weakness,' admitted Thomas, passing the plans over, 'but we will at least be serving Victoria Station. If the Metropolitan get permission for their extensions, they can bring it as far as Victoria, then passengers can change.'

'The railway begins at a terminus just outside Victoria?' asked Buckingham, studying the plans.

'Correct. It travels directly beneath Victoria Street, and diagonally below Parliament Square, to an intermediate station at Westminster Pier. A second line then proceeds beneath the Embankment to a terminus we shall build just south-west of Blackfriars Station. The first section will be 1 mile long; the second, 1 mile, 1 furlong and 6 chains.'

'What of the other specifications?' asked Buckingham.

'For both routes, the tunnel height will be 10 feet 6 inches – just fractionally wider than the carriages travelling through them. Depth will vary, but the base of the tunnel will always be between 15 feet and 35 feet below street level, so never disturbing sewers, which are laid lower. The curves are eminently negotiable, and likewise the gradients. The severest will be around 1 in 50.'

'When do you suggest taking these plans forward?'

'Our window is a small one,' said Thomas, 'so I recommend submitting these plans to Parliament by the end of November – five weeks from now – with a view to their being considered in the next session. Construction to begin by the end of next year.'

Buckingham nodded as he rolled up the plans. 'And?'

'And what, sir?'

'Is that everything?'

Thomas was uncertain what else there could be. 'That is the extent of my plans at present,' he said.

'Very well,' said Buckingham, frowning as he looked at his fellow directors. With no discussion, everyone returned to their seats and Thomas took a deep breath: expecting caution, but feeling well-equipped to deal with it.

'Apologies if we are missing something,' said Buckingham, 'but your plans leave us with a pressing question: when, and where, do we carry out our trial?'

Thomas hesitated. 'What trial?'

Buckingham sighed. 'You haven't legislated for a full-scale trial?'

'In honesty, sir, it's simply not necessary.'

'Ah, Thomas.'

'I mean it, sir. The Pneumatic Dispatch *is* the trial! Scaling up *will* work, as sure as air rushes into a vacuum! Besides, over a thousand people have travelled in the lines here and at Battersea. A *thousand people,* in *open* carriages, exposed directly to the atmosphere.'

'All of which satisfies us well enough,' said Sir Charles Rich. 'But will it convince our Parliamentarians? Will it sway the people they serve?'

'Even if it does,' said Latimer Clark, 'we haven't the strength to be permitted to carve railways through the centre of town. The Eversholt Street branch has only been operational for a few months, and the Post Office remain far from finding it indispensable. Take-up of the shares of our enlarged capital is nowhere near what we hoped—'

'It's time to take another risk,' interjected Thomas, sick of Latimer Clark's malicious caution. 'I have it on good authority that, given the numerous schemes being advanced in the wake of the Metropolitan, Parliament are convening a special Joint Select Committee to ensure that only the most sensible bills make it through.'

'Who told you this?' asked Latimer Clark.

'Lord Stanley of Alderley. He knows because he's going to be on it.'

The directors looked at each other in surprise.

'That's right,' said Thomas. 'Our only true friend at the Post Office, as it has turned out. The man whose enthusiasm has been keeping Sir Rowland's reluctance in check.'

'But Stanley is just one man,' said Buckingham. 'Given our rivals' might – especially John Fowler – we'll need more allies than merely him.'

'How about John Fowler himself?'

There was a baffled silence. Thomas couldn't resist a smile.

'Billy and I have just come from a meeting where John agreed to be named as co-engineer on the Oxford Street scheme,' he explained. 'I know it's strange, when he works for the Metropolitan, and is proposing to complete the inner circle with steam. But we all remember Fowler's Ghost – his doomed attempt to avoid using steam underground by storing heat in bricks. He has always known that safer, cleaner, more dependable power will one day be required for subterranean railways. That's why he wants to collaborate on the Oxford Street railway, even though it may take custom away from the Metropolitan – and even though we are rivalling him for the Thames Embankment.'

'Do you have anyone equivalent for the Embankment scheme itself?' asked Buckingham.

'There is Sir Joseph, of course, but also my co-engineer – George Stephenson's former assistant, Charles Liddell.'

'Very good,' said Buckingham, looking around the table. 'Gentlemen? Are we swayed? Who still insists upon a full-scale trial?'

To Thomas's dismay, all eight directors, including the chairman, raised their hands.

Buckingham gave a regretful sigh. 'I'm sorry, Thomas. But there you have it. Whatever else is in our favour, Parliament will never permit us to dig up Oxford Street, let alone interfere with the Embankment, if we haven't thoroughly demonstrated the viability of our system. To countenance your trying to persuade them otherwise would be irresponsible to our shareholders.'

Thomas began shaking, struggling to contain his frustration.

'We appreciate how vexing this must be for you,' said Sir Charles Rich. 'But please be assured that we remain committed to opening a pneumatic passenger line within two years – and as such, we will happily use capital directly from the PDC to fund a proper trial. It need be no longer than half a mile, but it must prove the capability of the full-size system to negotiate curves and gradients beyond those in your plans. Assuming this is satisfactory, we will then fully support submission of these plans next year – in time for approval in 1865.'

Thomas stared at the desk, thinking hard. He knew that the trial was a reasonable request. It was just the delay that made him anxious.

'I will happily organise the trial,' he conceded. 'But in terms of depositing the plans at Parliament, I must restate the importance of acting now. These schemes can only succeed if considered in the coming months. A year from now, the Embankment will have been appropriated by John Fowler, and some other steam-powered scheme will have beaten us to Oxford Street.'

'But what merit the trial,' said Buckingham, 'if it hasn't actually occurred by the time Parliament considers our proposals?'

'It would underline our confidence,' replied Thomas. 'Besides, the Committee is unlikely to convene until February or March, and we could readily have a trial underway by then. Imagine if they coincided – the upsurge of interest would virtually guarantee success.'

Thomas watched the directors exchange glances, the concern slowly ebbing from their features.

'What's the worst that can happen?' asked Buckingham. 'The trial isn't ready, so Parliament rejects our plans? Very well. We simply go back next year, with the trial a triumph, and offer new proposals that move with the times. Either way, Thomas is right. For these plans at least, there's no point waiting. Agreed?'

Buckingham received approval from each of the directors in turn. Only Latimer Clark remained unconvinced, but since he had no formal say, Buckingham declared the meeting over, and led the way towards the groundbreaking ceremony downstairs.

Gathering up his plans, Thomas glanced at his still-seated partner.

'It's your big moment, Josiah. You ought to be the first one there.'

Latimer Clark rose, his beard quivering with anger. 'Just so you know, if it were down to me, I'd have deferred any passenger lines for at least a year. Goods carriage remains our best chance of success, but even that is far from assured. By rights, those funds they'll be using for your trial line—'

'Thank you for your support.' Thomas smiled, pausing briefly to let his contempt sink in, then strode out of the room.

A minute later, they gathered at the south-eastern tip of Euston Station. A large portion of the street had been fenced off, and a small army of navvies stood ready on the periphery. After a brief speech from the chairman, Latimer Clark turned the first soil where the dig was to begin, and the dispatch tube, stretching all the way to St. Martins-le-Grand via Holborn, was shortly to be laid.

'So, Billy,' said Thomas, looking on at one remove. 'This trial line.'

'Back to Battersea, sir?'

Thomas shook his head. 'Too flat. Building a full-size tunnel with meaningful curves and gradients will require us to work with the lie of the land. We need somewhere big, open and, crucially, on a slope. Some kind of park. One whose owners will be open to enterprising new ideas.'

'Well then, sir,' said Billy, grinning. 'There's only one place for it.'

Chapter 19

I figured it needn't be too difficult. If I could just get them to believe the gist of my story, I was actually in quite a favourable position. The police were already there, and the fire brigade would follow. If only they'd hear me out, we could all head down to the carriage and dig up the bones together: not just proof positive of my story, but also job done as far as the skeletons were concerned. The only real downside was that I'd be left stuck in 1950, but was that really such a problem? I could start afresh and maybe even get back to working on the tube, shot of the draconian health and safety rules that had done for me in 2013.

'What I'm about to say sounds absurd,' I began. 'But do me the courtesy of coming down to the wood and you'll see it's all true.'

My measured words, combined with my failure to simply run away, brought a surprised silence to proceedings. Even the incensed young couple – Emily, who had encountered the skeleton, and her slick-haired boyfriend – seemed slightly pacified.

'I'm as much a victim as anyone,' I went on. 'I've travelled back from the year 2013, when I too was accosted by the skeletons – skeletons which, God's honour, are buried in a Victorian railway carriage, a *time machine*, in a wood near the Sydenham gate.'

Already some onlookers were stifling their laughter, but as long as I retained the straight-faced attention of the policeman and the couple, I had a chance. Perhaps the sheer improbability of it – the fact that no sane man would ever make this nonsense up – might yet win them over?

'I was assaulted twice, just as the young lady describes, and both times I escaped, only to find massive fires raging in the park: the skeletons' revenge for deserting them.'

'It's true!' cried a voice. 'The man from the future speaks the truth!'

Astonished, I looked round. The old, orange-toothed fellow in rags was vindicating my story.

'I saw the bones,' he confirmed, 'and the fire that followed. I knew it. By God, I've always known it!'

His witterings were scrambled, but the basic point was clear. I looked triumphantly at the constable, only to find him too now smirking.

'Dear oh dear,' he sighed. 'All these people you could have had, corroborating your little fantasy – and you chose mad old Monty.'

'Mad old Monty?'

'I saw them talking just before,' confirmed the girl's boyfriend.

'Priceless.' The policeman chuckled as he unhooked something from his belt. 'The tallest tale I've ever heard, substantiated by the maddest mind in Upper Norwood. I'm almost tempted not to cuff you, out of respect for the sheer audacity of it!'

'You'd better cuff him,' snarled the boyfriend, 'or I'll bloody well do it myself.'

'*Emily*,' I pleaded, daring to address the girl as the officer approached. 'Please tell them what you saw. You must know the hand was real. You even heard the voice!'

She gazed back vacantly, clearly knowing my words to be true, but so terrified that she'd sooner sacrifice me than face her fears.

I was left with only one option. Moments before, I'd planned to betray the skeletons by excavating them and their secrets. Now, their forgotten railway carriage was my only means of escaping a disbelieving world.

As the constable reached out to cuff me, I kicked him in the balls and pushed him into a patch of nettles. Shouting my apology, I sprinted away across the lower terrace, managing to evade the lunges of several passers-by. I took some stairs to the next level down, where I looked back to see the chasing mob just yards behind, at least a hundred strong. I ran as quickly as I could on the treacherous ground, but still they kept gaining, fuelled by fascination and anger.

Arriving in the northern enclosure, I veered to the right. Several times I stumbled on lumps of discarded iron, it only now dawning on me that the park had been closed for years because of World War Two. By the time I skirted the lake, breathless and heavy-legged, the vociferous rabble was nearly upon me.

'You'll never escape, son!' shouted the constable. 'You're in enough trouble as it is, so why not just give it up?'

I could feel the crowd swiping at me as the mound came into view.

'*Eeeh, reek.*'

The word was long, lingering and may well have originated in my imagination. Either way, it inspired me into one final sprint. Within moments I had crossed the gravelly path, climbed the mound, and begun frantically scouring the earth for the hole through which I'd been thrust minutes before.

Except that the hole wasn't there. In all directions, the mud was unbroken, showing no sign of having been recently disturbed.

The crowd clambered up behind me, led by the constable. Reaching the top, he stopped a few feet away, letting the mob fan out and encircle me.

Infuriated by the skeletons' contrariness, I stamped where the hand usually appeared. It had always felt like a reflex, triggered by pressure from above, but the mechanism was failing at the most critical time. I upped the tempo as the crowd thickened, but still the skeletons ignored me. I screamed in exasperation. Couldn't they see my predicament? I needed their sanctuary like never before – both for their sakes and mine.

'Come on, lad.' The constable grinned, dangling the handcuffs from his little finger. 'No getting away now.'

He stepped towards me and I stamped again.

'For God's sake! Let me in!'

'Who are you talking to, son?'

'Who do you think?' I pointed down as I pogoed. 'The skeletons!'

The constable glanced delightedly at his audience, who responded with a roar of hilarity.

'Fetch her!'

The words sliced through the laughter, shaking the ground with unignorable power.

'*Fetch her*!'

I knew what they were doing. They weren't just clarifying what needed to happen; they were buying me time.

I scoured the dumbstruck mob, hoping that the girl had been swept along, and saw her standing towards the front of the circle on the opposite side to the policeman, guarded by her boyfriend.

'*Fetch her*!'

'Stop saying that, you madman!' shrieked the constable.

I darted towards the girl, separating the people in front and pulling her free. The poor thing screamed, sending bats scarpering from the trees as I dragged her to the carriage.

'I'm sorry!' I shouted, the circle closing in. 'I'll take good care of her!'

I looked down, found my spot, and stamped again. On one side, the constable was an arm's length away. On the other, the boyfriend was right there. I stretched behind Emily and pulled her free arm back so he couldn't grab it, but still there was nothing from underground. I stamped to the right, then up, down, and back to the left.

Finally, just as the boyfriend and constable took hold, ready to tear us apart, the hole gurgled open. Two bony arms grabbed our legs and jerked us down with such force that the men lost their grip and fell into each other, heads clashing.

We hit the floor, and I looked up. The hole had already re-sealed itself. Emily was howling. As she scrambled to her feet, reaching up helplessly to the roof, I edged back into the shadows. There was nothing I could do but let her hysteria take its course, trusting that she would recognise that I was not a threat; that the two of us were in this together.

It wasn't long before a degree of calm was established. Within moments of darkness descending – broken only by my muted torch, shining sideways on the floor – the skeletons sat upright and the carriage continued its journey. The impossible sensation stunned Emily into silence, and I watched as she reeled with bewilderment, fascination, and a profound, inarticulate horror.

I took my place alongside the skeletons and waited. Our motion meant I had at least escaped the shackles of a 1950s jail, but who could say what lay ahead? There was as little point speculating as protesting.

The only certainty was that the skeletons had a plan, and the skeletons were going to have their way.

Chapter 20

Five months after unveiling his plans to the PDC directors, Thomas was at the Palace of Westminster, returning from the Committee meeting room to the public lobby.

It wasn't a short walk, but even by the time Billy rose in greeting, he hadn't formulated a single coherent thought. His dreams hadn't just been crushed; they'd scarcely even been acknowledged.

'How did it go?'

Thomas sighed. 'Truthfully, Billy, I haven't the first idea.'

'What did they ask?'

'I'll tell you what they *didn't* ask: why pneumatic power should prevail, and how these two railways could heal our sickly capital. There were just endless niggling questions about our experiments to date, and whether our tunnels could accommodate steam locomotives instead.'

'Didn't Stanley push it in our favour?'

'It's not my job to steer public interrogations.'

Thomas turned. The man himself was approaching down the gloomy corridor.

'Don't worry, we're not recalling you. Just taking a break, so I thought I'd say hello.'

Stanley's tone was ominous. Sensing the tension, Billy slipped away.

'What are our chances?' asked Thomas.

'Slim, if I'm honest,' replied the politician. 'And if I'm *really* honest, your chances are nil.'

Thomas stared back. Deep within, this was no surprise, otherwise the committee would have questioned him longer. But even so, Stanley's bluntness was a shock, and he felt an acidic anger begin to gnaw away inside. The right thing to do was so obvious, his railway so patently the only possible cure for the city's ills, how could others still fail to see it?

'You oughtn't feel disheartened,' said Stanley. 'Only a few privileged schemes reached the Committee stage. Well over two hundred fell short.'

'Why are you so certain we've failed?'

'It's the novelty. We hear what you say about the Eversholt Street line and those who have travelled on it, and we understand the scientific principle. Alas, we cannot act on inference alone. You need that trial.'

'But did I not say we'd happily run on steam if the trial failed?'

Stanley nodded.

'And you acknowledge that both lines meet a demonstrable need in terms of traffic relief?'

Again, Stanley nodded.

'Then why not give us a chance?'

'Because, being frank, other schemes are more impressive.'

'You just bemoaned its very novelty!' exclaimed Thomas. 'How much more impressive can a railway be?'

'It's a question of reliability.'

'But the pneumatic is—'

'I'm not talking about the railway, Thomas. I'm talking about making promises you can't keep. First, we at the GPO hear that the longer line will be ready by Christmas. But Christmas is two months ago, and the tube remains incomplete, so we struggle to believe your pledge that it will be operational two months from now. Likewise the trial. You cheerfully spread a rumour that it would be ready for today, but now you say April. Generating excitement is nothing without generating trust.'

'The delays are unfortunate,' replied Thomas, 'but they're not due to engineering issues. Both have been caused by landowner disputes on the route of the longer Post Office tube.'

Stanley looked puzzled. 'But why should that affect the Crystal Palace trial?'

The blood rushed to Thomas's cheeks. He wasn't used to being caught out, and it showed. For several seconds, he said nothing, searching in vain for a way out, but it was no use. He had to be honest.

'The decision came a fortnight ago,' he admitted. 'It's not just the compensation we're having to pay landowners; it's the expense of prolonging construction, and the lack of imminent profits. Naturally I argued back, but the directors were under pressure from Josiah and the shareholders. They suspended indefinitely their financial involvement in my passenger trial at the Crystal Palace – and any ensuing operational railways.'

'But wasn't that why you originally founded the PDC?'

Thomas nodded. 'And had I retained control of goods carriage, things would have been different. Alas, Josiah, in all his fastidious wisdom, has made such a mess of things that the company has had to compromise its original ambitions.'

'So who is to fund the Palace line now?'

'I am.'

Stanley was incredulous. 'You?'

'I'm contributing my own savings, borrowing more, and so are those PDC directors and shareholders who remain sufficiently committed to proceed. We're being helped by Staveley and Watt, who are providing the tunnel and fan respectively for no profit, and we've now got the Palace land for free, thanks to Sir Joseph.'

'So both the trial line, and the two railways we considered – the Oxford Street and City, the Victoria Station and Thames Embankment – all three are now distinct from the Pneumatic Dispatch Company?'

'That is correct.'

'But why didn't you say?'

'You didn't ask,' said Thomas, pausing before he added, 'and, I suppose, I feared it might harm our chances.'

'But at least it wouldn't have been dishonest!' Stanley held his hands to his head in exasperation. 'Honestly, Thomas, if only you could learn some patience, who knows how far you could go? You always react so defensively, even around me, and I'm one of your few allies! I didn't follow you out to offer empty commiserations, but to provide encouragement. And my first piece of advice is that it would serve you well to listen.'

Stung by Stanley's chastisement, Thomas took a moment before nodding. 'My apologies,' he said. 'I know I occasionally act somewhat rashly; even foolishly. But it's just a measure of my conviction; my belief in the importance of the pneumatic—'

'I'm well aware of all that,' said Stanley. 'But even so, you must respect the world as it is before you can make it how you'd like it to be.'

'I know. And you're quite right to upbraid me. Please, do go on.'

Stanley hesitated, then stepped in and looked around, rather furtively. 'My first recommendation,' he whispered, 'is to banish these two railways from your mind. Even if you had brought them forward after a successful trial, neither would have satisfied the Committee. The Thames Embankment route belongs to the Metropolitan District – the temptation of completing that inner circuit too great to resist. As for the Oxford Street proposal, our civic duty is to ensure that as little as possible of central London is dug up, and to maximum effect. And although your railway *would* relieve traffic, it would be too specific to Oxford Street and districts immediately to the south, since to the north, and further south, once the Metropolitan District opens, your rivals have it covered. Even if run on steam, your Oxford Street plan would have been rejected in favour of subterranean schemes addressing new parts of the city.'

'So what of the future?' asked Thomas.

'It's perfectly simple. Make your trial big, bold and public, then get a map and find yourself another route – this time ensuring it is absolutely new *and* needed.'

'Something suburban?'

Stanley shook his head. 'Given the novelty of your power source, you need something small and focused; a route that plays to your strengths. If you could find some such need in the centre of town—'

'But didn't you just dismiss such a possibility? Central London will soon be thoroughly encircled. There are scarcely any opportunities left.'

'Really?'

'*Really.* How many schemes did you say have been brought before Parliament this session? Two hundred and fifty?'

'Two hundred and fifty-*nine.*'

'Well, there you have it. How can any route have been overlooked? And even if it has, how can I ever acquaint myself with all those proposals to know where the opportunity exists?'

'If only you knew someone on the inside.'

Stanley's eye twinkled, and Thomas smiled. Finally, they were getting to the heart of the matter.

'Just the other day I spoke to Myles Fenton,' continued the politician, in an even softer whisper than before. 'General manager of the Metropolitan, but also former employee of the London and South Western. We were marvelling at how it was less than twenty years ago that Parliament prohibited any termini from being built in the centre of town, yet in that time our engineers have not only created underground railways, but are on the brink of connecting all the major stations.' He paused. 'Well, on the north side of river, at least. One terminus, of course, remains out on a limb.'

Thomas thought for a second. 'You mean Waterloo Bridge?'

Stanley nodded. 'Fenton's former stomping ground. It was always the station that suffered most from the 1846 restrictions, forcing passengers over the bridges at Westminster, Charing Cross and Waterloo, but for years the London and South Western thought that they themselves had the solution. After all, Waterloo Bridge was never intended to be a terminus; the idea was to run through it, across the river and into the City. Alas, those plans never materialised, and now the South Eastern have extended their lines into Charing Cross – quite literally blocking the South Western's way – Waterloo Bridge is doomed to remain the end of the line. All of which means that the paralysis on the river crossings – already at a standstill for two hours each morning and night – is only set to get worse, especially as the property developers burrow deeper into Surrey and Hampshire.'

Heart quickening, Thomas's thoughts lurched from bafflement at the overlooked obviousness of the diagnosis, to consideration of the cure, and a rapid understanding of just *why* no one had considered an onwards subterranean line from Waterloo.

'We'd have to build under the river,' he said.

'And?' Stanley shrugged. 'You're in the business of novelty. Surely the man who makes air power work should shy away from nothing? Besides, if we can have foot tunnels beneath the Thames, why not railways?'

'No comparable schemes have been brought forward?'

'None that are to be taken seriously.'

'So where would the line run? From Waterloo to . . .' He thought for a moment. 'Whitehall would seem sensible. Straight across the river from York Road, terminating at the Trafalgar Square end of Whitehall. That will serve most foot passengers, and give them access to the Metropolitan District below Charing Cross, for continuing east or west. The river there is also relatively narrow – and will be more so, with the Embankment.'

Stanley patted Thomas on the back. 'Of course, this

conversation never happened. I am risking my reputation by helping you. But after Myles told me that the Metropolitan had identified the need yet had too many other commitments to act – well, I couldn't resist.'

'And I am so grateful,' said Thomas, only half listening as Stanley retreated and the possibilities unfurled in his mind. The smaller scale of this imagined railway really would be ideal – the perfect, pioneering showcase for the simple reliability of air power.

'Good news, sir?' asked Billy, returning to see the dazed optimism on Thomas's face.

'We start at the Crystal Palace,' declared Thomas, striding towards the exit. 'We create the greatest railway sensation since Stephenson's Rocket, unveiled at the start of summer and kept running until early autumn. We make it enormously challenging, with tunnels fully buried, not just laid in trenches, and curves and gradients that take the breath away. Then, riding the wave of countrywide enthusiasm, we create the Waterloo and Whitehall Railway – my own company, independent of the PDC – and take our first step towards bringing pneumatic salvation to every last corner of the city.'

Outside, St. Margaret's Church gleamed in the midwinter sun, while the bell in the Parliamentary clocktower – Big Ben, as it was now popularly known – rang out the midday chimes.

Chapter 21

'What's going on?'

By the time Emily asked the obvious question, the acceleration had stopped and we were travelling at top speed.

'Who knows?' I replied. 'But the last time this happened, it took me back from 2013 to 1950 – just like I said.' I wanted to remind her of my honesty so she'd accept that I was as dazed as her. 'Sorry for dragging you down, by the way, but you heard the order.'

She glanced at me doubtfully.

'I tried ignoring them,' I said. 'But they have a plan and we're part of it.'

'Victorians,' she muttered, examining the seated corpses.

'Do you know what it could be? Why they were left to rot?'

'I was born in 1931,' she returned, witheringly. 'How should I know?'

I laughed as I picked up my torch. 'I just thought you might be better connected with the history.' I shone the light on my face. 'I'm Eric.'

She looked me over, then shifted her gaze to the skeleton beside me. 'You blend in well.'

'Careful.' I aimed the beam at her. 'Don't go insulting them.'

She gave a muted laugh. 'How animated are they?'

'They only move or speak when their plan demands it.'

She peered through the glass at the front. 'And what is their plan? You must have deduced something.'

I puffed out my cheeks. 'Well, I had assumed they wanted burying, but each time I tried to get one out, the others stopped me. Then we set off on this journey, since when the only thing that's roused them has been capturing you.'

Emily was reaching out, having spotted a disturbance in the air. 'What's happening to the soil?'

'It's going up to the roof,' I answered, illuminating the top of the carriage.

'But why?'

I was about to say I hadn't a clue, when the penny dropped.

'Because we're going back in time,' I said, delighted to put at least part of the jigsaw in place. 'The carriage and the tunnel are repairing themselves according to *when* we are in history.'

I lit up the heaps of debris on the floor, and we watched, wonderstruck, as several chunks of brick and wood floated up and arranged themselves seamlessly in the foot-wide hole above our heads.

'Extraordinary,' said Emily, taking the torch and kneeling between two skeletons. 'Look here . . .' She illuminated the window. 'The cracks in the glass are getting shorter.'

I peered over her. Sure enough, the fault lines were shrinking.

'Same with the seats.' She angled the torch down to reveal splits in the leather, sewing themselves back up. 'What of the passengers?'

She crossed to the gentleman opposite and shone the torch deep into his skull, leaning in so close that her nose was virtually inserted into the void vacated by his own.

'Careful,' I murmured, conscious of the skeletons' strength, but also enchanted by her cavalier spirit. 'Anything changing?'

'Nothing.' She held up the skeleton's right arm, marvelling at the connectedness of the bones. 'What do you want with us?' she asked.

The skeleton didn't reply.

'Go on,' she urged kindly, stroking the top of his skull. 'Give us a clue.'

But no clue was forthcoming. Emily sat back and sighed. 'So we just wait?'

I nodded. 'Wait for the next stop.'

A few seconds passed, then she smiled. 'I'm not scared any more.'

'Me neither.'

'Isn't that odd?'

'It's not about us,' I affirmed. 'We're part of it, the skeletons *are* angry, but we're not the enemy. If anything, we're on their side.'

She stood and probed around some more. 'We're passengers as well?'

'Personally, I feel more like we're drivers. Our presence is needed for the carriage to move, after all.'

'Drivers with no idea of their destination?' Emily stopped as a thought occurred. 'What if it's the actual driver we're looking for? The driver who deserted his passengers?' She walked to the front. 'But where would he even sit? This is just a standalone passenger carriage.'

'Except a passenger carriage wouldn't normally have those strange platforms at either end.'

'But either way, it's not a locomotive. Which begs the question: where's the rest of the train?' She turned and rattled the knees of a female skeleton in frustration – 'Why won't you tell us?' – before turning suddenly thoughtful. 'I wonder if Monty knows.'

I had to think for a second before realising who she meant. 'Mad old Monty,' I said, recalling the dishevelled old man above ground; the one who, in 1950, had supported me when I mentioned the skeletons. 'Why do they call him mad?'

'Because he is.'

'Yes, but *why*?'

Emily hesitated, as if making connections in her mind. 'Monty used to run a music shop in Sydenham, but he was also the Crystal Palace's resident organist. My mother said he used to live and breathe the building and its history. So when the Palace burnt down – 30th November, 1936 – he was sent quite mad. All he'd ever lived for had been decimated, and he spiralled into insanity. His shop fell into disrepair, and he spent all his time prowling the Palace grounds. Even in the war, when it was used for anti-aircraft fire, and became a vast scrap metal dump – even then, he just rambled round, chuntering about the good old days; spluttering doolally stories about what caused the fire.'

'And what *did* cause the fire?'

A knowing smile crept across Emily's lips. 'Nobody ever found out.'

'*Fetch him!*'

We jumped, grabbing each other as the skeletons commanded our attention, pointing to where the hole had reappeared. We'd been so distracted that we hadn't noticed the deceleration.

'Fetch who?' asked Emily.

'Fetch *him!*'

'This is what happened last time,' I explained, noticing that it was night-time overhead.

'But how do we get out?'

Feeling like an old hand, I led Emily to the middle of the carriage. As expected, the passengers rose and approached, but rather than encircle us both, they pushed Emily aside and focused on me.

'I could really use her help,' I said, as the skeletons grabbed my legs. 'If last time was any guide, it'll be much easier with two people.'

'*Eeeh, reek,*' the skeletons chanted. '*Fetch him!*'

That told us. I was their main man, and mere practicalities weren't going to change that. But if they didn't want Emily to help, why was she there at all?

'Take this,' she said, passing the torch through the ring of bones. I switched it off and took a deep breath as the skeletons tightened their grips and flung me up.

Outside, it was pitch black: the sky moonless and the glow of street lighting, wont to bounce off clouds or sneak through trees, totally absent. But despite not being able to see my surroundings, I assumed that the person who had tussled with the skeletons must still be close, possibly even hiding and watching as Emily had done.

I kept the torch off and tiptoed across the dry ground. There was hardly any sound from the road, but the wind in the overhanging branches whistled with a ghostliness apt for my purpose.

Feeling my way between the trees, I became aware of a sound on top of the breeze: *like* the wind, but coarser. Stepping this way and that, I traced it to its loudest point and stopped, flicking on the torch to illuminate a terrified pale face, lurching up towards me.

'Skeleton!' he gasped, grabbing my shoulders. 'A skeleton, I say!'

I'd been expecting to have to stop him fleeing, but he obviously hadn't seen where I'd come from. Dressed in a smart grey suit with a thin blue tie, he didn't look like he'd just had a traumatic entanglement with the undead. A second glance at his trousers, however – mud-splattered from the knee down – confirmed that he too had made the fatal misstep.

'A skeleton, I swear, real as anything!'

'Mad old Monty,' I whispered, pinpointing the resemblance.

He stepped back, wide-eyed with fear. 'Why did you call me that?'

It was an understandable question, since this Monty was handsome, healthy and young; not mad in the slightest.

'How do you know my name?'

Whatever the year, it was clearly before Monty had been sent mad by the big blaze at the Palace – although just how long before was a moot point.

'Well?' He looked me up and down in agitation. 'What are you all about?'

It was time to act. I knew that reasoning would not work, so I seized him at the waist and hauled him over my shoulder.

'What in the name of Sir Joseph Paxton are you doing?'

The hole was only a few feet away, but my fireman's lift was a shambles, particularly given Monty's youthful vigour. He easily managed to wriggle free, kicking me in the groin for good measure. I doubled up and he clambered away.

'You have to come and help us!' I cried, shining the torch at him.

'Help *us*? You and the skeleton? You're a team?'

'I'm a victim, like you. So's Emily – she's down there already. Once you've stumbled across them and been assaulted, you have to go down. Oh, and it's not just the one skeleton – there's nine of them.'

'And you've got the nerve to call *me* mad!'

'But it's true. I'm from the year 2013, when I too was attacked, just like you. They entrapped me and took me back to 1950, and now I'm here and you're next.' I stepped towards him. 'There's nothing to fear – at least, not that I know of.'

Monty burst out laughing and strode away.

'But you saw the hand!' I exclaimed, keeping pace. 'You know that much to be true. Why not believe the rest?'

'It's not that I don't believe you,' he shouted over his shoulder. 'It's just that I happen to rather cherish my life here, and don't especially want to sacrifice that.'

'What is it that you cherish?' I asked, in a flash of inspiration. 'What do you love the most?'

He stopped and faced me. 'I love my shop and I love my organ. Above all, I love the Crystal Palace.'

'And your organ is at the Palace?'

He shrugged, somewhat defensively. 'What of it?'

'Nothing. It's fine. You be on your way.'

He hesitated, looking bewildered, then headed up the hill. 'I'm late for work as it is. Good night, mister – and good luck with whatever it is that's troubling you.'

I let him get a few yards away then illuminated him with my torch.

'Before you go, just one more thing.'

He turned. 'Yes?'

'What's today's date?'

'November 30th.'

'And the year?'

'The *year*?'

'Yes. What year is it?'

'1936.'

I nodded. 'Just checking.'

Chapter 22

'Sir?'

Thomas looked up from his anxious reverie. Billy was silhouetted at the far end of the carriage, having slid open the doors that provided access from the open boarding platform.

'I'm doing my best, sir,' he said, 'but if you don't appear soon, I fear they'll be over the fences and all aboard – and our guest is due at any moment.'

Doing his best to banish his nerves, Thomas rose and inspected the carriage one final time. Seven months had elapsed since Lord Stanley pointed him towards the Waterloo and Whitehall scheme, and the Crystal Palace trial had been in progress for a little over two weeks. Despite intensive use during that time, the commodious little coach, made to order in Manchester, was as pristine as the day it arrived – gas lamps burning composedly, petite curtains hung just so, leather seats clean and comfortable, and windows gleaming spotlessly as the late summer sun blazed steeply in, filling half the carriage with scorching light, and consigning the other to deep shadow.

He stepped onto the vestibule outside and was greeted by a cheer from the crowd, spread out across the little bank that led up from the wooden fence bordering the platform.

'Ladies and gentlemen!' he shouted. 'May I say how gratified I am by today's turn-out, and how sorry I am to have to indulge your patience. Yes, the public notices say demonstrations commence at one o'clock, but today is an exception.'

There was a frustrated groan, and Thomas raised his hands.

'Please be assured that it shouldn't be more than thirty minutes until we let you on, and that the delay is caused by the visit of a very special guest; one who, like many of you, read the positive words of last week's *Illustrated London News*, and felt compelled to try the greatest railway novelty of the day.'

'Her Majesty!' guessed a woman, setting off a credulous and somewhat flattering murmur.

'Alas, not Her Majesty,' said Thomas with a laugh, 'but it is someone of prodigious significance to the Palace that watches over us. Not Sir Joseph Paxton – he's already been – but another, whose identity you shall discover presently. In the meantime, please take as thanks the promise of discounted tickets. Simply say the secret word "Paxton" when buying your return to the Penge gate, and you shall board for four pence, rather than the usual six.'

The people gave an approving roar.

'In the meantime, why not seek out some other diversion in the grounds? Up the hill is the English Landscape Garden, offering archery and croquet. Down the hill, a cricket match is just getting underway.'

Nobody was moving.

'There's also boating on the lake,' said Billy. 'Watched over by prehistoric monsters!'

'Or the rosary,' added Thomas. 'Or indeed the valley of—'

'We'll wait,' cried a man in the crowd.

'Hear, hear,' said another. 'There's nothing else as good as your railway, sir.'

Thomas smiled. The crowd's enthusiasm for his invention eclipsed everything else. It had been like this every day since the railway opened. It was as if people were entranced by the mere prospect of a ride; besotted by the sight of the quaint little station, cut into the side of a wooded mound, and sweetly mocked up with its own little platforms – resplendent with 'Sydenham Gate' station signs – ahead of an open tunnel entrance whose ornamented square surround and intricate brickwork surpassed the best adornments of the many other tunnels in the area.

Even the large valve hut and the tall, annexed engine shed, built partly below ground beside the tunnel mouth, had a certain magic about them. With the single carriage at its shimmering heart, the scene was so far removed from the dirt and darkness that characterised steam railways – especially those trundling beneath London's streets – that only the most stubborn sceptic could resist its charms.

Alerted by a whispering in the crowd, Thomas looked up to see a trio of men carving their way through the bodies. Adjusting his hat, he opened the gate that led onto the platforms.

'The most eminent civil engineer of our age!' he announced. 'Designer of bridges and railways throughout the land, inventor of railway points and the man who built – and then *moved* – the Crystal Palace. Sir Charles Fox!'

Thomas had only ever met Sir Charles in passing before, so was thankful the great man took his extravagant welcome in good humour, turning to acknowledge the crowd's ovation as he stepped through the gate.

'Mr. Rammell, I presume?' he asked, smiling warmly under big, brown eyes – a perfect match for his shock of brown hair.

Thomas bowed. 'An honour, sir.'

Sir Charles roared with laughter and stepped past. 'Well, well,' he said, examining the carriage and tunnel mouth. '*Most* splendid!'

Thomas darted to catch up, but his guest immediately turned, strode to the back of the carriage and crossed the tracks.

'Engines in disguise!' he exclaimed, observing the huts that housed the beating heart of the trial. '*Most* discreet.' He turned again to the coach, and the bristly fringe that encircled its rear, where the vestibule met the saloon. 'An airtight seal, to change the carriage into a piston. *How* ingenious!'

'I can show you into the engine house, if you like,' said Thomas. 'Perhaps we could—'

'You know why I'm here?' returned Sir Charles. 'Dispatched by the London and North Western?'

Thomas nodded. 'Is it just a general appraisal or are they planning something specific?'

'Well surely you already know they are disposed in your favour?'

'Indeed,' said Thomas. Euston had been the PDC's base for a while, and the company had always enjoyed a co-operative relationship with the LNWR.

'The plans are not yet clear,' Sir Charles continued, 'but the LNWR, serving so many major cities – Birmingham, Manchester, Liverpool – is exploring how passengers might continue their journeys on arrival in those towns. They believe this could be lucrative and, being far from convinced by underground steam, they have solicited my opinion on whether pneumatic power might be the solution.'

Thomas smiled, dazed and somewhat disbelieving. Sir Charles's presence had told him that the visit was significant, but nothing had prepared him for this. Having teetered on the brink of collapse earlier in the year, his grand project suddenly had the chance to take a giant stride forward.

'We should begin with a tour of the engine house,' Thomas said, summoning every last ounce of composure. 'Then perhaps a stroll above the tunnel—'

Sir Charles shook his head. 'I know how you generate the power. I know the challenges of the track. All I want to *do* is take a ride.'

Thomas turned to Billy – 'Get the power on; have us depart within a minute' – then ushered his guest into the carriage. 'The particulars are all determined by needing to keep the coach airtight,' he explained. 'Hence the glass doors at either end: far preferable to hinged wooden affairs.' He slid them shut. 'No air is getting past that.'

Sir Charles noticed the lengthways benches. 'Hence also the lack of side doors?'

'Precisely. Which in turn allows us to create two uninterrupted benches down either side, each seating up to thirty passengers and freeing the aisle for those wishing to stand.'

Sir Charles peered through the back doors. 'The platforms are not especially high above the tracks – yet access to the vestibule is on a level. The carriage must be hung tremendously low.'

'Again, it's a question of airtightness. To position the carriage at a normal height would require a larger tunnel, so creating more inefficiency in terms of air flow. As things stand, the tunnel diameter is only 10 feet 9 inches, and there's just a tiny gap between the base of the coach and the tracks. The wheels actually protrude into the carriage, encased in wood beneath the seats.'

'May I sit on one?'

'Naturally.' Thomas showed Sir Charles to a seat above the front left wheel.

'Aesthetically at least,' the great man said, 'your little railway is most delightful.'

'I've been lucky with the weather,' said Thomas, 'and of course the setting. I am so indebted to the Palace for giving me such freedom at no cost.'

'They know a kindred spirit when they see one.'

Billy stepped onto the front vestibule and turned an upright handle.

'Good heavens!' exclaimed Sir Charles immediately. 'We're moving.'

Thomas sat down opposite his guest. 'The noiselessness always catches people out.' He smiled and checked his watch. 'It's partly having the engine at one remove; partly the airtight carriage. A far cry from the usual cacophony!'

'This is gravity alone?'

Thomas nodded. 'A slight downwards incline to the tunnel.'

Billy stepped off the front platform.

'The young man doesn't travel with us?'

'No need. We exert all necessary control remotely.'

Half of the carriage had now entered the tunnel, and the speed continued to increase as Thomas directed Sir Charles's gaze to the back end. Once the whole coach was inside and the white light of the tunnel mouth began to recede from view, there was a muffled clatter and hissing below the train. A moment later, the two wooden lock gates either side of the tunnel mouth flipped inwards to make a perfect seal.

'Very deft,' said Sir Charles, beaming. 'And how very cosy, with only the gas lamps—'

He stopped, registering the forward surge.

'Oh my. *Most* smooth. One almost expects to hear the lapping of water – but this is even more graceful than sailing.' He shuffled in his seat. 'Only the merest vibration from the wheel, and the silence is—' Cupping his ear, he appeared to register the faint rustling that had become the railway's signature sound.

'The bristles of the collar, sir,' explained Thomas, 'brushing the inside of the tunnel.'

'Are we being blown or sucked?'

'Blown to the Penge gate, sucked back to the Sydenham gate. 600 yards each way. The fan, driven by the 40-horsepower engine, is turning 300 times per minute, giving a speed of over 20 miles per hour. We've been on a level now for a good 100 yards, meaning there is no residual momentum from gravity. We are entirely at the mercy of air.'

'What's the mechanism for admitting the air?'

'The clattering you heard just now – that was an iron grating below us, covering the air well that's linked to the engine house. Passing over it was the cue for the tunnel mouth to shut itself. That in turn switched the valves to allow air, captured from the periphery of the fan, to blow in through the well. The space behind us quickly became more pressurised than in front, so we were pushed forward, readily taking a sharp curve of 8 chains radius.'

Sir Charles stood and assessed their direction of travel. 'No curve now.'

'Correct. We're gun-barrel straight until 150 yards from the end, when there's another 8-chainer to take us into the station.'

'And now we're accelerating downhill.'

Thomas smiled at Sir Charles's attentiveness. These were not easy observations to make from within the carriage.

'This is the central section,' he explained. '1 in 15, steeper than any real railway, for 115 yards. Going down, it takes us to 30 miles an hour before we level out and slow ahead of the upwards climb that takes us round the curve, into our Penge Gate station.'

Sir Charles wandered up and down, gauging the forces at work on anyone required to stand. Once forty seconds had elapsed, Thomas confirmed that they were onto the final ascent.

'Our imminent arrival at Penge Gate will now be registered by the valvesman at Sydenham Gate,' he said, 'courtesy of the barometers in the tunnel. Seeing this, he will cease feeding air into the tunnel to assist our deceleration.'

'Most effective,' mused Sir Charles, as the carriage headed up the incline and began to slow, weighed down by gravity and unaided by air. The tunnel ahead was illuminated by light pouring through the already-open valve doors. 'Down to 5 or 6 miles an hour,' he inferred, scrutinising the passing brickwork.

The carriage emerged into daylight, the valve doors shut behind them, and an assistant leapt onto the boarding platform, winding down the brakes.

'A third of a mile,' declared Thomas, as they came to rest. 'Forty-eight seconds.'

Sir Charles peered out at the makeshift station, consisting simply of 20 yards of run-off track, a set of buffers, and a wooden shack that communicated by telegraph with Sydenham Gate.

'So much for the push,' he said. 'Now show me the pull.'

Thomas signalled to his assistant that they wished to make an immediate return, and the message was relayed to the shack. Moments later, having received confirmation that the Sydenham Gate engine house was ready, the lad went to the rear of the train – which now became the front – and brought up the brakes. The valve doors swung open and they re-entered the tunnel.

'As soon as the forward pressure was shut off,' explained Thomas, 'the valves were switched so the fan began sucking air out of the vacuum chamber. Then, the moment we passed into Penge Gate, and the valve doors closed behind us, air from the tunnel began being extracted via the vacuum chamber. The desired pressure was achieved in seconds.'

Behind them, the gates remained open, exposing the rear of the carriage to outside pressure, and so creating the differential that allowed the vacuum ahead to lure them on. The initial downwards section gave way to some level track, and then they began the steep, 1 in 15 gradient.

'Most commendable that you suck us back up,' said Sir Charles. 'And really: *what a sensation*! The absence of turbulence is enchanting, as is the consistency of speed. No sense of strain, or gravity fighting back. The vacuum is in complete control.' He turned to Thomas as the track levelled out. 'There is no denying the reports. It really is a *splendid* achievement.'

Thomas accepted his guest's praise with bewildered pride, troubled by how perfunctory it all felt. Had Sir Charles really seen enough to report back to the LNWR? Or was he secretly unimpressed, paying compliments out of mere kindness?

The valve doors at Sydenham Gate flew open and Billy brought the train to rest. Thomas slid open the glass doors.

'A most pleasing prelude,' said Sir Charles, stepping outside. 'Now, I should like to take up your offer of a walk above the route of the tunnel.'

Relieved that Sir Charles wished to stay a little longer, but puzzled by the word 'prelude', Thomas led him up the wooded bank behind the engine house. From there, they proceeded across the grassless ground above the tunnel, away from the waiting public.

For no better reason than to stir people's imaginations, the whole first section had been laid as deep underground as possible. From the starting point near the grounds' Sydenham entrance, the tunnel burrowed until its base was 17 feet from the surface, after which its depth lessened as the hill above sloped down to the open lawns on the eastern side of the Palace grounds. Here, the tunnel emerged from the hillside on an even level: a giant snake ensconced in a trench which concealed the lower brickwork, protected on either side by stout wooden fences. The downwards slope of the lawn, adjoining the cricket pitch, then provided the railway with its sternest test, as the half-buried tunnel descended with the 1 in 15 lie of the land.

'Reminds me of the old atmospheric,' remarked Sir Charles. 'The fences are like the rails, and the tunnel a much-magnified version of the tube that ran between them.'

They reached the point where the tunnel levelled out, along with the land, before the final approach to Penge Gate. Sir Charles looked back at the route, just as Thomas, to his astonishment, spotted a railway coach *beyond* the end of the tunnel. For a moment he thought it must be his own, having made an unordered trip down the hill, but this was no passenger carriage. Rather, it was a goods wagon, brimful with railway ballast.

'What on earth . . . ?'

Sir Charles turned back. 'Ah! *Splendid*. That, my good man, weighs approximately thirty tons: the equivalent of two carriages on the Metropolitan or five or six of your pneumatic affairs – which, including potential standers, equates to around 300 people. My challenge to you is to have that carriage – and the 300 imaginary people inside – sucked up to your Sydenham Gate station.'

Thomas wasn't sure what to say. He felt simultaneously shocked, flattered and intimidated, and walked on in an intrepid daze. The goods truck sat on a wheeled platform, mounted upon tracks perfectly aligned with his own. Stationed either side were upwards of ten men, ready to haul it onto the track.

'I apologise for the surprise,' said Sir Charles. 'But there are so many schemes, one must be ruthless. I know that this line may not have been designed with such a load in mind, but if you are an engineer worthy of respect, you will have over-compensated at every turn, meaning such a challenge ought not terrify you in the least.'

'Indeed,' muttered Thomas, and to an extent this was true. The Sydenham Gate engine, built ultimately to power a line between Waterloo and Whitehall, was running well under capacity. And yet, so absorbed had he been in the demonstrations – and the money-raising that went with it, replenishing depleted funds – it had never occurred to him that such an experiment might actually take place.

'The specifications are based on information we have gleaned from the reports, and include a brake platform, just like your own carriage.' Sir Charles gestured for his minions to transfer the carriage onto the pneumatic line. 'Even so,' he went on, 'I suggest you telegraph Sydenham Gate and have them push your carriage as far up the track as possible to allow us time to slow the ballast.'

Thomas commanded an assistant to advise his colleagues accordingly. 'Tell them to set the fan to maximum power.'

'Are you confident that will be enough, sir?'

'I have to be,' said Thomas, feeling almost drunk on the strange liberation of it all. Daunting as it was, he had no choice but to accept Sir Charles's challenge, and not just because refusal would be tantamount to an admission of failure. He had waited years for such an opportunity; he owed it to himself to believe. Besides, if he wasn't ready now . . .

'You should really have seen to this yourself,' said Sir Charles. 'Nothing can be left to chance when trying to persuade Parliament of your plans.'

'I know,' said Thomas. 'Alas, I have little spare money for such thoroughness. Even running the maximum number of demonstration trips, things are still tight.'

'But of course,' replied Sir Charles. 'My comments aren't meant as criticism, you understand; merely interested advice.'

Thomas smiled gratefully, sensing an unrevealed dimension to Fox's curiosity – something beyond his LNWR business – as word arrived that the passenger carriage was out of the way at Sydenham Gate, and the vacuum prepped. Sir Charles instructed one of his minions to lift the brakes on the ballast wagon in exactly ninety seconds' time.

'Sound the horn when she enters the tunnel,' he ordered. 'Meanwhile, we'll head back uphill to be there when – or rather if – she arrives.'

Sir Charles made this last remark with a cheeky grin, but it still unsettled Thomas as they set off towards Sydenham Gate. What if the carriage really did get stuck in the tunnel? Quite aside from the impact on his dealings with Sir Charles, there would be the effort of hauling it out and the ensuing delay. All those patiently waiting passengers would be inconvenienced and they, in turn, would tell others. He had assured himself he had nothing to lose, but was that really true? At long last, he had a firm foundation, and a solid idea of how to progress in the form of the Waterloo and Whitehall Railway. Why tempt disaster by entertaining the overtures of Sir Charles and the LNWR?

They reached the point where the line disappeared into the hillside and heard the distant hoot of a horn. Checking his watch, Thomas glanced back at the tunnel – dark-brown scything through faded green – and imagined the ballast wagon, a lonely pioneer, creeping through the darkness. Despite his misgivings, he couldn't help but smile. The sheer daring of it was as intoxicating as it was terrifying.

Climbing the hill, they headed across the line of the buried tunnel and joined the path that rose to intersect the Palace's great north fountain and Thomas's model railway station. The sound of expectant chatter came from up ahead, where those waiting for a ride had been told of the experiment and were watching for the emergence – or not – of the ballast from the airless depths.

Thomas joined the back of the crowd and checked the time: thirty-five seconds since the horn had sounded. Below him, the only sound came from the branches above the engine house, arcing wildly in the wind ejected by the fan as it sucked air out of the tunnel via the vacuum chamber below. Everything and everyone else – the workers on the platforms, the crowd on the bank – were lifelessly still.

Forty-five seconds: this was when most journeys concluded. A nearby murmur suggested that others registered this, but they weren't discouraged. The extra weight, one opined, meant that the ballast wagon was bound to take longer than the passenger carriage.

Alas, as Thomas knew all too well, watching the seconds tick by – forty-nine, fifty, fifty-one – the science wasn't that simple. For with the extra weight came additional power. Roughly, at least, the velocity of the goods wagon ought to have matched the passenger carriage, since the vacuum had intensified proportionately.

The watch kept ticking – fifty-three, fifty-four, fifty-five – and the crowd became disappointedly restless. But as they started to groan, the thick summer air filled with other-worldly sounds: a mighty mechanical sigh, monstrous yet gentle, like the tunnel was exhaling the tension of a hard day's work; then a harmonious clunking of rods and levers – prelude to the valve gates swinging open, and the ballast carriage sailing serenely through.

A huge roar went up as Billy leapt aboard and wound down the brakes just short of the passenger carriage. Heart pounding twenty to the dozen, Thomas embraced Sir Charles and screamed so loudly with joy that those around finally registered his presence, parting to cheer the two men through.

Never mind the parched soil underfoot; as Thomas walked down to the platform, the adulation whisked him up and swept him along on clouds of happiness, soaring with the air. Surely *this* was the watershed. Surely now the momentum was irrevocably his. With the Palace line so beloved by passengers, and its professional capability definitively proven, it was now as impossible for Parliament to reject the Waterloo to Whitehall proposal as it was certain that Sir Charles would deliver a favourable report to the London and North Western.

'Journey duration fifty-eight seconds,' declared Billy, as they reached the platform. 'Average speed, 15 miles per hour.'

Sir Charles congratulated Thomas again, but by now statistics were ceasing to matter. After years of frustration, the pneumatic railway had made the decisive transition from fancy to phenomenon, loved and admired by public and professionals alike.

Success – on the grandest of scales – was all but guaranteed.

Chapter 23

It was ten minutes since I'd waved Monty on his way, and the skeletons were yet to chivvy me along. Either they were showing uncharacteristic trust or, more likely, they were wise to what I was planning.

Once Monty had said it was 1936, I'd known what to expect, not least in terms of the Palace grounds. As I strolled up from the mound, past the lake and pond – the latter still missing its concert bowl – I took each surprise in my stride. Admittedly, I only glimpsed my surroundings sporadically, flashing the torch here and there, but I felt I had become anaesthetised to the shocks and spectacles: difficult to impress, like a tired tourist. Though it was good to see the Palace's northern gardens so well kept, my mind was too absorbed by the bigger questions – where the skeletons were taking us; why they needed us – to care much for the passing scenery.

All that changed – and then some – when I finally turned left, and stepped onto the lower terrace. Dimly floodlit, illuminated intermittently from within, the Crystal Palace towered and twinkled above me: a cathedral of iron and glass, utterly immense yet effortlessly compact.

I scanned down its length – well over a quarter of a mile – and thought back to the model in the museum, scarcely believing I was seeing it for real. There was the arched nave, running centrally from one end to the other above the perpendicular stacks of glass; and there, crossing the nave at its central point, was a gigantic arched transept, at least 50 metres high. Towards the far end was another arched intersection, half the height of that in centre, beyond which the fully-intact southern wing extended to the front of the lower terrace.

Seeking symmetry, I looked back to the near side, but the northern transept and wing weren't there. Instead, balance was achieved by the two massive water towers, which now stood at either end of the building – standing shadowy guard, reaching a good 80 metres into the overcast sky.

For several minutes I marvelled, amazed at how I had to crane my neck to see the upper reaches of the façade, but also spiritually captivated by how the glass – *so much glass* – reflected what little light reached it to give the whole building a sublime lunar glow. I tried dropping my gaze to the terrace around me – the statues better maintained than in 1950; the six fountains, symmetrically arranged either side of the central path, now filled with water – but it was no use. The Palace dominated everything. It swallowed my gaze again and again. No matter how often I managed to look away, I was still bewildered when I looked back: blown away by its scale, and the magnitude of imagination needed to build it. The place didn't just demand awe but respect. Its whole conception was an exercise in subtle grandeur, designed not as a show of strength but human ingenuity; engineering prowess matched by creative daring. The vastness didn't so much keep you out as reel you in, entangling you with its recesses and protuberances, sparking your curiosity even before you set foot inside.

Reaching the steps that led down to the bridge over the racing track, I wrenched my eyes off the Palace and gazed downhill. Unable to see the rest of the grounds in the dark, I thought back to what the park would become: the woody, littered wilderness where the Palace itself stood, and the sorry disrepair of the rest, haunted by the half-hearted ghosts of futile schemes which, over the years, would try and fail to rejuvenate this once-great lookout for all that was audacious and high-minded about human endeavour.

The path ahead became slowly clearer, bathed in a soft orange glow which illuminated the large circular fountain, and the surrounding clusters of quivering, windswept trees.

The fire had begun, seizing the Palace with accelerating ferocity. Historic as it was, however, I couldn't bring myself to watch. I felt short-changed, angry to have seen only a glimpse of the Palace as it was, but also privileged to have witnessed its last moments of shimmering tranquillity: a glory which, for the next seventy-seven years and beyond – for as long as anyone alive now was to live – would never be restored.

My mind rewound to Tom. For the first time since my journey began, I recalled his witterings about the park being diseased: how some kind of curse had hung over the area since the Palace's earliest days, accounting for the fires and all the rot that followed.

The old man's superstitious cobblers had suddenly become the hardest, fastest fact. He had sensed the effect; I now knew the cause. The whole pitiful history of the park had been triggered by a buried railway carriage whose rotting passengers were desperate for assistance. Whenever the ground above them was disturbed – whenever they reached out to the living, only to be deserted *yet again* – they vented their fury on whatever was in the park at the time, whether a palace of glass, or an old brick museum. 'Curse' wasn't the right word. This was more of a cry for help – and I was the man who had finally come good for them.

I looked again at the Palace. The fire seemed to be taking hold at the rear of the central transept, its flames leaping high into the air. A couple of deafening explosions ripped through the night air, intensifying the blaze many times over in the space of a few seconds.

I crossed the terrace, towards the Palace, at last under-standing all of what was at stake. The quest upon which I had unwittingly embarked was entwined not just with the skeletons' fate but that of the Palace itself, and my fondness for the magnificent old building consolidated my eagerness to discover the root cause of all this woe – while strengthening my sympathy for the stricken passengers. The museum, concert bowl and transmitter were one thing, but to be so angry that they destroyed the entire Palace? The enormity of the gesture focused my mind on the true horror of their suffering. It made me hope that, as Emily had surmised, our ultimate goal was indeed to find the 'driver' of the abandoned carriage.

With the heat starting to aggravate my lungs, I stopped by the side of the bandstand. On either side, two sets of steps rose to the upper terrace, where a pair of yet grander flights led all the way up to the first storey of the Palace. Beneath these, a shorter, single flight provided access to the lowest level of the centre transept, which by now was almost fully engulfed.

'We've had many a fireworks show down the years,' said a voice to my right. 'This beats 'em all.'

I looked round. Monty was standing on the opposite side of the bandstand, gazing into the depths of the fire. It wasn't clear if he'd been inside since I last saw him, but it was obvious that he understood the severity of the blaze. If he'd been able to act, however recklessly, he doubtless would have done so. As it was, he could only stare – dry-cheeked, yet clearly crying inside.

'I'd never seen it before today,' I said, walking over to him. 'Pictures, yes, but nothing prepared me for the beauty.'

Monty's face flickered. A strong north-westerly wind was urging the fire on, and the flames were consuming the iron and glass with astonishing rapidity. In many places it was impossible to distinguish the building's former outline. But here and there, you could see the glass melting and pouring off its immense iron frame. It was raw and utterly spectacular.

'It's spreading down the nave,' he said, looking up and down the building, 'North and south.'

I wanted to say something by way of consolation, but my emotions were scrambled by the breathtaking horror, not just of the sights but the sounds. The creaking of buckling arches, the cracking and crashing of shattering glass and collapsing ceilings: the effect was overpowering, and made a mockery of the howling fire engines weaving between the fountains below.

'They should just turn back,' said Monty. 'There's no fighting this.'

'I'm afraid you're right,' I said. 'The entire Palace, bar the towers and a bit of the south wing, is done for tonight. But at least there are no fatalities.'

Monty looked doubtful. 'Seventy of my friends are in there rehearsing. I'd have been with them if you hadn't held me up.'

As if on cue, a large crowd began pouring out of one of the northerly exits, spilling onto the lower terrace with coats in their arms and instruments over their shoulders.

'The man from the future speaks the truth,' Monty whispered to himself, reflecting for a moment before turning to me. 'That twinkle in your eye as you let me go. Did you know about this? Did you *start* this?'

'It wasn't me.'

'But you knew it was going to happen.'

'Once you had confirmed the date and year. As you can imagine, tonight's events are firmly etched on future memories. Besides, there's a pattern to these things.'

'These things?' He stared back quizzically, eyes slowly widening in fright as the events aligned in his mind. 'Oh God. It's me, isn't it? I'm what caused it.'

'Not you. The *skeletons*.'

'But they started it because *I* disturbed them.'

'Because you *abandoned* them – after they reached out to you.'

He staggered back, hands over mouth in dawning panic.

'Don't punish yourself,' I said, desperate to keep him level-headed. 'It's just bad luck. You're not the last and doubtless not the first. The blame lies with whoever deserted the skeletons in the first place. We're just accidental passengers – albeit with some kind of responsibility to help them.'

'Help them do what?'

'Whatever they ask.'

Monty looked at the Palace and shook his head defiantly. 'Surely we rebuild? This can't be the end.'

'But it is. There will be no new Crystal Palace in its place. After tonight, there's just war, then decades of disrepair – all because the skeletons are not at rest.'

Before I could explain any further, there was a deafening, discordant groan from inside the Palace: a succession of deep, droning, earth-shaking notes that echoed round the park like the soundtrack to the building's surrender.

'The organ,' mouthed Monty. '*My* organ.'

It was almost sadder to watch Monty than the Palace itself. There was such cruelty in the organ's audible, sorrowful end, I almost suspected the skeletons had planned it. It certainly played into my hands.

'Come with me,' I said. 'That's the only thing to do, if you really love the Palace. Come with me. Discover what caused this.'

Monty was trembling. He gazed at the highest point of the Palace façade, just as a line of iron girders came crashing to the ground.

'That's enough, gents,' warned a pair of approaching firemen. 'Getting dangerous now. Further back, please.'

I complied, swiftly retreating to the front of the lower terrace, where a growing crowd was assembling to watch the blaze. But Monty stayed stubbornly put, entering into a heated exchange with the firemen before being dragged forcibly back.

The density of onlookers meant I quickly lost sight of him, and for several seconds I weaved in and out, hunting the beleaguered organist. Just as panic began to set in, I stepped away from the crowd and spotted a forlorn figure walking north along the racing track below. I ran down and tried to catch up, but the gathering swarm of spectators once again intervened. By the time I finally reached the northern grounds, I'd lost sight of him altogether.

Cursing my carelessness, I switched on my torch and headed downhill between the lake and the maze. My best guess was that Monty, distracted and distraught, had taken off home. Remembering from Emily's account that he once ran a music shop in Sydenham, I turned right along the path that ran below the haunted mound, towards the gate where I hoped I might yet catch sight of him, retreating down the road.

I'd only gone a couple of paces when a noise on the slope made me turn. I lit up the wood and sought movement in the shadowy trees.

'Emily?' I asked, assuming that the skeletons had dispatched the cavalry. 'Is that you?'

I stepped forward a few places, flicking the beam from side to side until a figure appeared in the gloom.

I lifted the light to land on Monty's face, the grief in his expression now matched by an angry determination.

'Where have you been?' he demanded. 'We need to get going.'

Chapter 24

Monday 31st October, 1864

It was a month and a half after Sir Charles Fox's surprise inspection of the pneumatic railway trial, and the weather was ghastly. Even the resilient beauty of the Palace grounds had been tainted by the torrential downpours and mist that had gripped the Norwood hills for three days running. The English Landscape Garden on the northern periphery, not to mention the nearby valley of rhododendrons and cedars, had been wilting for weeks, and now a ferocious storm had come to see off summer's glories for good.

Practically, poor weather was no great concern to the Palace itself. It still retained a youthful allure for visitors from around the world, possessing so many riches in its colossal interior that it thrived all year round. For Thomas, however, such inclement conditions were extremely tiresome, and it was hard not to curse his luck as, balance awry from holding his umbrella, he negotiated the slippery paths – and thence the muddy bank – down to his model railway station.

The apparatus of his experiment, pleasingly quaint in the sun, looked downright absurd in the storm, with nobody present but the valvesman, visible through his hut windows, the engine operator, known by some trees blowing more wildly than others above the engine house, and Billy, standing alone in the sheltered ticket booth.

'Where is everyone?' asked Thomas, stepping through the

gate. 'It's three o'clock. We've still another hour to go. How many in the tunnel at the moment?'

'Three,' replied Billy.

'Only three?'

'I'm afraid so.'

'Dear oh dear. And it's been like this all afternoon?'

'You can scarcely blame them, sir.'

'But this is the last day! Last chance to ride the greatest railway novelty of our time until April next year!'

'Try not to be disheartened, sir. It's been a tremendous summer. We've just run into some rather sorry weather at the last.'

'It's not the weather, Billy.'

'No? Then what is it?'

'You know perfectly well! "The Pneumatic Dispatch Company" – wrong for starters – "now desire not only to pump and blow her Majesty's mails, but her Majesty's subjects generally through exhausted and flatulent tubes." That one flippant remark, Billy, made by that most pernicious of men, now lodged in the popular consciousness. "Flatulent tubes." That's all it took to puncture what we had.'

'Honestly, sir. Herapath's article was for specialists only.'

Thomas smiled as two more groups of passengers – a young couple, and a boy being held up by his parents – edged down the bank: enough for at least one more journey.

On a basic level, of course, Billy was right. The sudden decline in passenger numbers was due to more straightforward concerns than the facetious bleatings of *The Engineer*. The boom had continued right up to the weather turning, and he had every faith he could turn further profit out of his impulsive decision to revive the railway the following spring.

But if the public at large didn't care what *The Engineer* said, then those deciding the fate of his schemes certainly did. And in that context, John Herapath's vindictive précis, delivered despite a perfectly smooth trip six weeks before, was as destructive a blow as could be imagined.

Sir Charles Fox was proof. Despite his overflowing enthusiasm after the ballast run in early September, he hadn't expressed even the most perfunctory interest since, failing to respond to increasingly exasperated enquiries. He or the LNWR had clearly read the negative reports of Herapath and his weak-minded disciples, and been swayed into re-thinking their pneumatic future – despite first-hand evidence to the contrary.

Sir Charles wasn't the be-all and end-all, of course, but the sea-change in professional opinion also cast doubt over Thomas's own Waterloo and Whitehall scheme. He had hoped to deposit the plans with Parliament within the month, but such a move now seemed futile amid resurgent cynicism. Once upon a time, he would have gone ahead regardless. But former imprudence had taught him that even the greatest schemes needed a favourable following wind to get through Parliament, and the Waterloo scheme was too good, too *achievable*, to squander for want of such support. For all his impatience, there was simply no sensible choice but to wait another year, reprising the Palace trial to try to turn the fickle tide of professional support back in his favour.

If he was irritable, then, as the intrepid last-day travellers queued at the booth, chattering excitedly beneath their umbrellas, it was because his plans had once again faltered on the brink of fulfilment – and his patience with such setbacks had well and truly expired. From now on, he promised himself, he would be ruthless like never before, answering objections, overcoming obstacles and seizing opportunities without mercy, regardless of the consequences. Like a disease, steam was spreading fast and unopposed through London's subterranean arteries, and Thomas owed it to the world to waste no more time in making people see that *his* was the only safe way of doing things.

'Mr. Rammell! Up here!'

Thomas looked up to see four more passengers – a trio of friends, and a solitary gentleman – negotiating the muddy descent. Behind them, at the top of the bank, stood the Palace archivist Fotheringay – an eccentric, bespectacled fellow whose office was opposite Thomas's, in a building just beyond the southern end of the Palace. He was bellowing at full volume.

'There's someone—'

He was cut off by lightning and thunder.

'Say again!'

'There's someone up at the Palace—'

This time it was the sorrowful sigh of the railway, followed by the clatter of the valve gates as the petite carriage rolled into the station. Realising that to shout further was pointless, Thomas filed past the nine hardy souls waiting to board and clambered up the bank, umbrella in hand, only to lose his balance as another rumble of thunder shook the earth.

'This had better be good, Fotheringay!' he cried, lifting himself out of the mud. 'I look like I've been buried alive!'

'I wouldn't have ventured out if it weren't worthwhile,' said the archivist, helping Thomas onto the path. 'Sir Charles Fox is waiting in your office. He wouldn't say why and did offer to come back another day – but I thought you'd want to see him right away.'

'Indeed I do,' replied Thomas, nodding in acknowledge-ment as the three people who had just completed their journey filed past, grateful for the restorative sanctuary of his railway.

Down in the station, Billy was stepping off the front of the freshly departing train, having sealed the doors and taken up the brakes. He waved farewell to the passengers as they disappeared into the tunnel – rainwater pouring from its mouth – and the gates clanked shut behind them.

'Billy!' yelled Thomas. 'Sir Charles Fox is at the Palace! I'll be back for the last run!'

Billy gave the thumbs-up and returned into his booth while

Thomas and Fotheringay strode through the grounds to the Palace, the storm hovering unremittingly overhead. Such was his haste, Thomas quite forgot his dishevelment, and it wasn't until he entered his office, and Sir Charles looked him over in surprise, that he realised the full embarrassment of his muddied state.

'Oh goodness,' he blushed. 'I do apologise—'

'*Most* amusing!' exclaimed Sir Charles. 'The land around the railway must be utterly sodden.'

Casting his umbrella aside, Thomas went to the sink in the corner and washed his hands and face.

'I was at the Palace for a meeting,' said Sir Charles, 'so I thought I'd look in.'

'Very good of you,' said Thomas, quietly irked that Fox hadn't made a special visit.

'I was surprised to learn your railway is to return next year. I swear I've seen advertisements saying that this was the last day ever.'

'That was the original plan,' replied Thomas. 'I felt I had gained all I could. I was eager to move on. But then John Herapath published his piece in *The Engineer* and . . . well, after that, I fear I need another year to convince people that my plans are fit to proceed.' He dried himself with a towel. 'Besides, there's a demand for it, which I see no harm in meeting. The Palace are certainly pleased.'

'John Herapath's an old man now,' said Sir Charles. 'In his frustration, he's turning his fire on easy targets from years gone by. Anyone with a little discernment will know to ignore him.'

Thomas hung the towel over a radiator. 'So that's not what persuaded you?'

'Persuaded me of what?'

'I assumed you and the LNWR had lost interest.'

Sir Charles frowned. 'What gave you that idea?'

Thomas hesitated, the awkwardness acute. 'With respect, sir, after your initial enthusiasm, I expected a quicker response: if not definitive, then at least a gesture. But not only did I hear nothing, you failed to return my enquiries at your office.'

Sir Charles smiled inscrutably. 'As it happens, your inference is quite right. The LNWR have entirely lost interest in the pneumatic railway.'

Thomas stared back. 'But how, after your report?'

'You've seen my report?'

'No. But given your enthusiasm – and your stated immunity to Herapath's prejudice – I assume it was positive.'

'You assume wrong.'

Thomas clenched his fists, trying to disguise his rising temper.

'My professional duty was to present the facts,' explained Sir Charles. 'And though the trial thrives, it would still be an enormous risk to run such a railway through a major city. Likewise, although you are no longer formally associated with the PDC, they are still struggling with their bigger line.'

'Only because of legal barriers! Steam would struggle similarly. It's no reflection on air power. As for building in a major city—'

Thomas stopped, struck by the grin on his guest's face.

'I'm sorry,' said Sir Charles. 'I oughtn't be teasing you. It clearly means too much.'

'You didn't submit a negative report?'

'Oh I did, and venomously so. Indeed, I was so determined to ensure that the LNWR would give up their pneumatic designs, I even made a play of ignoring you – underlining my disdain for your invention, just to ensure I could have it all to myself.'

It took a moment to register, but once Sir Charles's meaning became clear, Thomas experienced a dizzy, weightless wonder as myriad points of confusion coalesced into sense.

'Please don't think ill of me,' the venerable engineer went on. 'I merely told them what they wanted to hear. And even if

I was a trifle dishonest, I feel no shame. I've been nurturing similar plans to theirs for twice as long. That's why they asked me to assist, and I was happy to oblige – until I experienced just how astonishing your railway really is.'

After almost two months of deflation, Thomas's heart surged with the same optimism he'd experienced on the day of the ballast test.

'You mention similar plans to the LNWR's,' he said, suppressing his leaping emotions and remaining business-like as he sat down behind his desk. 'What did you have in mind?'

'There are two I've been pondering for a while,' replied Sir Charles, taking a seat opposite. 'The first will connect Birkenhead to Liverpool, running beneath the Mersey. The second will link Victoria and Piccadilly stations in Manchester. Both are urgently needed, and both ideally suited to the pneumatic. Beyond those, I have a secondary notion of a similar line in Brighton.'

'Your idea is to work together?'

'In the first instance, I propose we become partners on your Waterloo and Whitehall scheme, acting immediately in order to get Parliamentary assent next year. Assuming that succeeds, we then deposit plans in November next year for my two railways – again sharing co-billing as engineers.' He smiled and sat back in his chair. 'Now of course I recognise that it's your system, so you're as free to reject these arrangements as you are to prevent me building a pneumatic railway at all. But I trust it's not impolite to observe that, notwithstanding your success here, you will be at a great disadvantage if you insist on working alone, with only the memory of your former PDC achievements to bolster your credentials.'

Thomas needed no persuading. From the instant Sir Charles made his offer he had known it would be folly to refuse. The great man's reputation made his co-operation a virtual guarantee of Parliamentary assent.

'It goes without saying that I would be honoured—'

Thomas stopped as he heard the sound of rapidly approaching footsteps.

'Sir,' panted Billy, appearing in the doorway, overalls saturated and splattered with mud.

'What is it?'

Billy looked anxiously at Sir Charles. Whatever he had to say, he wanted to say it in private. Thomas made his excuses and they stepped outside.

'It's the railway,' said Billy, wiping the rain from his eyes to reveal a stark, scared expression. 'You're needed right away.'

Thomas wanted to ask if it could wait, but Billy's panic rendered the question redundant. He stepped back inside.

'My apologies, sir, but I'm needed down at the track. There are people wanting to meet me in person.'

'Quite understandable,' said Sir Charles. 'Go and do what you must. I'm back at the Palace this Saturday for the Guy Fawkes celebrations. I suggest we reconvene then – say, 4pm? – to share our plans in more detail.'

'Certainly.' Thomas shook the great man's hand, then took his leave. He found Billy already outside the office building, heading back through the Palace.

Energy bubbling over, Thomas pursued his assistant into the southern end of the nave, keen to share the good news: what a perfect opportunity it was, and how determined he was to seize it, no matter what fate threw in his way.

Alas, Billy was in no mood for celebration. As they emerged into the pouring rain, beneath the arch of the south transept, he stopped beside one of the mighty sphinxes that guarded the grey gardens below, terror etched across his face.

'What is it?' asked Thomas. 'What's happened?'

Billy couldn't speak. He kept opening his mouth, about to talk, only to leave it hanging. Finally, he summoned strength enough to continue running downhill, imploring Thomas as he went.

'You have to come and see.'

Chapter 25

The skeletons pulled us in without any fuss. Within moments we were back on our way, gliding motionlessly through the timeless earth.

'We were right,' I explained to Emily. 'Monty caused the big one – 1936.'

I took a much-needed drag on my inhaler, while Emily introduced herself to the organist.

'I know how you must feel,' she said, 'but you've done the right thing in joining us.'

Monty paid no attention. He was too captivated by his magical surroundings: the skeletons, the carriage – above all, the forward movement.

'Everything alright while I was gone?' I asked, illuminating Emily with my torch.

'Quiet as the grave.'

'Back in time,' murmured Monty, watching the soil drift upwards. '1923 will be next.'

I smiled at Emily. Our latest recruit was clearly energised, his mind sharpened, not maddened, by being able to react positively to the Palace's destruction.

'I've never seen a railway carriage like it,' he said. 'I thought I knew all there was to know about the Palace, but this has completely eluded me.'

'Is it any wonder?' I said. 'Nine people left to rot. Whoever did this must have been desperate to cover it up.'

'We're stopping,' declared Emily. 'Quick!' She dragged me

to the centre. 'The darkness down here is creepy when you're gone. This time I want you up and down as quickly as possible!'

Still reeling from the emotional exertions of apprehending Monty, I shared Emily's impatience to make this next foray as straightforward as I could. Logic stated that the hole opened at the exact moment the intruder deserted the skeletons, so it was definitely possible to capture my prey more swiftly than I had managed so far – especially now I felt less need to explain myself, ever surer that our mission merited these audacious kidnappings.

The skeletons huddled round, hurling me up with a cry of 'Fetch him!' the second the hole gurgled open.

I flew into the air. It was the middle of the night on the surface, but my torch was still on from my last adventure. I spun round as I landed, and immediately spotted our next recruit: a grey-haired, tweed-jacketed, cloth-capped old fellow, standing just a metre away. His face was frozen in horror at the dual shocks of the skeletons' attack, and my having just geysered up from the bowels of the earth.

Seizing the moment, I launched forward and hauled him up at the waist.

'Help!' he cried. 'Mary, help!'

I shone the torch around. An old woman, clad in a thick brown overcoat, was standing a short distance away.

'Do something, Mary! He's trying to bury me! Bury me alive!'

'It's not what it looks like,' I said, smiling at the woman.

'He's already got one skeleton down there! Looks like I'm next!'

'Down there?' repeated Mary. 'Down where?'

'Down his hole!'

'What hole? What are you on about, Harold?'

'Never mind! Just do something!'

Mary darted forward, so I turned away and tried slotting Harold into the ground. A pair of skeletal hands duly seized his feet, but the old woman managed to hook her hands beneath his shoulders before he passed out of sight. A desperate tug of war duly ensued, stretching the screaming old man close to breaking point.

'You can't win!' I yelled at the woman. 'You have to let him go!'

But Mary wouldn't listen. Fearing the worst for Harold, I had no choice but to barge her out of the way, whereupon I turned and dived towards the disappearing old man, clinging on to his trailing hand.

The skeletons dragged us down in quick succession, and we clattered to the floor. I jumped off the poor fellow and warned Emily and Monty to give him space. His eyes flickered open.

'His name's Harold,' I said. 'So sorry, sir – but I had to get you. This seemed simplest.'

'There's nothing to fear,' said Emily. 'We can explain what's happening.'

The man sat up and gazed in astonishment at the skeletons, blinking again and again. 'I can't be that drunk,' he said. 'Can I?' He looked round some more. 'Where's Mary?'

'Mary's not here,' I said.

'Who's Mary?' asked Monty.

'She's my wife,' said the man, standing up. 'She needs to see this!'

'I'm afraid she can't,' I said.

'Why not? You just fetched me; why can't you fetch her?'

'That's not how it works. Any second now we're going to leave—'

In a flash, the skeletons dashed to the centre of the carriage, eight of them crouching to lift the ninth – the tall, solitary gentleman – towards the hole in the roof. He reached up, the sight of his arm so familiar to me, and plunged his hand into the mud. Moments later, he pulled in Harold's wife.

'There,' said Harold. 'Perfectly possible, you see?'

Mary landed, and the skeletons rushed back to their benches.

'Extraordinary!' she enthused, looking around. 'The hole vanished after you came in, but I stamped right away, and now—'

Registering the skeletons, she let out the most chilling scream I'd ever heard, stumbling back and falling into the lap of the lone gentleman passenger. She screamed some more and ran into Harold's arms.

'This has to be a nightmare!'

'That's what I thought,' said Harold. 'Either that or the booze.' He winked at me. 'We've been in the pub since seven.'

'What time is it now?' I asked.

'Gone midnight! But we can take it. Wouldn't have walked through the Palace grounds otherwise. We are both perfectly, immaculately *compos mentis*. Aren't we, dear?'

'Skeletons!' gasped Mary.

'Yes, dear,' said Harold. 'I know.'

'But why? How?'

'That's what we're here to find out,' I said. 'We've all come from different points in time, having all trodden on the spot exactly above that hole in the roof. All we know is that the skeletons aren't happy, and have a habit of taking out their displeasure—'

'But the *clothes*, Harold,' said Mary, clutching her husband close. 'I haven't seen bonnets like those since I was a child. They must have been here fifty, sixty years.'

'Fifty-nine,' said Harold. 'To be precise.'

I glanced at Emily, then back to Harold. 'Hold on. You knew they were here?'

Harold shook his head. 'I had no idea.'

'Then what are you jabbering on about?' asked his wife.

Harold stepped into the centre of the carriage and sighed. 'Honestly, dear. If I've told you about this once, I've told you a hundred times.'

'About what?' I asked.

'This railway line.'

The adrenalin fizzed through me. We had collected Harold

in 1923. Both he and Mary looked the better part of seventy.

'You mean the old whatsit railway trial?' said Mary.

Harold nodded. 'The pneumatic railway trial. Summer, 1864.' He sat down between two skeletons. 'I have no idea how the bodies came to be here. But this is where it used to be, and this is precisely what it looked like.'

'What was it?' I asked.

Harold was about to reply when the carriage started moving.

'Ah!' he exclaimed, sitting up straight. 'How I used to love it!'

'Love what, dear?' asked Mary.

'The smoothness!'

'What smoothness?'

He looked up at his wife, face alight with affectionate nostalgia. 'The smoothness of air, my love. The soft, strange smoothness of air.'

Chapter 26

Saturday 5th November, 1864

'Sir, it's nearly four,' said Billy. 'You need to be getting up to the Palace.'

It was five days since news of an emergency on the railway had caused Thomas to cut short his meeting with Sir Charles Fox.

'You're sure we need the extra hour?' he asked.

'To have it done by the end of next week,' said Billy, 'we need every last glimmer of daylight.'

They were standing by the cricket ground, where the first wave of navvies were demolishing the upper half of the tunnel. Behind them, stretching 70 yards down to the Penge gate, the tunnel remained fully intact but was no longer fenced in. Ahead, the brickwork fell away as it climbed the sloping lawn. Clusters of navvies were hard at work every 20 yards.

Thomas turned to Sid, the navvies' representative. 'Double,' he said, upping his previous offer of time and a half.

'Triple,' returned Sid, having previously intimated that they would accept double.

'Double – then half again,' offered Thomas.

'Working till five, men!' hollered Sid. 'Double time and a half. Anyone not interested: go at four, but don't bother coming back tomorrow. Pass it on!'

Ashamed to have been reduced to such unseemly

negotiations, Thomas led Billy briskly away, striding up towards the wooded mound that bordered the sloping lawns. Beside them, the tunnel diminished in size until it was a mere bricked-in shallow, after which the trench itself vanished, filled in with a black strip of soil that led into the side of the mound. A muddy brown splodge signified where the entrenched tunnel had formerly become a true subterranean railway.

'The first navvies will reach the Penge gate tomorrow lunchtime,' said Billy, 'at which point I'll have them return and start filling in the Sydenham Gate station. As for the later groups, they'll be charged with turfing over the scars we've left behind.'

'The tunnel itself is definitely secure?' asked Thomas, eyes glued to the abysmal blot on the steep rise ahead of them. 'We're sure of that?'

'Stop worrying, sir. It's all in hand.'

Thomas nodded. 'Where would I be without you, Billy?' he asked, marvelling at how efficiently his assistant had overseen the dismantling operation: a task Thomas himself would have struggled to discharge even half as dispassionately. As they had agreed on Monday night, it was all about haste – but not *too much* haste – and so, under Billy's supervision, it had been.

'Ahoy there!'

The voice was immediately recognisable.

'*Most* pleasant evening.'

For a fleeting moment Thomas was unperturbed, but then anxiety seized him. Yes, he had been expecting to see Sir Charles Fox – but up in the sanctuary of the Crystal Palace, not down here by the tunnel.

He turned to see the venerable old engineer just yards away, his elongated shadow cast across the filled-in trench.

'I decided to get off at Penge Lane and walk,' explained Sir Charles, gazing back at the disappearing tunnel. 'I thought it might be pleasant to admire the model railway in the setting sun.'

'We're digging it up,' said Thomas peremptorily, making sure to guide his guest around the side of the wooded mound, rather than over the top.

'That much I can see,' said Sir Charles.

'We began by filling in the subterranean section of tunnel, then worked towards the Penge gate, demolishing the brickwork and filling in the trench.'

Without missing a beat, he dispatched Billy to retrieve the Waterloo and Whitehall plans from the Palace. As he did so, the station formerly known as Sydenham Gate came into view, further deepening Sir Charles's perplexity.

For a couple of days the model railway station had resembled a muddy quarry, bereft of platforms – taken up as early as Tuesday morning – and all the works on the opposite bank. Valve room, engine house, fencing: all had disappeared, as had the tracks themselves and the gorgeous little carriage. As for the tunnel entrance, gone were the valve gates and elaborate brick surround; in their place, nothing but tightly packed soil.

'We're aiming to finish a week today to let the Palace gardeners re-nourish the soil before winter. Tomorrow we begin filling in the cutting. As of a few days' time, there'll be no way of knowing the station was ever here.'

'Your haste is commendable,' said Sir Charles. 'But I thought the line was merely falling into abeyance?'

'The railway isn't coming back.'

Sir Charles laughed. 'Evidently not.'

'I apologise for not informing you.'

'Quite right.'

Thomas flinched at the sharpness of Sir Charles's tone.

'Our interests are now mutual, Thomas. Your future is my future. To take such a decision unilaterally undermines our trust – particularly as I happened to see a certain merit in having a still-active trial to buoy up our plans.'

Shivering in the dying sunlight, Thomas fought to conceal his panic. Amid the tumult, he hadn't yet thought of a credible excuse for not informing Sir Charles. He hadn't even settled on a story explaining why they were dismantling the railway to begin with.

'In truth,' he began, pursuing the first idea that entered his head, '*you* are the reason I decided to take up the line. The very notion of a revival was a response to your apparent lack of interest, and dread that Herapath had turned professional opinion against me. Naturally, our meeting on Monday comprehensively allayed those fears, and after the final run I reassessed the wisdom of returning. Could the trial really still be of use? A working, profitable demonstration while we argue our case? Or might it not actually count *against* us: a sign of weakness, uncertainty – of something yet to be proven? In the end, I trusted my instincts. Better to say this is done, the point made, and so energise our more prestigious schemes with forward momentum. As for not telling you, I simply assumed you would endorse such bravado – given your faith in the system, and your self-professed influence.'

Sir Charles stared at the soil where the tunnel mouth had been, betraying nothing. For a tantalising second, Thomas feared that he sensed some other consideration lurking in the darkness.

'That all seems sensible,' he agreed finally. 'A confident gesture chimes nicely with my becoming involved.' He nodded as the argument settled in his mind. 'I'm just amazed at the swiftness.'

'I've waited a long time for a big stride forward,' said Thomas. 'I owe it to myself to be ruthless now the moment has arrived.'

'I take it the Palace raised no objections?'

'Not at all.'

'And what's become of the tunnel?'

'We've filled it in,' answered Thomas. 'I had the Palace's blessing. Better that, they agreed, than run the danger of dismantling it brick-by-brick. Should they ever need to excavate, I'll return to oversee it myself.'

'But why not just brick up the entrances? Why fill it with all that soil?'

'The tunnel wasn't built for long-term use. What if it became unstable? What if the land was built on? What of the trees' continued growth? One doesn't want it collapsing in a hundred years, injuring people ignorant of its very existence!'

Sir Charles gave a hesitant laugh, clearly wondering why his question had provoked such a fervent answer. But before he could query anything more, Billy reappeared with the plans, and Thomas suggested seeking more pleasant surroundings in which to examine them. Much to his relief, Sir Charles agreed.

As the two men walked away from the former station, conversation turned from the pneumatic railway to the Crystal Palace, prompted by the pair of giant fountains which came into view, either side of the wide central avenue that led up to the glittering building. Supplied by two broad cascades that ran over 500 feet downhill from a pair of iron water temples – themselves a good sixty feet high – the fountains were a perfect mirror of each other: the cascades adjacent to the central path, feeding the innermost of the two long, narrow wings that protruded from the circular hub of each basin.

'I remember it so well,' said Sir Charles, thinking back to the Palace's relocation from Hyde Park. 'Sir Joseph was obsessed – utterly obsessed – by the gardens at Versailles. Not just imitating them, but bettering them.'

'And how splendidly he succeeded,' said Thomas, trying hard to behave as normally as possible.

'Indeed,' said Sir Charles. 'Though I shan't deny having my doubts when he first revealed his plans. "I'm no gardener," I remember saying, "but surely one 800-foot-long fountain is sufficient. Do we really need the pair?"'

He laughed; Thomas joined in.

'Of course, there was no arguing with him. "Everything must be symmetrical," he said, "and that doesn't mean doing things by halves! Besides, the circular portions are *only* 468 feet in diameter." Only! As though that were somehow a disappointment!'

Thomas smiled. 'His imagination is a thing to behold.'

'Naturally, he soon discovered that he had over-reached himself – when the original water towers had to be abandoned. But then, what of it?' Sir Charles waved up the hill, towards the two mighty structures that had risen in their place. 'We had Brunel on hand to provide the solution.'

They took a seat beside the northern fountain, facing uphill towards the Palace. Almost all the benches along the embankment were occupied, the crowds eager to witness Darby's famous fireworks, along with the far rarer spectacle of Paxton's mighty fountains in full flow. Expense was the main cause of the latter's infrequency, but there was also the worry of wind. If the air were anything other than perfectly still, the jets could easily drench anyone within the grounds' perimeter.

'*Most* extraordinary,' reflected Sir Charles, 'the talent of the age. I wonder: has there ever been a time when men have been so happy to set themselves unprecedented goals – knowing perfectly well that somebody, somewhere, will find the means to do it?'

'Our resourcefulness is something to be treasured,' said Thomas. 'That's why the Palace is so important. An example for those who come after us.'

Sir Charles checked his pocket watch. 'The display is due to begin at half past. Not long now.' He lifted up his head, assessing the breeze. 'With such still air there's every chance the fountains might actually be turned on for once. I suggest we look at the plans before the display starts.'

'Good idea,' said Thomas, gazing absent-mindedly at the crowds behind them, streaming up the avenue and looking across the cricket pitch, towards his excavations. What might they be saying about the suddenness of the railway's removal?

Would any spot its now famous inventor, sitting beside the fountain? And if so, might they take the opportunity to query a strange coincidence from the beginning of the week?

'Mr. Rammell?'

Realising his distraction, Thomas turned back.

Sir Charles frowned. 'Is anything the matter?'

'My apologies,' said Thomas. 'Really, I'm quite alright. It's just been a long summer.'

Sir Charles hesitated, then tapped the plans which Thomas was holding. 'The Waterloo and Whitehall Railway. Tell me more.'

Grateful for the prompt, Thomas opened the file.

'What I'm proposing is an underwater tunnel,' he explained, 'connecting the terminus of the London and South Western with Whitehall. A straightforward line at first, disrupting minimal private property, but readily extendable. Indeed, I already have plans to take it to Charing Cross, Tottenham Court Road, and Newington Butts.'

'Do you have the South Western's approval?'

'Nothing formal, but I have the backing of two directors, Dutton and Mortimer, who are keen to ease their passengers' travails.' He unfolded the uppermost sheet of plans. 'As you can see, the proposal is for a single track. As one carriage moves through the tunnel, two others board at either station. The fan will be at Waterloo, because the land is cheaper. We'll therefore suck the trains to Waterloo, and blow them back to—'

All of a sudden, the two giant fountains burst into life, sending illuminated water plumes 200 feet into the darkening sky, and filling the twilight with an almighty aquatic roar. A little further up the hill, water began funnelling up through the hollow iron columns of the two domed temples, flowing back out to enshroud the structures in transparent sheets, then roaring downhill and cascading over a waterfall, into the fountains.

'How wonderful!' exclaimed Sir Charles.

Thomas smiled. It wasn't the first time he'd seen the jets in full flow, but the sensation never failed to astound him. It was difficult to comprehend the power that sent the water that high; gravity not just defied but humbled by human ingenuity.

'I'm so proud to have had the Palace as my home,' he remarked, quite without thinking. 'I've always known I'm capable of similar achievements, and yet . . .' He paused, knowing he should stop. 'Increasingly I feel haunted.'

Sir Charles turned towards him. 'Haunted by what?'

Thomas stared back, willing his mind to catch up with his mouth. 'By the misfortunes of the past – and the fear they'll drag me down again.'

Sir Charles studied him carefully. 'In the past you didn't have me. Whereas now you do. Or rather you will, if you can put a stop to these bouts of irrational apprehension.'

Irrational. Lodging the word in his mind, Thomas scrutinised Sir Charles and saw a face full of candour, free of any suspicion.

'I'm sorry,' he said, smiling meekly. 'To return to the Waterloo and Whitehall—'

'No, no,' said Sir Charles. 'Let's leave that for now. The light is too poor to see the plans. We'll review them later in your office – although, there is one thing I'm impatient for you to explain.'

Thomas's body tightened again with anxiety. Had Sir Charles somehow seen through the cover story? Had he found out the truth by other means?

'Do go on.'

'It's regarding the tunnel,' said Sir Charles.

Thomas's body tensed up some more.

'Assuming you're thinking similarly to Brunel – using a protective shield – I have some reservations about tunnelling beneath the Thames.'

Thomas exhaled, relieved yet simultaneously angry that he kept panicking. Sir Charles didn't know, and had no way of finding out, as long as he himself didn't give it away.

'For even though the river is narrower at Charing Cross than at Wapping,' continued Sir Charles, 'it would still take an eternity. The Thames Tunnel took nine years, so maybe five for us? And it would be dangerous. There'd be many lives lost.'

'Of course,' said Thomas. 'And I'd never consider imperilling so many.'

Sir Charles looked surprised. 'You have an alternative?'

Thomas nodded. 'Simpler, safer, quicker. For though the river is narrower at Whitehall, it is not by much: 1,000 feet, compared to the 1,300 feet of the Thames Tunnel. We require a new approach. One which gets the sub-aqueous tunnel built swiftly, and doesn't cause additional delay by interfering with the cut-and-cover work either side of the river.'

'But how can you dig such a tunnel any more quickly?'

'Who said we had to dig?'

Sir Charles stared at the fountain as the tower of water frothed ever higher. 'How else are we to drive a tunnel under the river?'

'By treating them as two separate things,' said Thomas. 'So we build the tunnel in sections, off-site, then float each part upriver to the appointed spot, where we will have driven down a set of foundation piers, and dredged out a surrounding channel. We then flood the sections of tunnel, letting them sink into place before draining them and securing the seals between each part.'

'That is all?'

'That is all. Think of it as the perfect, pioneering counterpart to the pneumatic railway itself.'

Sir Charles looked thoughtful.

'I confess I'm not the first to have thought of it,' said Thomas. 'But I am the first to think seriously of trying it.'

'You believe it can be done?'

The first firework of the night exploded above the fountain. Spirals of light shot through the crystalline water.

'I believe it as I believed in the pneumatic railway. I believe we must make it work, since it is the safest, most humane, option available. And I believe in its simplicity – in the fact that, with all due care, it *has* to work.'

'You are a remarkable man, Mr. Rammell,' said Sir Charles, watching the cacophonous, multi-coloured fireworks erupt over the floodlit Palace. 'There is much prodigious imagination in the world, but rarely is it matched by such tenacity, lateral-mindedness, and genuine concern for the common man. You are the best of our sort, and I should be honoured to work with you.'

'The honour is all mine,' said Thomas, as the explosions intensified, sending shivers through the sheets of water, and shaking the ground.

'Good gracious!' bellowed Sir Charles. 'It's enough to wake the dead!'

Thomas smiled, only belatedly registering the inadvertent double meaning, and even then retaining impeccable composure. Looking forward, and seeing Sir Charles's imagination ignite at the ingenuity of his own, had provided all the reassurance needed to set the seal on his recovery.

He had made it through the toughest test of his life. Now, with Sir Charles beside him, there was nothing to stop him achieving his ambitions.

Chapter 27

'How often did you ride on it?' I asked, as the buried carriage continued its graceful journey back in time.

'Just once,' said Harold. 'I must have been nine or ten. It was a memorable day; they were late opening because of some challenging load test. We went as a family – one of many great days out at the Palace. It was all so much better then. And as a child, having it all on my doorstep: I felt like I was at the centre of the world.'

'What do you remember about the trip?' asked Emily.

'He remembers everything,' said Mary bitterly. 'Hardly a week goes by without him wittering on about it!'

'You didn't travel on it yourself?'

'My folks didn't move here until the 1870s, by which time it was long gone.'

'Or so we thought,' said Harold.

'You never heard any rumblings?' I asked.

Harold looked pitifully at the skeletons. 'I've remembered it with a few people since, but nothing untoward was ever mentioned. There was no reason to think it wasn't just dismantled in the normal way.'

This last answer, while extraordinary, was no great surprise. It had long been obvious that the skeletons had been victims of a heinous cover-up. To learn of the pneumatic railway itself, however – an invention which even I, as a former tube driver, never knew existed – left me dumbstruck. The haunted, unconventional carriage had always felt alien, but never more so than now, knowing it had once been the centrepiece of a trial railway, sucked and blown through a tunnel, which, over time, had become as forgotten as the coach itself.

I turned to the nearest skeleton and gazed into his eye socket. 'What was it? What happened to—'

I noticed what looked like a tear – or was it condensation? – sliding down his speckled cheekbone.

'The motion's changing,' said Emily.

'Stopping?' asked Mary.

'*Accelerating.*'

'This is new,' I said. 'Normally we just—' I stopped to clear my throat; the air seemed more congested than before. 'Normally we just hit top speed, and that's it until we glide to rest.'

'Look.' Monty shone the torch through the cloudy air to reveal a whirl of particles: the larger ones in purposeful columns, shooting up to the roof; the smaller ones, the dust, swirling towards the two ranks of skeletons.

'It's repairing itself!' declared Mary.

This we had known for a while, but the speed was now making the process more spectacular *and* more perilous, as lumps of wood shot up to the roof, rearranging themselves as if the ruptures had never existed. Likewise the windows, where the cracks disappeared with a satisfying glassy crunch.

'When was the last big fire?' I asked, feeling distinctly wheezy. 'Before 1923?'

'1866,' said Harold. 'It was also the first. Enormous blaze. Did for the whole northern part of the Palace.'

'And the pneumatic railway trial began and ended in 1864?'

'Correct.'

'So our next stop is just two years after they were buried here.'

'You can tell,' said Monty, holding up the leg of a gentleman skeleton. 'His trousers: they're restoring themselves.'

All around the carriage, the skeletons' clothes were growing cleaner and smarter. Not only that, they were filling out in response to something happening beneath them. Recalling the clouds of dust that were drifting back to the skeletons, I looked again at the skull I had observed moments before. Sure enough, the cheekbone was no longer so bare. Instead, a brown moisture was spreading over the surface, obscuring the skull below. Lifting his sleeve, I found the same thing on his wrist bone – a squidgy layer, coarse and uneven, rapidly reforming as the dust particles collected themselves into patches of decayed flesh.

I stepped back, joining the others in the centre of the carriage. We watched in horrified silence as the process accelerated. On all sides, bony surfaces were being smothered by a kaleidoscope of blotchy, black-brown scars, thickening so swiftly that the corpses seemed to be inflating – a process aided, I surmised, by what was happening internally, where the outward changes were being mirrored by the restoration of their mouldy, insect-ridden innards.

Before long the nine bald corpses were approaching life-size, and the rotten skin began fizzing and squelching as the healing process took effect. The ruptures and blisters on hands and faces swallowed themselves up. The tips of fingers crackled with the return of filthy, flaky fingernails. The scalps sprouted tufts of wiry grey hair, creeping like worms out of the passengers' heads. And then, finally, as the carriage started to slow, ears and noses began to crawl out of cavities, and a dim whiteness bubbled up in the darkness of eye sockets.

We came to rest, whereupon the transformations ceased. The carriage looked almost as good as new. The floor was dusty but clear, with just one pile of soil below our now-solitary entrance hole. The windows had only a few cracks remaining and even boasted a shine where the dust wasn't too thick, while the brown leather benches, gas lamps and curtains were fully intact – the latter now a deep, luxurious purple, marred only by occasional cobwebs and a thin layer of dirt.

Against this almost civilised backdrop, the passengers looked more horrific than ever, frozen in a tantalising no man's land of decay. Grotesquely malformed, their corpses were yet sufficiently fleshy to conceal all traces of the skeletons underneath. While their sunken eyes were as dry as their lips, and their hair remained fearfully colourless, enough features *had* reappeared to give some semblance of life. The men's hairstyles were clear – side-partings, complemented by sporadic traces of facial hair – while the women's long, frizzy locks looked strangely elegant, even in their lifelessness.

Most disturbing of all was the fact that the corpses had resumed their usual poses, which now felt properly expressive: heads on shoulders and loving embraces, all accompanied by sad, sallow eyes. For all the torment that had prompted them to attack me and my fellow adventurers, the overwhelming impression was that they had died in stoic acceptance of their fate. Neither the ugliness of their desiccated mouths, hanging limply open, nor the gnarled noses and shapeless ears – not even the stomach-turning stench of the whole putrefying scene – could displace the aura of quiet bravery.

'How could it have been allowed to happen?' asked Emily.

'It must have been intentional,' said Monty, inspecting one of the pristine umbrellas. 'It's the only explanation for such barbarity.'

'But what possible reason could there be?' wondered Harold.

'Maybe the man responsible was just a maniac?'

'I'd hope even a maniac would think twice before choosing this as his means of murder.'

'For heaven's sake, it was an *accident*,' said Mary. 'Look outside – piles and piles of brick and soil. The tunnel collapsed and trapped the carriage.'

'But if it was an accident,' said Monty, 'why did no one save them?'

'Because we didn't have the faintest clue it was here!' said Harold. He crouched down in front of the skeleton boy. 'To think, these poor people were buried right under our noses. For several days – even weeks – I could have been the one to save them.'

'Someone knew,' reasoned Emily. 'The chap in charge, his closest associates: they must have decided not to rescue them. The question is, why? Why not dig? Why keep it secret, against near-impossible odds?

'To protect themselves?' I wondered.

'To protect his ideas,' asserted Harold. 'I remember now. The fellow in charge was pursuing some other scheme. Can't recall what – it never came to anything – but this was a prototype.'

'He covered this up to ensure his bigger plans weren't jeopardised?'

Harold shrugged. 'It's the only explanation that makes any sense.'

I stared at the rotting corpses, struggling to accept that anyone had it in them to let these people die – so claustrophobically, of starvation, suffocation, dehydration – simply for the sake of a doomed railway scheme. That the railway in question was so elegant, so seemingly humane, only compounded my confusion. But Harold's logic was unshakeable. The magnitude of the cover-up suggested the very highest stakes, and even the most benevolent Victorian railway entrepreneurs were a famously brutal bunch.

'If only I could remember his blasted name. Come on, dear . . .' Harold turned to his wife. 'I've mentioned it enough times.'

'Rammell!' came the answer – but not from Mary. Instead, a nine-strong chorus of corpses chanted the name: 'Rammell! Rammell! Rammell!'

'Thomas Webster Rammell,' repeated Harold. '*That's* the man!'

'Fetch him!' The corpses jumped to their feet, marching at

me like the zombies they had become. 'Fetch Rammell!' they wheezed again, as the hole up to the surface gurgled back into life. 'Rammell! Rammell! Rammell!'

They wrapped their cold, dry hands around my shins, and threw me up.

On the surface it was bright and cold, the sun low in the sky. The slopes leading away felt steeper than before – the little mound, if anything, higher – while the nearest trees had only recently been planted, and the grass underfoot was a different hue to further afield. The immediate area was deserted.

I thought of my mission. Previously, it had been simple because the skeletons' target was always nearby. But this challenge was altogether greater, especially since I was apparently expected to complete it alone.

Or was I? Just as the thought occurred, there was a whoosh of air behind me. I turned and, to my delight, saw Emily shooting out of the earth. But even while she was airborne, there was another sound – a gasp from overhead – which diverted my gaze to one of the older trees overhanging the hole, and a scruffy young girl, sitting astride a fat branch.

'I knew you were all still down there,' she hissed. 'Two years it's been covered up and forgotten. Two years—' She gasped again. 'But how still alive? Still alive, looking so well?' She jumped down and sprinted away. 'Ghosts!' she shrieked. 'Ghosts, ghosts, ghosts!'

Instinctively, I gave chase, but Emily held me back. 'We're not after her, remember?'

'But she knows about the carriage,' I said, as the girl passed out of sight. 'Maybe she can help us find this Rammell guy?'

'She's hysterical. We can't have her drawing attention to us. Our mission is likely to take time. Chances are, we'll have to go far beyond the Palace grounds. We need to find our footing and blend in.'

I looked down at the path. A few passers-by had appeared, peering in puzzlement at our outfits – my old tube overalls, and Emily's future-vintage 1950 coat.

'We need a change of clothes,' she murmured.

'And where do we find that?'

She thought for a moment, then stamped on the ground. Alas, the corpses weren't keeping pace.

'Rammell! *Fetch Rammell*!'

'Yes of course,' replied Emily, 'but first we need to get back in.'

The hole squelched open, and up sprang Monty.

'Now's my chance!' cried Emily, jumping feet-first into the ground, slithering through just as it shut.

'How splendid to see it so different!' said Monty, grinning as he surveyed the scene.

'Did you volunteer to come up?' I asked.

'They forced me, but I happily obliged. They want us all to chip in. "All change!" they said. "Get out. Get Rammell. All change!"'

This was good news. We needed as much manpower as possible, both for the hunt and the physical task of returning Rammell to the crime scene.

Monty and I helped Harold and Mary to land as they rocketed up in succession, already clothed in cobwebby Victorian garments. Emily appeared shortly afterwards, sporting a well-fitting, albeit slightly muddy, navy blue dress.

I looked again at the path. It seemed that any lingering interest in us had been superseded by altogether more dramatic news from the Palace.

'First word of the fire,' I surmised, as whispers were exchanged and people started striding towards the top of the park.

'How come there's a fire?' asked Mary. 'The corpses are getting their way.'

'But the girl in the tree who disturbed them still deserted them,' said Emily. 'Punishment must be exacted.' She passed me and Monty two armfuls of clothes, including hats and shoes, which she'd managed to bring with her out of the carriage. 'Best get changed behind the tree, chaps. I doubt you'll be readmitted until we've got our man.'

We did as we were told, hiding our old gear in a nearby bush. My brown outfit was pretty much a perfect fit, and my top hat perched snugly on my head. Only the shoes – the leather scuffed and cracked, presumably from repeated attempts to escape the carriage – showed any outward wear. While the ensemble was more than a tad whiffy, I welcomed the inconspicuousness. We didn't blend in perfectly, but the occasional ripped, discoloured or ill-fitting oddity was far from noticeable at first glance.

Deciding that the most unobtrusive tactic was to join the herds flocking towards the Palace, I led us on our way, admiring the immaculate surroundings as they unfurled around us. Just as it was hard now to recall the fleshy corpses as skeletons, so seeing the grounds in their sunlit prime eclipsed any memory of their ultimate dilapidation.

Skirting the back of the lake, I turned towards the indoor sports arena and saw instead a vast fountain, well over 200 metres long, with jets stationed all along its length, and broadening at its centre into a wide circular basin over 100 metres in diameter. Another, equally large fountain stood symmetrically behind it, on the site of the sports stadium, and though neither was in use, the sight alone was breathtaking. Beyond them, through a line of trees, I glimpsed the sculpted dinosaurs I'd encountered on my very first visit.

'Haven't seen those fountains for thirty years,' said Harold.

'Place is so much better with them,' said Mary, and it was true: on all sides, the grounds felt newly transparent and expansive.

The fountains were supplied by two long cascades, at the top of which were a pair of ornamental 'water temples', as Harold called them. We joined the central avenue just behind these, and were soon approaching the circular fountain I'd seen in 1950 and 1936. This time it was active, sending a tower of water at least 50 metres into the sky, and filling the air with a fine spray.

'The rosary!' exclaimed Mary, pointing out a circular iron structure, clad in rose bushes, off to the left. 'So beautiful in summer. Why on earth did they ever swap it for that stupid panorama building?'

We walked round the left-hand side of the fountain. Behind the rosary and its embankments of dormant flora, a single-storey glass and iron structure snaked uphill from the railway station, into the Palace's southern wing. My eyes followed the outline of the latter as we skirted round the rest of the fountain, slowly bringing into view the full, magnificent extent of the Crystal Palace itself.

Impressive as it had been at night in 1936, nothing had prepared me for its pristine polish, sparkling like a gem as it reached along the full length of the upper ridge, flanked by its two pepper-pot water towers at either end. The symmetrical majesty of the whole – complete, for the next few minutes at least, with its northern transept and wing – expressed the fathomless curiosity of the era in which we'd arrived.

'I feel young again,' said Mary, arm in arm with Harold, as we intersected two more fountains, right and left, and climbed onto the lower terrace.

There was real magic in how the fortress of glass commanded its gardens: casting sunlight back onto the lawns and flowerbeds, and animating the six fountains on the lower terrace, in whose frothing waters the rays twinkled and separated, bursting into rainbows which drenched the surrounding statues in colour and life. It seemed fitting that – as Monty had indicated – the Palace had been renowned for its fireworks. Light, and the spectacle of light, was the building's lifeblood; its purpose illumination, in every sense of the word.

'If only the skeletons could restore our youth, eh?' reflected Harold.

'I just want to freeze this moment,' said Monty. The Palace's organist-to-be looked like he was engulfed by an almost spiritual rapture, his tearful cheeks twinkling above a disbelieving grin. 'Why couldn't it have stayed like this?'

'Why couldn't it have stayed full stop?' asked Emily, her tone more angry than nostalgic. Like me, she knew what became of all this, and the bitterness in her voice re-focused attention on the task at hand.

'How do we get to Rammell?' I asked, watching the crowds start to flee the north transept, the back of which was now clearly ablaze.

'Well one thing's for certain,' said Harold. 'He's not just going to come along.'

'Why not?' asked Monty. 'Perhaps if we explain what's at stake, the ultimate consequences of his actions, we can appeal to his better instincts?'

'Better instincts?' Mary laughed. 'This villain Rammell sentenced nine innocent people to the ghastliest death, then covered the whole lot up. And all for some two-bit railway scheme!'

'He wouldn't believe our story anyway,' I said. 'Who would?'

'We have to assume he'll do anything to stop being discovered,' reasoned Harold, 'and that our plan is scuppered if he gets wind of what we're up to.'

'Then we have to kidnap him,' said Emily. 'Or trick him. Lure him here without realising why. Either way, we mustn't give him warning. We need to find him via the fewest possible people, making sure that even they don't suspect.'

'So where to start?' asked Mary.

'How about the Palace archives?' said Harold. 'They must have records of the railway, pointing us to what Rammell did next.'

'We'll need a back-up story,' I said. 'Something to explain—'

'Come on!' ordered Mary. 'We'll make it up as we go along.'

Hand in hand with Harold, she marched us to the upper terrace, where the long line of marble statues glinted in the fiery sunset.

'You're not suggesting we go in now?' I said. 'The Palace is on fire!'

'It's only the northern end.'

'But they won't let us!'

She started up the central stairs – the only option now that the steeper flights, which in 1936 had led into the first storey of the Palace, were no longer there.

'We mustn't draw attention to ourselves,' I said.

'Quite right,' said Mary. 'That's why this is the perfect course of action! Nobody will notice us snooping while there's a fire blazing.'

Before I could argue further, we passed under a row of open iron arches, through the doors, and into the Palace.

I looked up, expecting to be awed by the magnificent arch of the central transept, and the unfathomable vastness of the Palace's width. Instead, I found myself looking at a ceiling not many metres above my head, supported by iron columns and girders, and a solid brick wall no more than 10 metres away.

'The basement,' said Harold.

My eyes adjusted to the subdued light. On the left, lines of industrial machines stretched into the distance, their spluttering engines and hammering components resonating down the long, narrow interior. To the right were yet more machines – 'The Agricultural Implement Department' – similarly arranged.

'Before the Palace was here, the ground naturally sloped down to the gardens,' explained Monty, as we walked to a staircase on the right. 'Paxton realised that levelling it would mean compromising the view across the gardens from the floor of the interior.'

We began climbing the stairs; the daylight started to stream down upon us.

'So instead, he built the whole thing as high as he could, supporting the front with this basement level, to improve the view above.'

At the top of the stairs, I looked briefly to my left, where the

Palace grounds were visible through a glazed outer corridor, before becoming distracted by a dreamy echo that was filling the air.

Laughing to myself in anticipation, I stepped forwards and turned to the right.

There, ahead of me, was the interior of the Crystal Palace at its most spectacular point. Way above my head, the gigantic arched roof of the central transept – concertinaed glass, with iron framing – seemed almost to expand as I stared at it.

'And there she is,' said Monty, a fondness in his voice.

I lowered my eyes and immediately saw the focus of his affection: a huge concert platform, half-encircled by many thousands of sloping seats, at the centre of which was a gargantuan organ.

'The original instrument,' Monty said. 'And the best, according to some.'

He looked half-tempted to run up and hammer out a tune as we walked on, approaching the intersection of transept and nave. Looking back, I saw a stack of overhead galleries lined round the periphery of the transept, the uppermost almost as high as the roof itself. At the centre of the first of these was a royal box, while below and to the right was an enclosed 'Concert Room' – as if the stage behind me somehow wasn't enough.

'Fire!' came a cry, as the arched nave unfurled on either side. 'Everybody out of the fine arts courts!'

'Come on people! Out as quick as you can!'

The voices belonged to two gentlemen who were striding down the northern half of the nave, darting off every fifteen metres to bellow commands into rooms on either side. It was hard to see exactly what these 'courts' contained, such was the density of statues and plants surrounding each entrance, but I managed to distinguish two lines of miniature sphinxes, guarding the nearest court on my left, which was set behind a low wall covered in Egyptian carvings. On the right, meanwhile, the entrance consisted of a row of brown marble columns, supporting a sculpted frieze, with two small bronze statues stationed in recesses either side.

'Come on then,' said Mary to Harold. 'Which way?'

Harold turned through a circle, thinking hard.

'And don't say north,' added Mary, 'since that's plainly not going to work.'

'As I recall it,' her husband replied, 'the archive at this point was just beyond the south end of the nave.'

Mary set off.

'But I may be wrong.'

Harold could be wrong all he liked, I thought to myself as we continued on our way, unnoticed by the staff flocking past to help with the evacuation. From what I could see, the courts to the south were more industrial, more present day, than the historic and cultural exhibitions to the north. One was crammed full of the latest stationery implements, another was devoted to the art of ceramics, and yet another celebrated the manufacturing might of Sheffield. I desperately wanted to splinter off and explore each in turn, but Harold and Mary were firmly focused on our mission, and correctly so. The skeletons didn't take kindly to dawdling.

I unbuttoned the jacket I'd inherited from the solitary gentleman corpse. The Palace's affinity to a greenhouse was apparent not just in the sprawling trees, bushes and flowers that lined the nave, but also the temperature. The winter sun was oppressively hot through the glass, and I was grateful when eventually an overhead awning brought relief from the overwhelming daylight.

'There!' whispered Harold.

He was pointing at a moustachioed fellow, running towards us up the nave, having obviously heard of the fire at the opposite end of the building.

'That's Fotheringay, the archivist. Once a good friend of my father's.'

'Perfect!' Mary grinned as the man raced past us. 'We nip in while he's distracted!'

Continuing down the nave, we soon reached the intersection with the south transept. Here was yet another fountain, a miniature of the giants in the Palace grounds, covered by giant palm leaves and surrounded by more classical sculptures. A short way beyond was a two-storey gothic arcade, with statues lurking in its wooden arches, and a central doorway leading out of the nave.

Heading through this exit, we regrouped in a perimeter corridor. The outer glass wall of the Palace rose directly in front, while signs pointed right to the 'Saloon' and 'Retiring Rooms', and left to the 'South Wing Dining Room' and 'New Private Dining Rooms'. Guided by Harold, however, we went through a door straight ahead, leaving the Palace altogether and arriving in a small courtyard of brick buildings adjacent to the south water tower.

'Which one was it?' demanded Mary.

Harold scanned round, clearly trying to filter out his knowledge of the Palace as it had been in 1923. Seconds later, he marched towards a long, broad, barn-like building, and pulled open the door to reveal a carpeted corridor with offices either side. After another moment's pondering, he strode to the third room on the right, marked 'Palace Archive'.

'Not bad, eh?' He grinned as he pushed open the door.

Inside was a large oak table, surrounded by bookshelves and cabinets containing deep, wide drawers. My eyes immediately landed on a set of large, leather-bound volumes marked 'Newspaper clippings'. Thinking this a good place to start, we located the relevant volume – summer 1864 – and found a whole section dedicated to 'Mr. Rammell's Experimental Pneumatic Railway'. Most articles were from the *Illustrated London News*, but specialist publications were also included: *The Mechanics' Magazine*, *The Engineer*, and something called *Herapath's Railway Journal*. The majority were positive, with only a few dissenters.

I felt weirdly, possessively proud as I read about the luxurious carriage and the smoothness of its motion, both of which

I'd come to know in such a roundabout yet intimate way. Such was the strength of this strange nostalgia, I only just noticed a critical discrepancy. According to adverts ahead of its final day, the railway's closure was merely temporary; it was scheduled to return in 1865 for another summer season. That this hadn't happened – that Harold's memory was accurate – was then confirmed by articles from late 1864 referring to the line in the past tense, with no mention of a planned reprise.

'Why did he change his mind?' I wondered.

There was a noise outside like a stifled sneeze. Turning, we saw the door of the office opposite – which had been open – swinging to, as if its occupant had just returned. This in turn brought the nameplate into view: silver lettering emblazoned on a brown wooden panel:

Thomas Webster Rammell
Pneumatic Railway

'Surely not,' I whispered.

'It can't be that easy,' said Monty.

We exchanged intrepid glances. Should we risk knocking? What if it was him inside? I was about to lead us away when Mary hammered on the door.

'Hello?' she shouted. 'May we come in?' Blithely, she pushed the door open.

The office was bare, but for an empty chair and desk. This had clearly been Rammell's base during his experiment but, judging by the dust on the desk, it had not been occupied since.

Except, of course, at this moment it *was* occupied.

'Who's there?' I asked, peering over the edge of the desk – nothing there – then turning back and spotting a shadowy figure, hunched behind the door.

'It's her,' I said, closing the door to let the light fall on a whimpering young girl. 'The one who disturbed the corpses and triggered the fire.'

Her eyes were wide with fear. 'Ghosts!' she wheezed. 'Ghosts from the forgotten carriage!'

'Why were you spying on us?' I asked.

'I've . . . I've spent so long looking,' she stammered, clearly terrified out of her mind.

'We're not going to hurt you. And we are not ghosts.'

'But I saw you . . . Rising out of the carriage.'

'That's because we're victims. Victims, just like you. People the dead passengers grabbed.' I moved closer. 'We're from the future.'

The girl withdrew.

'We're here to do the passengers' bidding. We're here to fetch Thomas Webster Rammell.'

She stopped shaking. A grin started to spread over her face.

Just at that moment, the door opened and in walked Fotheringay. He looked from us down to the girl, eyes narrowing with anger.

'Did you hear what they said, sir?' she asked.

Fotheringay hesitated, and we held our breath. If the answer was yes, and word got back to Rammell, it could be the ruin of our mission.

He stepped towards the girl, bearing down on her with contempt. 'How many times?' he growled. 'You're not welcome here!'

'But they're ghosts, sir! Ghosts, come to catch the villain Rammell!'

A cold sweat crept across me – our secret was out! – but Fotheringay didn't flinch.

'You've had your final warning.' He hauled the girl up. 'Now, it's time to take you to those kind people who can make you better.'

The girl shrieked as Fotheringay lifted her over his shoulder. 'But it's them! They're the proof!'

Fotheringay turned to us and sighed. 'I do apologise. It seems you have become entangled in her pitiful delusions. Please be so kind as to wait here, and I'll return promptly.'

'Thank you,' I replied, unsure what else to say as Fotheringay carted the screaming girl away. I felt bad, but we couldn't possibly confirm her ravings. To do so would not only betray our motives but tar us with the same lunatic brush.

'Do you think he knows Rammell's secret?' asked Emily. 'Is that why he's so dismissive of her? Or does he genuinely just think she's mad?'

We stepped back into the archive. Could it really be that the man best placed to assist us was himself in on Rammell's cover-up? It seemed unlikely, but the risk was enormous.

'What say we leave right away?' suggested Monty, and I was about to agree – caution at all costs – when Fotheringay returned.

'Job done,' he declared. 'Unusually easy to find a police officer today. Which reminds me: you really shouldn't be here, what with the fire in the north wing. I know it would have to be quite a blaze to spread this far, but even so . . .'

He registered our bewilderment.

'Oh, I see. Still in a daze over that mad little witch, eh? I do apologise. She's quite obsessed. For two years she's been trying to convince us that something strange happened down at Mr. Rammell's railway – some balderdash about people going missing simultaneously.'

There didn't seem to be any subterfuge in Fotheringay's friendliness, and I was about to explain what we needed, stopping short of why, when he spotted the press clippings.

'Oh I see,' he said. 'You were here, reading about the rail-way, and that ghastly girl – always sniffing around – caught you in the act, and promptly worked you into her mania.'

'We are indebted to you for sparing us from her clutches,' I said.

'You're most welcome,' said Fotheringay, beaming at our endorsement of his heroism. 'What in particular did you want to know about the pneumatic trial?'

'Just curious,' replied Monty.

Fotheringay frowned.

'Is that strange?' I asked.

'It's just rather recent history, that's all. I'm surprised you didn't ride it, if you're that interested.'

'We did,' returned Harold. 'And I for one adored it. What we're actually trying to discover is where we might find Mr. Rammell today.'

Fotheringay's frown deepened.

'He's still alive, isn't he?' asked Emily.

'But of course.'

'Then what's so odd about asking?'

'Well, I assumed Mr. Rammell's whereabouts would be common knowledge – especially among enthusiasts. Even as we speak, he is in the centre of the capital, building not just the world's first fully-operational pneumatic passenger railway, but the world's first *sub-aqueous* railway of any kind.'

My heart skipped a beat. 'He's building a tunnel beneath the Thames?'

'He's building the tunnel in Poplar. Four separate sections, which he's then going to float upriver and sink into place.' The archivist smiled. 'The man's daring is an inspiration to us all. If there's one thing I know, it's that in a hundred years' time, Thomas Webster Rammell will be spoken of in the same breath as Brunel himself.'

This was high praise indeed, and Fotheringay had been so helpful I didn't want to disabuse him – still less reveal the truth about Rammell's murderous past. Instead, we thanked him for his time, and headed back into the Palace.

'Follow me!' commanded Mary, leading us along the back of the south nave, then through a chicane of corridors, down a level or two, until we trailed through the south wing: dominated by manufacturers' stalls, and innumerable refreshments outlets. Finally, adjacent to the front of the lower terrace, we headed downstairs, right and then left again, into a glass-covered walkway.

'The railway colonnade,' said Monty. 'I never thought I'd see it sparkling like this!'

'The railway?' I said. 'You mean, we're actually getting on a train?'

'No time to waste, is there?' said Harold.

'I suppose not,' I muttered, taking a surreptitious drag on my inhaler: daunted to be leaving the timeless sanctuary of the Crystal Palace, but also thrilled that our hunt for the skeletons' murderer was well and truly underway.

Chapter 28

An hour later, we trudged along Belvedere Road, taking a narrow alley down to the wide, busy, turbulent Thames. On our right, overlooking the river, a lighthouse-like brick tower hissed and growled with startling intensity.

'It's a lead works,' explained Harold, after I told him that the tower was long gone by 2013. 'The sound is molten lead, dropping into a water tank to produce gunshot.'

The stinking, cacophonous tower was entirely characteristic of the south London I'd observed on the journey into town, during which I'd had to take several additional drags on my inhaler to keep my asthma in check. Changing at Clapham Junction, then passing through Vauxhall, factory after factory had belched smoke into the cold winter air, charring the houses that were crammed in between their intransigent frames. Architecturally, the only source of respite was the front of Waterloo Bridge Station, as it now called itself, and even that was suffocated by the dismal greys and browns that dominated the surrounding district.

'Spy any works opposite?' I asked as we reached the riverside, standing between the lead works and the Red Lion Brewery: a smarter stone edifice, classical columns stacked above arches, and topped off by a big red lion, gazing proudly across the water. I could tell it occupied the site-to-be of the Royal Festival Hall, because opposite was the sophisticated skyline of the Strand: further away than in my day, the buildings lower and spires more prominent. Beautifully sunlit under relatively smokeless skies, it made the south bank feel more than ever like the poor relation of the north.

All around, the contrast was one of beauty versus industry, and it even pervaded the river crossings. To our right, the original Waterloo Bridge was similar in hue to the one I knew, but with more arches and classical ornamentation than its successor, while Hungerford Bridge loomed ominously on the left, its grim iron latticework feeding Charing Cross Station with a narrow walkway clamped inhospitably to its side. I remembered the latter from when I was a kid, before it was replaced by the fancier Jubilee Bridge. Seeing it again sparked a disorienting travel sickness – nostalgia for a time one hundred and thirty years in the future.

'There's plenty going on,' said Mary. 'But that's just the Embankment.'

I looked again at the Strand, and realised that the river owed its breadth not just to the undeveloped south, but the incompleteness of the Victoria Embankment, which was still very much under construction. Huge dams, scaffolds, and heaps of stone were dotted along the north bank for 100 metres before Waterloo Bridge, crawling with ant-like workers and continuing beyond as the river curved out of sight towards Blackfriars.

'We're sure Rammell's railway doesn't run inside the Embankment?' I asked.

'That's where the District line goes,' said Mary.

'Yes, but not for another couple of years.' said Harold.

'Then maybe Rammell's works are part of the Embankment?' I suggested. 'A failed predecessor to the District?'

'Fotheringay indicated that it *crosses* the river,' stressed Emily.

'What about over there?' Monty pointed to the other side of Hungerford Bridge, where some works protruded from the south bank *into* the river.

This looked promising, so we headed back round the rear of the brewery, passing under the railway bridge to arrive at the wooden fence on Belvedere Road that marked the end of the works.

Stretched out ahead was a vast trench – at least ten metres wide, and a good 15 metres deep. It ran down College Street and continued into a dammed enclosure beyond the shoreline. On the surface either side, continuous banks of displaced soil and clay waited to re-take their place in the ground, interrupted only by a large hoist that was lowering piles of bricks to a pair of workers in the trench. Around them, several dozen others were laying the curved base of a small tunnel upon pre-set foundations. Working inland from the riverbank, they'd progressed about 20 metres, raising the sides of the tunnel to one-fifth of their intended height.

'Connecting Waterloo to Whitehall,' observed Harold, nodding back towards the concertina roof of Waterloo Bridge Station, looming over nearby houses, then pointing out a matching dam on the northern shore opposite. 'This has got to be it.'

We meandered to the riverside, where I peered into the steep, deep trench. The tunnel base ended 5 metres beyond the shoreline, giving way to a brick abutment that extended further into the space vacated by the river.

'Can I help you?'

I looked back. For a moment I feared it was Rammell himself, but this fellow wore muddy overalls and had a rasping cockney growl. He kept checking over his shoulder, as if in charge of the navvies.

'Name's Sid,' he declared. 'And you are?'

'I'm curious about how you're laying the tunnel,' I said, thinking on my feet. 'I heard something about sinking it into place?'

'What's it to you?'

'I'm just interested. I have a fondness for subterranean railways.'

'You're not spies?'

'Spies?'

'I've been told to be on the lookout.'

'Why would we be *spies*?'

The man looked us over. His expression softened as he decided that – whatever else we may have been – we weren't secret agents.

'What you've heard is right,' he said. 'We've just finished driving down the concrete piers, three of 'em, at equal points across the riverbed.'

I looked at the river. A steam dredger was currently in action, about thirty metres from the shore.

'Obviously, the piers don't rise to the level of the bed itself,' continued Sid, 'so we're now dredging out a channel that'll expose the foundations. Once that's done, we'll float the tunnel sections upriver from the Millwall Iron Works – five miles, give or take – then sink 'em down onto the piers.'

'They'll automatically land end-to-end?' I asked.

'Should do. After which, we pump out the water, secure all the seals – tube to tube, tube to pier – and use the shore-side cofferdams to join them up with the land-lying tunnels.'

'So efficient,' I enthused.

'It is. Though it doesn't stop him getting us to work Sundays!'

'Him?'

'Mr. Rammell. Word is, he's worried about money. Wants to make headway to save his scheme.'

'Presumably he's not working today?'

'Mr. Rammell's *always* working,' replied Sid, checking on his men again. 'You'll find him over at Whitehall right now. He's different to others. More committed. More frantic. Good sort, though. Heart in the right place.'

This was all we needed. Having thanked Sid for indulging our idle curiosity, we walked away, tantalised by these glimpses of our quarry: first, his ingenious underwater tunnel, matching his ingenious railway, and then the revelation that he was in a hurry, fearing for his finances. Was that the cause of the railway's eventual failure? And what of his commendable dedication? Was that the same ruthlessness that had led to his unthinkable crime? My skin ran cold, thinking how Sid and his men were working in cheerful oblivion of their boss's murderous past.

We crossed the river along the western walkway of Hungerford Bridge – a short-lived mirror of the eastern footbridge, Harold explained, which soon succumbed to a widening of the railway tracks – and studied the recessed wharves that accounted for most of the riverbank up to Westminster. Construction of the Embankment was yet to begin along this stretch, and the sense of diminishment was remarkable. There was no elegant, Parisian, tree-lined thoroughfare; none of the stately statues, lampposts or benches punctuating the pavement behind stone river walls; not even a hint of the spacious, well-kept gardens that buffered the river and road from the stern government buildings that were themselves yet be built.

It was all so unimposing that Rammell's doomed little railway looked surprisingly mighty. Superficially, the details mirrored those to the south. A cofferdam pushed back the water, and a trench sliced into the land from the riverbank. But as more of the route curved into view, it was obvious that the northern works were far more advanced. The tunnel was complete as it left the river and snaked inland along the base of the trench, scything through derelict wharves then veering to the left, intersecting nearby buildings – several of whose neighbours had been demolished to make way – before joining an established road. Here, the tunnel stopped but the trench continued, widening just short of Whitehall into two branches with a scaffolded platform between.

Stepping off the bridge, we skirted the works all the way to Whitehall. It was astonishing how much progress had been made on a project of which nothing would be remembered. For all that Rammell eventually faded into obscurity, there was no doubting that, at this very moment, he was in his prime: powerful and, apparently, merciless.

'We go no further,' I said, once we reached the edge of the station works. 'Not till we have a plan.'

The others agreed, though Harold seemed distracted. His gaze was directed over my shoulder.

'Could that be him?'

Conspicuously, we each turned to stare. To the left of the station was a single-storey wooden hut, out of which a suited, bearded, fraught-looking man was walking towards makeshift wooden steps that led into the belly of the station-to-be. He had a younger companion by his side, who was calmly explaining some point of detail.

'It's got to be him,' I said, watching the older fellow – who faintly resembled my old friend Tom – descend the stairs. 'The navvies look nervous.'

'Keep it up, men!' bellowed the man. He reached the platform and waited as his sidekick unfolded some plans.

'Whoever it is,' said Monty, 'he has a visitor.'

I looked up. Stepping into the construction site was another suited man, tall and brown-haired. He peered into the trench.

'Thomas,' he cried, providing the confirmation we needed. 'Do you have a moment?'

Rammell returned swiftly to the surface and began an animated conversation with his guest.

'Well we can't just stand here,' said Monty.

'No,' agreed Emily. 'But equally, we can't let him out of our sight.'

'Two options,' I pressed. 'We kidnap him, or we trick him.'

'Kidnap!' replied Mary. 'Stick him in a wagon, whisk him back to Sydenham!'

'A wagon, dear?' asked Harold.

'We hire one!'

'And the money to pay for it?'

'We threaten the driver! I can be pretty terrifying when I want to.'

'That I know,' said Harold. 'It's just . . . Don't you think people might notice?'

'We do it at night! Follow him home at dusk – can't be long now – then pounce when no one's looking.'

'Too risky,' said Monty. 'Remember: once exposed, we're done for. We have to keep it within the law.'

'So we trick him,' I said. 'Lure him to the carriage, take him down from there.' I thought again. 'But how to get him to the Palace without saying why?'

'We could pretend we're organising a gathering of its famous associates,' suggested Harold.

'Not a chance!' said Mary.

'But if we flatter him. Claim we're writing a Palace history, and want to photograph one of its most illustrious sons at the scene of his triumph?'

'He'll see through it, dear. And even if he didn't, he'd still refuse: feign modesty, say he's fixed on the future. He won't risk returning, under any circumstances.'

A short distance away, Rammell was still chatting to the brown-haired man. Conscious that we were starting to look suspicious, I stared at the ground and sought clarity. In a bustling, unfamiliar London, our challenge was starting to feel insurmountable.

'We have to be honest,' I concluded. 'Say why we're here; why he must co-operate.'

'And go the same way as the girl?' exclaimed Mary. 'The man is a murderer, Eric. Given the choice of sending us to the asylum, or saving his scheme, I hardly think—'

'Eric's right,' said Emily suddenly. 'Our only option is to be honest – and it can work, provided we don't reveal everything at once. His guilt is our greatest barrier, but also *his* greatest weakness, given that this precious railway of his could never survive exposure of the truth. If we disclose enough to get him worried, but not enough to get us committed, he'll surely *want* to investigate further: see if we're just rumour-mongers, like the girl, or if we really know enough to bring down his scheme. We just need to pitch it so that his curiosity makes him return to the Crystal Palace – and then we spring our trap.'

'Perfect,' I said. 'But first contact must be got right: sudden and short. We petrify him with dramatic details – things the girl couldn't know – then leave his fear to fester.'

'Just one of us, then,' said Mary. 'And whoever goes should disguise themselves.'

'Yes!' said Monty. 'Intrigue at all costs. The more tangible we seem, the less it will scare him.'

'What kind of disguise?' I asked.

'The disguise that comes most naturally,' said Mary. 'Just like the girl in the archive said.'

'Which was what?'

'Spirits, remember? Come from the carriage to get revenge.'

I looked towards Rammell – still in heated conversation – and nodded.

'Ghosts we are,' I said. 'And as ghosts we shall confront him.'

Chapter 29

'There's no point pretending,' said Sir Charles. 'The situation is unchanged from Monday. You need to accept that the Manchester plan is dead.'

Thomas pressed his foot into the soft, moist clay. Two and a quarter years had passed since the Crystal Palace trial, and still he was fighting to bring his vision to life.

'I accept it,' he said finally. 'I just don't understand it.'

'Indeed not,' said Sir Charles with a sigh. 'Alas, such is the way of the world. The pneumatic is the best solution, but that counts for little if one's timing and good fortune aren't just so.'

'What of the Mersey scheme?'

'Nothing further to the October meeting, but the appetite for our proposed route remains.'

'Good,' said Thomas. After the battles he had waged, and calamities he had averted, success – *deserved* success – was the only thing in his mind. If Manchester was indeed dead, it only heightened his determination that Brighton, Liverpool, and above all the Waterloo and Whitehall would triumph – followed by grander railways throughout the land, and even reaching beneath the English Channel, into France and beyond.

'How are things here?' asked Sir Charles, taking the steps into the works. 'This, after all, is the flagship.'

'It's going well,' said Thomas, following. 'We've been buoyed by hearing that the worst of the financial dip is over. The line should now be open, bringing in revenue, within six months.'

Sir Charles looked around. 'The station is going to be tremendously compact.'

'Such is the beauty of having the fan at Waterloo. This week we'll finish the foundations, commence the iron and glass shell, and install the staircase frames, zigzagging up to the street.'

'And the tunnel?'

'Complete between here and the river.'

Sir Charles walked to the mouth and inspected the brickwork.

'Magnificent.' His praise echoed back and forth. 'So much smaller than the Metropolitan.'

'Now its elegance is apparent for all to see,' said Thomas, 'the investors will be queuing up – all the more so, once we've floated the tubes upriver from Poplar. The sense of inevitability will be impossible to resist, even for the London and South Western.'

Sir Charles smiled, but Thomas quickly sensed some uncertainty lurking behind the studied façade.

'The risk of charging ahead is paying off,' he said pointedly. 'Just as we planned.'

'Indeed so.'

'The directors do understand that, don't they?'

'Please, Thomas: stop being so anxious.'

'But I'm right, am I not? You're worried about Thursday's meeting.'

'Thursday's meeting is a mere formality. We shall be given the extra time, allowing additional investors to shore us up, and all will be well.'

'Maybe I should come along.'

'No.' Sir Charles spoke firmly. 'It will be more effective with you here: consumed, as you say, by the inevitability of your work.'

'But you'll definitely see me afterwards?'

'Thomas, *please*.' Sir Charles was exasperated. 'I didn't come here to discuss work, and I don't especially care for your distrustful tone.'

There was a brief, difficult silence before Thomas bowed in apology.

'I'm sorry,' he said. 'I am quite exhausted. What *did* you want to discuss?'

'I was simply passing, and wanted to share a couple of remarkable things that have just occurred at the Crystal Palace.'

'You mean the fire?'

'Ah – you've already heard.'

'They say the whole of the north wing *and* the north transept have been destroyed.'

'Indeed so. Some of the most exquisite parts of the whole building. It really is the most awful tragedy. For me, the nation, and most of all for Sir Joseph, God rest his soul.'

'I can scarcely believe it myself,' said Thomas. 'One almost feels that the Palace should be indestructible. Do you have any idea how it started?'

'None whatsoever. I suppose it will come out in due course.'

'Let us hope that it does – for the sake of the rest of the building.'

'Indeed so.'

'What was the other thing you wanted to relay?'

Sir Charles thought for a second. 'Ah, yes,' he said, a smile returning to his face. 'You'll like this. I happened to bump into dear old Fotheringay, just as the blaze was taking hold. He was with a lunatic girl, handing her to the police. Apparently, she'd just come from the scene of your little railway experiment, claiming to have encountered some kind of rotting corpse.'

Thomas stared back, seized by horror as his partner roared with laughter.

'She's been plaguing the Palace for a while,' Sir Charles went on, 'obsessed by a spate of disappearances two years ago, and convinced that the vanished met with peril on *your* pneumatic railway.' He chuckled. 'Well, today she started claiming that not only was she attacked by the one of the bodies, bursting out of the earth, but that she's actually seen ghosts of the deceased above ground! Can you imagine? Isn't that just the most marvellous tale you've ever heard?'

Thomas saw that his hands were shaking. Needing support, he summoned Billy, who listened attentively as Sir Charles repeated the story.

'What a terrible accusation!' exclaimed Billy. 'It must be the speed we took up the trial and cancelled the revival, sir. Gave people ideas.'

'Or the girl is simply prone to waking terrors,' said Sir Charles. 'That was Fotheringay's appraisal. Either way, don't let it worry you.'

'It does worry me,' snapped Thomas. 'My reputation is paramount.'

'Then be assured,' said Sir Charles, 'not a soul takes her seriously.'

'How can you be certain?'

'Oh come on, Thomas. Would you trust the word of someone who's just been locked up in Effra Hall?'

Thomas stopped shaking. 'She has?'

'Of course she has! The Palace managers have been tempted to have her committed for some time, but this latest turn left them with no choice. Nothing for her but the madhouse!'

At last, Thomas managed a smile. 'A splendid story indeed.'

'I think so,' said Sir Charles, checking his pocket-watch. 'Well, I must get on. I shall see you again on Thursday. In the meantime, try to relax. It's not good to see you so irritable.'

Thomas nodded, grateful for the concern, and Sir Charles

headed back up to Whitehall. As soon as he was out of sight, both master and assistant retreated into the privacy of the tunnel.

'How did she know, Billy?' asked Thomas. 'So yes, the ghostly visions are obviously in her mind. But how did she know about it all to start with? I thought we had it covered, but if she's worked it out, what's to say others—'

He froze as he caught sight of a suited figure, treading funereally out of the blackness of the tunnel, head bowed so only the top of his hat was visible.

'Who are you?' demanded Thomas. 'How did you get down here?'

There was no reply. The intruder simply continued his approach. Thomas and Billy glanced into the daylight, thinking to summon some muscle-bound navvies, only to turn back and discover the stranger – head still lowered – right in front of them.

'What is it that you want?' asked Thomas, registering the trespasser's clothes: smart at first sight but, on closer inspection, torn and soiled.

'Read it!' His voice was wispy and frail. Still, he didn't reveal his face.

'Read what?'

The man shot out his arm with mechanical malice, striking Thomas in the gut. There was a piece of paper in his hand, which Billy duly snatched.

'For Rammell!'

'Mr. Rammell is my master,' said Billy, unfolding the note. 'What's for him is for—'

He stopped as he read the words on the page.

'What is it?' asked Thomas.

Billy looked up in alarm, first at his master, then at the stranger, who was walking unhurriedly away.

'It's nothing,' he said, folding up the note.

'Show me.'

'Best not, sir.'

'*Billy.*' Thomas shoved his assistant against the wall and grabbed the note. Heart thumping, he turned to the light.

Midnight tonight: the grounds of the Crystal Palace.
You know the mound – you know the matter.
Be there, or expect the worst for the Waterloo and Whitehall.

Thomas's heart filled with dread. Without a second thought, he sprinted into the darkness, the bricks multiplying his and Billy's footsteps so it sounded like a whole army was pursuing the stranger. The line veered to the right, diverging from Great Scotland Yard above, and the mouth of the tunnel came into view. The intruder was silhouetted against the dying winter light.

'Wait, or I'll have you arrested!' cried Thomas, but the fugitive's unfaltering progress continued.

'We'll have him cornered in the cofferdam,' said Billy.

The man reached daylight and turned to face them.

Thomas accelerated one final time, and was about to launch his attack when the stranger raised his arms and rose smoothly off the ground, vanishing from view.

Dumbstruck, Thomas and Billy ran into the cofferdam. For several seconds they stumbled aimlessly around the stony riverbed, unable to see more than a few inches over the peak of the tunnel mouth.

'He must've had accomplices,' said Billy. 'They must've escaped along the top of the tunnel.'

The two men dashed to the landside wall and climbed up to the surface, but the stranger was nowhere to be seen.

'Who on earth was he?' wondered Billy.

'There's only one way to find out,' said Thomas.

Billy turned to his master with fear in his eyes. 'Please don't say you're serious, sir.'

'We've no alternative.'

'Let me see the note again.'

Thomas handed over the paper.

'It must be the girl,' concluded Billy. 'Escaped already.'

'If that *apparition* was any kind of human, Billy, it was a man.'

'Apparition?'

'The girl said ghosts.'

'Please, sir. It's not—'

'You saw how sinister he was, Billy! Those clothes; the calmness of his gait; the smoothness of that escape; his disappearance into thin air!'

'Trust me, sir. He's just another harmless pest. Perhaps he knows the girl. Maybe he's upset for her, or promised to continue her mischief-making now she's locked up. Maybe he's just been inspired by her infamy? Either way, his game is obvious: for want of any real evidence to take to the police, he's trying to scare you into some kind of disclosure.'

Thomas felt his insides twist and tighten with anxiety. 'I have to go back,' he said defiantly. 'Either that man was a ghost, in which case there's no avoiding him, or he was real, in which case his escape proves he is not working alone. And as long as there's more than just a lone lunatic spreading these rumours, we have to find out what they know and how they know it.'

'And then?'

'Then, we have to stop them. Before they do us lasting damage.'

'But to return to the crime scene, sir, after such a cowardly threat? It would be an admission of guilt. In fact, I'll wager that's it. Some rat from Herapath's has heard about the girl and wants to test her claims. Or maybe it's a rival, digging dirt to halt us.'

Thomas gazed across the busy river as the sun sank behind him. He drew his hands exhaustedly over his face. There was only one possible solution.

'Oh Billy,' he said, smiling weakly as a plan consolidated in his mind. 'What would I do without you?'

Chapter 30

'You're absolutely certain you gave nothing away?' whispered Mary.

'For heaven's sake, dear,' answered Harold. 'He's already said, several times: it went perfectly.'

This was true. As the first of the skeletons' recruits, I had volunteered myself to confront Rammell – and it had certainly felt like an effective exchange.

'Then where on earth is he?' wondered Mary.

I glanced at my watch, which I'd reset earlier to Big Ben. It was ten past midnight. The sky was clear and the haunted mound shimmered in the moonlight.

'Surely curiosity alone must make him come and check?' said Emily.

We'd been huddled behind the tree for thirty minutes. Our collective excitement had armed us against the bone-chilling cold as we waited, ready to force the wretched Rammell into the corpses' lair. But now the temperature, and the doubts, were pressing upon us.

'He must be too terrified to return,' I reasoned.

'Or not terrified enough,' said Harold. 'Maybe the precedent of the poor girl has allayed his fears. Maybe he's confident that, if we did broadcast our knowledge, we'd be hotfooted to the asylum before we could cause any—'

'There!'

Mary pointed through the branches. A silhouetted figure

was approaching the peak of the hill, hugging itself for warmth.

Without delay, I gave the cue for us to tiptoe into a circle around the site of the carriage. Then, with everyone in position, I signalled the advance: slow, steady, heads bowed. Once we had progressed far enough to be noticed, I clicked my fingers and we stopped.

'You left us for dead!' I wheezed, inadvertently mimicking the skeletons. 'And the world shall know it – if you don't do exactly as we ask.'

The figure turned to face me, dropping his hands to his sides. I braced myself for an attempted escape, but instead he stepped calmly towards me – the wrong direction for the corpses to intervene – and chuckled merrily. Unsure what he intended, I issued the command.

'Pounce!'

The others leapt upon him, trying to drag him towards the carriage. But rather than making a quick, clean grab, they instead became hopelessly entangled with each other. Moments later, our fugitive crawled out the far side of the scrum.

'Stop right there!' I cried.

I dashed round and stamped on his hand.

The man winced and looked up, exposing his face to the moonlight.

'Wait . . .' I let his hand go. 'It's his sidekick.'

'Sidekick?' the young man replied. He stood up and puffed out his chest. 'My name is Billy Gray, and I have the honour of working for Thomas Webster Rammell, civil engineer and railway pioneer.'

'We demanded Rammell!' shouted Mary.

'Mister Rammell won't go out of his way for pranksters.'

'We're no pranksters.'

'Really?' The young man eyed us up and down. 'Then why are you pretending to be ghosts?'

'Because we are – at least inasmuch as we represent your

master's victims.'

'What do you mean, *victims*?' The young man wore a look halfway between amusement and anxiety. 'Same claptrap as that lunatic girl, is it? Bodies underground?'

'Bodies beneath us here,' I confirmed. 'Except it's not claptrap. We know, because we've seen them. What's more, they've spoken to us and demanded Rammell.'

Billy Gray exploded with laughter, holding up his hands as he tried to control his hysteria. 'I'm sorry, but I've never heard anything like it!' He turned through a circle, taking us all in. 'Nothing bad happened here. I was present each day of the experiment, and every single one passed utterly without—'

I grabbed his arm and dragged him across the frosty earth.

'If the pneumatic railway was such an unblemished triumph,' I said, arriving at the point of contact, 'how do you explain this?'

I stamped my feet and waited. Nothing happened. Gray began sniggering.

'If only you knew how absurd you look, mister. If only you could—'

'Fetch Rammell!'

The command sliced through the air, cutting him off to brutal effect. Panicking, he looked at each of us in turn, as if hoping to spot someone impersonating the corpses.

'Fetch Rammell!'

The voice again. This time he glanced at the ground.

'You hear it?' I asked.

'Hear what?' He looked up at me and stepped away. 'Whatever you think you're hearing, it's in your head.' He stumbled and fell. 'But I'll tell you what . . .' He scrambled back up. 'If I ever hear another word of this nonsense I'll have the lot of you committed. Thomas Webster Rammell is a great man. He deserves better than you lot trying to destroy all he's worked for. There was no accident, there are no bodies, there are no voices!'

He sprinted away. Mary was first off the mark in pursuit, but Harold held her back.

'You heard the skeletons, dear,' he urged. 'They want Rammell, and Rammell alone.'

'But if we capture his assistant, surely Rammell will come after?'

'Rammell, and the police. We'd be locked up before we could prove our claims.'

'But now he's going to know everything anyway!'

'We should have seen this coming,' I said. 'The man's clearly not one to be easily outwitted.'

'Why don't we just dig up the carriage?' asked Emily. 'Expose his crime, plain and simple?'

'Because the Palace is in its pomp,' said Mary. 'There's no way we could dig for long enough without being noticed. Besides, that's not what the victims want.'

'We're weak,' said Monty. 'Easily dealt with, as long as we're just five random strangers, making outrageous claims. We need some credibility; something to strengthen our threat.'

'What about the victims' relatives?' I said.

My words hung in the air, and we exchanged bewildered smiles. How on earth hadn't we thought of it sooner? It was almost as if we too had been duped by Rammell's cover-up; quite forgetting that there must be dozens of people nearby who were once close to the decaying corpses.

'Assuming he hasn't done away with them,' I reasoned, 'the cover-up must have taken one of two forms. Either he devised alternative stories to explain the deaths, or he confessed all and somehow bought the relatives' silence. If it's the first, we'll win them over just by telling the truth. But if he's actually persuaded them to keep quiet, we'll have to work harder, convincing them their loved ones aren't at rest. Either way, if we succeed, it'll give us all the momentum we need.'

My words met with enthusiastic agreement from the rest of the group. At last, the plan was settled.

'Finding the relatives means first establishing who was on board,' I said, as we set off towards the sleeping Palace.

'The newspapers?' suggested Harold. 'Rammell might have placed make-believe deaths on record to aid his credibility.'

'Too far-fetched,' replied Emily. 'You'd need bodies for a start, and we know there were none. Far more likely, he bought their silence. Which means looking for a record of passengers, not deaths.'

'Back to the archives, then,' said Monty. 'Except – would they have kept such a register?'

'Even if they did, Rammell would surely have destroyed it by now,' I said. 'No matter how honest he's been with the relatives, he'd still not want to leave any incriminating patterns, for fear of attracting someone whose silence *hadn't* been bought.'

We stopped and stared at one another. The same idea had seized us all.

'We need to find that girl,' I said.

***

Shivering, Thomas watched the five ghostlike strangers leave the little hill, so concluding the most heart-stopping half-hour of his life. Quite aside from witnessing the scuffles between the strangers and Billy – unable to hear, he had sensed their encounter hadn't gone well – there was the agony of revisiting the place where his dreams had so nearly died. From the day he had handed the land back to the Palace, it had been his intention never to return. Now, however, he was not only back but dealing with the very calamity that had brought him so close to ruin.

'Sir?'

Thomas jumped as Billy appeared from the shadows. 'Well?' he demanded. 'What happened? Should we follow them?'

Billy shook his head. 'On the contrary, sir.' The young man

walked his master away from the wood, down towards the Penge gate. 'We need to take you far away from the Crystal Palace and ensure you never come back. You're not safe here.'

'What?' Thomas stopped. 'Where's your confidence gone, Billy? I thought you were convinced they were just petty troublemakers?'

'I don't know what they are,' said Billy, tenser than Thomas had ever known. 'But it *really* isn't safe for you.'

'They know the truth?'

'They know the bodies are there.'

'How?'

Billy hesitated.

'They've seen them?'

'Not seen. *Heard*.' Billy led his master onto the moonlit lawns. 'They've heard the dead speak. And so have I.'

Thomas froze again. 'You have?'

'It sounds mad, sir, but . . .' Billy hesitated. 'When you stand in a particular position, it seems to prompt them to call out.'

'You mean . . .' Thomas was suddenly so scared – his teeth chattering so hard – that he could hardly get the words out. 'The dead are not at rest?'

'It would appear not, sir.'

Thomas stared at the crystalline earth. There was only one question left to ask.

'What did they say?'

'They said . . .' Billy gulped. 'Their exact words were: "Fetch Rammell."'

Thomas began walking towards the Penge exit. He was terrified by the thought of being targeted, and sickened by his misfortune. Every last thing over which he and Billy had had control – covering up the emotional and physical scars of the unfortunate occurrence – remained resolutely intact. Instead, it was the victims themselves who, in defiance of the physical laws that had shaped his life's work, were threatening to destroy him.

'*Fetch Rammell*,' he repeated. 'What do they want me for?'

'I have no idea, sir. But given that they're clearly not at rest, the only thing I can think of—'

'I can't dig them up, Billy. It would expose everything and destroy the Waterloo and Whitehall. Besides, why should I? It wasn't even my fault.'

'Right, sir. And for that reason alone, we never do as they ask. We never give them Rammell.'

'That won't stop them asking.'

'But they only ask when a particular patch of ground is trodden upon.'

Thomas looked sideways at his assistant. 'Your point being?'

'Well, sir, between you and Sir Charles we've got ample goodwill at the Palace to be allowed to erect fencing round that area – with perhaps some extra trees and soil to stifle the voices. When they ask why, we say we felt duty-bound, two years on from the trial, to check on the stability of the ground. Having found it wanting, we're now making it good. And if anyone links it to the girl, we'll say her witterings reminded us that an inspection was overdue.'

'You believe the ghosts will be constrained by mere fencing?'

'Believe me, sir. Whoever those people were, they have no special powers.'

'What if they go to the relatives?'

'The relatives will be as dependable as ever – as long as they're not brought back to hear the voices. That's why we must get the fencing up immediately. I'll return later, as soon as it gets light, with some of the navvies from Whitehall. We'll have the whole thing done by midday, then I'll explain to the Palace once it's in place.'

They arrived at the gate. Thomas looked back at the shimmering Palace – still an exquisite sight, notwithstanding the damage done to its northern reaches.

'How I love it, Billy. And how sad to know I shall never return.'

But even as he spoke, his pounding heart eased. He would miss the Crystal Palace as he missed Paxton himself, yet its unsurpassable beauty would never lure him back. In his heart, the whole building had blazed away and melted to nothing: destroyed by the fire in his mind, and the deed he had done in the Palace's shadow.

Chapter 31

'This is the place,' said Mary. Clutching the girl's scrapbook in one hand, she knocked on the door with the other. 'Home of Hattie Fielding, wife of Frank.'

It was twelve hours after our midnight encounter with Rammell's flunky. We were on one of the roads surrounding Sydenham Station, standing outside a handsome new terraced house. The carriage – and in it, this poor woman's rotting husband – was less than a mile away. Somehow, the thought made Rammell's crime feel more chilling than ever.

The door opened and a fair-skinned young woman appeared. Her dark hair was tied back in a bun, and she wore a thick, brown winter dress, overlaid with a cream apron. She looked like she was in her early thirties. Beside her was a small boy, aged about four or five.

'Hattie Fielding?' asked Mary.

The woman nodded, peering quizzically at the rest of us.

'If you don't mind, madam, we've got some questions about your late husband.'

A look of alarm spread across Hattie's face. 'My husband?'

'That's right.'

She began shaking her head. 'No,' she said. 'Not interested.' She stepped back, about to swing the door shut, when the young boy spoke up.

'Questions about papa?' he asked.

The intervention seemed to catch Hattie off-guard. Her lower lip trembled.

'What kind of questions?'

'It's alright, Edward,' said Hattie. 'I'll find out. But you should go and play.'

She gestured for us to follow her up the stairs, sending her son into a disorderly kitchen, where another young mother took him under her wing. Already it was clear that Hattie knew something her son didn't: further confirmation, on top of what we'd read in the girl's scrapbook, that the victims' relatives were complicit in Rammell's cover-up.

'Don't tell me,' she said sternly once we had gathered in her room: a grotty, empty place with a faded photo of a young man by the bed. 'You're here because of that girl.' She looked us over. 'Well, you're embarrassing yourselves. That devious little witch spouts nothing but poisonous, hurtful nonsense. Now she's locked up you should know better than to follow her example.'

'Please, just give us a hearing,' said Harold. 'Then, if you want us to leave, we will happily do so.'

Hattie turned to the window.

'How did your husband die, Mrs. Fielding?' asked Mary.

Hattie's frame stiffened. 'In a fire. At a friend's house. A little over two years ago.'

'What proof do you have?'

'All the proof I need.'

'Was there a burial? Can we visit his grave?'

Hattie locked her hands behind her back. 'There was no body, so there was no burial.'

Mary took a few seconds to compose herself. 'What if we said that, in truth, your husband died on the pneumatic railway trial at the Crystal Palace?'

Hattie's forehead thudded against the window pane.

'And what if we knew this because we have encountered his remains?'

Hattie began shaking. 'I would ask you to leave.'

'Then leave we will,' said Harold. 'Although, with the greatest of respect, your lack of concern is startling.'

'Startling?' There were tears in the widow's eyes as she turned to face us. 'Why, when I have heard such claims before – from a certified lunatic? Why, when I have never had *any* reason to doubt the truth?'

'No reason to doubt the truth?' Mary opened the scrapbook.

'What is that?'

'It belongs to the girl you keep mentioning – Elizabeth Lovell, who was yesterday committed to Effra Hall lunatic asylum. We obtained it from her this morning, promising her freedom in return.'

Hattie's tired eyes narrowed yet further in alarm. '*Promised?*'

Mary nodded. 'These are the notes she made about the nine disappearances that occurred on or around 31st October, 1864 – and how each of their closest relatives responded when asked what became of their loved ones.'

'They all died in fires,' said Hattie abruptly. 'In each case no remains were found.' She nodded. 'The little devil told me that herself.'

'You don't find the coincidence odd?' asked Harold.

Hattie took a shallow, unsteady breath. 'There is only one absolute truth in all of this, which is that my dear Frank couldn't possibly have died on the pneumatic railway because he'd never have ridden it to begin with.' She looked at our doubtful faces. 'I mean it. Frank had a lifelong fear of going undergr—'

Her eyes landed on me. A second later, her jaw dropped open.

'What is it?' I asked.

'Dear God no . . .' Her terrified stare was fixed on my brown silk waistcoat. 'That button . . .'

She reached out a quivering hand, pointing to the single column of buttons. At first sight, there was nothing unusual about the arrangement. But as I peered closer, I saw that the lowest button was black, whereas all the others were a dark shade of brown. Slowly, she looked me up and down, taking in the whole of the outfit I was wearing. The tears started to roll from her eyes.

I couldn't think what to say. Here I was, appearing before a widow like the ghost of the husband she'd lost. The terror in her eyes shot right through me, and I felt an overpowering chill – as though I was as dead as the man whose clothes I wore.

'So now you see,' said Emily. 'We *were* down there with the corpses, and we've come back up so you can help us put it right.'

But still Hattie was unresponsive, and I began to sense something more in her horror. After all, assuming she had been in on the cover-up, the appearance of Frank's clothes – though emotionally charged – changed nothing.

'It's all in perfect condition,' she said, trembling. 'As fine as the last day I saw him.'

She spoke these words with a scary mix of incomprehension and iron-clad certainty. Like the ghost I was to her, I felt the truth bearing down on me with unavoidable force.

'You do know what happened?' I asked softly.

Hattie's face was as pale as those of the corpses in the carriage.

'I know of the accident,' she said. 'I know, because Rammell told me. But he never . . .'

The poor woman trailed off, breaking into sobs and looking away.

'It's alright, dear,' said Mary. 'Take your time.'

For over a minute, Hattie just wept, and the rest of us stared down at the patterned carpet in renewed disbelief. Finally, she drew up her shoulders and took a deep breath.

'The day he came here,' she said, turning back, 'he worked a kind of magic on me. I mean, yes, it was devastating. But his honesty blunted my anger. I should have gone to the police, but instead I just listened as he described what had happened, the tears welling up in his eyes.' She shook her head at the recollection. 'His sorrow seemed so sincere that to act against him would have compounded the crime. It was just an accident, after all. He wasn't to blame and, in his way, he was suffering as much as me.'

'How so?' asked Mary.

'Because his life's work was under threat. The air-powered railway: the safest form of travel ever invented.'

'But whose fault was it, if not Rammell's?'

'The tunnellers'. That was the crucial distinction. The tunnel collapsed because of shoddy building work – not any failing of the pneumatic method.' She sat on the bed and pointed to the armchair in the corner. 'I remember it so vividly – him sitting there, wiping away the tears, panicking that people wouldn't recognise the distinction. He worried that the disaster would be perceived as a failing of his system, meaning his important new lines – saving many thousands of lives – would never get built.'

'He made himself out to be as much of a victim as you?' I said.

Hattie thought for a moment. 'I suppose he did.'

'And that was all?' asked Mary. 'That persuaded you to keep quiet?'

Hattie said nothing.

'Was there money, too?'

'Yes, there was money. And yes, I needed it. Still do.'

'And still it comes?'

Hattie nodded. 'Regular as clockwork. But also . . .'

'Also what?'

She looked up. 'Also, it was Frank. He had no professional interest in the pneumatic railway – he worked as a post office clerk – but he loved it more than anything. It went back to his older brother dying of emphysema in 1846, not long after starting work at London Bridge. Frank was still young then. Highly impressionable. At the same time as steam was killing his brother, the old Croydon atmospheric was running through Sydenham.' She smiled at the memory. 'Well, you can imagine what the contrast did to his young mind. When Rammell started trying to revive air power, Frank was a keen supporter. We visited the miniature passenger trial in Battersea, and he adored every second. Even persuaded me to take a ride – despite being pregnant with Edward – and yes, it was quite magnificent. So when the pneumatic trial came to the Crystal Palace, we went many times – and we had been planning to go again that final day. But the weather was so terrible . . .' She looked out of the window. 'I tried persuading Frank not to bother, but it was no use. Edward and I stayed here, while he went off on his own.'

She stared into space. None of us dared say a word.

'So you see,' she continued finally. 'When Rammell came here, saying what had happened, and what was at stake, all I could think about was Frank. What he'd want me to do. So I accepted Rammell's apology. And I went with him to the other relatives, urging them not to jeopardise the air-powered railway either. After all, our loved ones were gone; the damage was done—'

Her eyes landed again on my waistcoat.

'The damage was done,' she repeated, voice cracking, 'yet Frank's clothes are intact.'

There was a brief, breathless pause, and then she threw her head forward and began sobbing again. Mary and Emily went to her aid, embracing her from either side, as the full extent of Rammell's cruelty became clear.

'How could he have been so cowardly?' she asked, the words coming in fits and starts. 'To come here, to this very room, where we raised our son, and tell me that the carriage was destroyed with the tunnel: flattened by bricks and earth, taking the passengers with it – crushed, suffocated, dead in an instant. When in truth . . .'

She pointed again at my suit, and there was another moment's hiatus. This time, however, Hattie rose in silence and went to the window, pressing her open palms against the glass.

'What must he have suffered?' she whispered. 'What must they all have gone through? The waiting for help, trusting that we would rescue them. And then the realisation that we weren't going to come.' Her voice was regaining its strength; despair alchemising into anger. 'Above all, the asking why: why haven't our loved ones saved us? Because they can't? Because they won't? Or because they were lied to?'

'The latter,' I said firmly.

She turned towards me. 'But how can you know?'

'Because they – or rather their *spirits* – have told us. "Fetch Rammell" was their instruction. That's why we're here today. We have come from the buried carriage to ask for your help – on your husband's behalf.'

She looked again at our clothes. 'What do you mean, *their spirits*?'

Realising that the time had come for a full explanation, I suggested she take a seat, then began by describing my first encounter with the skeletons.

By the time I'd finished, we were halfway to the next relative's house.

Chapter 32

'Over here!'

Thomas looked up to where a series of scaffolds jutted into the Thames, supporting four immense iron tubes. It was two and a half days since his midnight return to the Crystal Palace and, thanks to Billy's continuing heroics, his mind was now fully re-focused on the matter at hand – hence his visit to Poplar.

'Magnificent!' he shouted, addressing a group of men stationed in the mouth of the most distant tube.

'Climb up and take a closer look!' came the reply.

Thomas set off over the wet, gravelly earth. He gazed proudly at each tube in turn: the first, with just a portion of the frame in place; the second, with the iron complete; the third, also fully framed but sporadically thickened by external brickwork; and lastly, the fully complete fourth.

Steadying himself against the winds that buffeted the wooden latticework, he climbed up to the platform, where the diminutive Joseph Samuda – grey hair, perfectly angular sideburns – introduced his engineers, then led them all into the tube.

'224 feet long,' he explained, 'weighing 1,000 tons; internal diameter 12 feet 9 inches.' He drummed his fingers on the side. 'Three-quarter-inch boiler-plate iron surrounded by four layers of brickwork, bound by cement and hoops of angled iron, with another inner layer to be added once she is upriver and about to be sunk.' He smiled proudly. 'Quite the most secure tunnel you are ever likely to come across.'

'When can we float it?' asked Thomas. 'All three piers are now in place, and the channel should be dredged within the week.'

'Well, we're very nearly finished with it here. All that's required is to seal it, then lift it onto the river, and tow it upstream. That'll require some careful timing, but . . .' Samuda puffed out his cheeks. 'I'd say we could be with you within a fortnight.'

'A fortnight?'

'A fortnight, ten days. As I say, sir, it's not a short tube – and it's not a quiet river.'

'I want it within the week. And no more than three days to lay the brickwork once it's there. We have to be seen to be making—'

'Sir!'

Thomas turned to see Billy's silhouette approaching down the tube.

'Awfully sorry, sir, but you're needed outside.'

Thomas saw the anxiety in his assistant's eyes. He guessed immediately at the cause of the interruption, and an understanding nod from Billy confirmed it.

'I'm sorry, gentlemen,' he said, the tension returning to his muscles. 'I'll be back as soon as I can.'

'It's alright,' said Samuda. 'We shall begin hauling the bulkheads into position.'

Thomas thanked his associate and walked away with Billy, towards the landside mouth. 'They're here?'

'I'm afraid so, sir.'

'How did they find us?'

'Must've asked at Whitehall.'

'Damn it, Billy. This can't be allowed to happen! The more they ask after us, the more they're seen with us, the more people will suspect! We *have* to lock them up. Either that or silence them once and for all!'

'*Please*, sir.' Billy grabbed his master, just short of the daylight. 'Our greatest threat is your temper. No harm can be done with that fence in place. You must remember that as you step outside.'

Sensing a new dimension to Billy's alarm, Thomas alighted onto the scaffold, and looked down to see not only the five strangers, as expected, but an *additional* group behind them.

'Who are they?' he asked, but he had already begun counting, and the total rendered Billy's reply redundant. Here were the four people with whom he had made peace to cover up the deaths of the nine passengers on his experimental railway: their individual presence dangerous enough; their being together even worse.

'What do you want?' he shouted.

'Come down, and we'll tell you!' shouted an old woman, at the front of the group of strangers.

Limbs filling with the dual rushes of panic and anger, Thomas descended the ladder and ushered his visitors away from the busy factory entrance.

'I told you never to go looking for each other,' he raged at the bereaved relatives. 'It benefits no one! What's done is done, so why threaten my railways, the future of *your* city, just for the sake of—'

He stopped, perturbed by the relatives' silence. He looked to the troublemakers. 'I take it this is your handiwork?'

'Only partly,' said the old woman. 'After we'd spoken to Mrs. Fielding, the rest was all her own work.'

Thomas turned to the pale young woman he remembered as Hattie Fielding. 'Well?'

Hattie stood firm, saying nothing. Thomas felt his fear rising; and with it, his fury.

'You do realise this is the end of the money?' he said, addressing the relatives as one. 'If you don't all leave, this minute, and pretend this never happened, then I'll stop—'

Hattie suddenly charged at him, grabbing the lapels of his coat and spinning him up against the factory wall.

'"What's done is done,"' she cried. Her whole body was

quaking; her grip was unyielding. 'Those are the words you used to us all. And it is true – now. But it wasn't true then.'

Thomas felt his throat tighten. He was having difficulty breathing. He tried pushing Hattie away, but instead she flung him to the ground.

'It wasn't true, yet you said it anyway.'

What's done is done. Thomas thought back, as Billy helped him to his feet. The words resonated with something obscure: a sub-conscious fear, dismissed before it had ever surfaced into worry.

'I never lied to you,' he said. 'That was the whole point. I was honest. Foolishly so. I came to you of my own volition! I made no efforts to dissemble—'

Hattie pointed to one of the strangers: a young man, unremarkably attired in a gentleman's coat, waistcoat and trousers.

'Those clothes belong to my husband,' she declared, loudly and precisely, as if shielding herself from emotion. 'The waistcoat has a unique flaw which means it can be no one else's. He wore it on the day of the accident. Its existence above ground proves that these people had contact with the bodies. And its condition is proof that you lied.'

Thomas's confusion was slowly crystallising into terror. He looked at the ill-fitting clothes on the other strangers as each outfit was identified by one or other of the bereaved relatives.

'We now know the truth, Mr. Rammell,' continued Hattie, the poise in her voice faltering. 'The tunnel collapsed, but the carriage did not.' She took a deep breath, but it was clearly no use. 'Even while you were confessing to us . . .' Her eyes were filling with tears. 'Even while you were in my and Frank's bedroom, saying "what's done is done", even while I set off with you, helping to persuade these other poor people that you were right, even while they and I began convincing our friends and families about the made-up fires . . .' She sniffed back the sobs. 'Even then, Frank and the others were still alive – sitting there, in the carriage, wondering when we were going to rescue them.'

Thomas looked from Hattie to the other relatives – two ladies with their heads bowed, convulsing as they wept; the other, a stocky middle-aged man named Walter, staring dry-eyed back at him, his expression dark, fixed and fierce.

Somehow, Thomas needed to formulate a defence, but his mind was deadlocked by a vision of the nine passengers, lined along either side of the carriage, dying a quite different death to the one that had haunted him for so long.

'Imagine the suffering, Mr. Rammell,' said Walter, pushing past Hattie to bear down upon the engineer, who found himself incapable of moving away. 'Imagine the pain. You can't, can you? You can't even *imagine* what it must have been like. The hunger, the thirst, the suffocation . . .'

Walter raised his fist, about to land a blow, but Billy barged him away before he could strike. The two men began scuffling on the ground. For several seconds, Thomas simply looked on, as though the whole thing weren't really happening – paralysed by disbelief, both at what had happened, and that he, civil engineer, irreproachable force for good, driven by concern for the common man, was responsible.

'Billy!' he ordered. As he spoke, the guilt came flooding in, and he felt suddenly dizzy. 'Leave him!'

But Billy wouldn't listen. Instead, Thomas stumbled forward and pulled the two men apart. He lifted Walter up and looked him in the eye.

'I accept it, alright?' he said. 'I was wrong about what happened.'

There was a long pause as, one by one, the three other relatives came into view.

'But believe me, I never lied. All I've ever known about engineering made it certain: there was no way that one little carriage could have withstood the tunnel's collapse. It was too flimsy, too solitary, to fight such powerful forces.'

'Were you really that scientific?' asked Walter, the

bitterness in his stare matched by the venom in his voice. 'Or did you just convince yourself of whatever made it easiest to win our silence?'

'It was all about the engineering,' said Thomas. He was starting to tremble.

'But isn't an engineer's first duty to check?' demanded Hattie. 'To double-check? To triple-check? To ensure not the slightest thing is left to chance?'

Thomas raised his quivering hands to his head, desperately trying to steer his thoughts. 'If any part of me had honestly believed that any part of the carriage could have been salvaged, then clearly I would have done so.'

'Clearly?' repeated Walter.

Thomas no longer felt in control of his words. 'I am a good man, Walter,' he said weakly. 'I am not, nor have I ever been, in the business of making people suffer.' His voice cracked. 'My whole life's work has been a quest to—'

It was no good. The self-doubt was self-evident. He turned away and fell against the factory wall, letting the tears pour from his eyes. No matter how hard he tried, he simply couldn't tell what was true. Yes, he had been adamant on the plane of superficial reasoning, but was there not a deeper level? One on which he had deceived himself, silencing doubts so swiftly that he couldn't be sure if they had ever existed? Certainly, it wasn't *like* him to act so recklessly; at least, not where people's lives were concerned. But was it not that very belief that he was incapable of evil, fuelled by his beneficent work and the knowledge that the accident wasn't his fault, that had made it so easy to dismiss even the possibility that the carriage had survived?

'You didn't know.'

Thomas glanced up. Billy was beside him, whispering in his ear.

'I mean it, sir. Trust your memory like I trust mine. Neither of us knew. Perhaps we should have done. We certainly should have checked. But our errors were for the right reasons, and that's why we mustn't falter.'

Thomas was about to protest – to explain the extent of his sudden uncertainty – when Billy turned back to the bereaved.

'Have you gone to the police?' he asked.

'Not yet,' replied Hattie.

'Then don't. Whatever our dereliction of duty, there's as little merit in going to the police now as—'

'We've no intention of involving the police,' said Walter. 'This isn't about conventional justice.'

Thomas turned to face them. He felt goosebumps creep up his arm.

'"Fetch Rammell," our loved ones ordered,' said Hattie. 'So that is what we're here to do.'

Led by Walter, the bereaved relatives began closing in on Thomas, who wasn't sure whether to surrender or run.

'*Sir*,' urged Billy. 'You must hear what I said to you.'

Still, Thomas didn't move.

'Don't let your emotions scramble your better judgement. We've come too far.'

'At least allow me to apologise!' shouted Thomas.

The advancing assailants stopped.

'Please listen to me.'

'Why should we?' asked Walter.

'Because it's as I explained originally, only more so, for we are that much closer to success. If you condemn me, you will also destroy what I represent: not just the *idea* of pneumatic railways, but the Waterloo and Whitehall Railway and many others like it.' He turned to Hattie. 'Your husband understood this. He recognised—'

'How dare you!' yelled Hattie. 'You have no right to invoke Frank's memory!'

Thomas hesitated. If he was to stand any chance of success, he had to choose his words more carefully.

'I am responsible for the death of your loved ones,' he went on, feeling desperately short of breath. 'I accept that, and I am not asking for forgiveness. But you need to know what will happen if you expose my crime – how many more thousands of lives will be lost by allowing underground steam to spread unchecked through—'

***

'Wait!' I exclaimed. 'I've just realised.'

Rammell stopped, and the relatives looked towards me.

'Realised what?' asked Hattie.

'All these promises about the future; everything he's prattling on about – how his railway will transform the city, what'll happen if it *doesn't*. Utter rubbish!'

Rammell pretended to chuckle, but was obviously exasperated by my intervention. 'What kind of an argument is that?' he said, addressing the relatives. 'Who are these people anyway?'

'We're from the future,' replied Emily. 'We travelled back from the 20th and 21st centuries, propelled by the dead passengers in the carriage. And we can all testify that your precious pneumatic railway never gets built.'

'Never gets built?' repeated Rammell. 'And why exactly would that be?'

'No one can remember,' I said. 'That's just how forgotten you are.' I turned to the bereaved. 'But as of 2013, no air-powered underground railway has ever been built in London – which means you can obey the corpses' commands with a clear conscience.'

Rammell looked rapidly at each of us in turn, panic in his eyes, before facing the relatives with an awkward smile.

'Look,' he said, 'you have my word that the Waterloo and Whitehall is in perfect health. You need only step round the corner, see our tunnel taking shape, to know that success is inevitable. Why on earth would you trust these maniacs ahead of the evidence of your own eyes?'

'Well they have clearly been into the carriage,' answered

Hattie. 'And they insist your assistant heard the cry of "Fetch Rammell".'

'So I did,' conceded Billy Gray, 'and the restlessness of the dead is indeed extraordinary. But we have all heard such tales before; whereas time-travel?'

'But it's not the first time they've mentioned it. They've told many strange tales of the future. In particular, the passengers' curse – how, when ignored, they set fire to the Crystal Palace and its grounds.'

'A convenient little story,' sneered Gray, 'all too obviously inspired by the events of Sunday last.'

'But why would we make that up?' I asked. 'Why would we invent any of it?'

'Need I really explain? We all know the rivalry between different railway schemes. Every major undertaking of our time, including the old atmospheric, has been subject to some form of chicanery, be it espionage or straight-out sabotage.'

'It's true,' agreed Rammell. 'There are dozens of people desperate to scupper my pneumatic railway. I can quite believe that on hearing about that mad girl, any number would have dispatched their stooges to—'

'Enough!' shouted Walter suddenly. 'Enough of these endless excuses! We will not be reasoned with any longer.'

'But—'

'It's no use, Mr. Rammell,' said Hattie. 'Now we know the truth, everything else is irrelevant. All that matters is that our loved ones needed us when you deserted them, and we let them down.' She drew in a deep breath. 'We're most certainly not going to let them down again.'

Walter strode forward and grabbed Rammell by the shoulders. Feeling weirdly exalted that the moment had come at last, I seized the engineer's assistant while Hattie issued the orders.

'Emily – pass me the rope so I can tie these two villains up. Harold and Mary – head back to the wagon and tell them we'll be there presently.'

'But you must allow me to finish what I've started!' protested Rammell.

'And so you can, once you've faced your—'

***

'*Most* peculiar.'

The voice stopped Thomas's assailants in their tracks. One by one, they stepped aside to reveal Sir Charles Fox – standing a few feet away, examining the scene with a puzzled expression.

'Good day, one and all,' he said. 'Thomas, I was just wondering if we might speak briefly in private?'

Thomas needed no second invitation. 'Of course,' he replied, smiling anxiously at the relatives as he led Sir Charles around the corner. 'Incidentally,' he whispered, once they were out of sight, 'I know that all looked a little strange, but it's nothing you need worry about.'

'I'm not worried about it,' said Sir Charles. 'And nor should you be.'

They stopped. A chill crept through Thomas's body.

'I've just come from meeting the directors.'

'But the meeting's not until tomorrow.'

'They brought it forward.'

'Why?'

Sir Charles frowned. 'There's no easy way to say this.'

'Say what?'

'They're demanding construction cease immediately.'

'Cease?' repeated Thomas. 'For how long?'

'Indefinitely – with only a remote chance it will ever continue.'

Thomas blinked. After the turmoil of his previous exchange, this felt like some kind of nightmarish joke.

'I'm so very sorry,' said Sir Charles. 'I can only begin to imagine how this must feel.'

'But why?'

'Put simply, it's our failure to persuade the London and South Western to take a formal interest – and our inability to attract any more investors in their place.' He shrugged in weary resignation. 'Ultimately, it's just timing. Two years ago, we would have succeeded, but the financial crisis has taught people to stop speculating. We've reached a point where there's an established way of operating and the appetite for untested methods, however superior, has been sated. The focus now is squarely on application.'

'All of which I already know,' said Thomas. 'My question is: why has it failed now when, on Sunday, you assured me of the directors' confidence?'

Sir Charles touched his knuckles together. 'The truth is, I was a little dishonest. I believed it was in the railway's best interests to shield you from their deepening doubts.'

'The railway's best interests?'

'Really, Thomas: it's so awfully hard to say this. But as the financial crisis has unfolded, you have become ever more unbusinesslike in front of the directors. Your regard for practical matters has been eclipsed by an exasperated belief that the pneumatic must simply be *allowed* to work because you, and it, are somehow deserving. Now of course I sympathise, but the directors, for all their public spirit, are money men at heart. While your enthusiasm is inspiring to a point, it has lately tipped the other way: reinforcing their doubts that, in the present climate, this whole endeavour is too risky.'

'How can you be sure?'

'Because I have seen it, and my experience told me it had to stop.'

Thomas stared at the earth. His anger was neutered by the numbness of shock.

'So that's it? With all these extraordinary works completed, you are sincerely saying that the Waterloo and Whitehall Railway will never come to—'

He stopped as the two upheavals of the past hour collided in his mind.

'I am not blaming you,' said Sir Charles. 'And you must not blame yourself. Your behaviour hasn't *caused* the scheme's demise. Keeping you from the directors was merely my last, best hope of saving the railway. You do understand?'

Thomas wasn't listening. He was thinking back to the strangers' determined claim that the Waterloo and Whitehall never came to be built, and reeling at the coincidence of prophecy and fulfilment.

'I'll leave you to your thoughts, and go and tell Samuda.' Sir Charles set off towards the four giant tubes.

Immediately, Thomas summoned his assistant and updated him on the news.

'So the railway is dead anyway,' said Billy, once he'd heard all the details.

Thomas looked out over the river and let out a despairing sigh. 'I can't believe this is happening, Billy. After so many years, so many battles fought, the whole enterprise has collapsed in a matter of minutes. The railways themselves are done for, and the relatives are not to be silenced again – meaning you and I are going to jail, or worse.'

For a moment nothing was said. There was only the sound of the water, lapping softly against the shore.

'Are you sure they'll be the consequences, sir?' asked Billy. 'I mean, I agree – if we remain passive. But if we take control, who knows what reprieves we might expect?'

Thomas smiled at his assistant's naiveté. 'Ah, Billy. You're so very resilient. But from what Sir Charles said, the directors—'

'I'm not talking about that; I'm talking about the other problem. Think of the first time you met the relatives – how you won their co-operation, against insuperable odds. It's proof of your power.'

'My power?'

'The fact that you are a great man, working for the common

good. It's powerful because it's true, sir, and it can work for us again.'

'You think I should confess? Go to the police, or the papers, and admit what happened? How my lofty ideals led me astray?' Thomas puffed out his cheeks. 'Well, I suppose it might at least sway a jury to look kindly on us.'

'It could do more than that, sir.' Billy had a glint in his eye. 'It could rescue more than just you and me.'

Starting to understand, Thomas felt a smile creep across his face.

'The thing is, sir, it will require more than just confession. That might save us from the gallows, or even jail, but we'd still walk away defeated. To *really* turn it around, to win not just the world's pardon but its *blessing*, we need something bigger.'

'Bigger?'

'A gesture. A big, bold, penitent act which conveys your conflicting passions: your fathomless regret, yes, but also the courageous conviction behind what happened.'

Thomas turned to Billy. His grin was broadening by the second. 'But that's absurd.'

'Indeed, sir. So absurd, it just might work.'

'All done,' declared Sir Charles, returning from his conversation with Samuda. 'Naturally, he's shattered by the news, so I wonder if—'

Sir Charles broke off as the relatives appeared from around the corner, standing a short distance away in evident impatience.

'Who are those people?'

'Never mind that now,' said Thomas. 'All you need to know is that something extraordinary has happened; something that could change everything. I can't explain, otherwise the impact won't be so great. But please, do me this last favour: go back to the directors, and ask for one more day.'

Sir Charles shook his head. 'I'm sorry, Thomas. Their minds are fixed.'

'I don't mean an extra day's construction. We'll down tools immediately. Just ask them for one day's grace before they start closing us down. After all our work, and especially after you excluded me at the last, surely you can afford me this final courtesy?'

'One day's grace?'

'That's all.'

Sir Charles deliberated for a few seconds. 'One more day,' he said finally. 'What harm can it do?'

Delighted, Thomas bid him farewell until Friday, then walked over to the relatives.

'My apologies,' he said. 'Now, where were we?'

Hattie held up a line of rope.

'Ah yes, of course.' Thomas smiled and held out his hands. 'Here you go.'

The relatives looked at each other in bafflement.

'You're not going to fight?' asked Hattie.

Thomas shook his head. 'I have decided to do exactly as you wish.'

'You'll go back to the Crystal Palace? You'll hand yourself over to the bodies?'

'I'll go back to the Palace, and I shall do as they wish me to do – which, I assume, means laying them to rest. The only thing I ask is that you let me do it my way.'

'And what exactly does that entail?' asked Walter.

'I'd like to wait until Friday. The extra day will enable me to make the occasion as sombre and respectful as possible.'

'I should bloody well hope so.'

'Then I have your blessing to do as I see fit?'

'You have my blessing to do what's right by the dead!'

'Why the change of mind?' asked Hattie.

Thomas lowered his hands and looked her straight in the eye. 'Suddenly, Mrs. Fielding, the clouds in my mind just parted. "Fetch Rammell," the dead demanded – so Rammell they shall have.'

Chapter 33

'We had fun yesterday,' I said to Hattie, as we walked towards the Crystal Palace from her house in Sydenham. 'I can't explain how much it meant to each of us. A whole day, exploring the Palace and its gardens. It was like a dream come true. Thank you so much for the tour.'

'You're welcome,' said Hattie with a smile. 'It really was the least I could do.'

Ahead of us, the friends and families of the deceased mingled with my fellow time-travellers. In the forty-eight hours since we'd confronted Rammell at Poplar, the four relatives whom the engineer had paid to explain away the nine disappearances on his behalf had finally confessed the truth to their nearest and dearest. In all, fifteen bereaved individuals were attending today's event, each decked in the black of mourning. As for us, with no money to spend on new outfits, we'd been forced to wear the corpses' old garments. It felt odd but also fitting: a show of solidarity with the stricken passengers, to whom we'd become so close.

Reaching the edge of the Palace grounds, we joined the hordes flocking towards the Sydenham gate: a surprising number, even on such an enticingly sunny day.

'Did he take much persuading?' I asked.

'Persuading?' said Hattie.

'Digging during the day, at midday specifically – *the* most public time. I assumed you'd demanded it.'

'We would have done, but as with the day, he chose the

time himself. Said he felt duty-bound to make it as public as possible.'

'You think his intentions are that straightforward?'

'I don't know what to think. But I trust my Frank. He's in charge, as far as I'm concerned. As long as he's happy with what happens, I'll be happy too.'

We entered the Palace grounds and turned right, uphill, towards the carriage. The two of us became separated as the crowds forced themselves onto the same, ever-narrower paths – not a single person peeling off to view the fountains or the monsters, or to stroll around the cricket ground. Either there was a particularly riveting game of archery in progress in the English Landscape Garden, or all these people were making directly for the skeletons' mound.

'So I've been thinking.'

I looked round to see Emily walking beside me.

'Thinking about what?' I asked.

'How we get home.'

I smiled; it wasn't the first time we'd discussed it. 'We just have to trust to the skeletons,' I said. 'They brought us here; they'll take us back.'

'Which is all very well – but surely then we need to ask Rammell to let us in before he digs them—' She stopped, looking ahead towards the haunted hill. 'What on earth . . . ?'

My eyes widened as I followed her gaze. The onlookers were crammed twenty-deep around the mound, with the bulk on the southern slope, nearest the lake. You could see rumours rippling through the lines of people, many having herded themselves along without knowing why. Towering over everyone, on top of the mound, a large scaffold frame was draped in bunting, with a giant banner facing the crowd.

Led by the mourners, whose dress allowed us to weave through the hordes relatively easily, we ascended towards the front of the iron frame, bringing the banner into view:

THOMAS WEBSTER RAMMELL: 'I'M SORRY'

I was speechless. The breathtaking narcissism of the sign – difficult to digest, being so utterly inappropriate – was promptly underlined as we reached a dense scrum of photographers and reporters, jostling for the best view.

Seeing us arrive, Billy Gray called the men of the press to order and ushered us to the front, allowing us to see what lay below the frame: a roped-off area, within which a wooden platform stood just behind the critical patch of earth. Plainly, Rammell had not just reconciled himself to his solemn duties but was embracing them – even to the point of writing his own headlines.

Overcome by righteous bewilderment – whatever this charade was, it *wasn't* what the corpses had intended – I was on the brink of breaching the cordon and summoning the dead to fight the moral bankruptcy above ground, when Rammell appeared out of the trees. Head bowed, dressed in deepest mourning, he carried a gleaming spade between upturned palms. As he climbed onto the platform, his associates joined us at the front: his loyal assistant Gray, the brown-haired man we'd first seen at Whitehall, and the sharp-eyed factory owner from Poplar. They all looked deeply troubled, but Rammell himself was perfectly composed: unflinching as the crowd cheered, waiting patiently for the attentive hush that soon descended.

'Ladies and gentlemen,' he began, adopting an almost priestly monotone as he lifted his head. 'I am sorry. I, Thomas Webster Rammell, am sorry, from the very bottom of my heart.'

The crowd murmured, puzzled and intrigued.

'But of course, you ask: who is this Thomas Webster Rammell, and what has he to be sorry for?' He laid the spade down, pausing as he glanced at the ground in front.

'Well, without wishing to overstate the case, I – Thomas Webster Rammell – am the inventor of the pneumatic railway: the next great mode of subterranean transport. This air-powered marvel is the definitive alternative to the steam-driven leviathans that poison us at present. It is impeccably safe, clean and reliable.'

So he began, and so he continued, bragging about his invention while, behind me, Walter quizzed one of the reporters.

'What's the news?' I asked, once their conversation was over.

'There's a rumour that the Waterloo and Whitehall is in trouble,' whispered Walter. 'Word is, Rammell was told on Wednesday to cease construction immediately.'

'That was when we were at Poplar,' said Hattie.

Walter nodded. 'And when he received a visit from that brown-haired gentleman, remember?'

I looked across.

'That, Eric, is Sir Charles Fox: Rammell's partner on the Whitehall scheme.'

'Hence why he changed his mind,' I said. 'One last chance to salvage his railway.'

Hattie shook her head in disbelief; Walter was shaking with anger, his cheeks turning red.

'The man is a piece of evil!' he exclaimed. 'We've got to end this now!'

He strode forward, but I pulled him back.

'And so it is,' continued Rammell, glancing down anxiously. 'The first pneumatic route is nearly complete, linking Waterloo with Whitehall.'

'He can't be allowed to get away with it!' hissed Walter.

'And he won't.'

'But who's going to stop him, if not—?'

'Trust me,' I said. 'Trust *them*.'

'Who?'

'Our loved ones,' said Hattie. 'We've done what we need to do. We've fetched Rammell. Now it's over to them to decide if his actions pass muster.'

Walter considered for a moment, then relented and stepped back.

'But enough of that,' Rammell went on. 'We are not gathered here to laud the civilising power of my railways. Rather, we are here to set right a secret that has plagued me for two terrible years.'

The crowd became animated once again. Rammell had them in the palm of his hand.

'As you may know, the pneumatic system was trialled here in 1864. Thousands of people rode the railway, and every one felt cleansed and uplifted. But more than providing a pleasant diversion, it proved the system worked, and gave me the momentum to start building fully operational lines.'

He joined his hands and took a deep breath.

'It was Monday 31st October: our final day of service. The weather was abominable, but we opened anyway. If people were prepared to venture out in such conditions, they deserved to get what they'd come for. At around three o'clock, nine people entered the carriage: eight adults and one child, glad to escape the rain, and excited for the journey ahead. Off they went, through the gates and into the tunnel . . .' His voice cracked. 'Never to be seen again.'

There was a collective gasp.

'The tunnel collapsed, and with it the carriage, killing the passengers mere seconds into their journey. An unspeakable tragedy, but one which – crucially – wasn't my fault. For have no doubt: had the railway itself been responsible, I should have confessed immediately. But since it was *actually* the fault of slipshod tunnelling, what was I to do? Could I trust that people would make the distinction, or would my precious invention be undeservedly tarnished?'

Rammell's quandary was met by sympathetic nods and mutterings.

'Given that the damage was done, I chose to protect the pneumatic railway – and with it, the hopes of a million Londoners. We cancelled the day's remaining runs, citing the inclement weather, and quickly took up the line, filling in the tunnel entrances and reinforcing the ground. Then I approached those closest to the victims, explaining what had happened and why word must never get out, lest these nine deaths lead to thousands more.' He bowed towards the relatives. 'The four people concerned were most magnanimous, and for over two years my guilt lay buried until, just the other day, I discovered something so terrible that the pretence had to stop. Never mind the Waterloo and Whitehall Railway. Never mind my dream of a better future for all. Though harder-hearted creatures may yet have resisted, I had to confess.'

He seemed choked with emotion, but I couldn't tell if it was real.

'On Wednesday, I met a group of people who not only claimed to have encountered the decaying corpses of the deceased, but actually *wore their clothes*.'

This time, there was a whole succession of gasps: confusion, disbelief, dawning horror, spreading like waves through the crowd.

'It was a devastating sight, and could mean only one thing: that the carriage had *not* been crushed with the tunnel, but had instead—'

His eyes landed on the ground in front, and for a fleeting moment I thought his sorrow was genuine; that he was actually empathising with his victims.

'The carriage stayed intact,' he whispered, the crowd straining to hear, 'and the passengers were condemned to the most unimaginable of deaths.'

The silent air gradually filled with the sound of sobbing. All around, men, women and children were comforting each other. I assumed they were reflecting on the stranded passengers, but their stifled utterances – 'Poor, *poor* man', 'How *awful* for him' – indicated that the pity was aimed at the engineer himself: poor old Rammell, led such a merry dance by fate.

'But I know words alone will never make up for what I have done.' He lifted up the spade. 'Instead, I must take action.

Do now what I so wickedly failed to do then.'

I pushed forward to get a better look, watching Rammell descend with funereal deliberation. With the spade held across his hands, he stepped onto the open ground and I scrutinised his expression: free of fear, concentration absolute. In that moment more than any other, he seemed a product of his age: visionary, proud, persistent, and capable of the profoundest inhumanity as a result.

He approached the crucial spot and let his assistant guide him: 'Right a bit'; 'Left a bit'; 'A tad further forward'; 'That's it, sir. Right there.'

Rammell angled the spade down, holding the handle with his right hand and guiding it with his left. The tip hovered above the earth as he lifted his leg in readiness.

'May God have mercy on me,' he murmured, bringing down his foot with decisive force.

But before the spade had passed more than an inch into the earth, a rotting arm shot up and sought purchase – first on the spade, then on Rammell's calf. He screamed as he brought his other foot through, hopping to regain his balance and move away, but to no avail. The undead hand simply upped its power, tugging harder until his foot slipped clean off the spade and into the earth, taking the rest of the penitent engineer with it.

Chapter 34

Down and down Thomas slid, the moist soil pressing in, denying him air and silencing his screams. He tried desperately to writhe around, to offer some – *any* – resistance, but the pressure was too much for his body to withstand. Senses deadened, thoughts suspended by an advancing dizziness, he was about to pass out when his legs emerged into the space below, followed swiftly by his hips and belly.

But then his downwards progress stalled. A shot of pain scythed through his upstretched arms, and he realised he was still holding the spade, which had become lodged either side of the hole. Sensing escape, he tried pulling himself up, only to feel more squidgy fingers grip his ankles and wrench him back down.

'Billy! Pull the spade!'

'I'm trying!' came the muffled answer, but Thomas felt only a slight upwards thrust before yet more hands joined the clasping throng. The spade buckled and he tumbled into the carriage, landing on his rear with a numbing thud.

'Rope!' he cried, as his assailants padded back to their benches. 'Billy – get me a rope!'

For several seconds he stared up, thinking the situation still salvageable. Perhaps the corpses' vicious assault had actually been an act of grateful assistance, accelerating the burial process? But just as Billy's face appeared, the hole up to the surface shut itself with an unseemly squelch.

Darkness gripped the carriage: an all-engulfing blackness which seemed laden with a terrible finality. Dangerously exposed, Thomas sat up as alertly as his fear would allow, and imagined the benches running down either side, occupied by unseen adversaries. Even breathing shallowly, the atmosphere was putrid – musty, malodorous, quite possibly poisonous – and he fought hard not to choke as he stood and widened his stance, braced for an all-sided assault. Quite how he might defend himself wasn't clear, but he knew that his allies above ground would be working furiously to reopen the hole, so survival mightn't require more than a few moments' resistance.

The seconds passed. The corpses did nothing, and there was no sound of digging, frantic or otherwise. He entered an unsettling limbo, reproaching himself for not having asked *how* the strangers had got into the carriage; what the mechanism was by which the undead acted. He and Billy had been too preoccupied perfecting the theatre of the occasion to guard against potential traps.

Perhaps it was down to him to make the first move. But if so, what should it be? The corpses had demanded the strangers 'Fetch Rammell'; therefore, they wanted to see him. He had assumed they wanted digging up, but when he tried to oblige, they assaulted him. They obviously required something more before they would condescend to be exhumed.

'I'm sorry?' he said, wondering if the penitence he'd expressed above ground needed repeating below, face-to-decaying-face. 'I mean it. *I'm sorry*. Truly – from the bottom of my heart.'

He dropped to his knees and shuffled in a circle, addressing apologies to each invisible corpse. Still, however, there was no acknowledgement, let alone an escape route, so he went round again, reaching into the void, hoping some physical contact might legitimise his words.

'You must believe me. How I wish I could turn back time

and choose—'

His fingers met the coarse, crusty skin of a rotting head. He moved his hand a little to the right, feeling out a layer of sticky moisture, then off to the left, encountering bare human bone. Trembling, he was about to continue his latest apology when the corpse shoved him away, and the passengers spoke as one.

'All aboard!'

He stood and staggered round the carriage. It took an age to regain his balance as, absurdly, the carriage was beginning to move, seized by a smoothness that was as unmistakeable as it was impossible. Terrifyingly, for want of air or earth through which to move, and in defiance of all known laws of science, the subterranean pneumatic railway had resumed its operation.

'Make it stop,' he begged, oppressed by the silence, the darkness and above all the lack of control over his own invention: always ingenious, always startling, but never more so than now. 'Please, make it stop!'

Feeling his way, he made it to the corner of the carriage and sank onto his haunches, the continued acceleration reducing him from pioneer to powerless passenger. He buried his head in his knees and tried telling himself that this was still preferable to being clubbed to death by corpses, but it was no use. The experience felt so personal, so loaded with spite, that he almost wished they'd simply murder him instead. Heading blindly into an unknown realm of retribution, he was on the verge of throwing himself at their mercy, imploring them to be done with him, when the acceleration ended and the carriage began to slow.

Scarcely daring to believe it, he heaved a sigh of relief. That, surely, was that. The corpses had shown their strength, and it had been humbling and horrifying. Now, finally, they could proceed on an even footing. The train would stop, the hole reopen, and soon all nine corpses would be safely stowed in coffins.

And there it was. As the carriage came to rest, the darkness was relieved by the dimmest of lights, fading up to reveal the outline of the carriage.

Automatically, Thomas looked to the roof, expecting to see Billy peeking through, but there was no sign of the hole. Instead, extraordinarily, the light was coming from the gas lamps attached to the window frames: each one flickering back into life, returning colour to the familiar scene. There, at the far end, were the sliding doors through which he'd once passed so proudly. There, the deep purple curtains gathered neatly over the windows. There, the plush leather seats fusing comfort and convenience. It was all precisely as he remembered, yet something was missing: something he had expected to see, which would have extinguished his nostalgia in an instant.

'Surely not,' he whispered, finally registering both the miraculous disappearance of all nine corpses, and the carriage's unfeasible newness. Every surface – glass, wood, iron, leather – shone as brightly as when the carriage had first arrived from Manchester, and there was not the slightest scratch on the roof or windows, even though the compacted brickwork still pressed against the carriage sides.

Before he had a chance to reflect, there was a dazzling flash of light, accompanied by a portentous rumble. As his eyes readjusted, he saw that the carriage was no longer illuminated solely by the lamps, but that far greater light was flooding in from *outside*. Unfathomably, the debris had vanished and, in its place, rain was streaming down the windows, blurring the gloomy daylight beyond.

Heart pounding, he made for the sliding doors, still dry by virtue of the sheltered wooden platform that jutted out beyond. His first instinct was that the carriage had somehow extracted itself, and that any second Billy would appear to rescue him. But not only had the weather changed, the carriage was resting on tailor-made tracks, running beside a short brick platform that nestled in a bucolic, tree-lined cutting. Dashing to the opposite end, he saw the entrance to a tunnel, ornately built into a modestly-proportioned hill. On his left were two wooden shacks, one of which was exhaling smoke into the gloomy air.

Yelling out in shock, he swung onto one of the empty benches and summoned his sense. Despite appearances, there were two incontrovertible facts: the carriage couldn't possibly have moved, and it couldn't possibly be his Sydenham Gate station outside. At some point, he had fallen asleep – or been *made* to – and was now dreaming this horrific adventure, prompted by the strangers' wild stories of time-travel.

'Say again!'

He sat up with a start.

'There's someone up at the Palace—' came a second voice, cut short by another burst of thunder.

Reason as he might, there was no denying it. This was all too vivid to be anything other than real – too vivid and too accurate. That was *his* voice shouting 'Say again', and the response had come from the top of the cutting, where Fotheringay was trying to relay some exciting news.

He strode down the carriage and looked through the sliding doors. Sure enough, there he was, two and a bit years thinner, clambering up the bank. Haunted by every last twist of this traumatic day, he readily filled in the unheard conversation that followed: first, him berating Fotheringay for the disturbance; then, news of Sir Charles's appearance, and his pressing need to return to the Crystal Palace, leaving Billy to deal with the passengers.

The passengers. With horror, he lowered his eyes and saw nine people – the condemned! – marching directly towards the carriage.

Terrified of being discovered – how on earth should he explain himself? – he ran to the front and tried opening the glass doors. But despite having done so hundreds of times previously, he couldn't prise them apart. It was as if they were fixed shut, although no lock was visible, and he knew for a fact that none had ever been installed.

Checking back, no time left, he dived behind the end of one of the benches.

'Shelter at last!' joked Billy, sliding open the rear door and ushering in the passengers. Their footwear squeaked on the wooden floor.

'Homely,' enthused one, 'yet also luxurious.'

'I feel uplifted just coming aboard,' agreed another. 'All this space! So much more civilised than the Metropolitan.'

'Shutting the doors now,' said Billy. 'You'll be on your way presently.'

Peering round, Thomas saw his assistant leave and begin sealing the doors. Instinctively, he wanted to run and dive through the glass before it closed, but he knew that such an escape would be prohibited. Bit by bit, the corpses' intentions were becoming clear. In returning him to the moment immediately before disaster struck, he was being asked to avert the tragedy; to repent in the most direct possible way.

He fell back behind the bench. If that's what the undead wanted, he reasoned, that's what they would get. Never mind the chaos caused by interfering with history. Never mind that there was *another* him nearby, or that he was only there because, in his reality, the disaster had already occurred. If he could end this nightmare by doing now what he should have done then, why worry about the consequences?

The noise from the engine house throbbed through the carriage, and Billy appeared on the front platform, right in front of Thomas, beginning his muffled countdown.

'Ten, nine, eight, seven—'

Thomas leapt up and hammered on the glass. 'Wait!'

'Six, five, four—'

'Billy, please!' He tried squeezing the doors open. 'You must stop!'

Billy was oblivious.

'Three, two—'

'You don't know what you're doing!'

'One!'

Billy wound up the brakes and jumped off. Little by little, the carriage slid towards the sealed tunnel. Thomas shoved his elbow into the glass, but it wouldn't give. With the tunnel just yards away, he turned to the passengers, who were busily chatting in apparent ignorance of the panicked Rammell lookalike on board.

'This train!' he cried. 'I mean, this *trip*: it's not safe. If we pass through those gates . . .'

Still, nobody paid attention.

'I can't get out myself, but you can. We just need to wind down the brakes before—'

The passengers were now looking in his direction, but not so much *at* him as *through* him, marvelling at the tunnel gates as they swung open.

Dread deepening, he crouched beside a fresh-faced man, who was unique among the passengers in being on his own, and who must therefore have been Hattie's husband, Frank Fielding.

'Can you see me?' Thomas squeezed Fielding's hand but provoked no reaction. Like the rest of the carriage, the passengers were palpably there to him, but he was not permitted to interact.

The train rolled into the tunnel; the valve gates clattered shut. Enveloped by darkness, the carriage was now lit only by its lamps. Thomas felt a coldness creep across him as he recognised his powerlessness.

'What fun, to be blown along!' remarked a young boy, who had boarded with his parents.

He wasn't alone in his enthusiasm. All around, spirits were soon soaring, and Frank Fielding couldn't resist adding his warm, disarming voice to the chorus of praise.

'I shan't lie,' he said. 'This is far from my first trip on the pneumatic. But that's the joy of it: each trip feels like the first!'

'It's the freshness, isn't it?' said another. 'Airy, but still warm. Still cosy!'

'It just feels so clean.'

'I can't believe the smoothness. It's like—'

The carriage trembled as a muted groan echoed down the tunnel.

'The storm?' suggested Fielding.

'Surely not all the way down—'

The noise came again: louder, and definitely *not* the smooth, kettle-drum roll of thunder. This was chaotic, nearby, and intensely physical.

'What's happening?' asked the boy.

Another wave of noise crashed down around them, and this time it didn't stop.

'Look!' shouted Fielding. He pointed at the falling bricks that speckled the darkness outside. 'The tunnel's collapsing!'

The carriage came to a shuddering halt, and the passengers scrambled to either end, thumping on the glass and bellowing for help.

'It's filling up!' cried a woman, trying to open the doors at the back. 'The tunnel's filling up with debris!'

'Here too!' yelled someone at the front.

'We need to get out before it's blocked for good!'

'We'll be killed if we go out there!'

'And if we stay inside?'

There was a pause as they registered a battering above.

'The roof!' cried Fielding. 'Everyone onto the floor!'

They dived down face-first, shielding their heads with their hands, evidently fearing the carriage's total collapse. Thomas, however, didn't move. He simply stood and watched as the tunnel entombed the carriage at either end, with nothing more than a light drizzle of soil slithering through cracks in the creaking roof.

Once the barrage was finally over, the passengers raised their heads one by one, blinking incredulously at the miracle of their survival. Slowly, they climbed to their feet, dusting themselves down, exchanging bewildered stares and then embracing each other in astonished celebration. Not only had the carriage held up, they marvelled, but the gas lamps were still working!

'Thank God!' exclaimed one woman, reunited with her husband.

'Thank *Rammell*! To think this lightweight carriage can withstand such force! They say he's ill-starred, but his luck has turned with this!'

'How long until he fetches us?'

'Not long, I shouldn't think. Imagine the panic when we fail to appear at the Penge gate. I dare say they'll be digging already.'

'Do you think there'll be lots of people waiting for us when we get out?' asked their son, wide-eyed and grinning. 'Do you think we'll be famous?'

'More than likely, son,' replied the father. 'More than likely.'

Thomas wished the carriage would just collapse and bury them all – him included. The passengers' panic had been bad enough; to witness their relief was even worse. He had dwelt long and hard on the awfulness of their ultimate demise, but he'd never contemplated the immediate aftermath of the accident: the outbreak of false hope that compounded the terror of what still lay ahead.

'I am the man you are relying on,' he said softly. 'But I am not what you imagine me to be.'

He did not expect to be heard. He knew that this, here and now, was his punishment. Rather than intervene, it was time to step back and witness the consequences of his criminal inaction. He needed to open himself to empathy; to let the compassion find its way into his heart. Then, and only then, would the spirits guiding the carriage let him go.

He took his place on the bench, and watched in silence as the infectious energy of survival began to dissipate.

'It may be some time before they get us,' cautioned

Fielding. 'We need to stay calm. Conserve the air. Who knows what obstacles may block our rescuers?'

The passengers settled onto the benches, speaking only intermittently as the elation gave way to a deeper contemplation of what had just happened. As the seconds became minutes, and the minutes an hour, Thomas started to feel less separate. It was as if his punishment and their suffering were aligning themselves, and his fate was something beyond mere observation. By the time a full hour and a half had passed, he could see the first unvoiced doubts crossing the faces of his fellow travellers, and felt a deep, advancing dread that his own journey was also at an end; that within weeks he would become the tenth motionless corpse, waiting to be discovered by some mischief-maker from the future.

'What if they don't come?' asked the son, once two hours were up.

'Don't say such things,' replied his father.

'He's only saying what we're all thinking,' said the mother.

'But what's the alternative? If they don't come, what can we actually do?'

There was no reply. As the silent wait resumed, tears began to roll down the passengers' cheeks, and Thomas could bear it no longer. Tortured by the pointlessness of just sitting there, rotting, he wondered if one last plea might not yet save him from despair.

'I'm sorry,' he said, unsure who, or what, he was addressing. 'My previous apologies may have lacked sincerity, but now, having seen what you endured, please believe what I say. If you let me go, I give you my word that when I lay you to rest, it will be with everlasting respect for what you experienced.'

He didn't know what he was expecting. All he got were unconnected expressions of steadily mounting terror.

'Yes, my dying here makes sense,' he went on, 'but it's not *real* justice. Far better you let me go and allow me to explain what I made you suffer; for you to be pitied, and me punished, in the full glare of the world.'

Still there was no signal, and the continued unresponsiveness of his weeping victims pushed Thomas over the edge.

'*Don't make me suffer like you*!' he begged. 'There's not an ounce of merit in it – neither for you, me, nor the people of London. I have so much good work to do, the pneumatic railway is so important, you simply can't afford—'

He froze, unable to believe the words crossing his lips. What on earth was he doing, preaching to his victims about what they should and shouldn't do? How dare he start bleating about his concern for the common man, when common men, women and children were right in front of him, facing an unthinkable end because of his negligence?

He looked away, seized by self-disgust. Formerly, the knowledge of what he was trying to achieve had readily eclipsed all thought of the accident and those affected, but that delusion had decisively buckled under the scrutiny of the dead themselves. Though he certainly dreaded his railway's death more than his own, he no longer felt able to offer his selflessness as a defence. Instead, the benevolent ambition that had shaped his life was laid bare for what it had become – a wicked drug, which had intoxicated him once too often.

He bowed his head to consider his next words, and realised that there was nothing more to be said. It was time to unclutter his mind and place his duties as a human being ahead of his dreams as an engineer. It was time, finally, to forsake the pneumatic railway. Over the course of many years – from his first experience of the atmospheric, through his *New Plan*, right up to the trials at Battersea, Euston and the Crystal Palace – it had woven itself into who he was. Now he needed to untangle that web: to see himself as a man, not a mission, and the passengers as people, not martyrs.

He took a long, lingering breath – one of his last, he now knew, but no less welcome for that – and felt light-headed as he sat between two sets of passengers.

There would be pain aplenty over the coming hours, but for now he felt strangely liberated. Even as the unspoken horror grew around him, he blocked it from his mind. He had seen enough of the passengers' suffering. To watch any more would be mere voyeurism. Instead, there was nothing to do but close his eyes and wait in the carriage which, in finally disowning, he had made his home at last.

***

When Thomas next looked, the carriage was back in motion, accelerating quickly and serenely.

Outwardly, nothing had changed. The gas lamps were still burning brightly, and the passengers were arranged exactly as he'd last seen them, fear frozen on their faces. It was only a second later, when he looked again, that he realised they really were *frozen*: their expressions unchanging, even as the carriage travelled inexorably through the earth.

He approached the family of three and took the young boy's hand, which turned from warm to cold the moment he made contact. Simultaneously, the colour drained from his face, his muscles lost their tautness, and his posture quite gave way. The only accompanying sound was the rustle of his clothes readjusting themselves – a noise which was soon taken up by the rest of the carriage as the other passengers experienced the same abrupt, accelerated death, their bodies shrinking beneath their garments.

Thomas didn't dare speculate what any of it meant. All that mattered was that he was prepared to die down there, and in accepting his fate there was nothing to hope for, and nothing to fear, but that the wishes of the dead be granted.

The gas lamps died and the carriage returned to darkness. Not wanting to hide, Thomas remembered a pipe he had spotted protruding from one of the men's pockets. He swiftly located the accompanying matches and struck one after another, watching in pity as the faces of the nine bodies melted away: eyes receding, mouths, ears and noses shrivelling to crusty lumps; grey skin sinking into bones and unpeeling itself to reveal glistening, insect-ravaged flesh.

And then it stopped – the carriage, and the decay. The passengers were left stranded halfway between cold, pale cadavers and outright skeletons: four fully clothed, five miraculously disrobed.

Thomas sensed where they were, and stared expectantly at the gap in the wooden roof. The air filled with the sound of sliding and squelching, but the soil above didn't separate. Looking back down, he realised that the noise was actually coming from the corpses, who were shifting position. Some toppled to one side, others slumped forwards; a select few stayed just about upright. Their composition was changing, too, with wasted limbs collapsing into dust, joints falling to impossible angles, and clothes sliding off, onto the floor.

As the seconds passed, bare bones became more apparent, squeezing through remnants of skin, or falling through pockets of crumbling flesh to depart their hosts altogether.

At last, Thomas knew, he had won their forgiveness. The corpses were succumbing to the natural forces hitherto stifled by the revivifying power of injustice. As they continued to fall apart, some more dramatically than others, he frantically organised the splintered parts of the fully-collapsing corpses such that the remains of each were kept together. When finally the process was over, he stepped back and surveyed his work: nine bodies, in various states of togetherness, ready to be excavated at last.

But without an escape route – and without any undead passengers to conjure one up – how was he to get them out?

He stepped back, deep in thought, and promptly tripped over the answer: his spade, magically restored to straightness.

Chapter 35

'It's gone!' I repeated, as the people jostled round. 'It's just what happens, OK? When the corpses get what they want, the hole seals up.'

'So what's become of him?' asked Billy Gray, prodding the ground with his foot.

'Who knows?' replied Emily. 'Now they've got their man, it's anyone's guess.'

'I'll bet they've eaten him,' said an onlooker.

'They've eaten him!' cried another – and so news of Rammell's unappetising demise shot through the crowd, prompting another surge forward.

'Everyone back!' I cried. 'You saw as much as us. The corpses pulled Mr. Rammell into the carriage. There's not been a sound since. That's all we—'

The air resonated with a muffled, tinny banging.

'Could that be him?' asked Gray.

I frowned. 'They normally throw you out once they're done.'

'But who is it, if *not* him?'

It was a fair point. Gray's was the only logical conclusion, and it suggested that the carriage might finally have lost its supernatural aura.

'You have spare spades?' I asked.

He dashed behind the stage and returned with an armful of shovels. Joined by Sir Charles Fox and Joseph Samuda, Emily, Monty and I began digging, while Mary and Harold controlled the crowd.

It took several minutes to get through the soil, which was all the deeper because of the extra layer recently added. Finally, though, we uncovered part of the carriage roof, and with it the hole through which I'd plummeted so many times.

***

'Coming in, sir!'

Thomas watched in delight as Billy jumped feet-first into the carriage. He landed in a messy heap but managed not to dislodge any of the piles of carefully arranged body parts.

'What on earth has happened down here?' he asked, looking around in bewilderment. 'You were gone almost a minute!'

'Almost a minute?' Thomas laughed. 'I was gone far longer than that.'

He proceeded to explain everything that had occurred: the journey back in time, and how he had finally won the passengers' forgiveness by ceasing his protests and accepting his fate.

'So now what?' asked Billy. 'Are we still going to bury them?'

'Of course. We do what we came here for, just as we planned, and then—'

'It can't fail, sir.'

Thomas hesitated.

'You should see the sensation outside. Our plan is working to perfection!'

Thomas shook his head. 'This is the end, Billy. With these bodies, we bury not just the pneumatic's past but also its future.'

Billy was open-mouthed in shock. 'But I don't understand. How can you possibly—'

'My mind is decided. Having witnessed what we ignored for so long, I can't possibly profit from its exposure. We've trampled long enough on these people's memories.'

'But the facts remain, sir. This tragedy wasn't the fault of the pneumatic railway, and your invention can still transform our city. You've a duty to the citizens of London. It would be exceptionally indulgent for you to stop because of personal guilt – especially now you've made your peace with the dead. You, *we*, are better than that.'

Smiling, Thomas guided his assistant onto a bench and looked him in the eye. 'Belief in one's own virtue, Billy. Never trust it.'

'But it's real.'

'It misleads. Tell yourself you're doing right by the future, and who knows what liberties you'll take in the present? Presume something is right by the people at large, and who can say how many individuals will suffer in its interests? One must draw a line somewhere. The lessons of our past are too grave to ignore. We cannot trust ourselves to bear the burden of doing great work. We cannot be sure it won't deceive us.'

Billy looked close to tears. 'So what do we do?'

'We let the directors shut down the Waterloo and Whitehall, just as they wish.'

'And then?'

'Then, who can say? But one thing I know: I am not equipped to be the pioneer I believed I was, and it's with that knowledge that I shall proceed.'

***

'Keep back!' I yelled. 'This is private business.'

'But the hole *is* open?' asked an onlooker.

'It is.'

'And he's not been eaten?'

'Not as far as I can tell.'

'Then what *has* happened to him?'

'It's none of our business.'

'Hello there?'

The voice came from the carriage. I looked in. For the first time, it seemed curiously lifeless and plain. Billy Gray was peering up.

'I need a hand.'

'Rope!' I demanded.

Samuda obliged, and Monty, Emily and I hoisted up Thomas's assistant without any interference from the undead.

'What's happening?' I asked.

'You'll see,' said Gray, looking rather emotional. 'Sir Charles, Joseph: we need the boxes.'

Rammell's team set to work, fetching nine brown coffins and dragging them to the side of the little crater we had created. Emily and I offered to help, but Gray declined. It seemed important that we stayed out of it.

With the coffins in position, Rammell's assistant stood on the exposed carriage roof, feet either side of the hole.

'As you can see, ladies and gentlemen, we are about to begin the next phase—'

There was a communal gasp. Directly beneath Gray, a rotting head had popped up above the surface.

'Here goes!' cried Rammell. 'I'm starting with the most intact and working my way down. Steady, now!'

The engineer had forgotten his audience. With an embarrassed smile, Gray steadied the limp head and raised the body out of the hole.

The corpse was naked, much as I'd last seen it: still fleshy in parts, but with patches of bone amid the disappearing skin. It was, however, more weakly connected than before, making it instantly obvious that this gentleman carcass, along with his eight, reportedly even less 'intact' associates, was truly dead at last.

A hand touched my shoulder. I turned to see Hattie standing right behind me. Her face was whiter than any corpse.

'It's Frank,' she said, trembling. 'My dear, dear—'

The poor woman began sobbing uncontrollably, her eyes glued to her husband's body. Seeing what was happening, Gray signalled for her to help with the exhumation.

I pulled Emily close, and together we took in the horrific poignancy of the widow cushioning her husband into his box, gazing into his empty eyes while issuing broken apologies for not having rescued him.

'Ready for the next?' cried Rammell.

Gray glared down at his boss, reminding him about the sensitivity of surface events.

'Cover him up,' said Hattie, having kissed Frank one final time.

Samuda and Fox did the honours. They fastened the lid and carried the coffin away, making space for another.

And so the process continued, with Rammell passing up the corpses, and his associates, assisted by the bereaved, laying them to rest. After Frank came two clothed, one naked, but from the fifth on, the bodies deteriorated rapidly. Though the odd head, torso or leg still emerged intact, Rammell's team had to use bags to hoist up disengaged sets of bones and chunks of flesh. This in turn led to the unfortunate spectacle of relatives delving into sacks and bickering over which remains belonged to whom.

It all made for a curious mix of panic and peace-making, which my fellow adventurers and I felt too. Though delighted at the corpses' hard-won rest, their undead powers had been our lifeline. As each got locked away, we were losing more than just old skin and bone.

'We'll be OK,' I said. '1867 is exciting enough.'

'It'll have to be,' murmured Emily.

With the excavation complete, the coffins formed a nine-pointed star around the crater. The bereaved guarded the perimeter while Gray lowered the rope one final time.

'Here we go,' he said, calling to Samuda and Fox, who were poised behind him. 'Heave!'

Inch by inch, Rammell was dragged to the surface. Once most of his body was above ground, he heaved himself up and rose to his feet. His suit was ripped and caked in crisp brown mud; he looked utterly exhausted.

A round of applause broke out – more than one onlooker yelling 'Bravo!' – and the expectation was clearly that the engineer would pick up where he'd left off.

But the frown on Rammell's face was fixed, and his eyes flicked round with wide, guileless freedom. Instead of addressing the crowd, he walked slowly past the coffins and spoke to each of the relatives in turn.

Accomplished showman though he was, this was clearly no act. Not once did his attention stray to check how he was being received. Instead, his focus was unflinchingly on the bereaved, leaning in and listening attentively, shielding his ears from the cries of the onlookers.

'Something extraordinary happened down there,' I said to Emily. 'He went in proud, and he's come out humbled.'

Finishing his circuit, Rammell headed over towards us.

'My profoundest apologies,' he said. 'I realise I've never asked your names – although of all the things I've got to apologise for . . .'

'My name's Eric,' I said, smiling. 'And this is Emily, Monty, Mary and Harold.'

The engineer bowed to each of us in turn. 'I'm so very grateful.'

'No need to thank us,' said Monty. 'We were only following orders.'

'But I'm so glad you did. From the bottom of my heart.'

'It must be satisfying,' I said, 'knowing your railway's success is finally secured.'

Rammell looked taken aback. He had obviously expected to hear contempt, when in fact I spoke with total sincerity.

'Really,' he said, 'you must understand: I am *so* ashamed of this carnival. I couldn't possibly—'

'Why not?' I said. 'You've done what you needed to do – for the victims, for their relatives, for the Crystal Palace.'

Rammell hesitated. 'But how can you know that?'

'I defer to the passengers' judgement. Now they're properly dead, they must be happy. And if they're happy, we're happy.

You should feel free to move on.'

Rammell considered this for a moment, then shook my hand and bid us farewell. Acknowledging the crowd at last, he stepped back into the circle of coffins.

'I think he's a good man,' I said, as he began issuing instructions to his team. 'He's got an air about him. I hope he succeeds.'

'Well, we're going to have to find something to do,' said Emily. 'Perhaps you can help make it happen?'

I smiled, slightly nervously. Though meant as a joke, Emily's suggestion was as likely as anything else to come to pass.

'And so, to conclude,' said Rammell, raising his voice to address the crowd, 'we process to West Norwood Cemetery, where nine empty graves await our coffins.'

He caught my eye and I nodded back, providing the reassurance he apparently needed.

'The bereaved shall bear their loved ones' coffins,' he explained, 'assisted by our most capable navvies from the Waterloo and Whitehall Railway.'

A small army of uniformed workers appeared out of the trees, led by our old friend Sid. Marshalled by Samuda and Fox, they distributed themselves between the coffins, which were then hoisted onto thirty-six shoulders. The crowd settled into silence as Rammell led the strange parade off towards the Crystal Palace, and the coffin-bearers filed into line behind, setting forth with a sombre tread.

We headed down the familiar slope and took our place behind the last of the coffins. Emily and I went first, then Monty, Harold and Mary. It was a fair way to West Norwood, and would take a good couple of hours at our funereal pace. But as I took Emily's hand, I didn't much care. A protracted finale felt fitting. Besides, we had nothing else planned – neither now, nor indeed for the rest of our 19th-century lives.

'All aboard!'

The procession halted. The words – intoned in the distance by several croaky voices – brought yet deeper silence to an already noiseless scene.

'*All aboard!*'

The command was more insistent this time, prompting the coffin-bearers to stare in astonishment at the boxes they were carrying. At the front, Rammell stepped to one side and looked back at the cortege. Even from a distance, I could see he was perturbed by the return of the corpses' unmistakeable wheeze.

'*Eeeh, reek,*' came the chorus once more. '*All aboard.*'

Again, there was silence.

'They're talking to you,' whispered Emily.

'No,' I said. 'They're talking to *us*.'

Tentatively, I led us out of the line and signalled our intentions to Rammell. The engineer bowed in acknowledgement, then returned to the head of the procession.

Followed by our fellow adventurers, Emily and I wove through the crowd, back to the top of the mound. I turned to see the procession once more in motion. The corpses, seemingly, were content that we had grasped their final instruction.

'So it's farewell to 1867 after all,' said Emily, as we clustered round the crater.

I nodded, slightly saddened after all to be heading back to my own time. It wasn't that I wanted to stay in 1867. It was simply that I was going to miss my time-travelling companions, and all the excitement that had come with them. Even if I hadn't been jobless and friendless in 2013, it could never come close to what I'd just experienced.

'I knew they wouldn't let us down,' I said, trying to disguise my bittersweet emotions.

'But what do we actually do?' asked Harold.

'We jump in, dear!' said Mary. 'That's what they asked. All aboard!'

'But what if we end up trapped?' worried Monty. 'I mean,

without the skeletons inside to drive us—'

'*We* were the drivers,' I reminded him. 'The skeletons were always just the passengers.'

'So how do we do it?' Emily peered at the narrow hole in the bare carriage roof. 'One at a time, I suppose – and reverse order?'

I nodded. 'Mary, you go first. Then Harold, Monty, Emily, and me. Be sure to get out of the way when you land, so the next person can—'

'Sorry to interrupt, sir.'

The voice came from behind me. I turned to see Billy Gray, armed with a notepad and pencil.

'If you don't mind, sir, I'd like the exact date and time you were originally pulled into the carriage. That goes for each of you, if you don't mind.'

I looked to the others in bafflement.

'I know it's odd, sir,' continued Gray, rather hurriedly, 'and I'm as in the dark as you. But Mr. Rammell did say it would be in all your interests to oblige. And since the cortege is well on its way, I'd be grateful if you could—'

'Of course,' I said, passing on the required information, then waiting as the others followed suit.

'Much obliged,' said Gray, shaking our hands in turn. 'And all the very best to the five of you.'

He ran off down the hill, re-joining Rammell at the front of the procession, which was almost out of sight.

'What was that all about?' wondered Monty.

'Haven't the foggiest,' I said, watching Mary edge into the crater, held upright by Harold. As she alighted on the carriage roof, the crowd around us breached the peace with a respectful round of applause – for us, I realised, and all we'd done to expose the passengers' plight.

Responding to the prevailing solemnity, Mary lowered herself down without a word, dropping silently into the blackness below. She was followed swiftly by Harold, then rather more slowly by Monty, who seemed reluctant to forsake the 1867 Palace for the burnt-out ruins of 1936. Alas, as we all knew by now, there was no point resisting the passengers' will, and finally he too jumped in, leaving just me and Emily above ground.

'Your turn,' I said, guiding her into the crater, and onto the carriage roof.

'Let's jump in together.'

The crowd's applause intensified a little. I felt myself blushing.

'But will we fit?' I asked, looking down as we stood either side of the hole. It was going to be a tight squeeze.

'We'll fit,' she said, taking my hands. 'On the count of three. One . . .'

We each took a deep breath.

'Two . . .'

Emily kissed me on the lips.

'Three!'

We jumped forwards and dropped, falling smoothly and landing upright on the carriage floor. The darkness was absolute.

'You alright?' I asked.

There was no answer. I squeezed her hands, but they weren't there.

'Emily?'

I reached out, searching for her in the void. Looking up, I realised that the hole had already sealed itself.

'Monty? Mary? Anyone?'

I quickly determined that I was alone. As a whole new wave of confusion washed through me, the old acceleration returned: smooth as always, but faster and in the opposite direction to usual.

I came across some matches – presumably left by Rammell – and lit a succession to reveal the carriage deteriorating: cracks creeping across the windows, gas lamps wilting, dry wooden chunks falling from the roof, and lumps of earth hammering down in their wake. Fearing for my safety, I crouched in a corner and took a couple of drags on my inhaler as the repairs of previous journeys were fearsomely undone.

Mercifully, the trip didn't last long. After less than a minute, the carriage was back at rest, and an abundance of familiar details – the shapes of fractures, tears and piles of soil – confirmed that I had been whisked directly home.

My latest match fizzled out and I thought of the others. Never mind that we'd never said goodbye; were they even safe? I assumed the spirits had conjured up five incarnations of the carriage, each with a unique destination, but I had no guarantee, and nor could I ever have.

There was, however, no time for regrets. More moist earth was already falling from the roof, and an ominous chorus of creaks and groans drifted on the air. The carriage was no longer moving, but it was still imploding: hefty slabs of wood rained down, windows and walls ripped themselves open, and iron uprights buckled under pressure from above. Free of the skeletons' mitigating control, the weakened carriage was being effortlessly crushed.

I darted round, dodging the falling debris until I finally noticed the dim patch of moonlight that was shining through the reopened hole, enabling me to witness the collapse.

Recognising this as the skeletons' parting gift, I reached for the rim of the exposed roof, but it was too high, so I mounted a mud-coated bench and leapt up, clinging on to the damp, fragile wood. I tried pulling myself through, but one of my hands gave way, snapping off a large chunk of the roof and leaving me hanging by one arm. Crying out with effort, I hauled the other arm up and regained my grip – firmer, this time – only to realise that my arms were being forced together as the hole started to contract.

If I didn't act fast, I'd not only be properly trapped, but killed in the carriage's collapse. I heaved myself up, rising a couple of inches before reaching for safety and realising – with profound terror – that the roof was no longer exposed to the outside world. The 1867 dig meant nothing in 2013, and there was no way I could squeeze through several feet of mud without assistance from above or below.

For several seconds there was only the sound of shattering glass and splintering wood, and the certain knowledge that, at any moment, the carriage roof would give way and take me down with it.

But just as my helplessness reached its peak, I had a flash of clarity. There I was, feeling utterly alone, when actually, if these really were the moments immediately after my journey began, I most certainly *did* have assistance – hearty, well-equipped assistance to boot.

'Tom!' I yelled. 'I need the rope! I'm trapped!'

The soil was building up beneath my feet as earth poured in through the carriage's broken walls. I was no longer hanging but standing, though any upwards thrust I might have gained was negated as the hole tightened around me. I was being buried alive on all sides, and I knew that my next words would be my last.

'Tom!' I screamed. 'Anyone! Just a hand to pull me—'

The air in my lungs was forced out, and with it went my words. I felt light-headed, free and floating – not claustrophobic at all, but soaring on the air like a bird.

And then came the hand. A cold, wet hand, thrust in from above and clasping maniacally for its prey.

'Breathe in!' came the muffled advice, as the fingers dug down around my wrist. 'Here goes!'

The upwards pressure straightened my body, and I began squelching towards the surface, eyes and mouth jammed shut as the damp soil sprang into every crevice. Several times I stalled, prompting panic that Tom was about to withdraw his hand, thinking me beyond saving, but he was only ever redoubling his grip.

After a few more heaves my arms finally emerged into the cold night air. He took my other wrist and brought my head through. The rest of my body quickly followed, and within moments I was lying face-down on the earth, panting for air.

Turning over, I sat up and looked giddily towards the hole, just as it gurgled shut.

'Not a moment to spare,' I gasped, the oxygenated blood flooding ecstatically through my veins. I turned to face my rescuer. 'Thank you so much. I thought you were—'

I stopped. The light wasn't great, but it was enough to see that my saviour wasn't Tom. Instead, it was an old lady, grey hair glistening in the moonlight.

'Where is he?' I asked.

'Who?' Her voice was so soothing as to be almost familiar.

'Tom,' I said, checking my surroundings. 'I assumed, being 2013 . . .'

I trailed off. Something wasn't right. Although the carriage, before its collapse, matched what I'd originally discovered, the surface was different. The trees were more numerous, the flowerbeds better tended, and everything was illuminated by a succession of ornate lampposts beside the path. Above all, there was a glow that flickered through the lakeside branches; something shimmering in the higher reaches of the park.

'This *is* 2013?' I said, wondering if the skeletons hadn't accidentally whisked me to 1923, when the surroundings were so much prettier. 'I know it sounds absurd, but—'

'This is 2013,' she stated. Again, her voice was oddly recognisable.

'It's the middle of the night,' I said. 'Why are you in the park?'

She stepped closer. 'Because I was expecting you.'

Astonished, I backed away. 'How were you to know I was about to climb out of a buried railway carriage?'

She tilted her head. 'What railway carriage? Show me.'

My mind was in a whirl. Her words made no sense, but there was an authority in her tone that made me want to co-operate.

'It was destroyed when you were pulling me out,' I replied.

'Try showing me anyway.'

Thinking I might at least uncover part of the roof, I started digging with my hands.

'Keep going,' she said, after I'd spent a minute fruitlessly displacing wet soil.

'It's no use,' I replied, once I'd got a foot or so down. 'You'll just have to take my word for it. There *was—*'

My hands hit something: wooden, yes, but more substantial than a mere fragment of the carriage roof.

'What is it?' She flicked on a torch.

Digging deeper, I brushed the soil off a small wooden chest, with brass edges and a lock on the front. Realising that the woman had meant me to find it, I lifted out the container and laid it to one side.

'I have no idea what it is,' I replied. 'But I'm guessing you're about to tell me.'

Sure enough, the old lady's hand came out of the gloom. In it was a key, which I took and turned in the lock.

The chest opened with a squeak to reveal a collection of handwritten notes. Those on top were browner and more fragile than those underneath. With some trepidation, I sat on the ground and read the first.

To those who come after me –
with undying gratitude for all you did.
Elizabeth Lovell, 23rd March, 1923

'Elizabeth?' I said, struggling to reconcile the date on which the supposedly mad young girl had signed the letter with the year in which we had encountered her. I turned to the next note in hope of clarification.

To Eric, Emily and Monty –
we had the time of our lives.
Love, Mary and Harold, 30th November, 1936

Beneath that was a similarly gracious note from Monty, addressed to me and Emily, and dated 24th October, 1950.

I breathed out a great sigh of relief. Here, thank the Lord, were my fellow adventurers, writing notes through time to confirm that they had safely made it into, and out of, the carriage.

I turned to the fourth and final sheet, certain of what I was about to read, only to find it blank on both sides. Mystified, I looked to the old woman, who took the paper and, producing a pen from her coat, wrote something down. Moments later, she passed it back.

With love and thanks for all time.

Emily x

18th November, 2013

For several seconds I was unable to speak. Even though I knew it to be true, I was so disoriented that my mind couldn't take it in.

'But I've only just left you,' I protested. 'Not even five minutes ago!'

Emily lifted me up into a warm embrace.

'Thank goodness you're OK.' She wiped the mud from my face. 'I couldn't believe it just now. After all this time, I *almost* didn't get you out! Imagine the embarrassment!'

'The embarrassment?'

'Gosh, how I remember that outfit – the thing on which it all turned.' She stepped back and examined my dilapidated clothes. 'It seems like only yesterday to me too. Falling in, wondering where you were. Then travelling forwards and being rescued by my predecessor as the carriage collapsed. Even the digging, finding the chest. Sixty-three years ago, it was. 24th October, 1950. Yet still so very vivid.'

The date resonated, and not just because it belonged to one of the Palace fires. I'd seen it recently, written down.

I turned back to Monty's note, and there it was: 24th October, 1950.

'But Monty was pulled in during the 1936 fire,' I said.

'Yes, but just as I've only this moment signed my note, now you've appeared, so he only wrote *his* the day *I* reappeared.'

I finally realised what she meant by 'predecessor'. Emily had rescued me, just as she had been rescued by Monty, and Monty by Harold and Mary, and Harold and Mary by Elizabeth Lovell.

But that in itself raised a question, for strictly speaking Elizabeth wasn't one of us.

'Elizabeth was Harold and Mary's predecessor,' explained Emily, obviously sensing my confusion. 'In the wider sense.'

'What wider sense?'

'The chain of command. The line of succession.'

'Succession to what?'

She grinned and took my hand. 'There'll be time enough to explain. First, there's something I'm dying to show you.'

Chapter 36

Leaving the once-haunted mound behind, we strode onto the lawn to the east. Unlike in *my* 2013, the area was still home to a cricket pitch, complete with a quaint little pavilion on the Sydenham boundary. Ahead, the tree-lined avenue leading up from the Penge gate was distinguishable by twinkling lamps, which illuminated several intrepid pedestrians to reveal that the park was open, even at this ungodly hour. Beyond it, the freakish monsters were floodlit, frozen in time as they prowled through their rocky habitat, exuding an eerie prehistoric glow.

Excitement mounting, I looked to my right. At least, I figured, the sports centre and stadium would still be there, reliably ruining the view up the hill. But they too had vanished. In their place stood the two mighty fountains which we'd admired only the day before – or rather 146 years before – supplied by the immense cascades and water temples further uphill, and intersected by the steady climb of the central path.

Already, there was only one logical conclusion, but instead of focusing any further afield, I marched us towards the central path, eager to see it from the best possible vantage point. Once in place, I composed myself before lifting my eyes and looking up the hill.

There it was: the Crystal Palace in all its sparkling majesty, rising serenely above the grounds that lay before it. It was as incomprehensible as ever in size and beauty, the wonderful improbability of its very construction – all that, from iron and glass – now compounded by the mystery of how it came still to be there.

'Tell me this is real.'

'It's real,' said Emily, smiling as she guided me up the path. 'We fixed it. You, me and the others: we fixed the Crystal Palace.'

The future had changed. The park had been transformed, the Palace was gleaming, and it was all thanks to us. In holding Rammell to account we had appeased the skeletons' fiery rage, meaning that all parts of the Palace which had existed in 1867 remained intact, with only the north transept and wing still absent.

'This is more than just a fix,' I said, looking over to the illuminated rosary, and the twinkling glass colonnade that led up from the railway station. 'The Palace isn't just here. It's thriving.'

'And the area, too,' said Emily. 'Norwood is London's most prosperous suburb.'

'But in 1936,' I said, 'the 1936 *we* visited, the Palace was already showing signs of age.'

'Not in this reality,' said Emily. '*This* Crystal Palace has never once faltered. It's like the curse was replaced by a blessing.'

As we reached the lower terrace – the six symmetrical fountains in full flow, surrounded by immaculately preserved statues and urns – I turned and gazed downhill. It was true: astonishingly, the grounds were laid out exactly as they had been in 1867. I shut my eyes and tried imagining the old 2013, wondering if my predecessors had ever told the world about the alternative reality we had known and, indeed, prevented.

'Stop dawdling!'

I turned back. Emily was on the upper terrace, waiting outside the Palace.

'Come on,' she shouted. 'We're going in!'

'But surely it's locked?' I said, running up to join her.

'Why should that affect Palace royalty like us?'

She led me up the main bank of stairs. At the top, a security guard opened the door and we stepped inside.

'What do you mean, *Palace royalty*?' I asked, scanning up and down the long, dimly-lit basement, which seemed to have become a high-class shopping arcade, with stalls and glass façades reaching into the distance on either side.

'You'll see,' said Emily, heading up the stairs on the right.

I followed, pausing briefly to look out at the luminous grounds, then stepping into the great central transept. At the near end, banks of gleaming touch-screens and unmanned computers mingled with what looked like original 19th-century statues and foliage. Behind these, a full-sized spitfire was suspended from the ceiling, while at the far end, the giant organ and massive, raked concert seating radiated silver and gold into the night-time air, with massive stacks of speakers hung many metres above them.

We walked to the intersection of nave and transept, where a life-sized statue of Sir Joseph Paxton stood directly below the aeroplane. To the north, the fine arts courts still stretched away into the distance, set back on either side behind abundant bushes, benches and statuary. To the south, however, the two lines of illuminated overhead signs indicated the contents to be much changed. The nave itself remained relatively clear, but the space previously occupied by the industrial courts had become a mishmash of glass-fronted exhibition rooms – 'Warfare', 'Space', 'Technology', 'London' – interspersed with standalone structures, including 'The New Brunel Aquarium', 'The Charles Fox Studio Theatre' and, immediately on my right, 'The Fotheringay Archive'. At the far end, just beyond the palm-covered fountain, a giant cinema screen was attached to the wall.

'Eric,' urged Emily. '*Come on*! We've got people waiting.'

'People?'

But she wouldn't explain. Instead, she led me round the back of the archive room, down a flight of wide stone steps, and into a familiar square with a concertina glass roof: the same place, I realised with a shiver, where I'd first heard Tom sing and squeeze his way through 'Dem Bones'. In that incarnation, it had been an overgrown ruin, providing access to a forgotten subway that led under the road but no further. Now, however, the plaza and subway were not only spotless, but there was something on the other side. It was to this that we were headed.

'Surely not,' I said, as we passed through the vaulted underpass.

'What's up?' asked Emily.

I nodded towards the vast Victorian railway station sprawled out ahead: all sweeping staircases, gigantic arches and imposing walkways. It was empty for the night, but evidently still thriving, and fully equipped with all the regular station amenities I recognised from *my* 2013.

'Nothing but a housing estate here in my world,' I said.

'Really? I've always known it,' said Emily. 'The High Level Station, counterpart to the Low Level Station, down the hill. It must have been torn down after 1950 – in the old reality. Either way, no time to stand and marvel.'

She grabbed my arm and hauled me outside, where we crossed the road.

'Look back at the station,' she said.

I did as I was told. Like a squat Westminster Abbey, the station's two stumpy turrets guarded the front of the red brick and terracotta terminus, with long, flat roofs stretching away behind, nestled neatly in the hillside.

But there was something else too – *another* building, adjoining the High Level Station. It was of comparable size, hewn from similar brick, but altogether plainer. I may not have noticed it at all, indeed, but for the church-like doors that dominated its frontage, and the letters 'TWR' engraved proudly above.

'Now that building *did* take me by surprise,' said Emily.

TWR. The acronym had an obscure resonance which drew me magnetically to the wooden doors, and had me reaching for the handle. I hesitated briefly, looking back at Emily, who nodded her encouragement. Taking a deep breath, I swung the doors open.

The sight that greeted me made no sense whatsoever. At least thirty people were spread around the spacious entrance hall – some sitting, some standing, some arranged on spiral iron staircases. The moment I appeared, they erupted into raucous applause.

Emily nudged me. 'We all get welcomes, but this is the one we've been waiting for.' She stepped past and presented me to the crowd. 'The redeemer himself!' she cried, leading the crowd in three rounds of 'Hip Hip Hooray!'

Light-headed and bewildered, I smiled inanely as every man and woman in the room came up to introduce themselves, expressing delight at finally meeting me, before proceeding to Emily and congratulating her on sixty-three years' outstanding service. The moment I finished shaking hands, a chap approached with a digital camera.

'As dazed as you please, sir,' he said, snapping away. 'It's tradition to capture everyone while the confusion – and the mud – is still fresh!'

Looking down at myself, I realised that I was indeed still wearing the torn, tangled, dirt-encrusted remains of Frank Fielding's clothes.

'Welcome to your new job, Eric,' said Emily. 'And unlike those before you – save Rammell himself – yours is a job for life!'

Rammell? I thought again of the initials above the entrance.

'To your liking, Mr. Chairman?'

The photographer was showing me his camera, and the pick of the portraits he'd taken. Without thinking, I gave the nod and he slalomed away through the crowds.

'Come and look at this.' Emily grabbed my hand and led me to a curved reception desk. Behind it was a line of familiar photographic portraits.

Furthest to the left was Rammell himself, striking a stately pose, followed by Elizabeth Lovell, looking significantly older and calmer than I had known her. Next came Harold, Mary, Monty and Emily, each dressed as they had been when we separated, only with more muck covering their clothes. They all shared the same baffled expression that I myself wore in the portrait, taken moments before, that was already being added to the end of the line. Scanning back to the start, I read the plates beneath each picture:

THOMAS WEBSTER RAMMELL
Chairman, TWR: 7/1/1867 – 3/12/1889

ELIZABETH LOVELL
Chairman, TWR: 3/12/1889 – 23/3/1923

HAROLD KNIGHT
Co-Chairman TWR: 23/3/1923 – 30/11/1936

MARY KNIGHT
Co-Chairman TWR: 23/3/1923 – 30/11/1936

MONTY GARRARD
Chairman, TWR: 30/11/1936 – 24/10/1950

EMILY PRESTON
Chairman, TWR: 24/10/1950 – 18/11/2013

ERIC JAMES
Chairman, TWR: 18/11/2013 –

'The line of succession,' I said, beginning to understand at last. 'But succession to what?'

Emily retrieved a large leather book from behind the desk, and passed it to me. The initials 'TWR' were gold-stitched into the cover. Inside was a dedication:

To those who made me what I am today.
Thomas Webster Rammell
2nd December, 1889

'One day before he died,' said Emily.

I turned over to discover a chronological compendium of newspaper cuttings. First was an extract from *The Times*, dated Saturday 5th January, 1867 and entitled 'Rammell Redeemed: Penance at the Palace'. The story detailed everything from Rammell's confessional speech to his burying the bodies in West Norwood cemetery. It told of his alleged kidnapping by the undead, and the strange voices heard just prior to the disappearance underground of the five strangers to whom Rammell was 'profoundly indebted'.

The straightforward reportage was followed by a collection of enthusiastic editorials.

'Here is an engineer,' wrote one John Herapath, 'whose selfless vision is so grand that, weighed down by the burden of great public work, he made a serious error of judgement. For that, however, he has bravely repented, and our communal forgiveness must be granted.'

Another piece agreed that 'The very concealment of his murderous deeds is a measure of Mr. Rammell's benevolence. If those who perished at the Palace are not to have suffered in vain, it is imperative to support this honourable man, and ensure that his commendable railway transforms our capital precisely as he intends.'

Moving on, an article from later in 1867 – 'The Future Arrives' – breathlessly described the opening of the Waterloo and Whitehall Railway, whose success, according to subsequent pieces, was quickly rewarded with extensions both north and south of the river. Similar paeans then followed –

in 1868 and 1870 respectively – to the Mersey Tunnel, forged in the image of its sub-aqueous London predecessor, and the conversion of the Metropolitan Railway to an elaborated version of Rammell's system.

From there, page after page chronicled the spread of Rammell's railways through cities across the nation. The litany of successes was interrupted only by obituaries in the wake of his death, and an extraordinary article from 1900 explaining how 'electric traction' had been dismissed by the TWR company as an alternative to pneumatic power, chiefly because it couldn't match the latter's guarantee of perfect safety. The *pièce de résistance*, however, came in 1949, with a front-page splash headlined: 'Channel Tunnel Opens: TWR's Dream a Reality, Sixty Years After His Death'.

I shut the book. 'This is real?'

'It's real.'

'And this is the headquarters of TWR?'

'It is,' replied Emily. 'Always has been, and always will be. Unless you want to instigate a move.'

I looked again at the row of pictures. 'But why me? Why us?'

'It was Rammell's wish. When he finally decided to capitalise on what had happened, it was on condition that, in doing so, he repaid the debt he owed us. Without our words of reassurance and encouragement, he always said, he'd never have persisted with the Waterloo and Whitehall.'

This was a dizzying thought. A conversation which, for me, had occurred less than an hour before was now an entrenched part of history.

'Rammell wrote it into his company's constitution that the chairmanship should pass down through those who had helped him make amends. The chain would begin with Elizabeth when he died, then the five of us time-travellers would sequentially take the reins when we each returned from 1867. That's why Billy Gray took down our details before we left. So the company knew when control would pass over, ensuring each new chairperson was met directly off the train.'

I looked at the dates below the pictures and tallied the history.

'In case any of us didn't live long enough to greet the next, we each had to nominate someone to fill in until the next time-traveller emerged. The theory being that the line of succession would continue until your death, when the person of your choice takes over.'

I stared at my portrait. All this talk of the past and future was confounding any thought of the present.

'Don't worry.' Emily took my hand and guided me towards a nearby lift. 'I know how disorienting it is. Just be assured that everything is in hand. You have plenty of money waiting for you, plus somewhere to live on the edge of the park.'

We entered the lift and began descending.

'How will I know what to do?' I asked.

'I'll show you the ropes. And besides, you're the boss. You choose what to do, what to delegate. The role can be active or purely symbolic.' Emily chuckled. 'You could even go back to driving the trains.'

This sounded by far the most attractive option but, of course, came with a snag.

'I wouldn't be allowed,' I said.

'Why not?' A twinkle in Emily's eye reminded me of our altered reality. 'You do whatever you like. Besides, you scarcely need worry about your asthma. Parts of the network may be 146 years old, but it remains the healthiest subterranean railway in the world. To this day, people come down to the platforms purely to convalesce.'

The lift stopped, and the doors pinged open. We headed down a dark corridor to a door which released us into another, brighter walkway.

On the wall opposite was a large painted sign saying 'TWR HQ', but it still took me a moment – looking from side to side, processing the fluorescent lights, polished floors, and walls plastered in advertising – to realise that we had emerged into an actual underground station. Going by the overhead signs, Emily was leading me to the platforms, but I only managed to walk a few paces before slowing to a halt – distracted by the spotless surfaces and the freshness of the air.

'Behold your empire!' she said, pointing to a wall plan of the network.

I went across and examined the map. My empire looked good. The colour choices for the various lines were similar to those in my old reality, but the regularity of their arrangement was totally different: a startling sign of TWR's hegemony. As opposed to the mishmash of routes I'd known – some reactive, some generative, all spawned by different people at different times – here was a system born of a single mind. It took a while to find where we were, such was the density of stations in south London, but I finally located TWR HQ on the blue Palace Southern Line, sandwiched between Crystal Palace (Low Level) to the south, and Paxton Green to the north.

Leaving the map behind, Emily guided me down a curving corridor to the empty northbound platform, where a gleaming white train was sitting silently at rest. Looking up and down its surprisingly modest length, I couldn't help noticing how closely the cross-section of the train matched the tunnel mouths: a snugness aided by two bristly collars encircling its periphery at either end. The four carriages were open plan, with no doors between each, and seating along either side of the interior.

'Until recently,' explained Emily, 'the Palace Southern used Rammell's original wooden stock. With none of the usual wear and tear, the only risk was fire.'

I peered inside. A few midnight passengers looked by turns bewildered and irritated by me and my scruffy Victorian clothes.

'The network runs twenty-four hours a day,' Emily went on. 'But I've arranged for them to hold this train for you.'

'For me?'

Emily nodded. 'I thought you might like to have a go at the controls.'

Needing no second invitation, I set off towards the front – identifiable by a set of green lights at the tunnel mouth which, as at the opposite end, was blocked by a futuristic white shutter. The driver's compartment was just beyond the bristles, occupied by a slim, healthy-looking fellow, sipping on some thermos coffee.

'Good evening, Mr. Chairman.' He smiled as he threw open the door. 'Come on in. I'll show you the ropes!'

I stepped in, closely followed by Emily, and he introduced the tools of his trade. Central to everything was a long, flat computer screen displaying the Palace Southern 'up' and 'down' lines, stretching in parallel from Penge West to Oxford Circus, and curving to meet each other at either end.

'All stations on a given line are identical distances apart,' he explained, 'and everything happens in perfect synch. Right now, we're at rest, and so is everyone else.'

By the side of each station on both the up and down lines was a flashing green blip, with only one exception: our train, flashing red on the up at TWR HQ.

'Because we're not yet ready to depart, see? None of the trains, up or down, can move until all are green.'

'Are we ready now?'

The driver nodded, and hit a button in the centre of his dashboard. Our blip duly turned green, and the white shield ahead opened.

'Now, we just release the brakes and ease her into the tunnel.'

The train was sitting on a natural slope, enabling us to slide effortlessly into the darkness. The blips began moving round the circuit, flashing yellow then turning purple.

'Purple means the trains are now fully in the tunnels. The shields close behind all the trains, and the valves are switched so a supply of outside air from the surface is let in behind the sucked trains, and air captured from off the fans is pumped in behind the blown.' We started to pick up speed. 'That's what's happened to us, see. Air from off the fan is coming in behind, blowing us forward.'

I felt the motion working on my body. It was a magnificent kind of weightlessness.

'There are fans at every station, all dual action. So as the one at HQ blows us up to Paxton Green, it's simultaneously sucking another train from Paxton Green to HQ. Likewise, the Paxton Green fan is currently blowing an up train to West Dulwich, using the air it's simultaneously extracting out of the down tunnel to suck a train back the other way.'

'It's the ultimate refinement of Rammell's system,' enthused Emily. 'The air required to blow the up trains is exactly proportionate to that needed to vacuum back the downs.'

I could only laugh, staggered by the ingenuity and smoothness of our motion. It was like being back in the buried carriage, only somehow more impressive. Because now we were indeed moving through the earth, and yet that unforgettable sense of other-worldliness remained.

I felt the train stop accelerating, and just begin to slow.

'The fan at TWR HQ has been shut off,' said the driver, 'along with all other fans at all other stations. Each train, up and down, blown and sucked, now has enough momentum to carry it the rest of the way.'

I was delighted by the simplicity, but also slightly sceptical.

'There must be problems,' I remarked. 'People, for a start. They're unpredictable. What if one particularly crowded train holds all the others up?'

'Doesn't happen,' replied the driver. 'Passengers stay calm because they know the next service is always less than two minutes away.'

'But what about delays? Breakdowns?'

'All the fans have back-ups,' said Emily, 'and power is automatically switched when the sensors spot a problem with the pressure. The faults are fixed immediately, without disrupting the timetable, because the fans can be tended to independently of the trains. That's why there's never trouble. People genuinely trust the service.'

Given the chaos I'd once known on *my* underground railway, this was the most astonishing thing I'd ever heard. But the assuredness of our movement, plus the manifest, on-screen straightforwardness of the network in action, underlined Emily's claims.

Ahead of us, another shield opened and the light from the approaching station poured into the tunnel.

'The shield opening coincides with the start of the upwards slope,' said the driver, as we climbed gently into the station, continuing to slow until we had crossed the peak of the incline, halfway along the platform. 'Now we just apply the brakes against the *downwards* slope leading to the next bit of tunnel . . .' He brought the train to rest. 'And *hey presto*. Any questions?'

I shook my head. 'Crystal clear.'

'Then let's head back to HQ,' said Emily. 'And this time, you can take control.'

We headed to the opposite platform, and the front of the down train, where Emily asked the driver to make way.

I took my place at the console. Checking the passengers were clear of the doors, I pressed the 'Ready' button and focused on the screen, waiting for a few straggling red blips to turn green. Then the white shield opened and I took up the brakes, my heart leaping with delight as the train eased itself into the tunnel and our speck turned from green to yellow to purple.

Staring at the screen, I watched the blips move in synch around the circuit. The harmony was all the more entrancing now I was at the controls, and it was a struggle to believe anyone had ever contemplated an alternative; still harder to think that, in a different reality, such an alternative had actually been tolerated for a hundred and fifty years.

As our train flowed inexorably into the airless void created by the fan at TWR HQ, my thoughts wandered to the future. Tomorrow, I knew with joyful certainty, I would shed my senior responsibilities to become a full-time TWR driver, working my cares away on the Palace Southern. And I also knew that there would inevitably come a time when I'd have to tell my story. Not just the story I've disclosed in these pages, but also that which I've only had time to hint at: the story of the world I used to know.

It is this which will form the subject of my next book. For now, as a tease, I leave you with a thought that still occurs when I lie awake at night: the notion that somewhere out there, in this vast, misunderstood universe, my old reality might still exist. No longer with me in it, of course, since I am – as sure as the up train mirrors the down – sitting right here; but existing nonetheless. A reality where, below ground, electric trains rumble unreliably, noisily and dangerously through damp, rat-infested tunnels, inflicting daily misery on Londoners oblivious of anything better. A reality where, above ground, Paxton's mighty Crystal Palace is no more, destroyed in a series of ferocious, unexplained fires which left behind a wilderness that remains ruined to this day.

And as I dream of this reality, I think fondly of those who inhabit it, going about their business without the foggiest clue as to the profound connection between these apparently unrelated histories, and still less that the key to it all lies in a small patch of ground on the northern edge of Crystal Palace Park. A patch of ground beneath which sit nine skeletons, silently awake in the railway carriage that has been their tomb for a century and a half – forgotten, but far from gone, and holding the park in their spell until they are stumbled upon again, and have another chance to go back in time and confront their villain, and our hero, Thomas Webster Rammell.

Printed in Great Britain
by Amazon